Three brooding
at nothing t

Greek affairs

Claiming His Child

Three intensely emotional novels from
three fabulous authors: Julia James,
Catherine Spencer, Rebecca Winters

On sale 6th January

On sale 3rd February

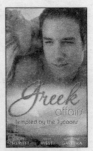

On sale 2nd March

On sale 6th April

On sale 4th May

On sale 1st June

Greek

affairs

Claiming His Child

JULIA
JAMES

CATHERINE
SPENCER

REBECCA
WINTERS

MILLS BOON

Mills & Boon, an imprint of Harlequin (UK) Limited, Eton House, 18-24 Paradise Road, Richmond, Surrey TW9 1SR

GREEK AFFAIRS: CLAIMING HIS CHILD
© Harlequin Enterprises II B.V./S.à.r.l. 2012

The Greek's Million-Dollar Baby Bargain © Julia James 2009
The Greek Millionaire's Secret Child
© Catherine Spencer Books Limited 2009
The Greek's Long-Lost Son © Rebecca Winters 2009

ISBN: 978 0 263 89631 2

025-0412

Harlequin (UK) policy is to use papers that are natural, renewable and recyclable products and made from wood grown in sustainable forests. The logging and manufacturing processes conform to the legal environmental regulations of the country of origin.

Printed and bound in Spain
by Blackprint CPI, Barcelona

THE GREEK'S MILLION-DOLLAR BABY BARGAIN

JULIA JAMES

Julia James lives in England with her family. Mills & Boon® novels were the first 'grown-up' books she read as a teenager, alongside Georgette Heyer and Daphne du Maurier, and she's been reading them ever since. Julia adores the English and Celtic countryside, in all its seasons, and is fascinated by all things historical, from castles to cottages. She also has a special love for the Mediterranean—'The most perfect landscape after England!'—and she considers both ideal settings for romances. In between writing she enjoys walking, gardening, needlework, baking extremely gooey cakes and trying to stay fit!

PROLOGUE

THE EXECUTIVE JET cut through the wintry night, heading north. Inside, its sole passenger stared through the darkened porthole. His face was sombre. His gaze unseeing. Looking inward, into the distant past.

Two boys, carefree, happy.

Brothers. Who'd thought they had all the time in the world. But for one time had run out.

A knife stabbed into the heart of the man sitting, staring unseeing into the night sky beyond the speeding plane.

Andreas! My brother!

But Andreas was gone, never to return. Leaving behind only a weeping mother, a stricken brother.

And one precious, most miraculously precious gift of consolation…

The front doorbell rang, peremptory and insistent. Ann paused in clearing the mess in the kitchen and glanced into the second-hand pram, checking that the noise hadn't woken Ari. She hurried to the front door, pushing back untidy wisps of hair, wondering as she opened it who on earth it could be.

But even as she opened the door she knew who it was. He stood, tall, and dark, face set like stone. Beyond him, at the kerb, a chauffeured car, sleek and expensive, looked utterly out of place in this run down part of town.

'Miss Turner?'

The voice was deep, and accented. It was also cold, and very hard.

Ann nodded briefly, dread suddenly pooling in her stomach.

'I am Nikos Theakis,' he announced, as the breath caught in her throat in a shocked rasp. 'I have come for the child.'

Nikos Theakis. The man she had most cause to hate in all the world.

Ann could only stare, frozen, as he stepped past her, inside, dominating the narrow hallway, glancing dismissively around the shabby interior before arrowing back on her, as she stood shocked into immobility. 'Where is he?' he demanded.

His eyes lasered into her—dark, overpowering. Her mind was reeling. Out of all the insane things to do at this moment all she could do was stare at him. Stare at six foot of lean packed male, sheathed in a business suit that shouted wealth, sable hair immaculately cut, and a face—Ann's stomach clenched—a face that widened her eyes involuntarily.

Night-dark eyes, a strong blade of a nose, high cheek-bones, steel-jaw and sculpted, sensual mouth.

She gulped mentally. Then, with a jolt of effort, she dragged her mind away. What the hell was she doing, staring at the man like that? As if he were anyone other than the man he had just announced himself to be.

Nikos Theakis—rich, powerful, arrogant and ruthless. The man who had ruined her sister's life.

Because he had. Ann knew. Her sister had told her time and again.

Carla, always the golden girl, vibrant and glamorous. Partying her way through life. Then the party had ended. She'd turned up late last summer at Ann's poky, dingy flat with no place else to go. Distraught.

'He said he was crazy about me. Crazy! But now I'm pregnant and he won't marry me! And I know why.' Her beautiful face had twisted in hatred. 'It's that snobby bully-boy brother of his! The almighty Nikos Theakis. Looking down his nose at me like I'm dirt!'

Shocked, Ann had listened while Carla's tearful tirade flowed on. She had tried to reassure her, to remind her that the father of her child had to support it financially—

'I want Andreas to *marry* me!' Carla had railed.

The months that had followed had not been easy. Carla had sunk into a depressive lethargy, forbidding Ann to make contact with the father of her child even to at least sort out maintenance for the baby.

'Andreas knows where I am,' she'd said dully. 'I want him to come and find me! I want him to come and marry me!'

But Andreas had not come, and Carla's difficult pregnancy had ended with an even more difficult labour that had left her with postnatal depression, brought on, Ann was sure, by Andreas' rejection of her. To Ann had fallen the task of looking after baby Ari—for Carla, it seemed, had failed to bond, sinking deeper into depression, refusing all treatment.

The cure, when it had come, had been dramatic. A knock at the door—a young man, handsome, but with a strained, uncertain manner.

'I—I am Andreas Theakis,' he'd told Ann.

That was all it had taken. Carla had flown to him, her face transfigured. Her life transfigured. Or so she had believed. In reality it had been a little less romantic than Ann had hoped. Andreas had wanted a paternity test done.

'I have to convince my brother...' he'd said uneasily to Ann. But Carla had been viciously triumphant.

'Oh, Ari is Andreas', all right! And Mr Almighty Nikos Theakis is going to get his comeuppance! Andreas will marry me now—he's promised me, because he wants his son—and there isn't a thing his damn brother can do about it!'

Had Carla been tempting fate, to be so triumphant? Ann wondered, with a bitter twist of misery. It had not taken the malign will of Nikos Theakis to keep his brother from marrying her sister. It had taken a moment's misjudgement by Andreas, whisking Carla away—glamorous once more, vibrant once more—in his powerful hire car on unfamiliar British roads. Nothing more than that.

And two lives snuffed out.

Ann had been at home with Ari, looking after him willingly while Andreas and Carla went off for the day together. He had been orphaned at a stroke.

Ann knew that the horror and grief of that day would never leave her. Andreas's body had been flown back to Greece. None of his family had come near Ann. Ann had been left to bury her sister on her own. Left to look after baby Ari, all alone in the world now, except for her. She had made no attempt to contact Andreas' family. They had clearly never wanted Carla—never wanted her child. Whereas she…

Ari was all the world to her. All she had left. Her one consolation in a sea of grief. Grief for her sister and for the man she had so desperately wanted to marry. Anger for his brother—who had stopped them doing so. The brother who was now standing in her own hallway, eyes like lasers.

Demanding to take Ari from her.

Getting no answer, Nikos glanced into the empty room beside the front door, then strode down the narrow hallway to the kitchen at the end. His expression hardened even more. The place was a mess. There was a sink full of washing up, a plastic covered table with food debris on it. But it was the pram that drew him. He strode up to it and looked down. Emotion knifed through him. Andreas' son! Out of this nightmare, one shining miracle. He gazed down at the sleeping baby, his heart full. Slowly, he reached a hand towards him.

'Don't touch him!' The shrill whisper made him halt, whipping his head round.

Ann Turner was in the kitchen doorway, one hand closed tightly around the jamb. Nikos's brows snapped together. Did the girl think he was going to take the boy there and then? Obviously he was not. He would return when he had all the papers drawn up, a suitable nanny engaged, and then make an orderly removal of his nephew. He was here now simply because he had had to come. He had had to see for himself, this baby who was the only consolation in the nightmare that had closed over the Theakis family with Andreas's death.

His eyes rested a moment on the figure in the doorway, his mouth tightening as his gaze flicked over her. She suited the place. Shabbily dressed, with her hair tied back, an unkempt mess, and baby food on her shapeless T-shirt. She couldn't have looked less like the girl who had got her avaricious claws into his brother. Carla Turner had been a gilded bird of paradise. This sister of hers was a scrawny street sparrow.

But Ann Turner's appearance was irrelevant—only the baby in her care was important.

She was standing aside from the door now. 'Mr Theakis, I want you to leave. I've nothing to say to you, and I don't want you disturbing Ari.' Her voice was sharp. Hostile.

For a moment he said nothing, just went on looking at her. Ann could feel the colour run into her cheeks. The shock of seeing him was still jolting through her and she was fighting for composure. And losing. That soul-searching gaze of his was transfixing her. Then, without a word, he started towards her. She pulled aside swiftly as he brushed past her, striding down towards the front door. But her relief was short lived. He merely wheeled into the living room.

She hurried after him, heart thumping. 'Mr Theakis, I asked

you to leave—' she began, but he cut her short with a peremptory lift of his hand, as if she were a servant who had spoken out of turn.

'I am here merely to see the child for myself, and to inform you of the arrangements that have been made to take him home.'

Ann stared. 'This *is* his home.'

Nikos Theakis glanced around him. The sagging sofa, the worn carpet and faded curtains were encompassed in his condemning glance. 'This, Miss Turner,' he said, his eyes coming back to her, resting on her as if she were a cockroach, 'is not a home. It is a slum.'

Ann coloured. Poverty wasn't a crime! But Nikos Theakis clearly thought otherwise. His eyes were pinning her as if she were on a dissecting board. Instantly she became conscious of her messy, drab appearance and unwashed hair—conscious, inexplicably, of a feminine shame that she should be caught looking so absolutely unappealing in front of a man as expensively and physically drop-dead gorgeous as Nikos Theakis. Angrily, she broke her gaze away. What did it matter what she looked like? Or him? This was a man who'd just announced to her his intention of stealing the baby she loved more than anyone in the whole world. Her only living family.

Then suddenly he was speaking again, and this time his tone was quite different from the curt, condemning one with which he'd informed her she was living in a slum.

'But how could it be otherwise?' he said smoothly, as Ann's eyes flew to him again. 'It is very hard, is it not, Miss Turner, to have the unwelcome burden of a small baby? What girl your age could want that?'

His smooth words backfired. Instinctive rage reared in Ann. Yes, it was hard work looking after a baby. But Ari was never a burden. Never.

Nikos Theakis was speaking again, in the same smooth voice. 'So I shall relieve you of this unwanted burden, Miss

Turner, and you may return again to the life of a young, idle and carefree girl.'

She stifled down the rage that his unctuous words aroused in her, trying to keep her voice steady.

'Mr Theakis, you rejected Ari's existence from the moment he was conceived,' she shot at him witheringly. 'Why the sudden concern about him now?'

Nikos's eyes darkened. 'Because now I have the DNA results forwarded to me from the laboratory. I know that he is indeed my brother's son.' There was no trace of smoothness in his accented voice now.

'My sister said so right from the beginning!' Ann protested.

The sculpted mouth curled contemptuously. 'You think I would trust the word of a whore?'

It was spoken in such a casual way Ann blanched. 'Don't speak of Carla like that!' she spat furiously.

His eyes skewered her. 'Your sister slept with any man rich enough to keep her in the lifestyle she hawked herself out for. Of course I warned my brother to check the child was his.'

'My sister is *dead!*' she rang back at him.

'As is my brother. Thanks to her.' The coldness in his voice was Arctic. 'And now only one person is important—my nephew.' Abruptly his manner changed again. That surface smoothness was back in his voice. 'Which is why he must return to Greece with me. To have the life that his father would have wanted. Surely, Miss Turner, you cannot disagree with that?'

He sounded so smooth, so reasonable—but Ann's hackles did not go down. 'Of course I disagree! Do you propose, Mr Theakis—' she was even more withering now '—to raise Ari yourself? Or will you just dump him on a nanny?'

The dark eyes flashed. Ann felt a stab of angry satisfaction go through her. *He doesn't like being challenged!*

'To assuage your concerns, Miss Turner—' the deep voice

was inflected with sardonic bite '—Ari will live in the family home. Yes, with a professional nanny but, most crucially, with my mother.' And suddenly his voice that was quite different from anything Ann had heard so far. 'Do I really need to tell you how desperate my mother is for the only consolation she has left to her after the death of her son? Her grief, Miss Turner, is terrible.'

Involuntarily, Ann felt her throat tighten.

'She is welcome to visit any time she wants—' she began, but Nikos Theakis cut right across her.

'Generous of you, indeed, Miss Turner. But let us cut to the chase,' he said bitingly, the Arctic chill back in his voice.

His eyes were pinning her again, but this time there was not disdain in them for her shabby, messy appearance. Now they held the same expression as when he had called her sister a whore…

His voice was harsh as he continued. 'I expected no less of you, and you have ensured that my expectations are fulfilled. So, tell me—what price do you set on the boy's head? I know you must have a high one—your sister's was marriage to my brother. Yours, however, can only be cash. Well, cash it will be.'

Ann stared disbelievingly as Nikos Theakis slid a long-fingered hand inside his immaculately tailored jacket and drew out a leather-bound chequebook and a gold fountain pen. Swiftly, with an incisive hand, he scrawled across a cheque, then placed it on the table. His face was unreadable as her gaze flickered to it. Ann stood in shock as he spoke again. 'I never haggle for what I want, Miss Turner,' he informed her harshly. 'This is my first and final offer. You will get not a penny more from me. I am offering you a million pounds for my nephew. Take it or leave it.'

Ann blinked. This wasn't real. That piece of paper on the table in front of her wasn't a cheque for a million pounds—

a million pounds to buy a child. As she still stared, Nikos Theakis spoke again.

'My nephew,' he said, and once more he had resumed that smooth tone of voice, 'will have an idyllic childhood. My mother is a very loving woman, and will embrace her grandson into her heart. He will live with her in her home in Greece, at the Theakis villa on my private island, wanting for nothing.' He gave a small chilly smile. 'So, you see, you may take the money, Miss Turner, with a clear conscience.'

Ann heard his terrible words but they didn't register. Nothing registered except that piece of paper on the table in front of her. He saw her fixation upon it and his expression tightened. The deep lines around his mouth were etched more harshly. She kept on staring at the cheque.

Monstrous! *Monstrous!* Emotion swirled inside her and she felt the pressure build up in her chest as though it would explode. Only when he moved to the door could she tear her eyes away.

'I will leave you for now, and return at the end of the week,' he announced. 'All the paperwork will be completed by then, and you will hand my nephew over to me.' His voice hardened again. 'Understand that a condition of your payment is that all connection with my nephew is severed—he will not benefit from any communication with his late mother's relatives. However, since my mother can have no idea of the sordid life your sister led, or your squalid circumstances, she has asked me to give you this letter from her.' He slid his hand inside his jacket once more, and withdrew a sealed envelope, placing it beside the cheque. 'Do not think to reply to it. And do not attempt to cash your cheque yet—it is post-dated until I have my nephew.'

Then he was gone, closing the door behind him. Numbly Ann heard his footsteps on the pathway, then the soft clunk of a car door and the hushed note of an engine.

Her eyes went back to the cheque, disbelief and loathing

filling her. Then slowly her eyes went to the letter. Numbly she picked it up and opened it. Her heart was wrung as she began to read Sophia Theakis' words.

You cannot imagine, my joy when Nikos told me of Andreas' son. I felt the mercy of God's grace upon me. To be blessed with making a loving home for this tragically bereaved infant would be a privilege I pray for. If you can see it in your heart, despite your own grief for your lost sister, to grant me this prayer, and allow me to lay the love I had for my own son before his son, you will have my eternal gratitude. He will be cherished and loved throughout his life.

Forgive, I beg you, the selfishness of a woman who has lost her son, and for whom old age beckons, in desiring her grandchild to raise. But you are young and have your whole life before you, and you must be free to live it without assuming the premature responsibilities of motherhood to your sister's child which will consume your precious youth...

Ann could taste the terrible mix of grief and hope in every sentence. Her heart constricted. What should she do? What was for the best? Did Ari really have a ready-made, loving home waiting for him with his grandmother? Would it be better for him than the home she provided, or only richer? A child needed love—emotional security, above all. Far more than material security.

Ann's face shadowed with memory. Carla had been her emotional security as a child—all that Ann had had—and she had clung to her sister as the only constant in an uncertain, unstable world after their mother's death. Andreas' mother's words echoed in her head, offering 'a loving home for this tragically bereaved infant'. Was that what would be best for her nephew? Was it what Ari's parents would have wanted for their son? Ann's heart squeezed. She knew the answer already.

Andreas *would* have wanted his son raised in his family, by his own mother who had so clearly loved him. In the short time that she had known Andreas he had often mentioned his mother, with love and affection clear in his voice. His mother, he had told Ann, would welcome the news of Carla's existence—and their child she would welcome with open arms and open heart.

And Carla? What would she have wanted? Ann knew the answer to that question too, and a hand clutched her own heart. Carla had spent her brief life trying to claw her way to the wealth she thought meant happiness—she would have given her right arm for her son to take his place in the heart of the Theakis clan.

She had given more. She had given her life.

How can I keep Carla's son away from what she would have wanted so much for him? How can I?

Slowly, inexorable logic crushed her desperation to find reasons to keep the baby she loved so much. How could she? It would be pure selfishness on her part. If a loving, financially secure home were being offered to Ari, which both his parents would have wanted for him, how could she keep him within her own impecunious protection? However much she loved Ari, one day he would grow up. How would he feel then, having been deprived of the birthright that should have been his? The time to decide was now, while he was a baby— before emotional ties could be formed, before he grew to love her, and could be wounded by parting with her. Now was the time, she knew, for her to be strong—to let him go to his grandmother, to be cherished and loved, protected and safe.

As every child should be.

And there was yet one more reason for giving Ari up to his grandmother. One that she could not ignore. One that the monstrous offer by Nikos Theakis made it impossible to ignore.

A million pounds. *So much money.* How could she possibly say no to that?

Nikos stood, as he had stood only a few days before, in the dingy living room of Ann Turner's flat, watching with rigid features as she signed away her custody rights to his nephew. But as she put her name to the last of the legal papers, and shakily got to her feet, he allowed himself the satisfaction of letting his opinion of her show in his face.

Ann flinched. It was quite visible. Then his lawyer was picking up the papers and placing them inside his briefcase. At the door, a young nanny held Ari. For a second the emotion was so overpoweringly strong that she swayed with the need to snatch him back. Never, never let him go! But it was too late. The nanny, with a last sympathetic smile at Ann, was going, followed by the lawyer.

At the doorway, Nikos paused. Ann Turner was clutching the back of the chair, her face white. For a second Nikos frowned, then his face cleared, resuming its expression.

'You may cash your cheque now, Miss Turner,' he said softly, and his words licked over her like a whip.

But Ann was beyond his scorn. Beyond anything but the silent scream in her head that she could not do what she had just done. Yet even as the scream sounded in her mind Nikos Theakis was walking out, the front door closing behind him.

Its echo haunted her, tearing at her through the years ahead.

CHAPTER ONE

Four years later...

THE FAMOUS LONDON toy shop was crowded with children and parents as Ann threaded her way through, studying the myriad toys on offer. Most were far too expensive, but some gave her excellent ideas. It was strange being back in England. She'd hardly been back here at all in the years since she'd taken Nikos Theakis' cheque—and given Ari away.

Four years—and still guilt assailed her over what she had done. *Oh, Carla, did I do the right thing? Tell me I did. Tell me that Ari is loved and happy.*

That was all that mattered—that he was growing up, as Nikos Theakis had said he would, in an idyllic childhood. Orphaned, yes, but with family to love him and material wealth in abundance. Not all children were so fortunate.

She steeled herself. Yes, that was what she had to remember. Yet it was with a heavy sigh that she continued her perambulation. Being back in England brought back all the memories of Ari as a baby. Would she even recognise him if she saw him now? Her heart ached. Of all the strictures that Nikos Theakis had laid upon her, the loss of contact had been the worst to bear. But it was the price she'd had to pay.

Familiar blackness filled her as she thought of the man who

had taken Ari from her. Remembered the vile things he'd said about Carla, the contempt in his eyes when she'd taken his cheque. His banning her from ever seeing Ari again.

Eyes shadowed, she rounded a display of soft toys, pausing to check the price and flinching when she saw it. Then, across the aisle, she heard a voice that stilled her utterly.

'Ari, my darling, speak English—remember we are in England now.'

As if in slow motion, Ann's head turned. A little way away was a huge railway track, laid out with trains whizzing around. Children crowded to see it. Right in her line of sight was a small child, flanked by two women with their backs to Ann.

'That's the train Uncle Nikki is buying me!' came a piping voice.

The younger woman beside him turned to smile. Ann saw her profile and gasped, her hand flying to her throat. Four years might have passed, but Ann recognised instantly the nanny who had taken Ari from her arms. The little boy beside her must be…must be…

She felt faint with shock, staring, transfixed. Even as emotion convulsed her, the nanny's gaze shifted outwards slightly and caught hers. Ann could see her expression change as she recognised her. Then the older woman saw the nanny's expression, and turned as well.

It was Ari's grandmother. It had to be! For a moment the older woman, elegantly beautiful, but with a frail air about her, returned Ann's stare with mild curiosity, and then her brow puckered questioningly. She murmured something to the nanny, who nodded slowly, assessingly, then walked across to Ann.

'You will excuse me, please,' she said in an accented voice, curious and a little hesitant, 'but…is it possible…? Could you possibly be…? You have a look about you of my grand-son.'

Ann swallowed, unable to move, her throat still tight as a

leash. Then, into her eyeline came another figure. Much taller, male, clad in a black cashmere overcoat, striding towards the train display from the cash desk. Ann's breath caught in her throat. Simultaneously the man's head skewed round, his eyes searching for his mother, absent from his nephew, who was still absorbed in watching the trains scurrying round the track. They lighted on Ann and he stopped dead.

In a second she made her decision. She took half a step forward.

'Yes, I am Ann Turner. Ari's aunt,' she announced.

After that it became a blur. The expression on Sophia Theakis' face turned to pleasure, and she reached out her hands to take Ann's and draw her forward. Immediately Nikos Theakis strode up, his face like thunder. But his attempt to intercept the greeting was too late.

Sophia Theakis held up one small but imperious hand to her son. 'Nikki, this is quite extraordinary,' she said, speaking English. 'Look, this is little Ari's aunt. I can scarcely believe it!'

Her son's face might have been carved from stone. 'Extraordinary indeed,' he drawled, and the menace in his voice vibrated like a warning.

But Sophia Theakis did not hear it. Instead, she was drawing Ann towards where her grandson was still riveted by the train display. She laid a gentle arm on his shoulder, spoke something low in Greek and turned him around. For the first time in four long years Ann looked into the face of the little boy she had last seen as a tiny baby.

His face blurred as her eyes hazed with tears. She dropped down to a crouch and took his little hands.

'Hello, Ari,' she said quietly.

The child frowned slightly. 'Ya-ya says you are my *thia*. But I haven't got a *thia*, only a *thios*—Uncle Nikki. Are you married to Uncle Nikki? *Then* you would be my *thia*,' he reasoned, with impeccable logic.

Ann shook her head slightly. His grandmother said something, again in Greek.

'But I haven't got a mummy any more. She and my Daddy live in heaven,' said the little boy.

'Your mummy had a sister, Ari,' said Ann, her voice husky as she spoke. 'That sister is me.'

'Where have you been?' demanded Ari. 'Why have you not been to see me?' He sounded indignant as well as confused.

'I live very far away, Ari,' said Ann, trying to give the child an explanation he could cope with.

'Ari.' Nikos Theakis' deep voice cut curtly across hers. 'We are keeping Ya-ya waiting and delaying your…aunt. She is a very busy woman. I will accompany her to her taxi.'

His voice was as grim as his face, and as he spoke Ann felt his hand clamp heavily around her forearm. Removing her from the scene of her crime was evidently his first concern. But he had reckoned without treachery from within.

'Nikos!' said his mother, surprise and disapproval in her soft voice. She spoke to him rapidly in Greek, with the expressive use of her hands. As she spoke Ann saw his face harden, grow even grimmer. He bit something back to her, and shot a glowering glance in Ann's direction. His mother raised astonished eyebrows, then said something again in Greek to her son.

Nikos Theakis' face set, then he gave a brief, curt nod. 'As you wish,' he said tightly, in English.

Sophia Theakis smiled, and then turned that smile on Ann. Graciously, she invited Ann to lunch, taking Ann's hands in hers.

'I have longed to meet you for many years, my dear child,' she said in her warm voice. She tucked Ann's hand in her arm. 'Come,' she said.

Ann was in a daze, scarcely able to believe what was happening. They left the store and were conveyed by chauffeured car to the hotel where the Theakis party were evidently staying—one of London's premier hotels, overlooking Green Park.

Ann only had eyes for Ari who, realising he had a brand-new admirer, took full advantage, chattering away to her. Yet, despite her undivided attention to the little boy, Ann could not help but feel the dark, glowering presence of his uncle, his anger at her vibrating from every pore, condemning her for her temerity in daring to be there. She ignored it. What did she care if Nikos Theakis were wishing her to oblivion? She returned the compliment tenfold!

Her only concern was Ari.

Her heart clenched again as she took in the miraculous reality of seeing her nephew here, now, in the flesh—a little boy, no longer a baby, no longer only a wrenching memory....

Lunch passed in a daze as well. What she ate she had no idea. She had no idea of anything except the fact she was sitting at a table with Ari, asking him all the questions a child his age would be ready to answer—his favourite toys and stories and activities. He regaled her copiously, prompted sometimes by his nanny, Tina, and sometimes by his grandmother.

His uncle, however, spoke only when referred to by his nephew. This, however, was not seldom, and Ann could see that Nikos Theakis was regarded as a high authority and the fount of great wisdom by his nephew. What she also had to accept—and she knew she should be glad of it—was how patient and attentive he was to Ari, and how Ari showed no timidity or reticence with him. As for his grandmother—it was obvious to Ann that Ari was the apple of her eye.

Across the years, the ghost of her voice, so heartrending in the letter she had written for Ann, echoed in her head: *He will be cherished and loved throughout his life.*

Oh, Carla, thought Ann, her throat catching with emotion. You can be happy—you can be happy at how safe and loved your son is!

A small beringed hand was laid lightly on her wrist. It was Ari's grandmother. 'You are thinking of your sister?' she said, her eyes kind.

Ann could only nod, unable to speak. The older woman smiled sadly.

'We do not know why they were taken from us—your sister and my dear son—but we know they gave us a gift beyond price. And I am so pleased—*so* pleased, my dear—that you are here with us now, after far, far too long away from Ari.'

Again, Ann could not speak—but this time not because of the emotion of grief. What could she say to this kind, sympathetic woman of how cruel the separation had been for her? How cruel, too, her surviving son's strictures on Carla and herself.

She looked away—and straight into dark, hard eyes. Time buckled, and it was if she were once more standing in front of Nikos Theakis in her dingy flat, with him looking at her as if she were a cockroach. Almost she dropped her eyes under that killing basilisk gaze, but then she rallied, her chin lifting slightly, her eyes clashing with his. Then, as she continued to hold his gaze defiantly, refusing to back down, his expression began to change. She didn't know what it was, but something shifted in those hooded night-dark eyes, and as it shifted something quivered down the length of her spine…something that suddenly made her snap her gaze away after all.

Then Ari made some childishly amusing remark, causing her to smile, as well as his grandmother and nanny, and the moment was gone.

As the meal came to an end, Sophia Theakis took Ann's hands again, drawing her to her feet.

'For the moment, alas, we must say goodbye again, while I place myself in the hands of my doctors.' She spoke lightly, but Ann wondered what it was that had brought her to London for medical treatment. Then Ari's grandmother was speaking again. 'But this must not be the end of our acquaintance.

Within a week I shall be returning to Greece for our Easter celebrations, and then, dear child, if it is at all possible, I shall count it the greatest pleasure if you will be my guest there. On Sospiris you shall finally have a chance to make up for the years you have lost with little Ari.' She smiled benignly.

'My son will make all the arrangements. Nikos—' She spoke swiftly in Greek, clearly giving him some kind of instruction. He nodded curtly at the end.

'I will indeed,' he said grimly. 'With the greatest pleasure, I will escort Miss Turner to her destination.'

Dark eyes rested on Ann, and she did not need to be a mind-reader to know where it was that Nikos Theakis wanted her destination to be. Somewhere exceedingly hot would do nicely. With flames.

Nikos closed his hand over the rich material of her coatsleeve, his grip tightening on the arm beneath. Tightly leashed anger lashed within him, as it had been doing since his incredulous gaze had first landed on the figure daring—*daring!*—to speak to his mother in the toy store.

Theos mou, he should have expected this! Should have expected that the girl would make such an attempt! Doubtless the million pounds he'd paid her off with had all been frittered away by now.

His brow darkened. Had it been deliberate? Positioning herself in that toy store, richly arrayed as she was in the spoils of her ill-gotten gains? Of course it had! Why was he even questioning it? What else would a girl like her have been doing in a toy store of all places? No, she must have plotted it deliberately, after discovering—he had yet to find out how!—that his mother was visiting London with Ari, and seeking the opportunity to put herself forward. More fool him for not having expected it. For letting her take him totally by surprise...

In more ways than one. For a moment Nikos felt again the second of the two shocks that had hit him as he'd recognised the woman accosting his mother. Not the rage that had signalled the moment he registered that it was Ann. But the other one. The one that had almost made him look twice, as if his eyes were deceiving him. Deceiving him that the woman with the knockout face and figure could possibly be the same drab, unkempt girl he'd last seen four years ago.

But then, he thought cynically, it was amazing what a million pounds to spend on herself could achieve by way of improvement! Sleek, beautiful hair, subtle make-up, flattering designer clothes and—his cynicism deepened—an expensive winter tan on flawless skin. Oh, yes, Miss Ann Turner with a million pounds at her disposal could well afford never to be drab and repellent ever again! Now she could look every inch a man-trap, like her trollop of a sister…

Not that she was anything like as blatant as her sister. Carla Turner had flaunted the kind of sugar-babe looks that pulled men in the most obvious way possible—including his gullible brother!—but Ann Turner was in a quite different style.

Classy.

The word came to him, and irritated him even more. Yet the woman whose arm his own was now pinioning had fitted in as effortlessly with the hotel dining room and their party as if she had been born to it.

His eyes went to her rigid profile, and assessed it.

Yes, classy. Her *soigné* hairstyle, the discretion of her make-up and the restrained chic of her outfit all created that image.

But it was more than just classiness…

His eyes lingered, and he felt again, angering him, the same reaction he'd felt as his eyes had first settled on her. He knew what it was, that reaction—it was a familiar one to him, and one he usually enjoyed. But *not* when it came in response to a woman like the one he was frog-marching out of the hotel and away from his family…who should never have been allowed to contaminate it in the first place.

What the hell had his mother been thinking of? But even as he posed the question he knew the answer. He'd deliberately sheltered her from the sexually sordid truth about Andreas' disastrous involvement with Carla Turner, and the financially sordid truth about her sister. So no wonder she had taken Ann Turner at face value.

Anger bit in him again—he would have loved to expose the girl for the worthless sham she was, but he would not upset his mother. His brother's death had nearly destroyed her, and Ari had become her only reason to keep going. With her health still frail, he would never upset her by exposing the truth about Ann Turner. But a free lunch was all the girl was going to get. Nothing more.

He thrust her inside a taxi at the hotel entrance, and came in after her. Immediately she slid to the farthest side of the seat, away from him. Illogically, the move annoyed him. Who did Ann Turner think she was to flinch away from him?

He ordered the taxi driver to 'just drive'. Then he turned on his target.

Ann tried to keep the maximum distance from him, but Nikos Theakis seemed to take up far too much space—exacerbated by the way he'd thrown his arm along the back of the seat, stretching out his long legs into the well of the cab.

Four years had made him even more formidable and grim-faced—and his impact was just as overpowering. He was still ludicrously good-looking, but now he looked tougher than ever. He must be into his thirties now, she reckoned swiftly, and the last remnants of youth were long gone. He looked hard, arrogant, and as self-assured as ever. Wealth and power radiated from him. A lot more radiated from him as well…

No! She crushed down the realisation. It was as inappropriate now as it had been four years ago. Worse than inappropriate—wrong. Wrong to pay the slightest attention to the fact that Nikos Theakis had the kind of looks to turn female heads for miles around. The *only* thing about Nikos Theakis she had to register was that she hated him…

Hated him for despising Carla, hated him for taking Ari from her, hated him for paying her to take him…

No—she wouldn't think about that either. It was gone, in the past. And the money was spent, too. All gone now. So she would not let him intimidate her now any more than he had four years ago. She sat in her corner, back stiff, and met his coruscating gaze unflinchingly. It seemed to make him angrier yet. With a rasp in his deep voice he began his attack.

'Doubtless, Miss Turner, you think yourself very clever indeed, insinuating yourself into my family thanks to my mother's innocence and kind nature!' His dark eyes narrowed viciously. 'But make no mistake. You will not be allowed to capitalise on scraping an acquaintance with her. This,' he assured her grimly, 'was your first and last meeting.'

Nikos Theakis' mouth tightened. Irrelevantly, Ann registered the sensual twist to it, and then he was continuing his condemnation of her.

'You have no place in my nephew's life—*no place*—do you understand? That was the agreement you made, was it not, four years ago, when you sold your dead sister's baby to me for cash?'

The scorn in his voice excoriated her. Ann felt herself flushing beneath its venom. She opened her mouth to retaliate, but his eyes flicked over her like a whip.

'And I can see just where the cash went.' His hand, resting along the back of the seat, dipped to touch the fleece of her coat's shoulder, trailing one finger down her upper arm. 'Cashmere,' he murmured, his tone changing suddenly from angry to smooth, his long lashes sweeping down over his eyes. 'So soft. So warm.' His mouth twisted. 'So expensive. Tell me,' he went on in that dangerous voice, 'has the million pounds all gone? Is that why you have decided to break your agreement and try to stick your greedy little fingers into the Theakis honey pot once more?'

The hand was still on Ann's sleeve, idly brushing the soft fabric. It should have been a harmless gesture, but it wasn't. It should have been intangible through the layers of her coat and the sleeve of her dress beneath, but it wasn't. Ann felt that light touch all the way through to her skin. Felt it, out of nowhere, cut right through her anger and resentment to reach the quick...

Her heart started to beat more heavily and her eyes were dragged to his. They were very dark, the eyes of Nikos Theakis, half closed as they surveyed her all over, from the pale gleaming crown of her gilt-blonde head, sweeping on across the fine bones of her face, dwelling a moment on her long-lashed grey eyes, then on down the slender curves of her body to the long, shapely length of her stockinged legs.

The breath caught in her throat. It was that moment again— the one that had happened so fleetingly, so briefly, at the end of lunch—the one that she had deliberately ignored, refused to acknowledge. But now she could not ignore it...

Four years ago this man had consigned her to the realms of the sexually repulsive. He'd cast one look at her messy, drab appearance and dismissed her.

He wasn't dismissing her now.

The dark eyes washed over her leisurely, keeping the breath stifled in her lungs, the muscles of her throat constricted. Her heart was giving slow, ponderous slugs as everything seemed to slow down, inside and out. The traffic noise faded, everything faded except the pulse in the hollow of her neck, the tightness of her lungs. She tried to fight it, tried to draw breath—but she couldn't. Could only go on sitting there as his eyes came back to her—reading her reaction.

He smiled.

It was not a nice smile, but it made a pool of heat flush all the way through Ann's body. He watched the heat flood through her as if it were a visible wave, his dark eyes veiled as they looked over her, through her.

The air in the taxi was thick, tangible. She felt his hand lift from her shoulder and reach a little further. Then the pad of his index finger was touching her cheek, drawing down it like a knife blade. Her eyes were locked on his—she could not break away.

She shivered.

The hand dropped, and rested again innocuously on the back of the taxi seat. But it had done its damage. She felt his touch sear her cheek as if his hand were still there. As if his touch had burnt into her skin…

'I will tell you how it will be, Miss Turner,' Nikos Theakis informed her, as though he were having a normal conversation with her. His voice had become flat and unemotional. All trace of his awareness of her as a female had vanished, as if a light had been switched off. 'There will be no more Theakis money for you. You have had your pay off. If you have squandered it, that is your misfortune. You will have no opportunity to take advantage of my mother's generosity and sentimental kind-heartedness.' His voice flattened even more, and the dark eyes beheld her opaquely. 'Accordingly, there will be no little holiday for you on Sospiris. No continuation of this touching reunion with the child you sold for a million pounds so that you could buy yourself a worthless lifestyle for a few years. No further contact with my nephew or my family at all. Do you understand me?'

Ann bit her lip. She longed to yell back at him but what was the point? She already knew she could not accept Mrs Theakis's invitation—it was *impossible,* impossible. She did not need Nikos Theakis telling her that, ordering her to stay away from Ari.

Seeing Ari again like this, out of the blue, had been a miracle—a wonderful gift. But that was all it was. Oh, now that Mrs Theakis had met her perhaps Ann would finally be allowed to write to Ari, send him presents, even occasionally see him—but she could never be part of his life. She knew that—accepted that. Had long ago accepted that.

So all she said now was a tight lipped, 'Yes, I understand, Mr Theakis.'

'That is as well,' he said curtly, lifting his hand to rap on the cabby's glass. 'I see we understand each other. Make sure it stays that way, Miss Turner.'

Then the taxi was stopping, and Nikos Theakis was climbing out, having pressed a twenty-pound note into the cabby's hand and told him to take his remaining passenger wherever the fare warranted. Then, briefly, he turned his attention back to Ann.

'Stay away from my family.'

Then he strode off into the London crowd, and Ann could see him no more.

For the second time in four years Nikos Theakis had walked out of her life.

He would walk back in far more swiftly.

CHAPTER TWO

ANN HAD JUST returned to her flat with a bagful of groceries. She had heard nothing more from Ari's grandmother, though she had posted a polite thank-you letter to the hotel, thanking her for lunch and for her kindness in letting her have such precious time with Ari. It saddened her profoundly that she would never know him as she longed to, but at least she knew now that he was having the happiest of childhoods, with a doting grandmother and, she forced herself to acknowledge, an uncle who clearly held his nephew in affection, despite his harsh condemnation of his mother and aunt.

She gained the kitchen and started to unpack the groceries. The front doorbell rang. Frowning slightly, for she was not expecting anyone, Ann trotted down the narrow hallway and cautiously opened the door.

But not cautiously enough. Like an action replay from four years ago, Nikos Theakis strode inside.

'We,' he announced balefully to an open-mouthed Ann, 'shall speak.'

'You want me to do what?' she demanded, staring down at Nikos Theakis disbelievingly. He was sitting in the armchair by the window of the living room, and his expensive, bespoke tailored presence was as dominatingly incongruous as it had been four years ago.

'Spend a month in Greece, at my mother's house on Sospiris,' repeated the man who'd told her to stay away from his family.

'Why?' she asked bluntly, folding her arms defensively over her chest. She was wearing jeans today, and the top she was wearing with them suddenly seemed to be showing off her figure voluptuously. Nikos Theakis' gaze had swept over her as he'd walked in and sat himself down without a by-your-leave, and she had not liked it.

But then there was nothing about Nikos Theakis she liked. Least of all the way he was speaking to her now.

He was angry. That was obvious. It was suppressed anger, but anger all the same, leashed on a tight rein. It had not stopped him flicking his gaze over her in a way that had brought a flush to her cheek—a flush that had nothing to do with the fact that she not expected to set eyes on him again and did not want to anyway. Even if her insides *had* given a sudden gulp as she'd rested her eyes on him…on his tall, powerful frame…the hard, handsome face and those night dark eyes.

Then all other thoughts had vanished from her head as he had dropped his bombshell.

'You are to come to Sospiris because,' he bit out, 'my mother insists! And,' he ground out even more bitingly, 'as her doctor informs me that her heart condition will be exacerbated by any emotional upset, I have no option but to concede to her wishes. Well?' he demanded, tight lipped. 'What are you waiting for? Start packing.'

Ann crushed her arms more tightly over her chest.

As if in an action replay from four years ago, Ann watched him reach into his suit jacket, take out his leather-bound chequebook, hook one leg over his knee to create a writing platform, and fill out a cheque with his gold fountain pen. He presented it to her with a contemptuous flourish.

'The fee, Miss Turner, for your very expensive and valuable time.'

His opinion of her cut through his voice.

Numbly she took the piece of paper he proffered her. The zeros blurred, then resolved themselves. She gave a faint sigh of shock and her eyes widened.

'Ten thousand pounds, Miss Turner.' Nikos Theakis' hatefully sarcastic voice floated over her head somewhere. 'Now, that is what I call an expenses-paid holiday…'

Slowly, Ann shifted her gaze so that she met his eyes. The expression in them could have incinerated her on the spot. Answering emotion seared her breast. With one part of her she wanted to rip the cheque into a dozen pieces and throw them in his cold, contemptuous face. And with another she felt a gush of excited anticipation at seeing her nephew again, combined with the sudden rush of realisation that she held ten thousand pounds in her hands. A fortune—and one that she knew exactly how to spend.

Just the way she had spent her last cheque from Nikos Theakis.

A smile of sweet pleasure broke across her face. 'Why, Mr Theakis,' she said saccharinely, knowing just how angry she could make him, and how satisfying that would be to her insulted soul, 'how very, very generous of you. I believe I shall start packing straight away.'

As she turned away, heading for the stairs, a word slithered out of the sculpted, sensual mouth. She couldn't tell what it was, because it was Greek. But it was enunciated with such deadly venom that she did not request a translation.

For a moment Ann stood transfixed, as if he'd struck her physically, not just verbally. Then, back stiffening, she gave a tiny, indifferent shrug of her shoulders and walked out of the room to begin her packing.

* * *

Ann craned her neck as the helicopter swooped in to land on the helipad behind the Theakis villa. Set in a huge, landscaped Mediterranean garden, on the tiny private island of Sospiris, the villa was breathtakingly beautiful—gleaming white, its walls and terraces splashed with bougainvillea, the vivid hues of an azure swimming pool competing with the even more azure hues of the Aegean all around. As they disembarked, she gazed around her, revelling not just in the beauty of the surroundings, but in the balmy warmth after the chill British spring.

Nikos Theakis watched her reaction as she stared about her, visibly delighted. 'Worth getting your greedy little claws into, Miss Turner?' he murmured.

Ann ignored him, as she had done her best to do all the way from London on the private jet that had flown them to the Greek mainland. He had returned the favour, occupying himself with his laptop and a pile of what she had assumed were business documents.

But if Nikos Theakis made it crystal clear she was here very nearly over his dead body, the warmth of his mother's greeting almost equalled the exuberance of her grandson's, who had swooped on his newly discovered aunt with a fierce hug from so little a body. As she crouched down to return his embrace, Ann's eyes misted.

Oh, Carla—if you could see your son now. How happy he is, how much he is part of the family you wanted for him. And this would have been Carla's home too—she would have been bringing her son up here, in this beautiful villa, married to Andreas, in the perfect life that her sister had so longed for. Instead a grave had been waiting for her, and for the man she'd so wanted to marry...

Anguish crushed Ann, then resolutely she put it aside. The past was gone—it could not be undone. Only the present was left, and the future that was Carla's and Andreas' son.

* * *

Nikos watched Ann Turner entering the salon that one of the house staff was ushering her into. He had seen nothing of her since he had handed her over to his mother on their arrival at the villa that afternoon, taking refuge from his grim mood by incarcerating himself in his study. Work, at least, had taken his mind off the unwelcome presence of a woman he wished to perdition, but who had, instead, succeeded in further insinuating himself into his family. Now, however, he was face to face with her again. His gaze surveyed her impassively. But impassiveness was not the hallmark of his mood. Resentment and grim anger were. And another thing he resented, even more than her presence.

Her impact on him as a woman.

His mouth tightened as he watched her approach his mother. Damn the girl—why did she have to look like that? Why couldn't she still look the way she had four years ago? Why did she have to be wand slender, with that incredible hair swept back off her face, her classically beautiful features set off by an aqua knee-length dress in some fine jersey material that skimmed her lissom body, making her look both subtly alluring and yet not obviously so. Why did he have to wonder what it might be like to sift his fingers through that long hair, inconveniently restrained in a velvet tie? Why did he have to speculate whether her breasts, scarcely outlined in the discreetly styled dress, would repay his personal investigation?

Forcibly, he dragged his eyes away from her towards his mother. She was smiling graciously at her guest, holding out a hand to invite her to join her on the sofa for pre-dinner drinks. Nikos felt his mood worsen. Watching his mother smile, bestow her kindness, her favour, on so worthless an object, galled him bitterly—yet there was nothing he could do about it. Not without hurting his mother, shocking her with the squalid truth about Ari's aunt.

No, like it or not—and he did *not*—he would have to endure

this farce, and make sure it ended as swiftly as possible, with the least opportunity for Ann Turner to get her greedy little claws yet deeper into both his coffers and his family.

She was greeting his mother prettily now, in halting phrase-book Greek, which set Nikos' teeth on edge but drew a warm smile of approval from his mother. Then she was taking the place indicated to her, and smiling her thanks as one of the staff offered her a drink. Moodily, Nikos seized his martini from the manservant's tray. He felt in need of its strengthening powers tonight.

'So, my dear child,' his mother was saying to her guest, 'I hope you have had an enjoyable afternoon with little Ari? Was I wrong to let him monopolise you so much on your very arrival? But he has been so eager for you to come.'

Ann smiled warmly. 'I've had a wonderful time! He is such a lovely little boy, Kyria Theakis,' she said spontaneously. 'Thank you—thank you so much for all you have done for him…'

Her voice threatened to break, and she fell silent.

'My dear,' said Sophia Theakis, reaching out her small hand to touch Ann's. 'He is our own precious child, is he not? We love him for himself—and for the memory he brings of those we have loved and who are no more.'

As tears pricked in Ann's eyes she felt her hand squeezed briefly, comfortingly. She blinked, looking away—straight into a pair of hard, dark eyes. Nikos Theakis' scathing gaze as he beheld this affecting scene.

Her own gaze hardened in response. She would not let this obnoxious man judge her—condemn her. She turned away, back to Mrs Theakis.

'Now,' Ari's grandmother went on, 'you must allow me to introduce my dear cousin, Eupheme, who is so very kind as to keep me company and take charge of the beautiful garden we have here which she created for us all.'

Another woman of late middle-age—who had, Ann

realised, just entered by a different door on the other side of the room—came forward now. Ann stood up and waited as Mrs Theakis performed the introductions. Again, Ann murmured in phrasebook Greek. It drew a kind smile from her hostess's companion, and an answer in Greek, which was swiftly translated for her by Mrs Theakis, who added that Cousin Eupheme spoke little English.

The topic of the conversation returned to Ari, and Ann was more than happy for it to do so, turning away from Nikos Theakis. Yet she felt him watching her like a malevolent bird of prey. The back of her neck prickled.

Why did the damn man get to her like this? She didn't like him—he didn't like her. God knew he had made that clear enough! Well, she didn't care about that—didn't care anything about him—cared only that she was here, in Ari's home, for the first time in her life. She would not let Nikos Theakis spoil so treasured an occasion for her.

This was difficult, for Nikos Theakis in a white dinner jacket that set off his natural tan and his strong, ludicrously good-looking features, was hard to ignore, though Ann did her dogged best. Surely she couldn't care less that he was a darkly stunning specimen of the male species, compelling and magnetic—this man who had called her sister a whore? Her mouth tightened as she took her place at the beautifully burnished dining table indoors.

Nevertheless, thanks to Mrs Theakis' impeccable skills as an experienced hostess, dinner passed comfortably enough, helped by the fact that Nikos Theakis contributed little more than his glowering presence at the table.

'You have arrived at a time that is both happy and sad for us, my child,' her hostess remarked at one point. 'Perhaps Tina has already told you that she is to be married from this house shortly? Her fiancé, Dr Forbes, is an archaeologist, excavating on our larger neighbour, Maxos. Indeed, she is spending the evening with him there tonight. I am happy for her, of course, but I confess I shall miss her—and Ari even more so, for she has been an essential part of his family since he came here. So your arrival will serve to divert him from his impending loss.'

'I'd be delighted to divert him,' enthused Ann, and the conversation moved on again.

After dinner, they removed to the salon for coffee, but it was not long before Ann, feeling the strain of the day, opted to retire to bed. As if the punctilious host, Nikos escorted her to the door in a parody of politeness. Away from his mother and Eupheme, Ann could feel once more the assessing, leisurely flick of his eyes over her, lingering a moment on the swell of her breasts. To her flustered dismay, she felt them tightening beneath his scrutiny.

'Another beautiful garment—and one that flatters your beauty,' he murmured in a low voice. 'I am glad to see you disposed so tastefully of my money...'

His smile was like the baring of a jackal's teeth. She turned her head sharply away and strode off across the wide, marble-floored hallway towards the staircase, sure that she heard a soft, jibing laugh behind her.

Damn him, why did he get to her like that? Why should she care what Nikos Theakis thought of her? He was nothing to her—*nothing*.

I'm here for Ari—that's all.

That was what she must remember—only that.

Tina reinforced Ann's determination the next day. The two women were on the beach in front of the villa, watching Ari industriously dig a very large, deep hole in the sand some little way away. Tina, so similar to her in age, with a friendly personality, was easy company. She was full of praise for both Mrs Theakis and Nikos Theakis. The former Ann could well understand, but her expression must have showed her doubt about the latter.

'Nikos is a fantastic employer,' enthused Tina. 'Incredibly generous. He's sponsoring Sam's dig, you know, and letting me have my reception at the villa. Plus he's wonderful with Ari, and is devoted to his mother's welfare too.'

Yes, thought Ann, *enough to force himself to pay me a ridiculous amount of money to come here because she wants me here!*

Aloud, she simply murmured, 'I suppose that's understandable, given Mrs Theakis' frail health.'

Tina's eyes lit. 'Is it, though? You know, I suspect that Mrs Theakis finds her poor health very useful! Nikos was dead set against the trip to London, saying it would be too tiring for her, but lo and behold Mrs Theakis' doctor recommended a heart specialist there, so off we all went! Mind you,' she went on, 'he's nowhere near so co-operative with other women! As you can imagine, with his looks and money, women are all over him—and desperate to become Mrs Nikos Theakis. But he won't be caught by any of them! He just enjoys them, then it's over. But of course he gets away with it. Men like that do.' She shrugged good-humouredly, then turned her attention back to her charge. 'Ari, pet, how's that hole coming along? Can we come and see it yet?'

The rest of the morning was spent with Ari, but after lunch, while Ari had his afternoon nap, Ann could no longer resist the lure of the swimming pool. Sliding into its silky azure depths, she did a few taxing lengths, then slowed to a leisurely breaststroke. Her wet hair streamed behind her, sleeked off her face, and the sun glittered in her eyes, warming her with its rays, as she moved soothingly, rhythmically through the water. A sense of well-being filled her at the peace and quiet and beauty of it all.

Until, with the strangest prickling in the back of her neck, she started to feel uneasy. Reaching the far end of the pool, she halted, holding the marble edge and looking around her.

She saw him immediately. On an upper terrace, one hand resting on the balustrade, looking down at her.

Nikos Theakis.

Instantly she felt vulnerable—exposed. Instinct told her to get out of the water as fast as she could and grab a towel. But that would mean he'd see her, and out of the pool she'd be even more exposed than with the translucent veil of the water. For a moment she hesitated, then, with a splash, she plunged back into the water, swimming again. After another two lengths she glanced surreptitiously up at the balcony again. To her relief, no one was there. Quickly, she got out of the pool and wrapped her towel around her tightly, recovering her composure.

She would not feel intimidated by Nikos Theakis! Recklessly, she settled down to sunbathe, lying on her tummy and loosening her bikini top to expose her back. As she lay soaking up the sun she started to feel drowsy in the quietness and warmth, and felt herself slipping away into sleep.

Dreams came, hazy and somnolent, drifting through her unconscious mind, scarcely registering.

Except one.

She felt in her dream a shadow falling over her, and then a hand stroking down the bare length of her sun-warm spine with a slow, caressing touch. She murmured something, nestling her face into the cushion. Then dreamless sleep closed over her once more.

Beside the lounger Nikos stood, watching her motionless form. His face was shuttered.

Why had he just done that? Why had he succumbed to the impulse he'd experienced when he'd taken a break from his work, gone out on to the terrace outside his office to get a breath of fresh air, and seen that lissom figure cutting smoothly through the water, the sunlight shimmering on her barely veiled body? He should have gone straight back indoors. Instead, he had gone on watching her, until she'd glanced up and caught him watching.

Abruptly, annoyed that she'd seen him looking at her, he'd gone back to his office. But he hadn't settled. And before ten minutes were up he'd pushed his chair back restlessly and gone out on the terrace again. She'd get out of the pool now, sunning herself.

His eyes had gone to her immediately. To the slender body, the sculpted perfection of her back, the narrow indent of her waist and the gentle swell of her hips, rounding down into long, gazelle legs.

He'd felt himself respond to the image, unable to look away, annoyed with himself for succumbing. Even more annoyed when he'd found he had started to walk down the flight of steps to the pool level, had strolled across to her, to see her in close-up, and worse, had succumbed to the impulse to lower a hand to her exposed nape, then glide it slowly, leisurely, down the elegant length of her spine.

She was like silk to touch…

He snapped his hand away.

Hell, this was not supposed to be happening. He shouldn't be responding to the damn girl! He was supposed to be ignoring her, being wise, totally wise, to the allure she held for him!

Because anything else was folly. Folly and madness. He knew exactly what Ann Turner was, and despite the beautiful packaging the woman inside was venal and worthless.

If she'd thrown that cheque back in his face—told him that no power on earth could part her from her nephew—then he might have thought better of her! But, no, she hadn't been able to take her eyes from the cheque…

For a long moment he simply stood, looking broodingly down on her sleeping, near naked form.

She really was lovely…so very tempting..

No. Cost him what it would, he must remember the only important thing about Ann Turner—she had sold her nephew to him for cash, and was here only because she was hoping for yet more money from the Theakis coffers. That was all he must keep in his mind.

Everything else was—irrelevant.

Abruptly, he turned away. There was work to be done. On swift, disciplined strides, he went back to his office, closing the doors to the terrace behind him with a decided snap.

Ann's sleep ended abruptly some time later when Ari, energy levels recharged from his nap, emerged with Tina, like a miniature rocket in swimming trunks and armbands. A hectic water playtime ensued, followed by refreshments at the edge of the pool, where they were joined by Ari's grandmother and Cousin Eupheme.

Sitting on a swing seat, Ari beside her, chattering away, Ann found herself thinking that although she had been here only such a short time, she fitted in as easily and naturally as if there had been no dark history keeping her away, parting her from Ari. But she knew exactly why she was feeling comfortably at ease now—because Nikos Theakis wasn't there, casting his malign, intimidating shadow over everything.

She had to face him again over dinner, however. She'd come up from the nursery quarters with Tina, who was not with her fiancé that evening, after helping her put Ari to bed. Once again she'd read him to sleep, and as she'd dropped one last light kiss on his forehead she'd felt a lump form in her throat.

Carla's son. Happy and secure.

Her memories swept back to the days of her own childhood, when her whole universe had been her older sister, to whom she had clung in the frightening, confused times they had both faced. In those fearful years where would she have been without Carla to hold her, to kiss her goodnight, to be all the family she had? And here, now, she was kissing Carla's son goodnight—who had no mother of his own.

But Ari's happy, she thought, fighting down the lump. *He does not miss the parents he never had. He has his grandmother, and his uncle, and a kind and affectionate nanny. And now, for this brief time, he has me.*

The briefness of her time with him clutched at her heart like a cold hand. Then anger stabbed in its stead. *Damn Nikos Theakis!* she thought. *Damn his arrogance and his pride and his despicable double-standard that lets him help himself to as many women as he pleases, but allows him to sneer from his golden throne at my sister, who had to make her own way in the world the best she could! He had kept her apart for Andreas, cheated them of what little time they could have had together...*

She sheered her mind away from the dark, familiar thoughts. Recriminations were pointless. The past was gone. Carla was gone, and so was Andreas. Only little Ari remained—and he was happy and content. That was enough. It would have to be.

There was no sign of Nikos Theakis when she and Tina first entered the salon, and Ann was relieved. Tina stepped out on to the terrace with Cousin Eupheme, who was telling her about some new plantings she was planning. Mrs Theakis called Ann to her side, smiling fondly at her.

'I am so glad to see you here at last, my dear. I am more sorry than I can say that so much time has passed without your taking your rightful place in Ari's life,' Mrs Theakis said sadly. Her beautiful dark eyes shadowed. 'I grieved so much,' she went on slowly, 'when Andreas was killed. It is the greatest tragedy of all—to lose a child. That is why, my dear, I begged you for the care of Andreas' son. Holding his child in my arms, I knew God had given me back my own son. You gave me a gift, that day, that I can never repay—'

She stopped, and Ann could see she was near to tears. Impulsively, she took the older woman's thin hand.

'I gave him to you with all my heart,' she said quietly.

There was a footfall, and a voice from the doorway spoke.

'Gave?' questioned Nikos Theakis.

The single word crawled like ice down Ann's spine.

His mother seemed not to hear him. Her face lightened. 'Nikki!' she exclaimed. 'There you are!' She made to get to her feet, and immediately, attentively, her son was there. But even as he moved, he did not stint from casting a look at Ann that might have withered her to the spot.

For the remainder of the evening, until she could retire, as early as she decently could, Ann did her absolute best to minimise the presence of Nikos Theakis. But when, having finally escaped, she stood on the balcony of her room, gazing out over the beautiful nightscape of gardens, beach and sea, emotion seethed in her.

Why do I let him get to me? Why?

It made her angry with herself that she could not ignore him, could not blank him out. She knew what he thought of Carla, what he thought of her—and why should she care? The soft wind winnowed at her hair, lifting it from her nape, making her give a tiny shiver that was not from cold. Why should she care that when she felt that dark, brooding gaze resting on her resentment and intimidation was not all she felt...?

Why could she feel the power of that dark gaze?

The wind came again, playing over her body, sifting her hair with long, sensuous fingers...

No! Her hands clenched over the balustrade. No! She turned away abruptly, heading indoors to make herself ready for bed. But when she lay sleepless, gazing up at the ceiling, that dark, brooding gaze was all that she could see.

CHAPTER THREE

THE NEXT MORNING saw a reprieve. Nikos, so she was informed by his mother over breakfast, had taken himself back to Theakis HQ in Athens. Immediately Ann relaxed, and spent a happy and peaceful three days, devoting herself entirely to Ari. But the following day, visiting Maxos for lunch and some light shopping with Ari and Tina, a helicopter heading out to Sospiris saw Ann's respite from Nikos over.

Worse was to come. The next day was to be an excursion that Ari had been enthusing about several times: a visit to the beach at the far end of the island. To Ann's absolute dismay, Mrs Theakis gave Tina leave to spend the day with her fiancé, and directed Nikos to drive Ann and Ari. Desperately, Ann tried to think of a way to get out of the coming ordeal, but how could she disappoint Ari?

Tense and reluctant, she climbed up with Ari into the canvas-topped Jeep—a mode of transport which had the little boy in transports of delight.

'It's really, really bumpy!' he enthused.

He was not exaggerating. And as Nikos Theakis, who had not yet said a word to her directly, set off at a greater speed than Ann liked along the unmade track heading across the island, she hung on grimly, repeatedly hurled against the metal doorframe as they took hairpin corners and avoided the larger potholes. Finally the Jeep swept to a halt on the stony upper reaches of a beach, and Ann looked around. They had descended into what was almost a hidden valley, between high cliffs that opened out into a patch of close-cropped grazing populated by a handful of goats. The banks of a dry stream bed were smothered in wild oleanders. Beyond, the grass and stones gave way to golden sand and then brilliant azure sea. It was very private, very remote, and incredibly beautiful.

Shakily, Ann got down, lifting Ari with her. He immediately sprinted off on to the beach, as Nikos hefted down a kit bag bulging with beach paraphernalia from the back of the Jeep. As she followed Ari she brushed the chalky dust off her long-sleeved T-shirt and long, loose cotton trousers, shaking out her windblown hair.

'The sea will wash off the dust,' Nikos said laconically beside her, as he fell into step at her side.

She ignored him. She had been doing her best to ignore him ever since the expedition started. Only for Ari's sake and his grandmother's would she be civil to this man. Without their presence she saw no reason to force herself to a hypocritical politeness she did not feel.

Nikos evidently thought otherwise. His hand closed over her arm, stopping her in her tracks. She tried to shake herself free, but his grip was like iron. He turned her towards him and she glared at him balefully. His own dark eyes glinted stonily back at her.

'Understand something. Had I my choice, you would not be here. But my mother wanted this outing to take place, and Ari, as you can see, is deliriously excited. Therefore, for his sake, you will be civil. You will not sulk, or behave badly. Farce it may be, but I will not have Ari upset. Do you understand me?'

'Why else do you think I'm here?' she shot back. 'It's only because of Ari and your mother.'

He stared at her grimly a moment. 'Good,' he said, and let her go, striding off.

She stared after him a moment, rubbing where he'd gripped her arm. A bruise was already coming up from all the bashing it had received on the journey here. She set off again, pausing to take off her canvas shoes as she reached the sand. It was slow progress in the deep soft sand, and by the time she caught up with them Nikos was already making camp in the lee of some rocks to the side of the beach, spreading out a rug over a groundsheet. Ari was helping—if upending the kit bag and rummaging through for spades and buckets could be considered helpful. Finding what he wanted, he immediately started to dig a hole. Ann watched him a moment, a smile playing on her lips. Ari definitely seemed to like his sand holes. As she turned to put her own beach bag down on the rug, she realised that Nikos was watching her, with a different expression from usual on his face. It seemed—assessing.

She busied herself unpacking her bag. She didn't really know what was expected of the day, and had had no intention of asking Nikos, so she had brought what she thought would be likely—including a swimsuit, which she was wearing under her clothes. But not the two-piece. Today's was a workmanlike one piece that was as unrevealing of her figure as a swimsuit could be. Whether she would have the nerve to strip down to it in Nikos Theakis' presence, she didn't know, but she did know that if Ari wanted her to come in the water with him she would not turn him down.

For something to do, and to stop feeling as awkward as she did, she went over to Ari and inspected the progress of his hole so far.

'Would you like me to help?' she offered. It seemed preferable to being stuck with his uncle's company.

Ari shook his head. 'You and Uncle Nikki have to dig your own holes, and the biggest hole wins,' he informed her.

'I'll start one here,' said Ann, moving a little away and dropping to her knees to begin. 'Your uncle can dig his own.'

There was a bite in her words as she spoke that she did not trouble to mute. Nor the unspoken coda—*and bury himself in it too, for all I care!*

She set to, scrabbling at the soft sand until a darker, more compact layer was exposed, which could be dug into satisfactorily. She dug industriously, using her bare hands, pausing only to retie her hair into a pigtail to stop it falling forward.

A shadow fell over her, and then Nikos was hunkering down to inspect both holes.

'Mine is deeper!' claimed Ari.

'You started earlier,' said Nikos. 'And you are using a spade.'

'Auntie Annie can have my spare spade,' said Ari generously, and pushed it across to Ann.

'Auntie Annie…' Nikos's voice was musing.

'Tina has started referring to me as that,' said Ann shortly, reaching for Ari's spare spade and thanking him.

Nikos's eyes rested on her unreadably. 'You do not seem like an "Auntie Annie,"' he said. 'Nor even like a plain and simple "Ann." Surely, once you were able to afford your new wealthy lifestyle, you aspired to a new name to reflect your new image? Even Anna would be more exotic.'

Ann ignored him, merely digging more vigorously.

Nikos levered himself back upright. Why had he let himself bait her like that? It was just that there was something about her today that was galling him more than ever. The intervening days had been intended to put a mental as well as physical distance from her, and though he had had been reluctant to leave her with his mother without his watchful eye, not only had he had things to do in Athens that could not be postponed easily, he'd also wanted a break from Ann Turner.

She was too disturbing to his peace of mind—and not just because of the threat she presented to his family. Ann Turner's presence on Sospiris disturbed him for quite another reason. One he was determined to crush just as ruthlessly as he would crush any attempt on her part to extract yet more money from the Theakis coffers.

While in Athens he had deliberately kept his evenings busy with social events. It was inconvenient, however, that he was currently between affairs. It would have suited him to have someone to take his mind off Ann Turner. She had occupied far too much of it already. Exasperatingly, any hopes that he'd had that when he returned to Sospiris he'd find her considerably less eye-drawing had evaporated on his return. The damn woman had just the same effect on him as before.

It rattled him.

It shouldn't be happening. He knew exactly what she was, and that should be sufficient—more than sufficient!—to put him off her big-time. And yet—

And yet he had found himself once again, covertly watching her—telling himself it was because he was keeping her under surveillance, to show her that every word she uttered was suspect, that he had the measure of her even if she were fooling his mother, and taking in the sculpted line of her jaw, the graceful fall of her hair, the wide-set grey eyes, the sensuous swell of her breasts.

And now it was even worse. His mother had manoeuvred him into taking Ari and the boy's pernicious aunt on this be-nighted jaunt. And for Ari's sake he could not refuse, nor spoil it for him by allowing his hostility to show.

His eyes rested on her bowed head. She was digging away as if possessed, refusing to pay him any attention. And that was another thing—the fact that she wasn't paying him any attention. Deliberately. Conspicuously. She was doing it on purpose, obviously, in an act of defiance—doubtless hoping that it would maybe convince him of a moral purity that was impossible for a woman who had sold her nephew for cash. Her hypocrisy infuriated him.

His mouth set. So Ann Turner, hypocrite and baby-seller, thought she could blank him, did she? Thought she could look through him, cut him, ignore him—defy him? Thought she'd run circles round him by ending up ensconced here, in the lap of luxury, ingratiating herself with his mother, his nephew—the nephew she'd *sold?*

Anger filled him as he watched them—the little boy that was all that was left of the brother he had lost, of the son his mother had lost, and the girl who had valued a million pounds more than an orphaned child, her blood kin. How dared she play the hypocrite? Not just with him, Nikos Theakis, who could see through her hypocrisy, but with the innocent Ari…

Harsh eyes looked at her.

You play with the child you sold to put designer clothes on your back, to jet you around the world…

A memory came back to him—one that filled him with deepest disgust, blackest rage.

Not of Ann Turner.

Of her sister.

A woman who had offered her body for cash—cash from any man who could afford it. Any man rich enough to keep her in the luxury she thought she was worth. Any man…

Bleak, empty eyes looked now on Carla's sister. So, just what was the beautiful, alluring Ann Turner prepared to do to get more money?

His mouth twisted into a travesty of a smile as the thought resolved slowly, temptingly, in his mind. What would she do if he made her an offer he'd make it very, very hard for her to refuse?

Very hard—

For a long moment he just went on looking down at the silvery-gold head. He could feel the blood stirring in his veins as he made his decision. Yes, that was exactly what he would do—make her an offer he would ensure it was impossible for her to refuse, and in so doing take the greatest satisfaction possible himself—in more ways than one! Indulge himself with her exactly as he wanted to. And all in the best possible cause—getting her claws out of his family. Permanently.

Ann sat back and looked at her hole. At least digging it seemed to have shut Nikos Theakis up in his attempts to talk to her.

She looked across at Ari. 'How's it coming?' she enquired.

He paused, and looked across at her. 'Is yours bigger?' he asked.

'I'm not sure,' she temporised.

'Uncle Nikki can judge,' said Ari.

Nikos had, to Ann's relief, returned to the camp, and was idly flicking through a business magazine. Now he looked up, and got to his feet. He strolled across the sand, and Ann did not like to see the way his legs seemed so long in his chinos, or the way his T-shirt moulded to his powerful torso.

Solemnly he inspected both sand holes. 'Ann's is wider, but Ari's is deeper,' he pronounced.

'I win!' shouted Ari excitedly. He turned to his aunt. 'You have to dig them the *deepest*,' he explained. He dropped his spade to the sand. 'Can we swim now, Uncle Nikki—can we?'

He'd spoken in Greek, and Ann could not understand him. Nikos glanced at Ann. 'Well, does your English *sang froid* run to a dip in the Aegean at this time of year?' he enquired laconically.

She gave a shrug. 'I'm happy to go in with Ari,' she said.

As well as not liking the way his legs seemed so long, or his torso so powerful, she also did not like the way he was looking at her. A veiled look that did things to her breathing she did not want it to.

'Good,' he said, and then he said something to Ari which Ann assumed was assent.

She had no objection to taking Ari into the water, however cold it might be. It would get her away from Nikos. He could sit in the sun and read his magazine and welcome. But as she scrambled to her feet, dusting sand off her knees and hands, she froze. Nikos, it seemed, was intending to go in the sea as well.

He was stripping off. Before her frozen eyes, he proceeded to divest himself of his chinos and polo shirt down to bare skin.

She stared, open-mouthed.

His body was fantastic. And there was so much of it! The golden shoulders were just as broad as she'd always known they'd be, his back long and smooth, his legs longer and not smooth—fuzzed with a sheen of dark hair over taut muscles that was echoed in the narrow arrowing above the waistband of his hip-hugging bathing trunks. Whether he worked out or it just came naturally, his abdominal muscles were unblemished by an ounce of fat, and the smooth, olive-hued pectorals were likewise perfect.

As he finished undressing, he glanced at Ann. For a moment his eyes stayed veiled, as if observing her reaction. Then, with an indolent, satisfied smile, he reached out one long index finger under her chin and closed her mouth.

'Your turn,' he invited softly. 'Or should I say—my turn?'

He stood, casually poised, with all the natural grace of a Greek statue but with absolutely none of its Platonic virtues, and waited for her to do likewise and disrobe—so he could watch her the way she had watched him.

As she stood stiff and immobile, he gave her a taunting smile.

'Don't worry, I've checked it out already. You pass muster.'

She started, confused. He enlightened her. 'By the pool. You were sunbathing.'

Colour mounted in her cheek as the penny dropped and subconscious memory flooded back. 'You touched me!' she

accused, outraged. God, she thought she'd been dreaming, and
all along the hand that she'd imagined stroking over her back
had been real. Had been his. Eyes flashing with anger she
dropped down to help Ari inflate his armbands and take his
T-shirt off.

She heard a mocking laugh, lightly running feet, and then,
her eyes automatically flying upwards, she saw Nikos Theakis
launching itself into the azure water, splashing loudly in the
quietness all around them. As he headed out to sea with long,
powerful strokes, Ann dragged her eyes away. Grimly, she
helped Ari get ready for swimming.

'You have to come in too!' said Ari.

'After lunch,' she said, sliding his armbands on and
checking their fit. 'Anyway, I take ages changing, and Uncle
Nikki is already in the water. I'll come and watch you both.'

Accepting this compromise, Ari hammered over the sand
to the water's edge, shouting enthusiastically in Greek to the
figure cutting through the water. Watching Ari plunge in, and
his uncle halt his swimming to meet him, Ann did her best to
ignore the way the sunlight played on the hard, lean torso,
glistening with water, and on the sleek, slicked back hair and
thick, sea-wet eyelashes.

Oh, God, he really is gorgeous to look at...

She felt her stomach hollow out, and not just with dismay...

Deliberately she flicked her gaze to Ari, keeping it fixed
on him. Against her will, she had to concede that Nikos
Theakis, unspeakable though he was, was a great companion
for a four-year-old child. Over and over again he hefted Ari
up and tossed him into the sea. Ari yelled with glee. He played
chasing games and piggybacking, and aeroplaned him around
above the water. Without her realising it, a smile came to her
lips as she watched them.

Then they were wading out of the water. Ari was rushing
up and giving her a wet hug, describing all the things that

Uncle Nikki and he had done, asking if she'd seen them, and she was taking off his armbands and wrapping his sturdy little body in a towel. At his uncle she did not look at all. Not at all.

But back at the camp she had to, like it or not.

Energy levels quite undimmed by his marine exertions, Ari hopped about from one foot to the other while Ann creamed sun lotion into him. The sun was getting higher now, and even his darker skin tone needed protection.

'Have you cream on your face, Ann?' The question made her look up, and immediately she wished she hadn't.

Nikos was standing, legs apart, his back to the sun, ruffling his hair dry with a towel. He looked—magnificent.

Ann tightened her mouth. 'Yes, I put it on before we set off.'

'You should top up,' Nikos told her. 'Even with your tan you can still burn, and that would ruin that flawless complexion of yours.'

Tight-lipped, Ann applied more sun lotion to herself, knowing the truth of what Nikos had said, despite the way he'd said it. Her complexion was none of his damn business...

Ari tugged at her sleeve. 'It's time to build a sandcastle,' he announced. 'A big one.'

Ann was only too willing. Anything to keep her busy and away from Nikos. She watched as Ari seized his spade and set off to select a good site, just beyond the sand holes, settling down to work. Ann reached for the sun lotion cap and started to screw it on, her eyes focussed on her task—focussed on whatever took her gaze away from where Nikos was lowering himself down with muscular grace on to the rug, leaning back against a large rock, legs stretching out in front of him. Perilously close to her.

But she refused to pull away, calmly returning the sun cream to her beach bag. As she did, Nikos spoke.

'So,' he drawled, 'do you intend to remain covered up neck to ankle the whole day?'

'I've told Ari I'll swim after lunch,' she said. Involuntarily her eyes flickered across to him as she got to her feet.

He lounged back, his drying hair feathering on his forehead, a pair of sunglasses over his nose, swimming trunks hugging his lean hips. The ultimate male. For a helpless moment she could only stare. Could only let him see her stare. Knowing that although she could not see his eyes, his could see her—see her reaction to him.

His mouth curved.

'Look all you want, Ann,' he said generously. 'I'm not going anywhere.' He gave a soft laugh and picked up his magazine again. 'Off you go now,' he said. 'Ari needs a labourer.'

Stiffly, Ann strode off, hating herself.

But not as much as she hated Nikos Theakis.

CHAPTER FOUR

SHE WENT ON hating him for the rest of the day, but she would not spoil it for Ari. Having built his huge and complex castle—a task which Ann had discovered she enjoyed hugely, despite the knowledge that Nikos was only a few metres away, and that Ari regularly invited him to comment approvingly on progress so far—Ari suddenly put down his spade and announced that he was hungry.

It was a general signal for lunch.

They wandered onto the stone terrace of a tiny beach hut which Ann had not even noticed on their arrival. It was set back on the shady side of the beach, above the pebbles, and was pleasantly cool now that the sun was high. Given the Theakis wealth, Ann half expected servants to jump out of nowhere and lay on a four-course luncheon for their lord and master, but their meal in fact came out of a cold bag Nikos had brought with him. It was very simple. A round, flattish loaf of fresh-baked Greek bread, sweet sun-ripe tomatoes, salty, oil-drenched feta cheese, some dry cured ham and a bottle of chilled white wine, with fruit to follow. Ari had a can of cola.

'It's a treat,' he announced smugly to Ann. 'Tina says it rots my teeth so I only have it for treats. Will you be looking after me when Tina marries Dr Sam, Auntie Annie?'

The question slipped out so suddenly that Ann had no time to think up a good answer. Ari's uncle supplied one instead.

'Your aunt isn't used to children, Ari,' he said. 'She wouldn't know how to look after you.'

For a second Ann's expression flickered. She was aware that Nikos was looking at her, a cynical glint in his eye. She ignored it.

'Your uncle is right, Ari,' she said gently. 'I'm sure Ya-ya will find another lovely nanny to look after you. And you'll see Tina still, won't you? She'll only be living on Maxos, and you can visit her in the motor boat.'

'It won't be the same.' His little lip quivered.

'Everything changes, Ari,' said his uncle. 'Some are sad changes, some are happy ones.' There was a strained note in his voice just for a moment.

The boy looked across at Ann. 'You're a happy change, coming to see me,' he said. 'Isn't she, Uncle Nikki?'

Get out of that one, thought Ann silently.

'It has its compensations,' he replied, and his glance flickered over her deliberately. Abruptly, Ann reached for another tomato and bit into it. Her bite was too vicious, and tomato juice and seeds spurted all over her T-shirt.

'Shame,' murmured Nikos Theakis insincerely. 'Now you'll have to take it off after all.'

In the end, she did. The afternoon simply got too hot, and before long Ari was clamouring to go into the sea again. Ann peeled off to her swimming suit, taking advantage of the fact that Nikos was now laying out his fabulous gold-hued body face down on a brilliant white towel for the sun to worship it.

'If you go in the water,' he advised lazily, not bothering to lift his head from the folded towel beneath it, 'don't go out of your depth. No further than that crooked rock to the left. Ari knows which one.'

'Or the sharks will get you,' contributed his nephew knowledgeably, if inaccurately, clearly having been told this to keep him close to shore. 'They lie in wait in deep water.'

Hurriedly she raced Ari down to the sea, welcoming the chill embrace of the water. Playing with Ari took her mind off Nikos, and she entered into his games with enthusiasm, whilst taking care to stay, as instructed, in her depth. Eventually Ari tired, and as they waded out of the sea Ann immediately became aware that she was under professional surveillance.

Nikos Theakis must have seen a multitude of female bodies, but he obviously liked to study each one as a connoisseur. Now he was studying hers, his arms folded behind his neck, using the casual strength of his own perfectly toned, sun-kissed abdominal muscles to hold his head sufficiently off the ground to survey her properly.

Ann attempted to adopt an air of indifference to his scrutiny, and failed. But she did manage to avoid looking at Nikos, instead taking Ari's armbands off and mopping him dry, letting him chatter away in Greek to his uncle before heading back to his sandcastle. Patting herself dry with Ari's towel, Ann knelt down, rummaging in her bag for a comb. Finding it, she straightened, squeezed out the worst of the moisture, and started to comb out her dripping wet hair.

Nikos sat up with an effortless jack-knife of his stomach muscles, hooking his hands loosely around wide splayed knees and looking at her with narrowed eyes, while she tried to look completely indifferent to his regard—and to him. But it was impossible. *He's even got beautiful feet,* Ann thought absently, trying not to look. Narrow, with sculpted arches. She looked away, but he had seen her. He limbered up, and crossed to where she was kneeling. Before she knew what he was doing he'd hunkered down, removed the large-toothed comb from her hand and taken over her task.

'Hold still,' he commanded, as she instinctively tried to get away. A large hand closed over her upper arm. She flinched.

With a frown, he scooped away the wet tangle of hair covering it, revealing the ugly bruise that had formed.

'What the hell?'

'Blame the driver,' she said briefly. 'I got a walloping against the door frame of the Jeep.'

He muttered something in Greek that was probably impolite. 'I'm sorry,' he said tersely. 'I didn't realise.'

She shrugged. 'I'll live,' she answered. 'Give me my comb back.'

He ignored her. Instead, his fingers gently skimmed the smooth skin of her shoulder.

'Your skin is like silk.' His voice was low, intimate. His touch made her shiver. But she didn't feel cold. Heat started to coil in every tensing muscle in her body. For a long moment their eyes met and held—night-dark speculative brown to startled, questioning blue-grey—then, as if in slow motion, Nikos lowered his mouth.

His kiss, on the cusp of her shoulder, was as soft as velvet. Ann's heart stopped beating. Somewhere, in some small, shrinking space, she knew she should jerk away, shout, scream—anything at all to stop what Nikos was so outrageously, unthinkably doing.

But it was impossible. Simply impossible. All she could do, as the world turned inside out, was to stay kneeling, frozen, weak in every limb, feeling the softness of his mouth on her flesh. She felt his lips part, so the soft, liquid warmth of the inside of his mouth was against her tender skin, moving over it, back and forth, moistening and caressing it. Slow bliss filled her. Then gently, very gently, he lifted his head and drew her around so that she was positioned in the vee of his open thighs as he knelt behind her, caging her. With long, even strokes he started to comb out her hair.

She couldn't move. Couldn't move to save her life. Every nerve in her body quivered with awareness. Around her the air hung like silk, shimmering in the heat. As he worked down from her scalp to the still dripping ends of her waist-length hair, gently teasing out every last tangle, she felt a drowsy languor steal over her as the sun beat down. With half closed eyes she could still see little Ari quit his sandcastle to go clambering over the rocks, examining the sea life. Behind her, another Theakis male was seducing her.

She had no doubt that that was what he was doing. Long after the last tangle was gone he went on combing down the length of her hair—soothingly, rhythmically, murmuring soft words in his own native language. It might have been a shopping list for all she knew. She knew it wasn't. He was telling her how much he wanted her, how much his body yearned for hers. How even now—had it not been for the child playing there on the rocks, for the interfering presence of the silky fabric of their bathing clothes—he would have lifted her back on to the hard muscle of his splayed thighs, thigh against thigh, cradling his hips against hers so that she could feel the hardening of his body against her contours.

He would take her soft breasts in the palms of his hands and caress them until her nipples hardened like peaks, and then he would roll them in his long fingers until she cried out, tiny moans in her throat that told him she was ready. Then his hand would splay down over the soft swell of her belly to ease her firm thighs apart, exposing the very heart of her, and he would let his clever, skilful fingers explore her secret folds until they found the pathway to delight. They would rouse her to such a point of glistening ecstasy that her back would arch away from him, her head would drop back, exposing the long line of her tender throat, which he would kiss and bite with soft, devouring kisses while her cry of ecstasy reverberated against his mouth as he possessed her with his body…

Ann felt the heat pool between her thighs and begin to

quicken. Her breasts tautened, nipples peaking beneath the damp swimsuit. Her head started to drop as the murmuring voice told her of all the delights he would give her, and her scalp tingled at the touch of the comb he wielded so soothingly. So arousingly.

Her body began to melt against his waiting hardness.

In slow motion she saw the little figure at the edge of her vision reach the top of the highest rock and wave triumphantly. Then, as her eyes widened in shock, she saw him wobble, arms flailing wildly, and start to tumble.

Which of them moved faster she didn't know. Ann only knew that she had hurled herself forward like a bullet from a gun, scrambling desperately over the rocks to try and break Ari's fall. She caught at him, gasping out words.

'I've got you. I've got you. You're safe.'

Then Ari was slithering down through her weakened arms, before being halted again by a pair of much stronger, harder arms, scooping him out of Ann's, holding his kicking, frightened little body against a broad, strong chest. Rapid Greek urgently reassured the child, soothing him.

Carefully, Nikos lowered the crying child down to a towel. Swiftly the pair of them examined him for damage, but apart from a nasty scrape down one calf Ari seemed nothing more than shocked. And being fussed over, plus a packet of crisps, soon put his woes behind him.

'Tina will put a plaster on it,' he informed his aunt and uncle as he inspected his scrape again, crunching crisps as he spoke.

'It won't need one, poppet,' Ann said reassuringly. 'It isn't bleeding.'

'It bleeds if I squeeze it,' Ari corrected her, and proceeded to demonstrate the truth of this with ghoulish pleasure.

Ann looked away, meeting Nikos' eye. For a moment a gleam of mutual humour passed between them, then he looked back at his nephew.

'Repellent boy,' he said.

Ari looked pleased.

The journey back to the villa was conducted at a far more sedate pace than their outward journey. Nikos was deaf to Ari's pleas to speed up, and took the rough road slowly this time.

'Thank you,' said Ann stiffly, conscious that Nikos had driven slowly for her.

She was still shaken. Not because of Ari's fall—though that had been a horribly sobering moment. Because of what had preceded it. *How* the *hell* had it happened? In the space of a handful of seconds she'd gone from being in control of herself to being...

Helpless. Completely helpless to do anything at all except let the extraordinary velvet seduction of the man take her over completely. Fatally. Lethally.

The moment the Jeep was back at the villa she was out of it, extracting Ari as fast as she could. To her relief, Nikos kept the engine running, and the moment Ari was down drove straight off round to the villa's garages. Ari, seizing Ann's hand, headed indoors, where he was intercepted by Maria, the nursery maid, who exclaimed dutifully at Ari's grievous wound, then whisked him off to get cleaned up. Gratefully, Ann escaped to her room. Under a punishingly hot shower she mercilessly berated herself. How *could* she have let Nikos Theakis do that to her? Touch her, caress her, kiss her...

And why had he done it? But she knew, with a hollowing damning of herself. It had been a power play, pure and simple. He'd done it deliberately, calculatingly, just to show her that he could. To show that she would succumb because he could make it impossible for her not to! That she was powerless against him...

I can't let him have that kind of power! I can't!

No—she had to fight it. And at least now, she told herself

urgently, in her head, she was now prepared for his new battle against her. He'd shown his hand, made his move, and that meant he could no longer launch a surprise attack on her the way he'd done on the beach. She was forewarned now, and that meant forearmed. All she had to do was be on her absolute guard against him.

Whatever it took.

Because the alternative was—unthinkable.

Nikos stared at his reflection in the bathroom mirror of his self-contained apartment in the villa, his razor stilled in one hand.

He was playing with fire.

His mouth tightened. That was the only word for it. He hadn't thought it would be. Had thought it would simply be a matter of killing two birds with one very satisfying stone—gratifying the increasingly persistent desire to enjoy a woman he wanted whilst simultaneously ensuring that Ann Turner was led very nicely up the garden path to a position where she could be ejected, once and for all, from his family.

But that incident on the beach had proved otherwise. Had proved that he was, indeed, playing with fire in what he was doing.

I was out of control so much I didn't even notice when Ari was in danger.

The words formed in his head, sobering and grim. A warning, clear as a bell. And one he would be insane not to heed.

Whatever Ann Turner had, he had to ensure that the only person who got burnt was her. Not him.

With controlled, precise strokes, he started to shave.

Outside the door to the salon, Ann paused. She could feel her chest was tight, her nerves taut. She wanted to bolt back to her room, but it was impossible. She had to get through this evening—the rest of her time on Sospiris. Ignoring completely the man who'd turned her into a quivering, sensuous, conscienceless fool.

Gritting her teeth, she walked in.

Her eyes went to him immediately, sucked to him. Her stomach hollowed, taking in, in a devastating instant, the way he stood there, casually dressed in dark blue trousers, open necked shirt, freshly shaved, lifting his martini glass to his mouth, his unreadable eyes resting on her. For a second so brief it hardly existed she felt his gaze make contact. Then it was gone. His attention was back on Tina, who was talking about archaeology.

Smiling awkwardly, Ann went across to Mrs Theakis and Cousin Eupheme.

How she got through dinner she wasn't sure, but she managed it somehow. Inevitably the conversation included a discussion of the day's expedition, and Ann had to fight the colour seeking to mount in her cheeks. Her comments were disjointed, and in the end she pleaded a headache from too much sun, and fled back to her room before coffee was served. She felt Nikos Theakis's dark gaze on her as she left the dining room.

For the next two days Ann stuck to Tina and Ari like glue. It was easy enough. The following day Ari had a playdate on Maxos, with the young son of wealthy friends of the Theakises, and after handing him over to the family's nanny at their sumptuous holiday villa, Tina took Ann off to spend the afternoon at the dig her fiancé was directing, before heading back to collect Ari again. That evening she was relieved to discover that Nikos was out.

'He is dining with the family that little Ari spent the day with,' said Mrs Theakis, when Ann joined her. 'One of their house guests has a *tendre* for him,' she said dryly. She looked directly at Ann. 'My son is very… popular with our sex, my dear. He has much of what they want. Most noticeably, con-

siderable wealth.' Was there the slightest snap in her voice as
she spoke? Ann wondered. Then another thought crossed her
mind—a horrible one.

Is she warning me off? She felt cold at the thought.

'And so handsome, too!' This from Cousin Eupheme, who
had, Ann had already observed, a visible soft spot for Nikos
Theakis.

'Yes,' allowed Mrs Theakis. 'It is a dangerous combination.
For him, that is. A man who is both rich and handsome.' Again
she looked directly at Ann, and now Ann knew that indeed she
was being specifically warned. 'Such a man can be tempted
not to treat women with the respect they should have from him.'

Ann stared. This was not what she had thought Mrs
Theakis had been going to say.

Mrs Theakis continued, in the same gentle, contemplative
voice she always used. 'I would hesitate to call my own son
spoilt, and yet— Ah, Yannis—*epharisto!*' This last to the
manservant, who had approached with the customary tray of
pre-dinner drinks.

To Ann's relief, the subject of the conversation turned,
with Mrs Theakis asking Ann what she had made of both
Tina's fiancé's dig and her fiancé himself. Tina was still with
Sam, Ann having brought Ari back to Sospiris on her own.
Ari had been full of his enjoyable adventures on his play-
date—except for one aspect.

'She kept kissing me, and I did not like it!' he'd complained.

'Who was that?' Ann had asked, amused.

'A grown-up lady. She asked me about Uncle Nikki. I said
he was busy working. That is what he tells Yannis to tell
ladies when they phone him. I told *her* that too. She did not
like it and went away. I was glad. I didn't like her kissing me.'
He looked at Ann. 'Uncle Nikki does not kiss. He hugs. And
he carries me on his shoulders. *If,*' he'd added, punctiliously,
'I do not pull his hair.'

Now, over dinner, Ann wondered what Ari's admirer was like. She would be elegant and well bred—one of his own circle. As socially acceptable as Carla, Ann thought darkly, had *not* been suitable to marry into the wealthy Theakis family.

There was no sign of Nikos the following day, or the one thereafter, and Ann assumed that he was still on Maxos. But wherever he was—providing it was not on Sospiris—she couldn't care less. It was taking all her strength, even with him not around, to force herself not to think about what had happened on the beach. But it was essential to banish the memory—vital not to think about Nikos Theakis. Not to conjure his image in her mind. Not to let him into her consciousness. To think of something else—anything else—that would take her mind into safer pathways again.

She was glad when Tina returned mid-morning, bearing with her an invitation to join her and her fiancé for the birthday celebrations of one of Sam's colleagues the following night.

'You will come, won't you?' Tina pressed. 'Oh, it won't be anything grand like here, of course, but it will be good fun, I promise!'

Mrs Theakis added her own urging. 'My dear—young people, and a lovely, lively evening for you!' She smiled her warm, kind smile at Ann.

So, in the early evening of the next day, she set off with Tina to cross the strait to Maxos in the Theakis launch. Ari had been consigned to Maria's care, and mollified with the reminder that the following day his playdate friend was coming over to Sospiris on a return invitation. Tina was looking very pretty, with her curly brown hair, and was wearing a flirty red sundress jazzed up with some locally crafted jewellery. Ann was a fair-haired foil, with an ivory-white lacy cross-over top and a floaty turquoise skirt which she'd bought the day they'd come over to Maxos between with Ari.

Sam met them at the harbour, his eyes dwelling with open

appreciation on his fiancée and with practised masculine appreciation on Ann's pale beauty. Gallantly, he offered an arm to each, and they started to stroll towards the quayside lined with tavernas. The Theakis launch had dropped them at the marina end of the harbour, which was visibly upmarket—as were the gleaming yachts at moorage and the smart bars along this section of the quayside. At that hour of the evening, with the dusk gathering in the sky and the last pale bars of daylight dying in the west, both Greeks and such tourists as there were at that season were making their traditional *volta*—the slow procession of both seeing and being seen.

Sam and Tina paused to greet acquaintances as they passed, and halfway along stopped more decisively when they were hailed by a party sitting outside a particularly smart cocktail bar.

Nikos Theakis had hailed them—sitting back, looking relaxed, his shirt open at the collar, a sweater loosely draped over broad shoulders, long legs extended, glass in his hand. A very elegant, sultry-looking brunette was sitting close enough beside him on the white cushioned padded cane seat to signal that her physical proximity to him was usually a lot closer.

'Tina,' said Nikos with smiling extravagance, his white teeth gleaming wolfishly, 'you're looking stunning tonight. Sam's a lucky man.' His dark eyes paid tribute to her, before moving on to exchange pleasantries with her fiancé. Then, without warning, his gaze flicked to Ann.

She'd been standing stiffly, trying to act normally, trying not to be instantly, horribly, mega-aware of Nikos Theakis's impact. She had been quite unprepared for this, and was desperately scrabbling for her guard.

Too late. Those dark long-lashed eyes rested on her, and sucked hers into his gaze.

For a blinding moment it felt intimate—shockingly, searingly intimate. As if there was no one else there at all. As if his eyes were branding her.

Then, abruptly, his head turned towards the woman at his side, whose hand, Ann slowly registered, was now curved possessively around his forearm.

'Nikos, darling,' she announced in overloud English, 'we mustn't keep your nephew's nanny and her friends from their evening out—you'll lose your reputation for being such a generous employer to your household staff!'

At her side, Ann could feel Sam tense with anger at this dismissive put-down of his fiancée.

'True,' Sam said with deceptive ease. 'But one must, of course, also be careful not to *gain* reputations, either—such as one for hunting rich husbands, Kyria Constantis.'

He bestowed a sardonic smile on the woman, whose expression darkened furiously, and strode off, taking his fiancée and Ann with him. Only Ann, it seemed, registered the low chuckle that emanated from Nikos Theakis, and the hiss of outrage from his companion at the scarcely veiled insult.

'Isn't Elena Constantis a complete cow?' Tina quizzed Ann, visibly pleased that her fiancé had supported her so ruthlessly.

'Nikos doesn't seem to think so,' retorted Ann. She was still trying to recover from that scorching eye contact—which had seared so effortlessly through the guard she'd barely had time to scrabble for—and she was also trying to ignore the fact that she had seen Nikos Theakis cosying up to another woman.

Too late she caught the fatal admission she'd just made. Using the word 'another'....as if she herself had *anything* to do with the man in that way.

Tina was speaking again, and Ann latched on to the diversion. Unfortunately, she was still on the same subject.

'Oh, Nikos won't marry Elena Constantis—however much she wants him to. Apart from anything else he'd never marry someone Ari didn't approve of, and Ari's made it clear he doesn't like Elena Constantis. He says she keeps trying to kiss him.'

Ann felt her spirits lift illogically, though she knew there was absolutely no reason for it. She made herself remember that as they reached the taverna where Sam's colleagues were gathering. She was glad of the party. The mix of professional archaeologists and students was a lively, polyglot gathering, and the taverna in the old port was a world away from the swish marina. Not a place for a Theakis, thought Ann, and found the thought reassuring.

As the evening wore on, and the local wine went round, she felt herself relaxing. It was good to get away from the constant threat of encountering Nikos, from keeping her guard high, as she must around him.

The convivial meal culminated in a large birthday cake, with ouzo, brandy and coffee doing the rounds, followed by some very inexpert and woozy dancing to bouzoukis. It was all very good humoured, but finally the taverna owner could bear it no longer. With a clap of his hands he banished them all back to their table, and summoned the males of his establishment, who obligingly formed the appropriate line in front of their enthusiastic audience.

A voice in Greek from the doorway halted them. Ann looked round. Half shadowed against the night, a tall figure peeled itself away from the entrance.

The taverna owner hurried forward, exclaiming volubly in his own language, and held out his arms welcomingly.

Nikos Theakis strolled in.

CHAPTER FIVE

ANN WAS SITTING sandwiched between Tina and one of Sam's colleagues, and as she realised what was happening she felt her stomach hollow.

It was the last thing she had expected. The last thing she had been prepared for.

What is he doing here?

The question ricocheted through her like an assassin's bullet shot out of nowhere. Then something else fired straight through her. Far worse than shock. She could feel it in every nerve-ending in her skin, every synapse in her wine-inflamed brain. It was a quickening of her breath, her pulse, making her instantly, totally aware of him as if everyone else in the taverna had ceased to exist. Dismay washed through her, but it was too late—far too late. All she could do was gaze helplessly at him, as he raised a hand in casual greeting to Sam and the others and made some remark in Greek to the taverna owner. The latter smiled vigorously, and gestured Nikos further in. The honoured guest murmured his thanks, casually deposited his sweater on a spare chair, and took his place in the row of men.

The music started again.

The hypnotic thrum of the music started to reverberate through the room, and very slowly the line of men, shoulder to shoulder, started to weave to the soft, but intensely rhythmic music. Hypnotically, the music started to quicken, becoming insistent, mesmerising. Overpowering.

Ann watched, feeling her heart swelling. Even without the presence of Nikos Theakis she would have been riveted by the unconscious grace, the intense dignity, the suffused sensuality of the dancers. These men dancing were real men. Every one of them. Masculinity and virility radiated from each of them, from the oldest white-haired elder to the youngest teenage grandson. As their interlinked bodies stepped with flawless unison through the paces Ann could feel the tension mount, excitement thrum in the air.

It was a magnificent sight. And none so magnificent than that of Nikos Theakis, dancing like one of his own ancestors, binding the stones of Greece to the wine-dark sea of Homer, grace and power and sensuality personified.

In the subdued light his white shirt gleamed like a sail, its open collar exposing the powerful column of his throat and his raised arms, embracing the shoulder of the man next to him in the line stretching the material over his muscled torso. The way his dark head turned, the way his long legs flexed and stepped—Ann felt her stomach clench. He was stunningly, overpoweringly beautiful. Heat flowed through her body. She couldn't take her eyes off him. Not for a moment, not for a second. She didn't care if people saw her looking. Didn't care if Nikos Theakis saw her watching him. And if his eyes met hers, held them completely, totally, never letting her go, as if she were their captive…

It was as if he were dancing for her, displaying his prowess, his masculinity, for her alone…

She felt dazed—dazzled and aware.

Responding to him. Weakening to him.

As the music and the dance reached its rampant finale to a volley of applause and vociferous appreciation by its audience, she dropped her head, shaken with what she was feeling. Yet there was still that quickening in her veins that seemed to make the whole world more vivid.

She lifted her head again, and her eyes clashed straight into his.

He had joined the party at the table, finding a space, somehow, immediately opposite her. For a moment—how long or brief it was she could not tell—he simply held her gaze.

Then he was accepting a glass of brandy from the taverna owner, exchanging something with him in Greek which brought a comment from Sam in the same language. Nikos made an airy gesture with his free hand, lounging back in his seat.

'It is my pleasure—a token of appreciation for all the hard work you and your team put in on the excavation,' he said smoothly, and Ann gathered that he'd picked up the tab for the evening.

It brought back the question that had originally struck her when he'd strolled in. Why was he here? Why wasn't he with the elegant, chic Elena Constantis? And where was she? She would not have relinquished her prize easily. And why should Nikos have relinquished her?

He wasn't looking at her now, and she was grateful. He was talking across the table to Sam and a couple of his colleagues, asking them about progress on the dig. She dragged her eyes away, occupying herself with drinking her coffee until the party finally broke up. Outside, after the warmth of the taverna, the night air struck chill. But Ann was glad of it. There was enough heat in her body.

Her blood.

Yet the fresh air seemed to bring on an increase in the effects of her evening's consumption of wine. Where was Tina? She looked around, but Tina was standing beside Sam, who had his arm around her.

'I've told Tina she can stay here with Sam,' said a deep, accented voice behind her.

She turned abruptly. Nikos was draping his sweater casually around his shoulders. 'I'll see you back to Sospiris,' he said to her.

Where her stomach had been, a hollow opened up. Dismay filled it. And something else. Something she really, really didn't want—

Her hands clutched at her bag. 'No, really—that's quite unnecessary,' she began, flustered.

But her protest was ignored. Nikos was saying something to the taverna-owner again. And when she looked pleadingly at Tina the other girl was grinning delightedly up at Sam. Ann felt the words die on her lips. Of course Tina would be pleased that her boss had given her the night off! How selfish would it be to expect her to give that up? And it was only a short journey across on the launch. She could survive that.

But why was Nikos Theakis coming back to Sospiris anyway? Why wasn't he with Elena Constantis?

Mentally, she shook herself. *Who cares? What does it matter? It's nothing to do with me! I've just got to tough it out and get to the other side, that's all.*

'Ready?'

A hand was on her spine. Large, warm. Its heat reached through her thin top. She jerked forward, managing to get out a last 'goodnight' to Tina and Sam and the others, who were heading back to their accommodation on the edge of the town. Then the hand was pressing into her back, urging her forward. She took a jerky step and started walking. The hand dropped.

Self-consciousness possessed her. She felt dangerously affected by the wine, the chill evening air in her lungs—the heat in her veins. Her pulse seemed to have the hypnotic rhythm of the bouzouki music in it still. Yet, though she felt hot, she shivered.

'Wait,' said Nikos beside her, unknotting his sweater,

draping it around her shoulders like a shawl. She felt his body heat in the fabric.

'No—I—'

He ignored her protest, starting to walk on again along the harbour's edge. There were still a few people around, but most of the restaurants were shut, only some of the bars open. Lights played on the dark water, and out at the end of the quay Ann could make out the harbour lights, marking the entrance. She could see the Theakis launch at its mooring, and as they neared a figure stood up from a bench, extinguished a cigarette, and greeted his boss in Greek. Nikos returned the greeting laconically, and stepped down into the launch, holding his hand to help Ann in. Reluctantly she took it, letting go of it again as soon as possible. She took her seat, tucking her skirt around her and holding on to the sleeves of Nikos' sweater.

It seemed strangely, disturbingly intimate to be wearing it like that.

The engine was gunned, roaring to life, and they were nosing out into the harbour. Ann felt the wind lift at her hair as they picked up speed, and she reached up a hand to hold it back. At least, she thought gratefully, the noise of the engine made it hard to speak. But awareness of Nikos' presence beside her dominated her. For something to do, she gazed up at the sky, looking at the bright stars. Abruptly the launch hit a swell, side on, and bucked. Caught off balance, Ann jerked in her seat. Immediately the hand was back on her spine, steadying her. She stiffened instantly, reaching for the gunwale, waiting for the hand at her back to drop.

But it stayed where it was.

'Thank you, but I'm fine now,' she said tightly.

'Focus on the horizon. You won't feel dizzy then,' said Nikos. He had leant towards her, to speak above the noise of the engine.

She gritted her teeth, doing as he bade. Ahead of them the dark mass of Sospiris gradually grew closer. But horribly, horribly slowly. The hand was still at her spine, but she would not, *would not,* tell him to take it away. Would not pay him any attention. Would completely ignore him.

It was impossible to ignore the presence of Nikos Theakis beside her, his hand at her back, even though she was straining away from him as much as she could. His long legs were braced, one arm stretched out along the gunwale. Impossible to ignore the subtle scent of him—a mix of brandy, expensive aftershave, and something more. A scent of masculinity…

Never had the crossing seemed to take so long.

At her side, Nikos wondered to himself whether he were insane.

The evidence was certainly in favour of that judgement. Ever since he'd looked himself in the eye in his bathroom mirror and told himself he was playing with fire, he'd known what the smart thing to do would be. It would be to take full advantage of the fortuitous presence of Elena Constantis— even if it did only fuel her ambitions. It did not, most *definitely* did not, include what he'd done this evening, seeking Ann out. What he was doing right now.

Let alone what he wanted to do…

He dragged his mind away. He shouldn't be here—he knew that. He shouldn't have murmured insincere apologies to Elena, ignoring the snap of frustrated anger in her eyes. He shouldn't have found his steps taking him in the direction of the old port, shouldn't have found himself outside the taverna where he'd known the archaeologists would be. And when he'd heard the familiar, hypnotic, compelling age-old music coming out of the doors and windows he definitely should not have gone inside. And when he'd gone inside he should never have succumbed to the impulse to join in the dancing.

And he should never have allowed himself the pleasure of watching Ann Turner unable to tear her eyes away from him…

But that was just what he had allowed himself to do—and why? Because he'd wanted to. He'd seen her, and wanted her.

Very simple. Very stupid.

Wasn't that why he'd been avoiding the girl as much as he could since the afternoon on the beach, spending time instead with Elena? He was playing with fire again. Because that incident had shown him vividly, urgently, that his grand plan for her was far too incendiary—for him. Yes, seducing the girl and keeping her as his mistress would be an excellent way of getting rid of her, spiking her guns, but the seduction had to be one way only. *He* would be seducing *her*—*not* the other way round. That was essential. He and he alone had to be calling the shots.

More logic impressed itself upon him impeccably, giving him exactly the answers he wanted to questions he didn't want to ask in the first place. He spelt it out to himself. It was exactly because Ann Turner was what she was—a woman who would sell her own sister's baby for cash—that he had fought his attraction to her. Of course he had! She was the very last woman he should sully himself with—however deceptively beautiful her packaging. But it had been precisely *because* he'd fought his attraction to her that it was now so powerful. He could see it with absolute clarity. Logic carried him forward inexorably. Which therefore meant that his reaction to her on the beach had been so extreme only because he'd been trying to suppress his attraction to her. And so now, if he simply gave free rein to his desire, stopped trying to suppress it, his reaction to her would be nothing more than what he was familiar with, comfortable with. The normal reaction he had to a woman he found sexually enticing…

Satisfaction eased through him. Problem analysed. Problem solved. He wanted Ann Turner. There were very good reasons for permitting himself to do so—and no good reason for denying himself what he wanted.

A highly pleasurable bedding. Followed by an equally satisfying removal of a thorn in his side. Once Ann Turner was his mistress, his mother would not invite her to Sospiris again...

His eyes moved over her. She was all unseeing of him. Beneath his palm the fine material of her top fluttered in the wind. Almost he pressed his hand forward, to feel the warmth of her flesh soft beneath his palm, the heat of her pliant body. For nothing more than an instant unease ghosted through his mind as the dark mass of Sospiris loomed closer and the launch came in under its lee, heading to the quay.

Then it was gone. Stavros cut the throttle, nosing the craft forward until he could reach for the mooring. They were back at Sospiris, and the night—Nikos got easily to his feet to alight, holding down his hand to Ann—the night had scarcely begun.

CHAPTER SIX

WITH DEEP RELUCTANCE Ann took the outstretched hand. It
was warm, and large, and the strong fingers folded over hers
effortlessly, drawing her up on to the stone quay. For a few
seconds she felt unsteady, after the rocking of the boat, and
yet again she stiffened as his hand moved to her spine again,
performing the dual office of steadying her and impelling her
forward with smooth pressure.

'Mind the steps,' his low voice reminded her. It was not a
drawl, precisely, but it was lazily spoken, with a note to it that
she was deeply aware of.

His hand was there again, and though with any other man
it would not have signified anything other than common
courtesy, with Nikos she knew it was quite, quite different. It
was his brand on her. A brand that went right through the thin
layer of her top.

In deafening silence she walked up the steps, gained the
level ground at the top as he guided her through the stone
archway that led into the main gardens. She went docilely, as
if there was nothing awkward in the slightest about Nikos
Theakis walking through the villa's midnight gardens, with
the scent of jasmine and honeysuckle filling the night air so
that her breath caught the scent, rich and fragrant.

'Eupheme planted them there deliberately,' Nikos remarked.

'So that you walk, as it were, into a wall of scent at just that point. The night air always gives so much more intense a fragrance, does it not?'

He paused on a little stone concourse, where massed vegetation softened the stone walls, the tiny white flowers of jasmine like miniature stars beneath the sky. Another, wider, shallower flight of stone steps led down from here into the garden spreading away below, and where they stood was a vantage point over the whole expanse. Without realising it, Ann paused as well, automatically taking in the landscaped vista beyond, from the artfully winding pathways, the sculpted vegetation, the little walls festooned in bougainvillea, their brilliant hues dimmed now, and out towards the stand of cypress trees at the garden's far edge, their narrow forms spearing the night sky.

There was no moon, but starlight gleamed on the sea beyond, and caught, too, the iridescent surface of the swimming pool, nestled into its terrace between the villa and the garden.

Ann gazed out over the vista. 'It really is beautiful,' she said. It was impossible not to say so. Impossible not to stand there drinking it in and feel the heady intoxication of the flowers' fragrance, the even headier intoxication of her blood. She wasn't sure how much wine she had drunk—she could feel it suffusing her veins, feel it swirling gently through her— but it seemed to have put the world into a strange, seductive blend whereby she seemed both supersensitive to everything around her and yet everything seemed dissociated from her, unreal almost…as if she were drifting through it like a veil.

But she knew she should not go on standing here beside Nikos, gazing out over the starlit garden with the scent of flowers in her nostrils, the soft music of the cicadas playing in the vegetation. She should, in fact, walk briskly away along the stone pathway to the terrace and get inside the villa, go straight to her bedroom. Where, equally briskly, she should take off her make-up, brush out her hair, get into her night-dress, get into bed, and go peacefully, immediately to sleep.

That, she knew, was precisely what she should do. Right now.

Not stand here in the soft Aegean night, feeling the wine whispering in her head, feeling the dark, solid presence of Nikos Theakis standing beside her. His hand was still grazing her back, so close that all she had to do was turn slightly towards him to let that warm, strong hand press her against him, to let her hand splay against the fine cotton of his shirt, feeling the hard wall of his chest beneath as she lifted her gaze to him, to drink in the shadowed planes of his face, the dark sweep of lashes across those eyes that could sear right through her, making her breath catch in her throat, making her sway, as if she were a flower on the breeze. His arm would encircle her pliant body, and his sensual, sculpted mouth would come down on hers—

She jerked forward—a single step. But it was enough to shake her back to reality.

'I must go in,' she said. Her voice sounded abrupt. She gazed at the long façade of the villa, brow furrowing slightly. Where, exactly, was she to get inside?

'This way.' His voice was smooth, assured.

Automatically she went the way he indicated, walking slightly in front of him until the path converged on the main terrace. Even though she had broken the moment, she still seemed to be in that state of hypersensitivity, feeling his presence behind her in every follicle in her body. Yet to everything else she seemed quite blind. So much so that when he stepped past her, to halt her progress and slide open the French window they were adjacent to, indicating she should step through, she did so.

And stopped. This was not a salon or a hallway, or any room she was familiar with.

It was a bedroom.

She turned. Nikos was smoothly sliding shut the French window again.

And walking towards her.

She stepped backwards. It was automatic, instinctive.

'What—?'

He gave a low, brief laugh. 'Don't be naïve, Ann. What do you think?' There was amusement in his voice.

He came up to her, looking down at her. There was a single low lamp burning by the bed—a wide double bed, swathed in a dark coverlet, sombre and masculine—dimmed right down. By its light his face seemed more planed than ever, with shadows etching his features. She felt weak suddenly, overcome. Gazing at him, lips parting.

Her breath quickened.

He saw it, saw her reaction. Saw how it came even without conscious volition.

'This has been waiting for us since the beach,' he said, his voice low, with a timbre that she could feel in her spine. 'Then was not the time—but now… Now, Ann, we have all the time we need.'

Dark long lashes swept down over her. He reached forward, his hands closing over the loose arms of his sweater, still draped around her shoulders. She had long ceased to be conscious of it, having had so much else to dominate her awareness, but now she was vividly aware of it again, and even more vividly, breathlessly aware of the slight but inexorable pull he exerted through the sleeves, around her neck and shoulders.

Drawing her forward.

For a moment, a balance of time she could not say lasted either a few fleeting seconds or a long, long interval of consciousness, she felt herself resist. Felt her mind fill with the realisation that she must step back again and flee to the door behind her. Flee away from this man on whom her eyes were fixed as he drew her casually towards him, until he was discarding the sweater, sliding his hands along the slender column of her torso, his fingers splaying around her ribs. Sensation rippled down her as her breath caught again, mouth parting yet again, as she felt his thumb grazing the swelling underside of her breasts.

He held her there, in position for him, as his hooded gaze held hers, and he casually, leisurely, let his thumbs glide across the tautening material of her top.

She felt her nipples flower, the delicate tissues of her breasts engorge. And he felt it too, for he gave a smile. Slow and sensual. Watching her reaction.

'Very nice, Ann,' he murmured. 'Very nice indeed. As is this…' he continued, in the same considering tone.

His mouth came down in slow and sensual possession. As if he had every right to taste her, every right to let his lips smooth over hers, explore their contours, then ease them apart to taste the nectar within. Every right to overwhelm all her senses and render her helpless, unresisting, capable of nothing except feeling the exquisite sensuality of his kiss, tasting her, possessing her…arousing her…

She could feel the blood surge in her veins like a hot tide, drowning out everything. Everything except what was happening. Nikos Theakis was kissing her…holding her… seducing her…

She knew it was happening, but she could not stop it. It was too overpowering, too overwhelming. All rational thought, such as was left, was gone—dissolved away. All that existed was sensation—sweet, arousing, seductive. She could no more resist it than honey poured over a hot spoon could resist melting.

He let her go, and for a moment she only swayed blindly, held in his sensual grip. Then his hands were sliding around her spine, unfastening the tie of her crossover top, drawing each section of the lacy fabric away to reveal her bra beneath, straining over her engorged breasts. Smoothly he eased the top from her, over each shoulder, discarding it carelessly. Then his hands were at her spine again, slipping the fastening of her bra.

Her swollen breasts fell free, her bra following her top to the floor, and she was standing there, bared to the waist, the coral peaks of her nipples full and erect.

Dark eyes washed over her, flaring as they did so.

'Perfect,' he murmured. 'Quite, quite perfect…'

With a leisurely motion he lifted his hand, letting the backs of his fingers drift against the fullness of the twin orbs. She gave a low, incoherent moan in her throat, her eyes fluttering as the exquisite sensation he aroused shimmered through her. A low laugh came from him.

'Oh, Ann—do you have any idea how disturbing your breasts have been to my peace of mind? And now—now I can have my fill of them.'

His fingers drifted over them again, gently scissoring her nipples. The low moan in her throat came again. Heat beat up in her, and she felt her breasts react more strongly still, straining forward, as if eager for his touch. Her mind was in meltdown—inchoate, formless, distilled to pure, exquisite sensation and the heady, erotic knowledge that she was standing here, naked to the waist, while Nikos Theakis caressed the breasts he had bared for his pleasure.

Another low moan came from her parted lips, and this time it was as a signal to him. He swept her up, her skirt trailing to the floor, swung her around and then lowered her down on to the bed. Her hands splayed upwards, above her head, lifting her breasts, and for a moment he just gazed down on her, his eyes narrowed to a beam of intense focus that quickened the blood in her, susurrated on her skin. She could only lie there, gazing up at him, letting her eyes twine with his, letting the desire flaring in them accentuate her own desire so that it flooded out all the last, fleeing shards of her resistance, drowned them out. Her desire was all-possessing, all consuming—to reach for that tall, strong body looming over her, to close her hands over the sinewed arms, draw it down to her, feel its hard muscled weight press down on her...

'Nikos—'

Where had that word come from, murmuring from her lips? Had she really spoken his name. Pleaded it? Invited it—?

Invited *him?*

Invited him to do what he was doing now—stripping the clothes from his body so that her eyes widened, as they had widened once before on the beach, as his flawless body was revealed to her. Her eyes gloried in his arrant masculinity and his eyes never left hers, never strayed from the body she was displaying for him. Prepared now, he lowered himself down beside her, his hand splaying once more over each breast, his body moving over hers, his mouth finding hers.

He renewed his possession skilfully, expertly, with lips and tongue, soft and gliding, arousing and desiring. He drew from her a response she had not known was possible, engendered a sensuous bliss she had not known existed till that moment. His hands explored her body, turning it in his strong, assured grasp, unwinding her from her long skirt until she was boneless beneath him, until her body was a mesh of arousal. His hands smoothed over her, making him master of every portion of her body, easing her thighs apart, long, skilled fingers teasing the delicate folds concealed.

She gasped in pleasure, her head rolling back into the softness of the pillow, lips parting as the breath exhaled from her. She heard him give a low laugh, and then his lips were almost at hers, and he was teasing them with his even as his hand was performing the same office between her thighs, teasing the dewing flesh.

He murmured something to her, but she was beyond hearing, beyond anything but drowning in the sensations he was engendering. She moaned again, fingers clenching into the pillow as his fingers began their skilful, unbearable work. He eased her thighs yet further apart, gained deeper access to her, finding the throbbing nub of her desire. Arousingly he caressed it as her breath quickened to gasping, her body threshing in a flux of desire as he arched over her, his hand sliding away from her, letting the tip of his manhood take its place. Instinctively, blindly, her hands splayed over his hard, taut buttocks, holding him there, and her hips lifted to him in a gesture as old as time. Her mouth was questing against his, her breasts straining against the muscled wall of his chest, her peaked nipples crushed against it.

Fire licked through her. Her body was aflame, aching for his possession. She strained against him and his mouth was lifting from hers, saying something. She knew not what, but there was promise in it, promise and purpose…

Her head threshed from side to side as wave after wave of pleasure broke through her. She cried out, head lifting back, eyes fluttering shut, as her whole being focused on the sensation searing through it.

Then he was driving into her, strong and insistent, thrusting up into her. She heard him cry out above her, felt his body explode inside hers. She cried out with him, the universe burning all around them as their bodies convulsed one within the other. It went on—a tidal wave crashing again and again through her flesh.

Her head fell back again as the final wave died away. Long moments later, he slid his hand up over her throat, his fingers curving up around the line of her jaw to cup her. Slowly, shudderingly, her pounding heart started to ease. Her panting breath to steady. She lay exhausted, shaken, as he released her, gazing blindly up at him. Shock glazed her eyes. The world returned to her, and she realised what she had done.

Had sex with a man who held her in absolute contempt.

A man whom she had more cause to hate than any man alive.

Cold drenched through her, replacing the heat of her sated body with a chill that seemed to go down to her guts, pooling into ice. Disbelief and a dismay so wrenching that it seemed to convulse her stomach choked her lungs.

Oh, God, what have I done?

Her shocked eyes could only stare upwards to the man on whose bed she was lying, whose body was still pinning her, filling her...

For an endless moment the world froze in horror. Only around the edges, like a miasma, it was haunted by the imprint of a quite, quite different emotion—an emotion that had possessed her, consumed her, enveloped her into a world she had never known existed. A world against whose loss now she heard a faint, anguished cry, as if she were losing something incredibly rare and precious, as if the loss of it were unbearable...

But filling her consciousness, spreading through it like an ugly stain, was the overpowering emotion of dismay—and shock and disbelief that she could have done what she had just done. Limp with horror at herself, she could only lie there, all limbs exhausted, staring blindly up into the face looking down at her.

For a moment there was no motion. None at all. Then abruptly, roughly, her body was away from the weight bearing on her. Nikos was striding away, across the huge room, thrusting open the door into the *en suite* bathroom, and closing it sharply behind him.

For a handful of seconds she could only lie there, still, inert, motionless. Then, forcing her frozen mind to act, she clambered up, urgently scrabbling for her clothes, forcing herself into them with unbearable haste and clumsiness, not bothering with underwear, just winding her top and her skirt around her to cover her nakedness. From the bathroom she could hear the sound of a shower starting. Her eyes flew past the door opposite the French window to the terrace, and she saw the door which surely must lead to the rest of the villa.

She hurried to it, half tripping, heart racing, lungs still choking, and yanked it open, finding herself, to her abject relief, in a service corridor. She didn't know where she was going but it didn't matter—she simply hurtled along it, desperately hoping that at this late hour she would encounter no one until she came upon part of the villa she recognised and could navigate to her own guest bedroom from there. Minutes later she was shutting the door and collapsing down on her own bed, shaking like a leaf, her arms wrapped around herself, as if stanching a wound. She started to rock.

Words whipped through her, over and over again, more and more cruel.

What have I done? What have I done?

Nikos stood beneath the pounding water of the shower. Its needles should be knives. Knives to carve into his greedy flesh the punishment he deserved.

How the hell could he have been so stupid? Hadn't he known—hadn't he told himself, staring into the mirror above the basin in that very bathroom a handful of days ago, that he was playing with fire? And now what had he gone and done? Knowingly, deliberately fooled himself on the way back to the villa with the kind of self-flattering logic that, had it been a dodgy business proposal, he'd have seen through in an instant. But which, because it was his damn male desire—never thwarted before, never not satiated, whenever and with whoever he wanted—he'd seized on it as if it were legal writ!

His mind sheered away. Sheered away from remembering the moment when he'd realised that not only did he *have* to take her, right there, right then, but worse—far, far worse— the moment when the world had simply whited out.

It's never been like that before.

The words formed in his mind as the stinging needles pounded down on him.

Never had the moment of sexual fulfilment been like that—so intense, so overpowering, so consuming that he'd cried out, unable to stop himself.

Until the moment when consciousness had knifed back into him and he'd stared down at her and realised, with harsh, pitiless self-condemnation, that he had just walked over the edge of a cliff.

Angrily his hand fisted, and he thumped it against the wall of the shower stall.

I damn well knew I should have left her alone. I damn well knew it!

But even as the words formed, so did others. Others that made him abruptly cut off the water, grab a towel, and pat himself dry, roughly towelling the moisture out of his hair. Then he cast the towels aside and yanked open the bathroom door.

He knew he should never have touched Ann Turner. He knew he should never have taken her to his bed. Knew he should never have had sex with her.

But he knew something else as well as he strode out of the bathroom.

He wanted her again.

CHAPTER SEVEN

THE SUN WAS SCARCELY UP, but Ann was lying in bed, wakeful and tormented. She would have to go. Leave Sospiris. There was no other option. She couldn't stay here now!

I'll have to think of something—something to tell Ari, Mrs Theakis. Something—anything!

Except the truth. Even as she lay there she felt a semi-hysterical bubble inside her at the thought of Mrs Theakis knowing…

She shuddered in horror, feeling her skin flush.

How am I going to face her? How can I even have breakfast with her—knowing what I did, where I was?

And yet she was going to have to. Going to have to somehow get through the morning, behave normally, then dream up some plausible reason why she had to go back to England.

A spear stabbed her. Ari! Ari would be so upset, so distressed! Wasn't it bad enough he was about to lose Tina? Now she was proposing to walk out on him as well.

For ever.

Because unless by some miracle Mrs Theakis invited her here again when Nikos was somewhere else—like Australia, or better still Antarctica!—or perhaps herself come to London some time, then how could she possibly ever see Ari again? She could never go anywhere near Nikos Theakis again—never!

Abruptly, another emotion stabbed into her. One that was shocking, unforgivable—shameless!

Never to see Nikos again—

Instantly, viciously, she slammed down on the emotion, crushing it brutally, punishingly. How could she stoop so low? How could she? And how could a man who thought her the lowest of the low, who had said such cruel, vile things about her sister, a man she had hated for four long years, have possibly made love to her the way he had?

Her face hardened. Made love? Was she stupid or something? Nikos Theakis hadn't 'made love' to her! He'd had sex with her! That was all he'd done—all he'd wanted. Bitter humiliation seared through her. Oh, how could she have fallen into bed with him like that? Just because he looked like a Greek god. Just because she felt weak at the knees because he was so devastating a male that any woman, *every* woman, would turn and stare at him and yearn for him to look their way…

Anguished, hating herself almost as much as she hated Nikos Theakis, Ann went on staring at the ceiling, counting the hours till she could escape from Sospiris. Escape from Nikos.

But what had seemed imperative as she lay sleepless and tormented on her bed became far, far more difficult when she had to face Mrs Theakis at breakfast.

'Leave us?' Sophia Theakis' eyes widened in surprise. 'Surely not?' Her gaze shifted as the doors to the morning room opened. 'Nikos! Ann is saying that she may have to return to London.'

Ann felt herself freeze. Not for all the power on earth would she turn her head to see Nikos stalk in. But nothing could stop her hearing his deep voiced reply as he took his place. 'Out of the question. It was agreed that she would stay until after Tina's wedding so that Ari would be least unsettled. Is that not so, Ann?'

Her head swivelled. And immediately, fight it as she might,

she felt colour stain vividly across her cheekbones at the sight of him. He was casually dressed in a pale cream polo shirt with a discreetly expensive logo on it, hair still damp and jaw freshly shaved. At once, vivid and hot, sprang the memory of his roughened skin against her last night as his mouth possessed hers… Her colour deepened.

His eyes were holding hers, challenging them—branding them.

She bit her lip, and saw something flare deep within. 'I—I—' she began, then floundered. Rational thought, speech, was impossible. 'It's just that—' she tried again, and failed.

Another expression shot through Nikos's eyes. She could have sworn it was satisfaction.

'Good,' he said. 'Then that is settled. You will stay, as agreed, until after Tina's wedding. And then…' His eyes flicked to her momentarily, as his hand reached for the jug of freshly squeezed orange juice in front of him. 'Then we shall see. Who knows, Ann, what will happen after Tina's wedding, hmm? In the meantime today, with Ari occupied with his playmate from Maxos arriving with Tina later this morning, it is more than time, I think, that I showed you something more of Sospiris than you have already seen.'

Calmly, he started to drink his orange juice. Numbly, Ann turned back to Mrs Theakis, as though she might somehow save her from so dire a fate. But as she turned she caught for a fleeting moment a strange, assessing look in the older woman's eyes, as they hovered between her guest and her son. Then an instant later it was gone, and Ann could only think— only hope!—she had imagined it.

Sophia Theakis' expression had changed to a serene smile. 'That is a lovely idea, Nikos. Sospiris has many hidden beauties, Ann,' she said benignly, 'and I'm sure my son will show you all of them.'

With monumental effort, Ann schooled her face into com-plaisance. Inside, she felt like jelly.

Nikos gunned the Jeep impatiently. Where was she? If she was planning on trying to get out of this, he would simply go and fetch her. But she would come. His mother would see to it.

For a moment his expression wavered. It was not comfort-able, being under the eye of his mother in these circumstances. But it was for her sake that he was doing this—even though, of course, she could not know that. But for her to be burdened indefinitely, leached off by the female she thought so well of just because he could not open her eyes to Ann Turner's true character, was not something he was prepared to tolerate. What he *was* prepared to tolerate, however, was his own dis-approval of the course of action he had decided to pursue—a course of action that he'd already taken a decision on as he'd walked back into the bedroom the night before.

To hell with it! To hell with warnings about playing with fire—it was too damn late for that. He'd not just played with fire—he'd set the bed ablaze! And it, and he, had gone up in a sheet of flame. So any warnings, any regrets, were too little, too late. If there was one thing that was now absolutely clear—had become forcibly even more crystal-clear when he'd seen his empty bed and realised that Ann had run away—it was that he was counting the hours until he could possess her again.

The remainder of his night had been a sleepless one, but not because he had been repining his seduction any more—it had been because his bed was empty, and he very definitely did not want it to be empty. He'd almost gone after her. Why she had done a runner he had no idea—unless it was to see whether he would come chasing after her. Or—a sudden frown had knitted his brow darkly—was she belatedly, seeking to assume a virtue she had just very amply demon-strated she did not have?

He brushed the thought aside. Of course Ann Turner possessed not a shred of virtue! How could she, when she had sold her own flesh and blood for cold hard cash? For a fleeting moment something jarred in his brain. The vivid memory of their union burned again in his mind. Could the woman who had so inflamed him, with whom he had cried out at the searing moment of their fulfilment—a fulfilment deeper and more intense than any he had experienced—really be the same woman whose grasping fingers had greedily closed over the cheques he had so contemptuously handed her?

And yet she was. She was that same woman. However much she inflamed him he must never forget that—not for a moment.

Certainly not now, as she finally emerged from the villa, her face set, not meeting his eyes, simply clambering up into the Jeep without a word, ignoring his hand reaching across the seat to help her in. Angry irritation flared briefly in Nikos at her obvious intention of refusing to acknowledge him. He released the handbrake, let in the clutch and sheered off, his eyes behind the sunglasses hard. He drove fast, not bothering to take the bumpy track easily, and was conscious that Ann was hanging on grimly, refusing to ask him to slow down.

He didn't stop until he slewed the Jeep to a halt at the far end of the island, down by Ari's 'secret beach'. He'd brought Ann here deliberately. Not only would they not be disturbed, but the beach hut was ideal for his purposes. It was not luxurious, but it contained the essentials—mainly a bed.

As he cut the engine, tossing his dark glasses on to the dashboard, a silence seemed to descend along with the settling cloud of white dust around the car.

He turned towards Ann. She was still sitting with one hand clutched at the doorframe, the other planted on the dash to steady herself. Her expression was stony. She was wearing, Nikos realised, exactly the same outfit she'd worn when they'd brought Ari here—beige cotton trousers and a long-sleeved T-shirt. His eyes glinted mordantly. Did she think such a drab outfit would put him off? And why, pray, the cold shoulder? The glint came again, and there was a spark of anger in it now. 'Cold' had not been the word for her last night.

Time to stop this, right now.

'Ann,' he began, his voice edged, 'I don't know what you think you're playing at, but—'

Her head swivelled. The expression in her eyes was scorching.

'Playing at?' she threw back at him. 'I'm not *playing at* anything! I have absolutely no idea what the hell you think you're doing, but—'

He laughed. He couldn't help it. The scorching look in her eyes intensified. Absently, he noticed how it made them even more luminous.

'What I think I'm doing, Ann,' he said—and now the edge in his voice had gone, replaced by something very different, 'is this—'

He reached for her. Unable to help himself. He'd been wanting to do it since he'd walked into breakfast and seen her there, feeling a punch to his system that had made him want to walk right up to her and sweep her to him.

She was pliant in his arms as he drew her to him, and satisfaction surged through him as he lowered his mouth to hers. The next moment she had gone rigid—as rigid as a board—and her hands were balling against his chest, her mouth jerking away.

'Let me go! Let me—'

His mouth silenced her, catching her lips and his hand at her back slid up to hold the base of her skull, fingers spearing into her silken hair. God, she felt so good to kiss! So sweet and soft and honeyed—

Her momentary resistance had vanished, melted away into his kiss, and he took instant possession. He felt her hands splaying out, pressing through his polo shirt against the wall of his chest.

He kissed her thoroughly, deeply—arousingly. And not just arousing her. His own body was responding as though a switch had been thrown, and desire swept through him.

Eventually, breathlessly, he surfaced, holding her still, gazing down into her eyes. They were huge.

'You were saying?' he said. The amusement was in his voice again, but different now—husky and low.

For a moment she just gazed at him blindly. Then, with a little choke, she tugged free. He let her go—he had proved his point. Handsomely.

Her face was strained. 'I don't want this.' Her voice was faint, hands knotting in her lap. 'I don't want it.'

His eyes glinted. 'Ann, no games. Not now. Last night proved that amply.' The glint intensified. 'Very amply.'

He started to reach for her again, but this time she was faster. She thrust open the Jeep door and leapt down. Nikos stared with a mix of exasperation and incredulity as she started to march back along the track. Was the girl mad? It would take a good hour to walk back to the villa, and the sun was getting high in the sky. He gave a rasp of irritation and went after her. She was only doing it as some kind of grand gesture, though heaven knew why.

He caught up with her in seconds and turned her round towards him. She was rigid, face clenched.

'Take your hands off me,' she gritted, eyes sparking. 'I told you I don't want this! What part of that don't you understand?' she bit out.

Something shifted in his eyes. 'This,' he said. Deliberately, quite deliberately, he lifted a hand to her face, letting the other one drop from her arm so that she was quite free. His eyes never leaving her, he simply drew his index finger down her cheek—lightly, like a feather.

He saw her eyes flicker, saw her pupils dilate. Then he let his hand fall.

She didn't turn, or run, or march away. She simply stood there, on the track, the sun pouring down on her pale hair, swaying slightly. There was a helpless look on her face.

'That's the part I don't understand, Ann,' he said, his voice low. 'The part where I only have to touch you and you respond to me. Or not even touch you…'

His gaze held hers, lambent with desire for her. 'Do you think I haven't wanted you from when I first saw how beautiful you had become? All that was required was—opportunity.' His hand lifted to her face again. This time he slid his fingers around her jaw, feathering her hair, his thumb playing with the tender lobe of her ear. She did not move. Very slowly, her eyelashes lowered over her eyes. His other hand lifted, his thumb going to her lips, tracing across their fullness. Then, as she still stood there motionless, eyes shut in the silence all around, he gently pressed down on her lower lip with the pad of his thumb, even as his mouth came down sensuously, languorously, to take its place.

He felt her give. Felt her mouth slowly start to move against his. Felt the stiffness leave her body, the rigidity ease, dissolve. She was dissolving against him. She was exploring, tasting every moment of the sweet, delectable arousing. How long he kissed her, standing as they were alone, at the edge of the deserted beach, he did not know. Only knew that at some point he let his mouth ease from hers, felt his hand slip into hers, take it lightly, loosely, but enough to lead her, as if she were still in a daze, towards the little stone building. She came willingly, unresistingly.

Just as he had known she would.

Light filtered through the wooden shutters. It slanted narrow fingers across the bed, casting planes of dark and shade across the strong face lying so close to Ann's. She lay looking at it a moment. The eyes were shut and the features in repose. He looked—replete. The word came to her, and she knew it was apt. For herself she was—drained. Drained of everything— all emotion, all will. She could only go on lying there, her naked body held slackly against his. Her mind was a miasma, floating adrift in a strange state. She'd gone, she knew, beyond conscious thought—because what *could* she think? What was it possible to think, rationally, about what she had done? What was happening? It wasn't possible, that was all.

It was barely sane…

Because how could it be sane to sink again into the bliss she had known last night when that bliss came courtesy of a man who made his contempt of her no secret? And yet that man, that harsh, condemning man, so sneeringly offering her money for Ari, for her time here on Sospiris, seemed a universe away from the man who had initiated her into an ecstasy she had never known existed…

She felt something squeeze inside her that was almost pain.

But it's the same man… The whisper formed in her head, and she felt that strange, squeezing pain again.

Her eyes shadowed. *Is it the same man—is it?*

Her head told her yes, but her body—oh, her body denied it with all its power.

Without conscious thought, she let her hand press against his warm, hard body, smoothed the golden skin. He was so beautiful to touch. She felt her heart give that little squeeze again, felt a strange catch in her breath, as if in wonder—in homage—at such perfection.

The long lashes lifted from his eyes, and immediately his gaze focussed on her. Equally immediately she felt as if those incredible dark eyes were piercing right into her. She felt naked—

'Ann—'

It was all he said, but it was said in a voice that sounded

as replete as he was. He glided the hand resting on her upper arm along its smooth surface. It was not sexual, not arousing. It was just because she was there. In his bed. Beside him.

'Ann,' he said again, and drew her more closely against him, settling himself into the bedding, feeling her slender body curved against his. It felt good—but then everything about her felt good. Idly, he went on smoothing his palm along her upper arm. He felt full, at rest. And after a while he started to caress her again.

This time arousingly.

And yet again Ann went with him where he wanted to go.

The Jeep was rattling over the trackway again, heading back to the villa. Nikos was driving a lot more sedately now—and why not? His ill-tempered mood of the outward journey had disappeared completely. Of course it had! Ann's ludicrous and incomprehensible show of resistance had taken him nothing more than a few moments to dispose of. Why she'd done it he had no idea, and he didn't much care. It had obviously been some kind of ploy, and it had equally obviously been completely pointless. Anyway, it was irrelevant now. All that mattered was that it was over and would not be returning.

A smile played around his mouth. No, Ann had proved—conclusively and incontrovertibly—that she was completely incapable of resisting him. Which was exactly what he'd known all along.

Just as he'd known—the smile around his mouth deepened—that his decision to stick to the strategy of making Ann Turner his mistress was the right one. Every cell in his body told him blatantly that it was certainly the right one for him personally.

As his mistress, Ann Turner was malleable, enjoyable—definitely enjoyable!—and above all disposable. His strategy was foolproof. He'd been mad to think it had any risk to it.

Not only was he now going to be able to stop Ann Turner from being a thorn in his flesh, but her own exquisite flesh was his to enjoy—to enjoy with an intensity that had proved as real today as it had last night. Just why there was such an extraordinary intensity he didn't much care—he wasn't about to question it, just make the most of it.

Whenever he could.

His smile faded, replaced by a tightening of his mouth. Now, that was going to be an impediment he didn't welcome. But it would have to be managed, all the same, until he could take Ann back to Athens with him.

He turned his head to speak to her.

'We're going to have to be discreet, you understand? But I will see what can be done to make time for you.'

A looming hairpin bend made him look back at the road. Then, having negotiated it, he said, having got no response to his comment, 'Ann?'

He glanced at her again. She appeared not to have heard him.

'Ann?' he said again, now with a slight edge in his voice.

'Yes, I heard you. Thank you,' she answered.

Nikos considered her profile. Was she put out because he'd said they would need to be discreet? Perhaps she didn't understand that there was no way he was going to expose his mother to what they were doing? Or perhaps she thought he was not intending to continue with her—or that the necessity for discretion was in fact a lack of appreciation for her on his part? Well, that could easily be sorted—no problem. He knew exactly what would keep her sweet.

And it wasn't just sex…

Ann sat on her bed, the shutters of her bedroom window drawn, locking out the light of the day. Locking out the world. She had told a maid she'd passed on her way in that she had a migraine and would be keeping to her room.

Blankness enveloped her. She knew with one part of her mind that it was a kind of safety mechanism, like anaesthesia, blocking everything else out. The blankness made her calm—very calm. In a little while, but not just now, she would think about what she had to do. But not just yet. Not quite yet. Soon.

She ought to go down and see Ari. After all, that was why she was here. But she couldn't face it. She needed time—time here on her own, with the world locked out, safe.

Safe from Nikos.

But she wasn't safe from him. She had proved that, conclusively and indelibly. He only had to touch her and she was lost.

And there was no point bewailing it, no point being angry with herself, feeling ashamed. She had tried to resist him, tried to reject him, and failed. Failed completely.

How could any woman say no to Nikos Theakis when he wanted her?

But somehow, cost what it would, she was going to have to find the strength to do just that.

A bleak look crossed her eyes.

She couldn't cope. That was the only thing she knew about this whole situation.

But why? That was the question that wrung her mind. Why?

Why had Nikos Theakis seduced her?

It didn't make sense. He could have his pick of women—women from his own world—so why bother with her, a woman he openly despised? Surely not just to prove to her that he could? He hadn't liked her attempt to reject him—was that it? His male ego demanded her submission to him? Was that all it was? He wanted her to be as susceptible to him as every other woman must surely be?

Well, she thought heavily, he had all the proof he needed of that now! His ego could rest easy—she could no more say no to him than honey could refuse to melt over a hot spoon!

Restlessly, she got to her feet, starting to pace around the room. The blankness was leaving her now, and she wished it wasn't. It was like anaesthesia wearing off…

With every portion of her body she could feel the physical evidence of what she had done—her muscles were stretched, her lips beestung, and between her thighs a low throbbing beat to her pulse. She headed for the bathroom. A shower would help, surely? And it would give her something to do—something other than letting impossible thoughts go round and round in her head, like rats in a trap.

When she emerged from the shower they were still going round, but they no longer mattered. How could it matter that she did not know why Nikos Theakis was so determined to prove her vulnerability to him? How could it matter that he only had to touch her for her to melt into his caress?

Because from now on it wasn't going to happen. From now on, even if she had to lie and be evasive, say whatever it took, she would not spend one minute alone with Nikos. Not a single minute.

She dared not.

She knew it was cowardice, but so what? If that was what was necessary to keep her safe, but still with Ari, then so be it. It would be hard, but so what? If she could just hold to her line then she would be safe. There was nothing Nikos could do to her if she refused ever to be alone with him.

It was either that or leaving Sospiris. And she wouldn't be chased off by him! She *wouldn't!* This was her only opportunity to see her nephew, her sister's son, and nothing would make her give that up!

Resolution filled her. She was here for Ari—that was all, and that was what she must remember. Nothing else.

She kept her mind focussed on that resolution as, deliberately trying to divert her mind from the tormenting channels it was running in so fixedly, she occupied herself in catching up with her correspondence—including the large number of postcards she had bought on Maxos. Writing them did her good—it reminded her of the world far beyond Sospiris, touching essential base with her real life.

She ought to go down for nursery tea, she knew, but she was too chary of Tina's astute eyes. Surely it must be branded across her forehead just what she had gone and done? No, Ari had his playmate. He would not notice his aunt's absence particularly, and she had already said she had a migraine. She had better make the most of it and keep to her room. Hiding.

She knew that was what she was doing but she needed to do it. Strengthen her resolve. Prepare her mental barriers.

And pray they would hold.

Nikos strolled along the corridor, his mood enjoyably anticipatory. It had been annoying to discover, on emerging from his office for his mother's pre-prandial drinks, that Ann was apparently in her room with a migraine, and was not coming down to dinner. Damn—evidently Ann had indeed understood the need for discretion. If he'd only known sooner she was in her room, and not with Ari, he could easily have slipped along there at some point. He'd had to endure a dinner without her that had seemed to go on for ever until now, pleading some late night work he had to attend to, he could head straight for Ann's room.

Outside her door, he knocked briefly, then walked in. Already he was eager for her—the beach chalet seemed far too long ago.

His eyes went to her immediately. She was in bed waiting for him, idly flicking through an English language magazine.

'*Kalispera,* Ann,' he said, as he walked into the room.

The magazine dropped as if it were a hot stone, and her head snapped up. Shock emptied her face. He strolled across the room and sat down on the bed.

'I'm sorry you've had to wait for me—I only learnt at

dinner that you were keeping to your room. I'd been working till then. My apologies.' He leant forward, unable to resist the pleasure of making skin contact, drawing the back of his hand down her cheek.

She jerked, as if an electric shock had gone through her. Nikos smiled. That was good. Responsive.

Just the way he wanted her.

Then, as if his touch had thrown a switch, she spoke.

'What the hell do you think you're doing here?' Her voice was half a croak, half a whisper.

He gave a low laugh. 'Don't panic. I've been very discreet, the way I told you we would need to be.'

'*Discreet.*' She said the word as if it were an expletive.

He gave a shrug. 'It's inconvenient, yes, but there it is. My mother has certain codes of behaviour, and I would not wish to breach them openly.'

Even as he spoke he was conscious of a sense of discomfort. He did not relish this aspect of the business—but it was for his mother's sake in the long run that he made Ann Turner his mistress and got her greedy claws out of the Theakis family by putting her beyond the pale of his mother's misplaced forbearance of her.

'Inconvenient—' Her voice was hollow now, and she was staring at him with a peculiar expression in her face.

'Ann,' he said, making his tone temporising, 'for the time being it's unavoidable. But as soon as Tina's wedding is over I'll take you to Athens and—'

'Take me to Athens?' Her voice had changed to incomprehension.

It started to irritate Nikos. Why did she have to repeat everything he said to her?

'Well, Athens first, and then wherever you'd like to go—though of course I'd have to fit any vacation around my obligations to business, alas. But all the same—'

He never finished his sentence.

Her face snapped shut. Like a door closing. Shutting him out. Very decidedly out.

'I,' she bit out, and her eyes were hard suddenly—like stones, 'am not going *anywhere* with you. I am *not*—' she made the emphasis as if it was a razor slicing down '—going to have some hole and corner affair with you! Get out—get out of my room, right now!'

His eyes flashed impatiently. 'Ann—enough. We've been through this little farce once already today. I don't appreciate games—especially when they've already been played out. It's going to be difficult enough as it is, finding time together, without you doing your pointless denial routine. So—'

He didn't get any further. She was scrambling out of bed, the other side from him. Immediately Nikos's eyes went to her body, its slender form outlined beneath the diaphanous nightgown by the lamp from her bedside, to the tender mounds of her breasts, the slender wand of her waist and the graceful swell of her hips with the darkened vee between the perfect column of her thighs, all barely veiled by the translucent fabric. He felt himself respond—*Theos,* she was so beautiful! Desire surged through him. He wanted her—was hungry for her, could not wait for her.

'Ann—' Her name came, husked, raw. He started to move, levering off the bed, heading round its foot towards her, to reach her, touch her, to fold her to him, feel that beautiful, arousing body in his arms, that sweet, honeyed mouth opening to his...

And then, to his disbelief, even as his eyes devoured her she gave a little cry and hurled herself into the *en suite* bathroom. Nikos heard the frantic turning of the key in the lock, and then there was silence. For a long, incredulous moment he could only stare at the locked door.

Anger surged through him. Anger, disbelief—and intense, obliterating frustration.

Then, like a zombie, he walked out of the room.

Still not believing what had just happened.

CHAPTER EIGHT

'OH, ARI, THAT'S *very* good. Well done!'

Ann was on the terrace outside the nursery, shaded from the sun by an awning. Ari was colouring a drawing of his beloved trains.

'Why not write their names under the picture?' said Ann. She started to write a dotted outline that Ari could use to trace the shapes of the letters. Tina looked up from where she was checking off 'Things to do' for her wedding.

'You know about children, don't you? Using dots for letters?' she observed.

Ann smiled. 'It's a good way to get them to control the shape, I think.' She watched attentively as Ari started to write. It was good to be here with him. Good to be with the lively little boy who was the whole purpose of her presence here at the Theakis villa. The *sole* purpose.

A purpose which did *not* include providing on-tap sex for Nikos Theakis whenever he felt like waltzing into her bedroom! No, she mustn't remember that—and she mustn't let in, not even by a hair's breadth, the emotions that went with the memory. She must just shut it out. Ruthlessly. With an impermeable seal.

Nikos had used the term 'denial' and she clung to it. Yes, denial was exactly what she had to do. Deny everything. Deny she had ever felt such insane weakness for the man. Deny she could still, if for a moment she allowed it, feel the haunting echo of his touch, his caresses, his intoxicating invasion…possession.

Her eyes hardened. Possession. Yes, that was a good word. As in helping himself to her. Just because she was convenient—handy. Deliberately she let her hackles bristle. Nikos Theakis was a man so arrogant that he actually thought he could just help himself to sex with her! It didn't even bother him that he held her in total contempt for having taken his money from him! A chilling thought went through her. Was it because of what he thought of her that he also thought he could just help himself to her body? Was it because he held her in such contempt that he saw no problem with casually seducing her?

A shadow seemed to fall across her, making her shiver inwardly. To be held in such contempt that he thought he could use her sexually for his fleeting convenience…

'Kyria Ann?'

She surfaced from her dark cogitations to find one of the maids hovering.

'Please come…' said the girl in hesitant English.

Wondering why, but getting to her feet all the same, nodding to Tina and murmuring to Ari that she would be back soon, Ann followed the maid back indoors. Did Mrs Theakis want to see her? But the room she was shown into was not Sophia Theakis' sitting room.

It was Nikos Theakis's office. And seated at the desk, the flickering computer screen to his side, his planed face illuminated through the half-closed slats of the Venetian blinds at the window, was Nikos.

Too late she made the realisation as she stepped inside. The maid closed the door behind her. Too late she instantly turned to leave.

'Don't bolt, Ann. I have something to say to you. Sit down.'

The voice was clipped and impersonal.

She looked across at him. He was formally dressed in a business suit. She hadn't seen him so formal since they had arrived. And she had forgotten just how formidable he could look—every inch the captain of industry, born to give orders and have them obeyed by a host of minions doing his bidding.

Well, she wasn't one of them! Automatically she felt her hackles rise, and she stiffened.

'There's nothing I want to hear from you,' she said tersely.

Something flickered in his darkly veiled eyes, and she felt a shimmer go through her.

He did not reply, instead sliding open a drawer in the desk and removing an object. It was long and slim. He placed it at the front of the desk, facing her.

'This, Ann,' he said, and his eyes did not change expression, 'is yours.'

Warily, as if it might be a loaded gun, she reached for it. What was it? And why was Nikos telling her it was hers? She picked it up and realised that it was a case of some kind. It could be a case for spectacles, or a pen. But why should that make it hers?

She opened the case.

And stared disbelievingly.

A ribbon of white fire glittered in the dim light.

'What is this?' Ann heard her own voice speaking.

'A diamond necklace. Whilst I appreciate you prefer to operate on a cash basis, that is not something I am prepared to do in these circumstances. But you are welcome to see the receipt for the necklace—to know how much I consider you are worth. You can be flattered, Ann—it's a considerable amount.'

She dragged her eyes from the necklace, glittering against the dark velvet of the interior of the jewel case. She looked at him. There was a glitter in his eyes too, as if reflecting the diamonds he was offering her. She felt an emotion spear through her. She did not know its name—only that it was powerful. Very powerful.

'You see…' said Nikos, and he shifted very slightly in his seat, the hand that was resting on the polished mahogany surface of his desk flexing minutely. His eyes with that dark glitter were still resting on her. 'I have decided to cut to the chase. As a businessman I apply the motivations that are sufficient for each transaction to succeed. Your motivation, Ann, is consistent—money. Money is what drives your actions—whether it is giving up your sister's child, or giving up your invaluable time to come to Sospiris. And therefore I apply it now to this transaction—albeit in a form that is, let us say, an alternative to cash. So—' he took a sharp intake of breath '—now that we have successfully concluded this transaction, you must excuse me. I am leaving for Athens shortly. But I will be back later tonight. Wear the necklace when I come to you, Ann.' He paused, and the dark glitter intensified. 'Just the necklace.'

She went on standing there, immobile, incapable of moving, incapable of anything except feeling the emotion spearing through her. Then, from somewhere, she found her voice.

'You think a diamond necklace will get you into my bed?'

She said it flatly, getting the words out past the emotion that was seizing on them even as she spoke them.

'Why not? Your track record shows you are very amenable to such an approach to life.' There was a twist to his mouth as he answered her, his voice terse.

It made the emotion spear deeper into her. Her eyes went to the necklace again—the necklace Nikos was offering her in exchange for sex. Emotion bit again—a different one. One that seemed to touch the very quick of her. But she must not allow that emotion—only the other one, which was as sharp as the point of a spear.

Her eyes pulled away, back to the man sitting in his handmade suit at his antique desk, rich and powerful and arrogant. The man who had kissed her deeply, caressed the intimacies of her body, who had melded his body with hers, who had transported her to an ecstasy she had never known existed.

Who was offering her a diamond necklace for sex...

Carefully, very carefully, she snapped shut the lid of the box and placed it back in front of him.

'I am not,' she said, 'a whore.'

His expression did not change. 'Your sister,' he said softly— so softly that it raised the hairs on the back of her neck— 'possessed at least one virtue. She did not try and disguise the truth about herself. But you, Ann—you are a hypocrite. Worse even than your sister. Your sister sold her body—you, you sold your own flesh and blood. You sold her child.' His gaze seared her. 'So do not stand there and attempt to look *virtuous* or *insulted*—' each word dripped from him with acid contempt '—because I'm offering you what your sister was happy enough to take from any man she could persuade to make a similar offer!'

Like a floodgate breaking, emotion surged in Ann. Powerful and overpowering.

'Don't speak of Carla like that! And take your diamonds and *choke* on them!'

She whirled around, blind with fury.

How she got out of there she didn't know, but the moment she was in the corridor all she could do was stand there, shaking. Then, looking wildly around her, she plunged through the villa until she found her own bedroom, and there, safe in its sanctuary, she threw herself down on her bed.

Hot, hard tears convulsed in her throat. Fevered and furious. Choking her as they racked her. Face down on her pillow she cried tears for Carla, dead in her grave, whom even death could not save from the vile insults of Nikos Theakis—

a man who could take a woman to ecstasy, a paradise of the senses, and yet think her nothing more than a whore...

It was like acid poured on a wound, burning and biting into raw flesh.

She fisted her hands, pushing herself up on her elbows, neck straining, staring at the headboard, tears staining her cheeks.

Why—*why* should she be reacting like this? She'd known Nikos despised her for what she had done—and she had already castigated herself for succumbing to a man who could still take a woman to bed that he thought so contemptuously of.

And yet this was different. Offering her a diamond necklace, in exchange for her body. Expecting her to accept it.

And why? Because it brought home to her the brutal reality of it—that was all she was to Nikos Theakis. Nothing more.

Rage, convulsing and blinding, shook through her. But beneath the rage was another emotion. The one she had felt reach the very quick of her. The one that brought not fury but something quite different. That made her want to curl up into a ball and clasp her arms around her, as if to stanch a wound.

A wound that had gone much, much deeper than should ever be possible.

Nikos sat at his desk. He hadn't moved a muscle since she'd gone storming out of his office.

Without the diamond necklace.

He shifted his eyes so they rested on the jewel case.

Why hadn't she taken it?

It didn't make sense.. Everything he knew about her—everything she had proved to him—had told him that she would snatch the necklace from his hand as eagerly as she'd taken his cheques.

Even more eagerly.

The expression in his eyes changed minutely. After all, it was not as if she had found being in his bed repulsive...

But it was a mistake to admit any thoughts about Ann
Turner in his bed. Immediately, hungrily, appetite leapt within
him. It had been twenty-four long, deprived hours since he had
taken her to the beach chalet, and his body was protesting the
absence of a repeat encounter. It had protested quite enough
last night, when he had been left unsatisfied, thwarted. But
then at least he had had the prospect of remedying the situation by dint of the means he'd just put into play.

Cutting to the chase had been exactly what he'd intended.
No more prevaricating, manipulating games from Ann Turner.
Just cutting to the chase and giving her exactly what she was
so obviously angling for—what was so obviously the reason
behind all her ploys of denial and evasion. Because what
other reason could there be for her evasion of him? Her denial
of her response to him? He only had to touch her for her to
light up like a flame—and, *Theos mou,* it was the same for
him! One touch from her and he wanted her instantly—totally.

The way he did right now.

He shifted restlessly, his thoughts biting with a poisonous
mix of frustration and incomprehension.

Why had she refused the necklace? What did she think she
was going to achieve by refusing it?

His mouth thinned. Well, there was one thing she was
going to achieve, that was for sure.

He seized up the house phone. As Yannis answered, Nikos
barked down it, 'Phone Kyria Constantis and inform her that
she is invited to dine here tonight.' Then he put the receiver
down. He glowered darkly into the space in front of the desk,
where Ann Turner had refused to take the necklace.

So she didn't want the necklace, and she didn't want him.
His mouth tightened even more. There were plenty of women
who *did* want him. And tonight Ann Turner would get an
eyeful of one of them.

CHAPTER NINE

ELENA CONSTANTIS WAS speaking Greek, clearly intent on cutting out Ann and Tina. Ann was glad of it. Glad that she could focus her whole attention on Tina, discussing her forthcoming wedding, and give none at all—not the slightest iota—to the man to whom Elena Constantis was devoting *her* attention at the dinner table.

She was welcome to him.

Every woman on God's earth was welcome to him.

Emotions still roiled within her like bilge water—dark and angry. She had got through the remainder of the day somehow, but she wasn't even sure how. She'd had to stay in her room until she could finally face going back downstairs, face washed, breathing controlled. But it had still been hard. Hard to behave normally, and harder still now, in Nikos's loathsome presence at dinner.

Abruptly, Elena switched back to English—and to Ann.

'Will you be looking after darling little Ari as his new nanny?' she enquired in saccharine tones.

'I am his aunt, but I'm only visiting, Kyria Constantis,' replied Ann. 'I have no qualifications to be a professional nanny.'

The Greek woman's eyes hardened a moment. 'Yes, even on a salary as generous as working for a family such as the Theakises would bring you, it would be difficult to afford designer clothes,' she purred. Her heavily mascaraed eyes flicked over Ann's dress, then became tinged with satisfaction. 'I do love your outfit—I had one very similar when that particular collection came out. When was it now? Oh, five years ago, I believe. It has scarcely dated at all!'

'Yes,' responded Ann, not rising to the pinprick. 'Some fashions last longer than others.'

Longer than those who bought them—

The unbidden thought rose in her mind, making her throat tighten suddenly and her vision blur. Emotionally raw as she was, despite her outward display of calm, as she blinked to clear her eyes she diverted her thoughts from their painful subject and became aware of Nikos Theakis' dark gaze resting on her. Or rather on her dress. He was staring at it critically.

Ann's mouth thinned. *Oh, yes, go on, do,* she thought viciously. *Cost it down to the last penny—something to condemn me for!* Why should she care what he thought of her?

I won't let myself be hurt by what he did today! I won't! I knew all along that he despised me for taking his money, and I knew it was just sex that he wanted me for! Just sex—a passing appetite. He helped himself, and didn't have to think twice about it, because he thought he only had to toss me a diamond necklace and I'd roll over for him! Because that's the sort of woman he thinks I am.

So how can a man like that hurt me?

A silent shudder went through her. Thank God she had the strength to know she must not have anything more to do with Nikos Theakis! Had had that strength even when he was sitting on her very bed, reaching for her, and her whole body was suddenly aflame. Because if she hadn't, if she had allowed Nikos to sweep away her frail, pathetic defences against him, as he had done on the beach she would never have known just how low he thought her.

But now she did. Bald, brutal knowledge. And she had to

cling on to it with all her might. Like clutching a scorpion to her breast.

Somehow she got through the rest of the meal. But that night, as she lay in her bed in the beautiful guest bedroom, despite all the luxury of the Theakis villa around her she felt very alone.

Nikos would not be alone, she knew, with a tearing feeling inside her that she knew she must not, *must* not feel. No, tonight he would have Elena to keep him company! It would be Elena who would know the sensual bliss of his touch, the lush pleasure of his kisses, his caressing. Her body which would catch fire, burn in the flames he would arouse—her throat that would cry out at the moment of consummation, of ecstasy.

The pang came again, like a stiletto blade sliding between her ribs, seeking the quick of her flesh. Restlessly she turned over, pulling the bed coverings around her, wanting only the oblivion of sleep.

When it came, it brought no peace. Only the torment of dreams—dreams she would have given a diamond necklace *not* to have! And it brought too—dimly, like an excess thudding of her heart—a sound penetrating her unconsciousness that she did not quite believe: the thudding of helicopter rotors.

But in the morning she discovered that the Theakis helicopter had indeed been busy. Not only had it ferried Elena Constantis back to Maxos just after midnight, but it had also just departed again, this time taking Nikos with it.

'He must spend some time in the office, he tells me,' said Mrs Theakis to Ann over breakfast. 'He will be back for Tina's wedding, of course. Now, my dear,' she went on, 'how are you feeling this morning?'

She gave her customary serene smile, but even as Ann managed to murmur politely that she felt better, thank you, simultaneously trying not to show the relief on her face at hearing that Nikos had left Sospiris, she was sure she saw an assessing flicker in her hostess's expression. Then it was gone.

For the next few days Ann devoted herself entirely to Ari, glad to do so. But if during the day she told herself—over and over again—how glad she was too for the respite from Nikos's presence, at night her unconscious mind was a traitor to her, giving back in dreams what was a treacherous torment, a coruscating humiliation to remember. The sensual bliss she had felt in his arms. She awoke restless, aching, yet knowing she must not, *must not* feel that way…

And not just her unconscious mind was traitor to her. For when, the day before Tina's family were due to arrive for the forthcoming wedding, Ann came down to dinner, she discovered Nikos had returned to Sospiris.

She was taken by surprise—she had thought she had another twenty-four hours to steel herself. But she had no time at all—none. And that—surely only that?—must be why she felt her heart crunch in her chest. Just shock and being unprepared. That was all. Not because her eyes went to him immediately and her stomach hollowed, as she took in his tall, commanding figure, sheathed in that hand-made business suit of his, with a dark silk tie echoing the raven satin of his hair, the planed face, the sculpted mouth, the hooded long-lashed eyes that flicked devastatingly to her.

She felt them scorch her, as if a laser had gone through her, and in them was something that made her breath catch.

No! Her own weakness appalled her. God, she'd had days to collect herself, compose herself.

Cure herself.

Because cure herself she must. No other possibility was acceptable. She had to cure herself so that she could look at Nikos Theakis and see him as Tina saw him—as nothing more than a ridiculously handsome male who could turn female heads for miles around, but not hers. Her he left cold—quite, quite cold.

Except that *cold* was not the sensation flushing through her now. Not in the slightest.

It was heat beating up through her, invading her skin, her body cells, her mind, her brain.

Taking her over.

'Ah, Ann, my dear—there you are.' As ever, it was Sophia Theakis' placid voice that made her surface, made her brain work again, made her drag her eyes from the man who had magnetised them with his presence.

Another presence helped distract her as well. A little figure came running across to her.

'Uncle Nikki is back! And Dr Sam is coming too! And I am staying up, and I am *not* going to fall asleep and go splat into my dinner, like Uncle Nikki says!'

Ann stooped to catch up Ari and return his hug. His presence at dinner was a godsend, and so was Sam's. He arrived shortly, escorted in by Tina, who was looking very fetching in a blush-pink dress that suited her dusky curls. They made a striking couple, and Ann felt a strange pang go through her as they stood together, so obviously a pair, Tina's hand hooked into Sam's arm, and their shoulders brushing.

Lucky Tina, came the thought again. But she put it aside, knowing she had to focus only on getting through this meal without looking anywhere near Nikos.

Somehow she did, and it was mostly thanks to Ari, who held centre stage, having both his uncle and a clearly amused Sam to entertain with his chatter. As the lengthy meal drew to a close, however, despite his assurance that he would not fall asleep, Ann could see Ari getting sleepier and sleepier. It gave her just the opportunity she needed to murmur to Tina that she should stay with Sam while she put Ari to bed. Scooping up the nearly somnolent infant, she bore him off, smiling her goodnights to everyone round the table except the man at the head of it. He, with her blessing, could fall off a cliff for all she cared.

At least, she thought darkly, Nikos was ignoring her as

much as she was ignoring him. And with Tina's parents and immediate family arriving the next day, surely there should be people enough to make it possible for her to go on avoiding him?

But her hopes were dashed the very next morning.

'My dear,' said Mrs Theakis to her during breakfast, at which Ann was doing her best to continue her policy of ignoring Nikos, even though his presence was about as easy to ignore as a jackal's at a watering hole. 'It would afford me a great pleasure to be allowed to make you a present of a new gown to wear for Tina's wedding reception evening party.'

Immediately Ann demurred. 'Oh, no, really—it's very kind of you, but I brought an evening gown with me, just in case.'

Mrs Theakis gave an airy wave of her beringed hand. 'I am sure that a new one would be far more fun for you.' She smiled.

'No—really. The one I have is fine, I promise you,' insisted Ann. Not only did she *not* want Ari's grandmother spending money on her, she was also painfully conscious of what would obviously be Nikos's caustic disapproval of her getting yet more out of the Theakis family.

The next moment she was even more grateful that she had refused.

'Nikos is going to Athens today—he could take you with him and help you choose a new dress,' said Mrs Theakis encouragingly.

Ann's expression was a study. 'No—please—really,' she stammered out.

To her intense relief Mrs Theakis dropped the subject, but as Ann headed back to her room after breakfast to brush her teeth, she was intercepted at her bedroom door.

'Show me this dress of yours,' said a brusque, terse voice behind her. She turned sharply. Nikos was bearing down on her. 'My mother is clearly too tactful to say that she would like you to wear something appropriate for Tina's reception. If I can't reassure her, then—like it or not—I'll have to let her splash out on a new one for you,' he said, with evident disapproval.

Ann's eyes snapped. 'It's a perfectly respectable evening gown, thank you very much!'

'I'll be the judge of that,' said Nikos darkly, and pushed past her into the room.

It was hard to see him there again, dominating the space as he dominated every space. He had not been inside since the night he'd walked in for a bit of sex on the side…

The last thing she wanted was to see him there again, but if it meant that she could evade the unthinkable prospect of going to Athens with him to buy a new dress she would endure it. Stiffly, Ann marched to the wardrobe and leafed through her clothes, taking out the evening gown she had brought with her from London. It was a beautiful gown—in deep turquoise layered chiffon, with one shoulder bare and the other a broad pleat of material. The bodice was a little too low cut for her liking, but she had made a tuck in the shoulder strap to hoist the bodice higher, reducing her décolletage. Originally, too, the long skirt had been split to the thigh, but Ann had painstakingly sewn up the two sections to make it much less revealing.

A sudden oath sounded behind her, startling her. Before she could stop him, Nikos had snatched the dress from her.

'Where did you get this?' he snarled.

Ann looked askance at his incomprehensible anger. Then, before she could gather an answer, he provided one himself.

'Don't bother to answer with a lie! I recognised it immediately!' His voice was harsh and grating. 'Your sister wore it the night she got her avaricious claws into my brother!'

Ann could only stare. Shock and fury etched her face. Anger flashed again in Nikos' eyes. He threw the dress to the floor, and Ann, giving a little cry, made an instinctive movement to pick it up from where it lay crumpled in a heap. But hard hands came around her elbows, pinning her immobile.

'Were you planning it deliberately?' The snarl was in his voice, in his contorted face. 'Flaunting that dress in front of me—in front of my mother!'

Ann's face worked. 'I didn't have the faintest idea of—'

He thrust her away. 'No? Then why choose to bring it here?' he demanded.

'Because it's a beautiful dress, that's all!' she answered agitatedly. 'I didn't know—' She took a heavy, ragged breath. 'I didn't know you'd recognise it….'

Her mind raced on. How had he recognised it at all? How on earth should *he* know what dress her sister had been wearing when she'd met his brother?

A sound came from his throat. It was one of revulsion.

'Oh, I would recognise that dress, all right.' His voice was like a razorblade. Dark eyes bored into hers. 'It's indelibly etched on my memory.' The razor scraped across her flesh. 'Especially when your sister was taking it off in front of me…'

Ann stared. There was ice forming in her stomach.

Nikos's eyes were dark. Black, like pits. He started to speak.

'Andreas and I were guests on a yacht, cruising off Monte Carlo. The owner—a business associate we were currently in negotiation with—was the kind of man who liked to have a lot of girls on tap for any guests who might not have brought their own partners for the occasion. I don't have to tell you what kind of girls they were, do I?' His voice was mordant, his eyes still boring into hers. 'The kind that like to party at other people's expense. But let us say they pay for their passage in their own way…'

A breath was raked into him. 'Your sister targeted me right from the outset. Girls like her are amateurs only in name— she had done her research. She knew exactly who I was, how much I was worth, and that on that occasion I had no female partner with me. Her mistake, however—' his voice twisted

'—was in thinking I would have any interest in a girl like her. My indifference didn't put her off, though—she took it as a personal challenge.' His lips curled. 'On the last night, as we headed back to Monaco, I went back to my cabin and she was there, waiting for me. Wearing that dress.'

His eyes flicked to the vivid heap of material on the floor. Then they whipped back to Ann. His voice dropped to Arctic.

'She came on to me, stripping the dress off her body, determined to seduce me—determined to get into my bed and get the reward she wanted for it. When I turned her down, telling her to get dressed and get out, she spat at me that she'd make me sorry. I threw her out and thought I'd done with her. The next day—' his expression was like granite '—I woke to discover she'd taken off with Andreas.'

His eyes narrowed to slits as he iced his words at Ann. 'Your bitch of a sister helped herself to *my brother* out of spite. Because I refused to take her as my mistress and drape her in the diamonds she sold her body for!'

As his ugly words fell into the silence between them Ann felt sick. Through the agonising tightness in her throat, she forced herself to speak.

'She cared for Andreas—I know she did. I saw them together.'

'She cared for his money, that was all. The Theakis wealth. That's what she got pregnant for.'

His stark, cruel denunciation stabbed as punishingly as it had done four years ago, when Nikos Theakis had come to take Ari from her. She looked away, down at the crumpled dress on the floor. Slowly she bent to pick it up. She couldn't wear it now. She stared at it a moment. Then she turned back to Nikos. His face was still stark.

Was that really what Carla had done—tried to get Nikos to make her his mistress, and then turned to Andreas out of spite when she was rejected?

It was horrible to think of—horrible to think of the world Carla had lived in—a world where she had been regarded as some toy by rich men, as one of any number of girls provided for entertainment. Paying her way on a luxury yacht by making herself sexually available, out to get what she could, any way she could, from the rich men there…

I never wanted to think about Carla like that. It was always too horrible—too sordid. But that's the way Nikos saw her— with his own eyes…

Sombrely she put the dress away, smoothing down its folds. 'I won't wear it,' she said in a low voice.

But words grated from him. 'No—wear it, Ann. Wear it and look in the mirror when you do. And see the woman you are. Like your sister—beautiful on the outside, but on the inside—'

He stopped, mouth tightening. For a moment his eyes burned into hers, and she felt slain by them. Then, without another word, he walked from her room.

Her thoughts that day remained sombre, disturbed. Nikos had ripped a veil from her—a veil she had kept in place of her own volition. She had known what was beneath, but had not wanted to look. But it was there, all the same. Indelible. Staining her sister's memory.

No wonder he hated her so much.

The words formed in her mind, weaving in and out of her thoughts, haunting her. She tried not to hear them, but they would not leave her.

She did her best, though—busying herself first with Ari, who was getting progressively more excited as the day went on, then with greeting Tina's family, and then with the enlarged company for dinner. She remained unobtrusive, for the focus of attention was—as it should be—on Tina. For herself she was more than happy to stay on the sidelines, and take care of Ari.

The following day was very similar, with Tina's family

relaxing, making the villa seem very full. Sam came over for lunch, and Ari was in his element, introducing him to any of Tina's family who had not already met him.

'This is Dr Sam.' He beamed. 'He is not a sore tummy doctor. He is an old things doctor. Very old things. Older than Ya-ya.'

This, of course, drew amused laughter—including from Mrs Theakis. She was being—Ann would never have thought otherwise—an exceptionally kindly hostess to her new guests. But what Ann also had to acknowledge was that so was her son. He was as welcoming and as pleasant as any guest could wish. There was no trace of arrogance about him, nothing of the rich man condescending to his employee's relations.

Ann found herself watching him. She told herself she was merely watching *out* for him—making sure she kept a physical distance from him, making sure she said nothing that might draw his unwelcome attention to her. But she knew it was more than that. She knew that seeing him talking, smiling—even laughing—his manner relaxed and easy, was doing things to her insides.

Like tying them into knots. Tight knots. Squeezing hard.

Deliberately she stayed at the edges of the company and the conversation, effacing herself as much as she could. This worked until Tina's mother, directly addressing her, said, 'Tina says she is so relieved you are here, Ann—to take Ari's mind off the fact that she is leaving.'

Ann smiled a little ruefully, first glancing to see that Ari himself was out of earshot, his eyes only for the radio controlled car that Tina's parents had brought for him as a present.

'Tina must not worry too much. Ari will get used to her absence,' she said. 'It may sound upsetting to an adult, but at his age he will adapt very quickly to new circumstances.'

'I do hope you are right,' said Tina's mother doubtfully.

Ann sought to reassure her. 'Well, I lost my mother at four—Ari's age. And I have to say I have almost no memories of her—certainly not of losing her. My "memories" of her are really my sister's. She told me about her. It was much worse for Carla—Ari's mother. She was nearly nine, and felt our mother's death very badly.'

'Oh, how very sad! And for your father, of course.'

'He wasn't there any more. He left when I was born,' replied Ann.

'Good heavens—how dreadful for you two girls, left alone. What happened to you?'

Ann didn't really want to answer Tina's mother's enquiry, but it was made with concern and sympathy, so she answered briefly. 'We were fostered. Luckily Carla and I were able to stay together, which doesn't always happen when children are taken into care.'

Tina's mother smiled sympathetically. 'You must have been very close to your sister?'

'Yes.'

It was all Ann could say. She looked away—and found her gaze colliding, as if with a stone wall, with Nikos'. He was looking at her, his expression strange. She snapped her eyes away immediately, and to her relief Mrs Theakis moved the conversation onwards again.

Tina's wedding day dawned as another beautifully warm and sunny day, with the villa and its beautiful gardens creating a fairytale setting. With the civil ceremony having been conducted on Maxos, for the Greek authorities, Tina and Sam returned to the villa later in the day for an Anglican blessing, held under a vast gazebo erected on the largest terrace and conducted by Sam's uncle, a Church of England canon, attended by all their family and friends, as well as the Theakis family.

Ann sat beside Mrs Theakis, with little Ari, very smartly dressed, on her lap. Less happily, Nikos was on her other side. She sat very stiffly, drawing herself away from him, but his presence was overpowering all the same, and she was horribly conscious of it through the ceremony. But not enough to distract her from the beauty of the ceremony itself. Canon Forbes blessed the bridal couple and at the end, as Ann watched Sam's strong hands gently cradling Tina's face to kiss it, gazing down with love and happiness reflected like a shining mirror from his bride's eyes, she felt her own swell with tears. She had held them at bay throughout the service, but now they spilled over. Silently they coursed down her cheeks. Surreptitiously she dashed them away with her finger. Then, a moment later, a large silk handkerchief was pressed silently into her hand.

'My mother and Eupheme came better prepared,' said a low, deep voice at her ear.

Ann glanced at the older women, and indeed, as Nikos had indicated, both were shedding unashamed tears of emotion, delicately mopped with lawn handkerchiefs. As her gaze moved back to the bridal couple it brushed past Nikos. For a second she wasn't sure she could credit what she thought she had just seen in his face as he stared at Tina and Sam. Some strong emotion she could put no name to. Then, as she was still staring, his gaze suddenly flicked back to her.

The same emotion was still in it.

CHAPTER TEN

THE WEDDING RECEPTION was a lavish affair. Everyone was in evening dress, and Ann, though she wished she had another dress to wear, had no option but to put on Carla's dress. When she did, gazing at herself, her hair dressed in a low chignon at the nape of her neck, she was glad. It was a beautiful dress! And she knew she looked beautiful in it.

If there were dark associations with it, she would ignore them.

Just as she would ignore the man who had told her about them.

As she had been since Tina's family had arrived, Ann was glad to be unobtrusive, looking after Ari. Glad too that Nikos was spending his time being a highly hospitable host, which kept him well away from her. After the lengthy wedding dinner came dancing under the stars. Ari, though getting sleepy, wanted to dance, and Ann smilingly obliged, letting him lead her out importantly, and count with great concentration the *'one,* two, three' of the slow waltz being played as she held out her hands and he lifted his to hers. The steps brought them close to Tina—who was dancing, Ann realised too late, with Nikos, while her new husband bestowed his favours on one of the other female guests.

'Oh, Ari,' cried Tina laughingly. 'Dancing with Auntie Annie and not with me! I'm jealous!'

Immediately Ari let go of Ann. 'Tina is next,' he explained to her, and defected to his nanny. Tina disengaged from Nikos and swept off with Ari. Ann made to slip away, but suddenly her wrist was taken.

'I believe we have changed partners,' he said.

And took her in his arms.

It was done in a moment. She could not stop him without tugging free, making a scene. And she couldn't—not now, at Tina's wedding. But her body had gone rigid instantly, stiffening like steel. It annoyed him, she could tell, for his eyes had darkened, his mouth had tightened. She didn't care, though. Why should she? And anyway, she must not look at him—must not let her eyes anywhere near his face, which was so close, must not meet his gaze, above all must not be conscious in any way whatsoever of the touch of his hand at her waist, his clasp of her hand. She mustn't—just mustn't.

But it was useless. Every cell in her body screamed to her of his closeness, the warmth of his body, the firm pressure of the hand at her waist, guiding her steps, the warm touch of the hand holding hers as they turned—she stiffly, he with the same fluid grace that she had last seen when he'd joined his countrymen dancing in the taverna.

The night he'd seduced her...

Weakness rushed through her, and if her limbs hadn't been as stiff as steel she would have collapsed, falling forward against him, requiring his strength to effortlessly support her.

The music lilted through her brain, her blood, and the rhythm turned them so that imperceptibly, treacherously, she felt it loosen her limbs, dissolving their stiff rigidity—seducing her all on its own.

He felt it—his hand tightened at her waist, ineluctably drawing her against him. She tried to counter by bringing the hand she was holding inwards, as if to ward him off, but it only meant that his clasp enfolded her hand the more, and worse—worse—caught their hands between her breast and his chest. Desperately she found her other hand clutching at his shoulder, at the smooth, rich material of his tuxedo jacket.

Her heart had started to slug. She could not stop it.

Nor could she stop her head tilting, her eyes going to his. And drowning.

And it was bliss—magical, beautiful, wonderful!—to be held in his arms and wafted around the floor, the soft folds of her chiffon rustling and lifting and floating, the lush, seductive strains of the music cradling her even as his arms cradled her.

She couldn't resist it. Couldn't! Had no strength, no will. None. So she gave herself to it.

How long the dance lasted she could not tell, because she had stepped out of time. And not just out of time—out of reality. The reality of what had happened between her and Nikos—the sordid reality of what he thought of her—the angry, bitter reality of her loathing of him—seemed to have vanished. While the music lasted reality was banished. Only the magic remained—the magic of being in his arms, his embrace, of gazing up at him, lips parted, as his eyes fixed on hers in that wonderful, magical, drowning gaze that absorbed everything that existed.

Then, out of nowhere, the music stopped—and so did the magic. Blinking, she realised she had stopped moving, become aware of the world again, of the other people there and little Ari, tugging at her dress.

Dazed, unfocussed, she looked down. Ari's face was alight with excitement.

'The fireworks are starting!' He tugged her towards the stone balustrade looking out over the sea in the direction of Maxos.

There was a sudden 'whoosh' and a collective gasp—including a squeal from Ari—and the fireworks started. It was a spectacular display, probably visible from Maxos, and Ann appreciated that it was a generous gesture by the Theakis family to the townsfolk, as well as to Tina and Sam. It went on for ages, dazzling the night sky, and Ann was grateful. It gave her time to try and calm down—not that it ever stopped her being punishingly aware of Nikos, so close to her. But since he was holding Ari, who was squealing in excited delight throughout, at least it meant he couldn't try and touch her.

But would he want to, anyway? Since she had refused his diamonds he had not made the slightest attempt to come near her. He was obviously perfectly happy to go off with the likes of Elena Constantis—and who knew how many other women?

So why had he danced with her?

There had been no reason for him to take her in his arms and waltz with her, as if…as if… She felt her heart squeeze suddenly, painfully. As if it were the most romantic thing in the world—the most magical, the most wonderful. The pain clutched her again. As if he had never offered her a diamond necklace for sex and told her she was a hypocrite not to take it…

That was what she must remember! Nothing else! Not those few stupid, foolish minutes in his arms as the lilting music had danced in her veins and the magic had woven its velvet dreams into her head.

With a stupendous crescendo the fireworks ended. Ann turned away from the balcony and saw that Ari was almost asleep on Nikos's chest.

'Bedtime, poppet,' she said, and moved reluctantly to take him from Nikos.

'I'll carry him,' came the reply, and he started to thread his way towards the French windows leading inside. 'He's already asleep.'

Ann followed him inside. She'd half thought to stay out with the party, simply to keep away from Nikos, but Ari had reached out a hand for her.

'Auntie Annie put me to bed,' he said drowsily, but with a plaintive note. So she followed Nikos, her chiffon skirts sussurrating.

It was so quiet in the nursery quarters—and quite deserted. She found herself tensing, realising how alone she was here with Nikos.

It took only a very little time to see Ari into bed. He was already asleep as Nikos laid him carefully down, then stepped away to let Ann gently ease him into his pyjamas, lightly sponging his face and hands, then tucking him in with his teddy. For a moment, forgetting Nikos' presence, she soothed Ari's hair, feeling the soft silkiness beneath her fingers. His lashes were so long, she thought—almost as long as his uncle's...

She bent to drop a silent kiss on Ari's forehead, then straightened. Nikos was standing at the foot of Ari's bed, watching her. For a moment—a strange, breathless moment— she met his eyes. The light was dim, with only Ari's night-light on. She could not read the expression in his face, or in his eyes, knew only that she could not look away.

It was not like any look they had exchanged before. This was—different. She didn't know why, could only feel the difference. Feel the vibration that went through her—not just through her body, but somewhere deeper.

Then Ari stirred in his sleep and the moment was gone. Leaving only a whisper behind of an emotion she could not name. Different from any she had ever known. It was strange—disturbing. And something more. Something had seemed to come like a lift to her heart, like music she had never heard before, impressing deep upon her...haunting her like a ghost—a ghost of something that had never been.... could never be.

Jerkily, she moved to shake out and fold Ari's clothes, smoothing their creases and draping them over a chair. It was displacement activity, she knew. To give her time to recover her composure after that strange, disturbing moment—and more practically, to give Nikos time to leave.

But when she could no longer keep smoothing Ari's clothes she had to turn round—to see, with a quiver going through her, that Nikos had not moved. He was still standing there, watching her.

She made herself speak. 'You can go back to the party. I'm staying with Ari. I moved my things into Tina's room so as to be next door to him.' Her words sounded dislocated, disjointed. Awkward.

A second later she wished them desperately unsaid. Oh, God, had he thought she was telling him deliberately where she was going to sleep, hoping he'd come to her? Or, worse, would he now think he could?

But he didn't reply to what she had said. Instead, his eyes still resting on her, he spoke. His voice was low, grating—almost reluctant, as if he spoke against his will.

'You were right to wear that dress. You look—breathtaking.' There was a pause—minute, but telling. 'Nothing like your sister looked in it. Nothing at all...' His voice seemed to trail away.

She couldn't speak, did not know what to say. The silence stretched between them, the tension thick. For a moment longer he just went on standing there, looking at her, as she stood immobile, motionless. Then, with the slightest alteration of expression, his gaze loosed hers at last and he left the room.

For quite some time Ann could only stand there, still immobile. There seemed to be a hollow somewhere inside her, but she wasn't sure where.

Or why.

Nikos stood on the terrace outside his bedroom, his hands curved over the stone balustrade, looking out to sea. The scent of jasmine and honeysuckle caught at his senses. And not just at his senses—his memory. How short a time ago he had stood here with Ann, waiting to take her into his arms, his bed, seducing her in the sweet Aegean night—

He had not wanted the music to end. He had not wanted to let her go. She had seemed so—different. Not the woman he knew her to be. And just now, when he'd watched her put Ari to bed, how tenderly she'd kissed him, how naturally her affection for him had seemed to show. It had made strange, disquieting thoughts form in his head. Questions he wanted her to answer—but why he wanted her to answer them he would not ask himself.

He went on gazing out over the sea, disturbed, unsettled. Restless.

The next day seemed very flat, and when Tina's family had left after lunch, profusely thanking Mrs Theakis and Nikos for their wonderful hospitality, it seemed even flatter. Ari felt it most, Ann knew.

The reality of Tina actually leaving was hitting him, and though Ann reassured him that she was only on her honeymoon, and would be back soon from a Nile cruise, he was fretful and disconsolate—tired, too, after his exciting day and very late night. She was patient and forbearing with him, but it was hard going.

At least she didn't have to face Nikos, however. Once lunch was over and Tina's family had left for the rest of their holiday, at a popular resort on another Greek island, he kept to his office.

The next day was easier, with Ann getting Ari to draw pictures of Tina and Sam beside huge pyramids. But Ann was worried about him. Who would look after him when she herself had gone—as go, soon, she surely must? It would not be kind to stay so long that Ari got too used to her...

But at lunchtime Sophia Theakis dropped a bombshell.

'Now, Ari, my darling,' she said, smiling mysteriously, 'there is a wonderful surprise in store for you. A holiday, just for you!'

Ari's eyes were huge with excitement. 'Where? Where?' he cried.

Ann could only stare, wonderingly. She realised that Nikos had paused at the head of the table, and was staring equally bemused at his mother. He started to speak, clearly wanting to know more, but his mother silenced him by addressing her grandson.

'Somewhere little boys will *love* to go! You are going—' her eyes twinkled even more '—with Uncle Nikos and Auntie Annie to the best theme park in Paris!'

Immediately Ari cried out in blissful glee—but his uncle cut right across him. The Greek that followed was intense on his part and unruffled on his mother's—she was adamant. As for Ann, she could only sit there in disbelieving dismay. Her mind raced frantically. Of course Ari's grandmother could have no idea—none at all!—just *why* it was so impossible, so completely, utterly impossible, for her and Nikos to go off together with Ari.

The moment lunch was over, Ann handed Ari to Maria and hurried to Nikos' office. She didn't want to—the last thing she wanted to do was speak to him deliberately, let alone in the place where he had so cruelly offered her diamonds for sex— but there was no alternative.

At his desk, Nikos knew it was going to be Ann at the door—and he knew why. 'Come in.' His command was terse, and as she marched inside her expression was grim.

'I am *not* going to Paris with you!' she said immediately.

Just as immediately, Nikos found his own expression hardening. Gone in a flash was that unsettling sense of there having been something different about Ann. He was back on familiar territory again. All too familiar. Ann Turner defying him. Refusing him. Refusing to hand over her baby nephew.

Refusing to come out to Sospiris at his mother's invitation. Refusing to admit she wanted him. Refusing to accept his diamonds—refusing, now, to go to Paris with him…

Always damn well refusing him!

He was fed up to the back teeth with it all. He leant back in his leather chair, hands resting palm-down on the surface of the desk.

'I have no intention,' he spelt out, eyeballing her, 'of having my mother upset. Nor Ari. So you'll come with us to Paris, and that is all there is to it.'

Her eyes flashed furiously. 'You cannot *possibly* want to do what your mother's planned? You objected fast enough when she announced it!'

He had. It was true. An instinctive objection, and one that he had not been able to express in any way other than by claiming pressure of work. But his mother had calmly informed him that she'd checked with his PA and been told that there was no pressing business to prevent him taking time out for the coming week.

'I repeat,' he said brusquely, 'I will not have my mother upset. Nor Ari. We have no alternative but to go through with this farce. God knows—' his voice was edged suddenly '—it's been a farce right from the start!' He took a short breath, silencing her evident desire to riposte by raising a hand peremptorily. 'However,' he continued, 'from Paris you will go back to London. You've already spent more time with Ari than is good for him. Now, that is all there is to be said on the subject. And since,' he finished with heavy mordancy, 'I am to be away from my desk from tomorrow, I have a great deal of work to get through today!'

It was a dismissal, and he looked at her pointedly. For a moment she just stood there, visibly fulminating.

'Ann,' he said, and there was something in his voice that crawled over her skin, 'if you are waiting for me to make you a cash offer for your compliance, you will, I warn you, be disappointed. You've already been paid for your time with my family—consider Paris as part of that holiday.'

His eyes rested on her, and for a moment two spots of colour burned in her cheeks as her lips pressed together tightly. Then, without a further word, she turned on her heel and left.

CHAPTER ELEVEN

'COME *ON*, AUNTIE Annie! Come *on!*' Ari's piping voice was breathless with excitement. Ann finished replaiting her hair, and smiled down at him.

'Nearly ready. Why not go and check if your uncle is?'

Ari zoomed off to the connecting suite in the hotel, repeating his urging. Ann took a big breath to steady herself. She was here, in Paris, about to set off for the theme park—and she was with Nikos. She didn't want to be, but she was. And she just had to cope.

Somehow.

Ari, however, was of course ecstatic with excitement as they made their way into the heartland of any child's dreams. Open-mouthed, he stared around, exclaiming at every scene.

In the central concourse, Nikos hunkered down beside him with the park map opened out. 'OK, Ari, what ride do you want to do first?'

There followed two hours of breathless bliss for Ari, though for Ann, on those rides where Ari was snuggled between them, she felt that Nikos was far too physically close to her—especially when his arm reached around the back of the car, dangerously near her shoulders. But for Ari's sake she bore it stoically and tried not to tense too obviously.

And yet Nikos, she noticed, seemed to take her presence in his stride. She knew she was doing it for Ari, but Ann found, against her will, that as the afternoon wore on her tension was wearing off. She even caught herself exchanging amused smiles with Nikos when Ari made some childish expression of delight.

As the afternoon waned, Ari started to flag. Nikos hefted him up on his shoulders, and they made their way to the exit, buying a helium-filled balloon on route. Back at the hotel, Nikos had booked Ari a 'fun tea,' and afterwards, tired out from all the excitement, he went willingly to bed.

'Asleep?' The deep voice sounded from the communicating doorway.

Ann stood up from where she had been sitting on Ari's bed. She nodded.

'Exhausted by an excess of fun,' said Nikos. He strolled in and looked down at the sleeping boy. Something shifted in his eyes suddenly.

'I see Andreas in him—' He stopped. As if he had said what he shouldn't. His tone changed, deliberately lightening. 'He's had a good day—no doubt about that.'

'Yes,' said Ann. Her voice was stilted. It was the first time she had been in Nikos's company today without Ari's presence as an essential diversion.

'I've ordered dinner to be served in my suite in about an hour. That way we don't have to worry about organising a babysitting service—just keep the communicating door open.'

'Oh,' said Ann. She hadn't really known what to expect. Obviously she didn't actually want to have dinner with Nikos, but at least there would be waiting staff present.

But when, having spent the hour having a bath, she nerved herself to go through, it was to find that no servers were present. The table was beautifully laid, the first course set out already, and the second course was being kept hot on a side table. Almost she retreated, then steeled herself. She could get through this if she tried.

Nikos was pouring from a bottle of wine. He didn't ask whether Ann wanted any, just set a full glass at her place opposite him. He must have showered, Ann realised, for his hair was damply feathering, and he was freshly shaved too. He'd changed into an open necked shirt and dark blue trousers. He looked—she gulped silently—devastating.

But then he always did! It didn't matter what or where or when! He always, *always* made her stomach hollow.

Always had. Always would.

She picked up her knife and fork and started to eat her first course.

'No toast?'

She paused, looking up. 'What?'

Nikos picked up his wine glass. 'To Ari's holiday.'

It was impossible to disagree. Reluctantly she picked up her wine glass, and took a small sip in acknowledgement.

'One thing I'll say for you freely, Ann—you make an effort for him.'

'It would be hard not to,' she answered quietly. It was bizarre to hear a compliment, however mild, come out of Nikos.

'Yes,' he agreed. He paused. 'I hope the menu is to your liking?'

'Oh, yes, it's fine. Thank you. It's delicious.'

'Better than in the park,' he commented wryly.

'Well, I suppose they are catering for children, so fast food is the order of the day. The ice-creams were good, though.'

'Ari certainly thought so. Though he got most of it on his face!'

She smiled. 'I think a lot reached his tummy too.'

'It didn't stop him putting away a good tea, all the same.'

'No—having fun must make you extra hungry.'

'And sleepy. He was out like a light.'

'Recharging his batteries. Ready for tomorrow.'

It was so strange—exchanging pleasantries like this, even stilted ones. But what was the alternative? Ripping apart the frail veneer that kept them civil like this? Dragging everything vicious and ugly that lay between them back out into the open? No, better—easier—to do what she was doing now. What she had done all day since they'd left Sospiris. Behave as though the enmity between them did not exist.

'What's the schedule for tomorrow?' she ventured. 'By the way, I should point out to you that Ari has spotted there's a swimming pool in the hotel!'

A smile tugged at Nikos's mouth. Ann tried not to think how it made her stomach tug too.

'Are you volunteering me?' he asked, eyebrows raising with quizzical humour.

'No, I don't mind taking him in the least. I want to make the most of him while I—' She broke off. She had been refusing to let herself think that these were the last few days she would have with Ari, not knowing when she might see him again—or even if. No! She mustn't think like that. Ari's grandmother had promised, as Ann had taken leave of her that morning, that she would not lose touch. But would Nikos let that happen? Anxiety gnawed at her.

She looked down, continuing with her eating. Nikos made no reply, just watched her mechanically lifting her fork to her mouth and back.

She was back to being different again. It was because of Ari, he knew. That was obvious. When the boy was there she slipped into the 'different' Ann that she had started to be during Tina's wedding. A frown creased his brow as memory teased at him. She'd made some remark to Tina's mother—something that had struck him at the time. He reached for his wine and took a draught.

'You said you lost your mother when you were young?'

The words came out balder than he'd intended. Her head snapped up. She looked taken aback, and momentarily blank.

'You said it to Tina's mother,' he prompted.

Ann frowned. 'What of it?' Why on earth had he suddenly said that? Out of nowhere.

'You said you were taken into care?'

Ann stiffened. 'Yes. Why do you ask?'

He was looking at her strangely. 'Because I realise how little I know about you, Ann.'

'Why should you want to?' she countered. Nikos Theakis knew all he considered he needed to know about her. Why should he suddenly want to know more? What for? He'd never evinced the slightest interest before—why now?

'Because—' Nikos began, then stopped. Why *did* he want to know? What was it to him what Ann Turner's background was? What her childhood had been? It was irrelevant—she was the person she was. That was all. Desirable, hypocritical, venal. He had proof of all those three qualities. They were enough for any woman!

But was it enough for him to know? Was there more about her?

'You said something about foster parents?' The prompting came again.

'Yes.' It was a bald reply, and all he got.

'Were they good to you?' Why had he said that? Why did he care?

She gave a little shrug. 'Some were better than others.'

He frowned. 'You had more than one set?'

'We were moved at least three times. The last—' She broke off.

'Yes?'

Unconsciously Ann reached for her wine and took a mouthful. She needed it.

'The last placement was very good for me. I thrived. I was

happiest there. The foster mother was kind, and I liked her. The foster father—' She broke off again. Took another mouthful of wine.

'The foster father…?' Again Nikos was prompting her.

Something flashed in her eyes. Hard. Like a knife-blade. He wanted to know? OK, he could know. 'The foster father was fine—with me.' She took a constricted breath that razored in her throat. She breathed out harshly. 'That was because I was too young for him. He liked young teenage girls—like Carla.'

Nikos's expression had stilled. 'Are you saying—?' he said slowly.

'Yes.' It was all she said. All she had to say.

'But surely there were social workers for you both, if you were in state care? Why didn't your sister—?'

Ann's gaze was unblinking. 'Carla didn't tell them. She knew I was happy in that placement. So for my sake she…put up with it. She didn't want us moved again, unsettled. And the risk of separation was always there. It's hard for fostered siblings to be kept together—there's such a shortage of foster carers. She thought that at least we were together, and that— well, she could stick it out. So she did. For two years. Until she was old enough to leave at sixteen.' A final breath exhaled from her. 'Then she got out of there like a bat out of hell. But not before telling our foster father that she would be keeping a lookout for me like a hawk, and if he made the slightest move on me now that I was older she'd see him in jail. So he never touched me—and I never knew about what had happened to Carla until I was old enough to leave care. I found out when Carla called the social workers in, and the police, and got the man prosecuted. So he couldn't prey on any other girls they took in.'

Nikos paused. 'His wife colluded?'

Ann shook her head. 'She didn't know. She really, really didn't know. When the case came to court, and Carla and I had to give our testimony, she looked as if her very soul had been destroyed. It was heartbreaking for her. She felt guilty because she'd failed to care for the children in her charge, because she'd been so blind to her husband's nature.'

Nikos was silent. Silenced. Ann had resumed eating. Focussing only on her food, her face blank. Slowly, he spoke.

'I didn't know.' The words seemed inadequate even as he said them.

Ann glanced at him. 'Why should you? If you want to apply popular psychology you could say that because a man used Carla she decided that in future she'd use them. Which she did. Does it excuse her? I don't know.'

'Perhaps,' said Nikos slowly, as if his thoughts were rearranging themselves in his head, 'it explains her.'

'Maybe it does. But then maybe she just wanted the good things in life. We weren't materially deprived in care, but we didn't have anything of our own. Carla was always hungry for material goods. Maybe she wanted to taste luxury the easy way.'

His expression had changed. He was looking at her. Different thoughts were in his head now. Memory was suddenly vivid in his mind. Four years ago he'd stood in Ann Turner's dingy flat and seen only a place utterly unfit in which to bring up his brother's son. His only urge had been to get Ari out of there. Now, in his mind's eye, he saw it differently. As the place Ann had *had* to live in. The rundown area, the shabby furniture, the primitive kitchen, worn carpets, peeling wallpaper—all the signs of poverty and squalor.

No wonder she had wanted out...

His eyes rested on her as she went on eating.

If I'd been as poor as she was, would I, too, have been tempted to do what she did...sell Ari for a million?

The thought sat in his head with a weight he did not want to feel. But felt all the same.

What did he know of poverty? He'd been born to immense wealth, immense privilege. What must it be like to have to live in a place like that? To have your world confined to such conditions? Dreary, cramped, dingy, squalid.

And then someone offered you a million pounds…

So you could taste luxury the easy way…

Ann had finished eating, setting aside her knife and fork. She lifted her head.

'Would you like me to serve the next course?'

Her voice was quite steady, as if they had not just been talking about what had happened to her sister as a vulnerable young teenager.

Nikos nodded. 'Yes, thank you.'

She busied herself clearing away their plates and moving to the sideboard. Nikos joined her, lifting the lids of the chafing dishes. His thoughts were troubled, confused. Unsettling. Making him think things he found uncomfortable.

Briskly, Ann took the filled plates back to the table. Nikos poured out more wine. They settled down to eat the next course. After a few moments Ann said, 'There are several shows on in the park that I'm sure Ari would love. If you can't face them I can take him, if you like.'

'No, the pleasure is in seeing his pleasure,' returned Nikos.

He spoke in a deliberately easy manner. It was clear that Ann wanted to change the subject, and he could understand why. But even as they resumed their deliberately light conversation about Ari his thoughts were running as a background process in his mind. Like an underground river—eroding what he had taken for the solid rock of his certainties about her. Her sister.

He thought of what he'd known of Carla Turner. Yet she had protected her young sister's happiness by sacrificing herself to the lusts of a pervert exploiting the very children he had been appointed to care for. Had that loss of innocence she'd suffered made her the woman she'd become? Irremediably scarred by what a man had done to her?

And Ann? What of her? Taking the money he'd offered her as her only chance to escape the poverty she'd been trapped in?

Again he felt the certainties he had held for so long shift, become unstable. Reshape themselves.

But what shape would they finally take? He did not know. Could not tell. Could only let them run in the background of his mind while he dined with a woman he both desired and despised.

The next day was spent entirely at Ari's pleasure: a second visit to the theme park, a swim in the hotel pool, and a dare-devil circus dinner show in the evening. Then came a day at a second theme park, rounded off with a candlelit parade and supper at the main park. Back in their suite, Ari was asleep in minutes.

Ann kissed him tenderly, an ache filling her heart. This was their last day here—which meant tomorrow she must return to London. Leave Ari.

Leave Nikos—

The ache in her heart seemed to intensify…

'Come and have some coffee.' Nikos's deep voice came from the doorway. She straightened, composing herself. Her expression did not falter even as her eyes went straight to Nikos'. As if a magnet drew them thither.

But then he drew *all* women's eyes.

She went through to the reception room. After all, this would be the last time she would spend with him. The sense of loss increased even as she berated herself for letting it in.

'So,' said Nikos, relaxing back, taking his coffee cup, 'do you think Ari is theme parked out?'

She made her voice sound normal—the way she had done all the time here. 'For now, yes. But as soon as you get him home he'll be asking you when you're going to take him again!'

He laughed, and Ann had to drop her eyes. The aching feeling inside her was getting stronger. She must crush it. Because there was no place for it. This time tomorrow she would be back in London, with her own life—her real life—taking her over again. That was what she must remember.

Remember what Nikos Theakis thought of her…

'Well, next year, perhaps,' he allowed. 'But I admit I'm looking forward to being in central Paris tomorrow. Tell me, do you know the city?'

She shook her head. 'I've never been there.'

'Never been?' He sounded surprised, as if it were odd she'd never been. 'Well, then, it will be my pleasure to show the city to you both—you and Ari.'

She swallowed. 'It might be better if I got a midday flight back to London,' she said. 'I don't want to arrive too late.'

He was looking at her. His eyes were veiled suddenly. 'Ari's holiday is not yet over,' he said. 'There is no question of you abandoning him yet.'

'I didn't mean I wanted to leave him,' she said defensively.

For a moment his eyes rested on her with that same veiled expression. Then, lifting his coffee cup, he said, 'Good, then that is settled. Tomorrow we remove to central Paris and do our sightseeing.'

Ann felt her mood lift—she knew she shouldn't let it, but it was too late.

A reprieve—

As she thought the word, she wished it unthought. But she knew it was true, for all that.

CHAPTER TWELVE

IF SHE'D WONDERED whether a city with so sophisticated a reputation as Paris might not have much to appeal to a young child, Ann swiftly discovered her mistake. The next day, after they'd taken a taxi into the centre of the city and checked into a hotel so world-famous it made her eyes stretch, Ari could not wait to get out and about.

The Metro was an immediate hit, and so was the Eiffel Tower—especially lunching halfway up. Then came a ride on a *bâteau mouche* on the River Seine, followed by a stroll through the Tuileries gardens, ending up at a café on the Rue de Rivoli, where Ari wolfed down an ice-cream, and Ann contented herself with a *café au lait,* nobly resisting the mouthwatering array of patisserie—which Nikos, to her chagrin, did not.

'You should succumb to temptation, Ann,' he murmured, his eyes glinting.

She pressed her lips together. Why couldn't Nikos be the way he'd been on Sospiris—raking at her, castigating her sister, insulting her with diamonds? Why did he have to be like this now, with that lazy glint in his eye and his casual companionableness, and their mutual conspiracy towards Ari that they were the best of friends? Making remarks that sounded innocuous but which carried a subtext a mile high?

Was he doing it on purpose? she wondered bleakly. Baiting her? Taunting her? Yet the humour in his glint belied so malign a purpose. Hinting at a purpose that made her insides give a little skip.

But what was the point? What was the point of reacting to the male gorgeousness that was Nikos Theakis? She was here with him for Ari's sake, that was all. She forced her heart to harden. Nothing could take away the poison that lay between them, however superficially nice Nikos was being.

Yet that evening, with Ari fast asleep in the exquisitely appointed bedroom Ann shared with him in the suite Nikos had taken for them all, the soft knock on her door took her by surprise.

'We can dine downstairs,' Nikos informed her. 'I've booked one of the hotel's babysitters to be up here until we return. And since, Ann, this is a grand hotel, we shall dine in grand style.' His eyes held hers a moment—a brief, dangerous moment. 'Wear the turquoise evening gown again—you won't be overdressed, I promise you.'

She should, she knew, have made some excuse. Pleaded a headache, or tiredness—anything to avoid dining with Nikos Theakis *en grande tenue* at this world famous hotel in the heart of Paris. And yet she didn't.

He certainly drew all eyes as they made their way into the three-Michelin-starred restaurant at the hotel. But then Nikos Theakis in a tuxedo was a sight to rivet female eyes for miles around.

For herself, she had definitely had to *avert* her gaze, as her eyes had gone to him in the suite, taking in in an instant just how much the superbly tailored jacket enhanced his superbly structured torso, how the gleaming white of his shirt emphasised the sleek muscled chest, and the immaculate dark trousers sheathed his long legs. Keeping her composure in the face of such incentive to lose it had helped minimise the impact of his own sweeping glance over her, wearing once more, as she had done for Tina's wedding reception, the beautiful layered chiffon gown that fell in Grecian folds to her ankles, skimming her breasts and baring one shoulder. She'd dressed her hair loose tonight, and it cascaded down her back, loosely pulled around her bared shoulder. Her make-up, too, she'd applied with particular care—this was, after all, Paris, which must put any woman on her mettle. Especially when she was dining with so superb a specimen of manhood as she was tonight.

The food, she discovered, entirely justified the prestige which the restaurant was held, and when it came to the exquisitely prepared creamy *bavarois,* adorned with a net of spun sugar and laced with vividly hued coulis, she did not hesitate. She dipped her spoon into the heavenly concoction—only to find Nikos's amused, long-lashed gaze on her.

'Enjoy,' he murmured, and his eyes gave their familiar glint.

She felt her breath catch in her throat, two flares of colour flag in her cheeks, then she dipped her head to taste the mouthful of dessert. It was as gorgeous to eat as to look at, and it did not last long. She surfaced to see Nikos still watching with amusement, lounging back in his seat, a glass of Sauternes between his fingers.

But even as she met his gaze it changed. Amusement flickered to something else, and now the catch in Ann's throat was enough to still her breath. Then, abruptly, the gaze was gone. He took a mouthful of his wine, his gaze turned inward. Then that expression, too, changed.

'So—' he tilted his chair further back, easing his shoulders more, relaxation in every line of his lithe, powerful body '—what shall we do tomorrow, Ann?'

'Anywhere by Metro will keep Ari happy.' She smiled, grateful for the safety of talking about Ari instead of having Nikos looking at her with his long-lashed, gold-glinting eyes.

'I just hope he doesn't realise one can take the Metro all the way back out to the theme parks!' said Nikos feelingly.

She laughed. 'Ari heaven! But then this whole holiday has been wonderful for him! Any child would have adored it.'

For a moment there was a shadow in her eyes. It was only fleeting, but Nikos noticed it, all the same.

'What is it?' he asked.

She gave a half smile, a little rueful. 'He doesn't know how fortunate he is, compared with so many other children.'

Nikos's face was sombre a moment. 'True, he has every material blessing. But no parents.'

Ann bit her lip. 'Yes, but there are many children with neither families nor material security. Still,' she went on, 'who would begrudge him for a second the happiness he has? And he isn't spoilt—not in the slightest.'

'No,' agreed Nikos. 'He isn't. We have done our best, myself, my mother and Tina, to ensure he is not a spoilt brat.'

'Never!' exclaimed Ann feelingly. 'He's an angelic child.'

There was a tug at Nikos' mouth. 'Now, there speaks a doting aunt!' Then, as it had before, his expression changed. 'And you are, aren't you, Ann? It's not a show for my benefit, is it? You really do love him.'

'Is that so surprising?' she asked steadily.

His eyes rested on her, with that same expression in them that she could not read. 'Perhaps not,' he answered.

Was there reluctance in his voice? Of course there must be, thought Ann. It would gall him to think she really cared for the nephew she had sold, as he so scathingly reminded her whenever it suited him, for hard cash.

And suddenly, out of nowhere, Ann found herself wanting to dispel that view of her as heartless and mercenary.

'I think you have come to love Ari,' he said slowly. 'Being with him as you have been on Sospiris and here, now, day after day. I think you have come to love him now that he is no longer a baby—a burden on your life imposed on you by your sister's death, a responsibility you could not evade.'

His eyes were resting on her, still with that unreadable expression in them, and Ann could only let him speak—even though she wanted to shout out that he was wrong, *wrong!* That she had never, ever regarded Ari as a burden, that he had been the most precious thing in her life, and that giving him up had nearly broken her...

But Nikos was still speaking, his tone sombre, and as she listened her eyes widened in amazement.

'When I came to you that night, Ann, four years ago, fresh off the plane, I'd spent the entire journey in a state of agonising grief for my brother's death. There was only one other emotion in me.' He looked at her, his eyes heavy. 'Fear,' he said.

She stared, not understanding.

'Yes, fear. And anger—not just at your sister, for what she'd done to my brother, but at myself. Harsh, unforgiving anger. Because...' He took a ragged breath. 'It was I who had ensured that Ari was illegitimate. I was so sure that Carla had lied through her teeth to Andreas that she was pregnant by him, and not any of the dozens of men she got through, I persuaded him to wait until the child was born and only then have DNA tests done—convinced as I was that they would be negative, and he would not need to marry a woman like her and ruin his life. So when I arrived that night, Ann, my anger at myself for having myself ensured my dead brother's son was a bastard warred only with my fear—my fear of you.'

'Me?' Ann's voice was disbelieving.

Long lashes swept down over his eyes, and his mouth twisted.

'Yes, Ann—you. A drab slip of a girl, living in a dingy slum, holding a baby in her arms that I desperately, desperately wanted—needed!—and which you could have denied me.' He took another heavy breath. 'Surely, Ann, you knew how powerful your position was? The moment I showed my hand and told you I wanted to take Ari you must have known?'

'Known what?' she said blankly.

'That you were holding me to ransom! *Theos mou,* Ann— you had legal possession of my brother's son. When your sister was killed you became Ari's legal guardian—and as such, the moment you knew I wanted him, you had unlimited power over me. Had Andreas and Carla been married, I could have wrested Ari from you with ease—what court in the world would have awarded custody to a penniless girl in comparison with what I could offer my nephew? But as Ari's guardian, as you were, you held every card.'

Incredulity flared in her face. He saw it, and gave a brief, hollow laugh.

'I came to you that day with only one weapon in my hand. My money.' His mouth twisted again as he spoke. 'Fear that you would turn me down, laugh in my face, made me harsh to you, Ann. Whatever your sister had done, you were hardly responsible—I knew and accepted that! Yet my anger at her, my fear of you—of the power you held to deny me what I needed most, my brother's son—made me angry with you, too. But…' His eyes closed momentarily as he faced truths he had not wanted to face—truths that told him baldly, bleakly, just why he had so wanted to hate and despise Ann Turner for selling her baby nephew to him. 'I had a lucky escape that day—and do not think I did not know it. I found a woman young enough, poor enough, to bribe with a pittance.'

Ann swallowed. A million pounds? A pittance? But Nikos was talking again. His voice was darkly bitter—at himself.

'Do you not realise how I cheated you that day, Ann? You could have held out for far, far more. I would have given the world for Ari. You could have sent me off, left me to sweat with no room to manoeuvre, once you realised how desperately I wanted Ari. You could have raised the bidding—not just to sell him to me, but for a share in the Theakis wealth. You could have gone to the press, Ann—kicked up a storm, a hideous scandal over our heads, raking up everything your sister had been. You could have hired a team of crack lawyers to get your fingers into the Theakis fortune on behalf of the child for whom you were legal guardian, illegitimate though he was. Just thinking of what you held the power to do that day made me so harsh to you. Even as you took that cheque for a paltry million pounds from my hand I hated you for the power you had over me.'

He stilled, the strong emotion in his face fading—but not completely.

'And I hated you for selling Ari to me—even though it was what I wanted—so swiftly and so cheaply. I've condemned you ever since for it.'

She swallowed. There seemed to be a stone lodged in her throat, making it hard—impossible—to breathe.

'I...I noticed,' she said.

His eyes were on her, heavy, and it was a weight she could scarcely bear.

'But what right have I, Ann—I who have only ever known wealth and ease and luxury, all my life, through no effort of my own, merely inheriting it—what right have I to condemn someone born to poverty for taking easy money when it came their way? Would I, Ann, in your position, have been any more virtuous? Would I have turned down the money dangled so temptingly in front of me so that I could live the rest of my life in poverty? Raising my sister's orphaned child, giving up my life to my nephew just so that his rich uncle would not condemn me? Would I have been any better than you?' He paused. 'I would not like to be put to that test, Ann—as you were.'

Her mouth was working. She had to speak—had to! Had to tell him that—

But Nikos was speaking again. His voice was urgent, suddenly—persuasive. Compelling.

'I want to put it behind us Ann. Nothing—nothing that I've seen of you, known of you, since you came to Sospiris—gives me any further cause to think ill of you. Indeed—' his voice twisted '—you have even proved to me you do not have your sister's morals when it comes to sex, haven't you?'

She felt colour flare out along her cheeks, felt Nikos' gold-glinting eyes rest mordantly on her.

'Was that the moment I was forced to rethink my opinion of you, Ann?' he mused. 'The moment you rejected the diamond necklace I wanted to give you, which I thought you would seize with both your greedy little hands? I didn't want you to reject it—I wanted you to take it.'

'Yes,' she answered tightly, the colour still flaring in her cheeks. 'I'm aware of that.'

His lips twitched. 'Not because I wanted to confirm my low opinion of you, Ann. Because…' The long lashes swept down again, making her breath catch though she shouldn't let it—she shouldn't, she mustn't. 'Because I wanted you back in my bed—any way I could get you there.'

His hand reached across the table. A single finger stroked along the back of her hand. She felt the lightness of his touch as if it were searing heat.

'I still want you, Ann.' His voice was low, intense.

The breath stilled in her lungs. She could not breathe, nor speak, though she should do both…

He was holding her with his gaze, as if her entire weight were suspended. Words came from him, seductive, sensuous.

'You are so beautiful. So incredibly beautiful—'

His eyes swept over her, making her weak—so weak.

But she could not be weak—*must* not. However much her head was swirling with the same overwhelming emotion as when he had danced with her, taken her into his arms in those magical, dreamlike moments.

'It's…it's not a good idea,' she said. Her voice seemed strained, tortured.

But Nikos wasn't listening. His mouth was lowering to hers.

She made one last, frail attempt.

'Ari…' she breathed.

But all at once they had left the restaurant, were standing in the little entrance hallway outside the suite. She was fighting for sanity, but it would not come. It had fled, far away, and she could not get it back. Dimly she heard voices speaking French—one Nikos, the other the hotel babysitter—and then the woman was slipping past her, letting herself out, and Ann could not say a word, not a word, until Nikos came out of the lounge. And then she still could not say a word, could only let him take her hand and lead her across the lounge and into his bedroom.

And there she could speak only one word—only one.

'Nikos,' she breathed.

She was his. His again. But not as she had been before. Because now his heart was not hardened towards her. Now she was not the woman he must take control of to prevent her exploiting him and his mother any further. She was not the woman he'd cynically, deliberately seduced, succumbing to a desire that he'd needed a reason to slake, allowing him to take her, enjoy her—and still despise her.

Now she was his only because he wanted her—wanted to move his hand over her bare shoulder, feeling the softness of her pale skin, easing aside the chiffon material to free her other shoulder so he could glide his lips along it, even as his fingers went to the zip at the back of the dress. He slid it down in one single long movement, so that the dress fell from her in a shimmer of gossamer, and he turned her, boneless in his hands, to face him.

His breath caught. She was so beautiful! Her rounded breasts, bared to him again, were already swelling to his gaze, and the slender pliancy of her waist awaited his caress. Around her hips there was only a wisp of lace, enticing more than it revealed.

She opened to him willingly, ardently, and his mouth played with hers, each touch, each intimate caress, arousing him yet more and more.

And then her fingers were at his throat, teasing apart the tight knot of his dress tie, slipping the buttons of his shirt, first one and then another, until even as he was kissing her she was baring his body for her own delight, easing his shirt from the confines of his belted hips. He revelled in the feel of her delicate fingertips exploring his torso, revelled yet more in the flatness of her palms smoothing over him, and then, pulling away from her, he shrugged off his jacket, the remains of his shirt.

She stood watching him, even as she had watched him strip down on the beach on Sospiris, when he had first realised his own desire for her. His hands went to his waist, unbuckling his belt, slipping the metal hook, the zip…

He watched her watching him…

With a little cry she turned away, as if she had been caught out, guilty, and he gave a laugh, catching her in his arms even as she turned.

'No shyness! This is for us both, my most beautiful Ann…'

He swept her up, taking her across to the bed, pulling back the coverings and lowering her down on to the sheets where she lay, hair spilling like a silvered flag, her pale body exquisitely beautiful to him. Then he stripped off the rest of his clothes and came down beside her.

He feasted on her. Every morsel of her body was his delight, his pleasure, his to enjoy. As was his body for her. Caressing and arousing, he felt the blood pulse strongly in his veins, and desire—strong and untrammelled—coursed powerfully through him. She was everything he wanted—*everything!*

The bounty of her breasts, the glory of her hair, the sweetness of her mouth, the silk of her skin, and—most glorious of all—the richness of her dewing body, opening to his, drawing him in. She clung to him, hands meshed with his so tightly their palms were sealed, her spine arching, lips parted, eyes glazed as she gazed up into his eyes that were devouring hers. And all the time he thrust within her, taking her with him, onwards, onwards to that place that awaited them both.

It took them in, turning the world to searing glory in a heat so fierce he cried out—a low, guttural cry that found an echo, higher, finer, which melded into the fire in which they writhed together.

And then the coming down—the slow, heavy exhaustion of the body that took him back from the furnace and made him fold her sated body to his, panting, breathless, still quivering, clinging to him as if he were the only still point after the passion that had consumed them both.

She lay in the circle of his arms, exhausted, weak, and gradually he could feel his hectic pulse slow. His own breathing started to ease, and his eyelids felt heavy, so very heavy, so that all he could do was pull the covers over them, hold her stilling body more tightly to him yet, and give himself up into the oblivion that reached for him. His last awareness was of how good, how very, very good it felt to have her body so close, so closely entwined with his.

The place it should be.

The place it would be.

CHAPTER THIRTEEN

ARI WAS CHATTERING, telling them all about what he had seen from the rooftop of Notre Dame, and Ann and Nikos were smiling indulgently at him. But beneath the table in the restaurant where they were having lunch, they were holding hands.

Such a simple gesture, thought Ann, and yet it felt so magical. But then the whole world had turned to magic.

She'd been mad, she knew, to succumb as she had last night. But how could she have resisted? It was impossible to resist Nikos Theakis. Impossible! Even while he had made no secret of his contempt for her it had been all but impossible to resist him—but now... Her insides squeezed flutteringly. Now that he was being so...so *nice* to her, the very thought of trying to resist him was...impossible.

Yet even as she'd given herself to him—unresisting, quickening with a desire that had swept her into his arms, his bed—she'd known not just that she was mad, but that she was lighting a fire that would be far, far harder to douse this time. Before, she had found the strength to resist him in his vileness to her.

But now, how many days—how many nights—did they have left? Nikos had said nothing of how long he wanted to stay in Paris, but Tina would be back from honeymoon soon, and surely then he'd be returning to Greece with Ari?

Perhaps only a few days—only one or two—but I will take

them—take them and not think about anything else—anything else at all!

It was, she knew, the only policy that made sense in the middle of this madness she was permitting. But what else could she do? It was too late now for sanity to prevail. Last night had proved that—overwhelmingly, consumingly—with memories so vivid, so wonderful, she dared not let them into her head now, lest they show blatantly in her eyes, her expression. And then Nikos would know, and then desire would leap between them, as it had done again and again through out the long, magical night they had spent together, until dawn had crept in over the rooftops of Paris.

But if the night had been for Nikos, then the day must only be for Ari—the reason they were here.

After lunch they went to the Luxembourg Gardens on the Left Bank, where Ari enjoyed himself at a children's playground and sandpit until it was time for an ice-cream while he watched the marionette theatre, hardly needing his uncle's translation of the traditional fairy tale depicted. After that came another ride on his beloved Metro, to a destination that left Ari speechless with glee—the descent into the sewers of Paris.

'I will explain everything to you while we are here, but it is not to be a subject for discussion over meals, Ari!' said his uncle sternly.

Nevertheless, the subject recurred, as Ann had known it would, over Ari's bathtime. He watched with a knowing eye as the water drained away, and explained its destination to her.

'Very good, Ari,' said Nikos from the doorway. 'And now I shall read your bedtime story while Auntie Annie makes herself even more beautiful than she always is.'

His eyes went to her, and their message was clear.

That evening they dined in the suite, with Ari fast asleep in Ann's room. They did not linger over their meal, superb as it was, washed down by vintage champagne. Instead, Nikos suffered her to swiftly check on Ari, before taking her to bed. And there in his arms she found a bliss that was unimaginable, sweeter, more wonderful, more thrilling than even the night before.

Afterwards, lying in the cradle of his arms, she wondered anew at the insanity of what she was committing, but she knew it was too late, and she was too helpless to resist. She shut her eyes to everything but the moment, content only to feel Nikos' strong arms enfolding her, to feel the beat of his heart beneath her cheek, the scent and taste of his body in her mouth as sleep washed over her.

But that sleep was rudely disturbed when more than the morning's sunlight pierced her slumber. Ari, waking to every expectation of another fun-filled day, had come to find her.

He bounced vigorously on the bed. 'Time to get up! Time to get up!' he enthused, landing with a thump.

As Ann stirred, and Nikos too, she saw Ari regarding them with keen interest.

'Mummies and daddies sleep in the same bed,' he pronounced.

'Well, so do uncles and aunties sometimes,' responded Nikos, sitting up, stretching his fantastic physique and looking not a whit abashed at being so discovered.

'Where are we going today?' asked Ari, accepting his uncle's comment without demur.

'A surprise,' said Nikos promptly.

He would not be drawn, despite his nephew's constant plaguing, but after breakfast a car was waiting for them, and it drove them out of Paris.

The surprise was another theme park.

'You're a glutton for punishment,' murmured Ann to Nikos, as they set off round the park for a day of rides and children's treats.

'But I have my reward waiting for me,' he replied, his dark

eyes glinting, and Ann felt heat flush through her skin. But even as it did she saw his expression change, become almost thoughtful for a moment, as if something had struck him.

She saw that look again during the day, from time to time, and sometimes, despite Ari's unbridled glee, Nikos seemed abstracted—his mind elsewhere. Perhaps he was thinking about work? thought Ann. Because surely he must be keen to get back to Athens?

She felt a pang go through her at the thought. Was this their last day together—tonight their last night? And what would come tomorrow? A car to the airport and Nikos and Ari heading back to Greece? Herself on a flight to London? To see Ari again—when?

And Nikos?

It was like a knife blade slipping into her. Silent. Deadly. And as it did so she felt the breath empty her lungs.

I can't bear to lose him!

She knew with every fibre of her being that there could never be another man like him in her life.

Knew as if a cold hand clutched her that for him she was just one more woman.

Yet it was so easy to forget that—dangerously easy. Not just when she clung to him in passion, or in the aftermath of passion, but during the day, when they were with Ari, together. As if—her heart squeezed—as if they were a family...

But they weren't—it was temporary, illusory, and that was all.

And yet the following day, when Nikos announced at breakfast that they were going to spend the weekend in Normandy, her spirits soared.

The elegant château hotel Nikos had booked was only a few miles from the coast, and their days were spent with Ari on the wide sandy beaches, and the nights entwined in the four-poster bed—with Ari, fast asleep from his exertions, in the connecting room.

It was over breakfast in their bedroom on the last morning that Nikos spoke to her. Ari was next door, watching cartoons on satellite TV.

'So, our little holiday is over and we must go home.'

Immediately Ann felt a chill numbness seize her. So this was the moment she had been dreading. The parting of the ways was upon her. She to return to London, Nikos and Ari to Greece. Even though she had known this moment must come, yet now it was here she felt as if a knife were sliding slowly into her.

Worse, far worse, than she had ever imagined it would be.

She felt the blood drumming in her head and fought for composure—outward at least, for inward was impossible. Yet even as she tried to control herself she became aware of what Nikos was saying next.

His eyes were resting on her with a strange expression in them. 'I want you to come back with us. Make your home on Sospiris.'

She could only stare, wordlessly.

His mouth twisted with wry self-mockery. 'Yes, you can stare, Ann. After everything I've thrown at you about *not* thinking you can insinuate yourself into our family. But obviously things are different now. Your making your home on Sospiris is the ideal answer. It ticks every box. You will be with Ari, and he with you. You get on excellently with my mother and Eupheme, and they both sing your praises—more than I have done!' he allowed, with the same wry expression. Then his expression changed. 'And best of all, Ann—' he picked up her hand and grazed the tips of her fingers sensuously with his lips '—we can still be together.'

His eyes were lambent, clear in their intent.

She waited for the leap in her spirits to come, for relief to flood through her at the blissful knowledge that she was not to be sent away after all, that Nikos still wanted her.

But it didn't come. Only a cold chill seeped through her skin. She heard herself speak, and hardly believed the words she was saying.

'I can't come back to Sospiris.'

She watched his expression change, as if everything were happening in slow motion.

'What are you saying?'

'I can't come back to Sospiris.' The brief words sounded so blunt, so harsh, but she said them again all the same.

His brows drew together, and he let go of her hand. In an instant he was not Nikos her lover, but Nikos Theakis to whom people did not say no...

Not even the woman he wanted to keep as an on-tap mistress in his home, spending her days with his nephew and her nights in his bed. A convenient mistress—there when he wanted her, while he wanted her. And when he no longer did—well, she'd still be looking after Ari.

She took a breath. A sharp one that cut like a knife. 'I have a life of my own. One I can't abandon indefinitely.'

His face had stilled. 'So this was nothing more than a passing amusement for you, was it?'

His voice cut as sharply as the breath in her lungs.

'There's nothing else it could be, Nikos. It's been a... a holiday. Wonderful, but—' another breath razored in her lungs '—now it's over.'

Even as she spoke her mind was shouting at her—urgently, desperately! *Don't say such things! Don't turn down what he is offering! Take it, grab it, seize it with both hands!*

But if she did—

The cold iced through her again. The icy cold of standing on the top of an Arctic crevasse. One wrong step and she would plunge down into its fatal depths. Her eyes went to him—went to the man who, night after night, had taken her into such bliss as she had never known, never could know again, whose arms had embraced her, whose kisses had melted her, whose smile alone warmed her like a living flame.

If I go back to Sospiris now—if I continue our affair—there can be only one ending, one fate for me.

A fate as clear to her here, now, as if it were already fulfilled. She said the words in her mind—forced herself to say them, to make very, very sure she faced up to them.

If I go back to Sospiris I will fall in love with him. Because already I stand on the brink of it—already I feel his power over me. But to him I will only ever be one more woman out of many. And one day he will have no more interest in me...

'And what about Ari?' Nikos's voice, still cutting, still cold, sounded again. 'You're just going to walk away from him?'

She felt her heart squeeze. 'It's for the best. I won't be out of his life. I can visit—or perhaps we can meet up. Your mother has been most generous in assuring me I am welcome for another holiday.'

'And that's all? All you're prepared to do? Very well.'

Abruptly, he got to his feet, looking down at her a moment. His face was closed. Closed to her completely. The way it had been for so, so long, until this brief, precarious truce had formed between them and this even briefer affair.

'Then there is no more to be said,' he finished. For one last moment he looked down at her, and for a second so brief she knew she must have only imagined it she saw something in his eyes—something that shook her. Then it was gone. Shuttered and veiled and closed down.

'You can have the task of telling Ari,' he said curtly. 'Since I'll be the one to mop his tears at losing you.'

She said nothing. Her heart was heavy enough as it was. Inside her head the voice was still shouting—telling her it wasn't too late, that there was still time to say she'd been an idiot, that of *course* she would jump ten feet at the chance to live on Sospiris, to take of him anything and everything she could, while she could, and not count the cost—never count the cost—until the bill had to be paid…

But when it does, it will be agony. So go—go now—while you can—while you can escape. Escape a fate that will be un-bearable—year after year of watching Ari grow and knowing that Nikos has left you far behind…

She couldn't face it. Not even to stop Ari's tears, which came, as Nikos had said they would, despite all she could say to comfort him.

'I'll come and see you again, poppet. You know I will. Ya-ya has said so. And when you go back home Tina will be back—she'll want to know all about your lovely, lovely holiday…'

'But I want *you,* too—as well as Tina!' wailed Ari discon-solately.

Parting from him at the airport tore her, and yet again the voice in her head shouted at her to change her mind, recant, to go with them back to Greece, not board a lonely flight to London. But she had to do it—she knew she had to do it.

The pain now is bad, but it is to save myself worse pain. So I have to clutch that sanity, that sense, and take the lesser pain now. Whatever it costs me. Before it's too late.

But even as her plane landed at Heathrow, she knew, with a crushing of her heart, that it was already far too late. She was not standing on the brink of the abyss. She had already fallen deep, deep, *deep* into its fatal heart.

'Uncle Nikki, when will Auntie Annie come back?'

Ari's plaintive question cut Nikos to the quick.

'Not for a while,' he answered. 'But,' he said, forcing his voice to lighten, 'I've got nice news for you, Ari. Tina is going to come back to look after you. She'll come across from Maxos every day in the launch. In the evenings Maria will put you to bed, and get you up in the morning, but all day you'll have Tina.'

'I want Auntie Annie too,' said Ari dolefully.

'Well, we can't have her.' Nikos's voice was short.

No, neither Ari nor he could have Ann any more.

The familiar reaction kicked again, as it had done every time since he'd returned to Sospiris and faced up to the fact that Ann wasn't there any more. The villa, despite the presence of Ari, his mother, her cousin and all the staff, felt deserted—echoingly empty.

He wanted Ann there. Badly. He wanted her in the villa, just being there. He wanted her and he could not have her—and the knowledge kicked in him like a stubborn mule.

Why? Why the hell had she not wanted to come back here? Why the hell had she not wanted to be with Ari? And why the hell had she not wanted to be with *him?* Emotion roiled in him, angry and resentful—and more than that, but he would not acknowledge it.

Why had she walked out on him? Why?

The question went round in his head, over and over again, as if there might be an answer. But there wasn't one. How could there be?

We were good together! Hell, we were more than good, we were—

But his thoughts broke off, as if hitting a wall. A wall he didn't want to think about. Instead his mind went back to brooding—resentful, unforgiving—at Ann Turner, who had come willingly, so willingly, to his bed, whose possession had filled him with a searing fulfilment the very memory of which kept him sleepless, and who had lain in his arms as if there was no other place she could ever be. Yet she had walked out on him. Just—gone.

As if what we had was nothing to her. Nothing.

His brow darkened.

Why? Why had she done it? His face hardened. She'd said she loved Ari, but she'd been prepared to abandon him in tears. What kind of love was that? None. Ari clearly meant nothing to her.

Nor do I.

He felt the knife thrust again in his side. He tried to yank it out. Why should he care? He didn't care.

But even as he scored the words in his mind he knew them for the lie they were. He wanted Ann. He wanted her now, here—with him, with Ari, in his home, his life.

And he didn't have her.

He went back to his resentful brooding, his face closed and dark.

Work was all he could do, so he did it.

After five days on Sospiris—knowing he was being like a bear with a sore head, and knowing that the fact that his mother had received his curtly uttered intelligence that Ann had returned to London with nothing more than a placid calm only, illogically, made his mood worsen—he decided to take himself off to Athens.

His mother was just as placid and calm about his removal as she had been about Ann's desertion. And it aggravated him just as much. At the doorway of the salon he turned abruptly.

'I asked Ann to come and live here, to make her home here,' he said, out of the blue. He paused. 'She said no.'

His mother's eyebrows rose. 'Did she?'

'I thought she'd snap at it. Devoted to Ari as she is.' His brow darkened. 'As she claimed to be.'

'Well, she has her own life to lead,' Sophia Theakis replied tranquilly.

'She could have led it here,' her son retorted brusquely. 'And I could have—' He broke off.

'Perhaps,' his mother said gently, 'you didn't make your… request…sound sufficiently inviting?'

Nikos glowered at her. 'I told her it was the ideal solution. Ideal for her, and for Ari, and for m—' He broke off yet again.

His mother folded her hands into her lap. 'Nikos, my darling.' Her voice was different now. 'It's not something to undertake lightly. You must understand that. If Ann makes her home with us, here, not only does she have to give up her own life, but she has to think very carefully about what her life will be like here. We are not talking about a brief holiday—we are talking about years. Because the longer she is here, the more Ari would feel her loss if she were to leave again.'

'She doesn't have to leave again! She can just live here,' Nikos said stubbornly.

His mother looked at him. 'As what, Nikos? My permanent house guest?'

'No. As my—' He broke off.

For one long moment mother and son looked at each other. Then, his mouth pressed tightly, he spoke. 'I know what I want of her,' he said.

She looked at him measuringly. 'Do you?'

'Yes. And it is *not* the assumption you are making!'

The ghost of a smile played at Sophia Theakis's lips. 'But perhaps, my darling, I am not the only one making such assumptions?'

His brow furrowed. 'I don't understand what you mean,' he replied shortly.

His mother gave a gentle sigh. 'Think about it, my darling boy, on your way to Athens. Now, off you go—I'm sure you are keeping your pilot waiting.'

He took his leave, brow still furrowed. What did his mother mean? That *he* was making assumptions? Assumptions that Ann would want to be with him as much as he wanted to be with her? Angry resentment bit again. That was exactly the assumption he'd made. Of course he had! He'd had every reason to assume she shared his feelings!

Because why wouldn't she? He'd come to terms—belatedly, but finally—with the bitter circumstances surrounding Ari's birth. And if he could not exonerate Carla Turner's exploitation of Andreas, at least he could now pity her for what she had endured for her sister's sake. As for Ann, he'd come to terms, too, with why she'd taken his money—and why he'd hated her for the power she'd had to deny him his brother's child, then gone on hating her because he'd realised, when she'd come to Sospiris, that he desired the woman he had told himself he could only despise.

But that was all in the past! He no longer needed to despise Ann—now he could desire her to his heart's content. His face darkened again. Except she did not want his desire any more. She'd had enough. Taken what she'd wanted of him, enjoyed him, and gone.

Why? That was the question, stark and unanswerable, that went round and round in his head, as remorseless as the pounding blades of the helicopter taking him back to Athens. *Why?*

But it wasn't until that evening—sitting at his desk in his apartment, catching up with his personal finances for something to occupy a mind that wanted only to brood on Ann Turner's defection—that he got the answer to his question. And when he did, his fury with her knew no bounds.

CHAPTER FOURTEEN

IT WAS RAINING. Ann stared out of the window at the heavy skies and the soaking rain coming down in rods. She should go and finish her packing, ready to leave London. She felt her heart clench. What would she give to be heading back to Sospiris? No, she mustn't let her mind go there. Not in memory or in imagination or in anything at all. Nothing—nothing to do with anything about Sospiris, anything about Ari, and nothing at all, not an iota or a speck or a single mote, about Nikos Theakis.

But it was hopeless—hopeless to tell herself that. She had no power to ban him from her mind any more than she'd had the power to resist him when he'd wanted her for his bed. The only strength she'd found was in leaving him, and that had taken all she had. But it had been in vain.

The hammering at the door—demanding and peremptory—made her start. She got to her feet, making her way out of the room and along the narrow corridor to the front door—opening it.

Nikos Theakis was there.

Just as he had four long years ago he strode in, not waiting for an invitation. Ann could only stare, her heart pounding wildly, the blood leaping in her veins, her senses overcome with shock—with far more than shock. She hurried after him into the living room. Why, why was he here? What did it mean?

Hope—wild, insane—pierced her...

And crashed and burned. He turned, eyes blazing. But not with desire. Not with the emotion she had for a brief, fragile moment so desperately hoped for. Instead, with an emotion she had once been only too familiar with.

Loathing. Rage. Contempt.

Words seared from his mouth, twisted in fury, and his eyes darkened with blackest anger.

'You despicable little bitch!'

Her breath caught audibly. Then her face contorted. *'What?'* she demanded. Shock was slamming through her.

'What?' he echoed. 'You dare—*dare*—to stand there and plead ignorance? Did you think I wouldn't find out?'

'Find out what?' Shock was still numbing her. And something quite different from shock. Something that made her whole body, her whole being quiveringly, shakingly aware of the tall, dark figure that was dominating the space, taking it over. Her eyes were drawn helplessly, hopelessly, to his planed face, its features stark with fury. Even consumed with anger as he was, she could feel her senses leap at the sight of him.

'Don't stand there looking ignorant and virtuous! *Theos mou,* to think I was taken in by you. To think I found excuses for you. Justified your actions. *Forgave* you! And all along—'

Greek broke from him—ugly and harsh, withering her even though she understood not a word of it. He took two strides and was in front of her, hands curving over her shoulders like talons of steel.

'How dare you target my mother? Go sleazing to her with whatever disgusting tale you've trotted out?' His eyes were blazing—blazing with fury and an emotion that seared her to the spot. 'To think I wondered why you walked out on me in Paris. I wondered what could be so wonderful about your life without me that you could just dump me—abandon the child you prattled about loving. And now I know. *Now I know!*'

Breath razored from him. 'Did you think I wouldn't find out?' He gave a harsh, vicious laugh. 'Well, for your information I handle my mother's personal finances! Everything about her bank accounts goes through me. So tell me—' he shook her again, face black '—what lies did you spout to get her to part with so much money?'

Ann's eyes flashed fire. 'It was a *gift!* And I never, *never* asked for it! I didn't even know she'd given it until I got back here and found her cheque waiting for me in the post.'

'Which you cashed.' The words ground from him, enraged.

'Of course I cashed it. Just like I cashed the cheque you gave me to go out to Sospiris. And the cheque you gave me for taking Ari from me.'

'To fund your luxury lifestyle on other people's money!' His head twisted to take in the passport and travel documents on the table. 'And now you are fully funded to go off travelling again.' His hands dropped from her shoulders. 'So where is it to be this time? The Caribbean? The Maldives? The South Seas? What expensive destination are you heading for this time around?' Contempt dripped from his voice, lacing the anger beneath with savagery.

Ann's face set. 'South Africa,' she said.

'South Africa?' he echoed sneeringly. 'Isn't it the wrong time of year for there? Save it for the European winter—the Cape is very clement in December.'

'I'm not going to the Cape. I'm going inland. Up-country.'

'Ah—a safari!' His voice was withering her.

'No. I'm going back to work.'

His eyes flashed like dark lightning. '*Work?* You wouldn't know the meaning of the word. What kind of "work" do you intend to tell me that you do?'

'I teach. I train teachers. And I look after children.'

Derision etched his face. 'As if I would believe that! With all the money you've extracted from my gullible mother you can live a life of ease for the next two years at least!'

She shut her eyes. She'd had enough. Snapping open her eyes again, she shot back at him. '*That money was not for me.* Nor was the money you handed me to go to Sospiris—*nor* the money you gave me four years ago! I gave it away—all of it. To charity.'

He stilled. Then, as she watched him, feeling her heart pumping in her chest, a laugh broke from him. She could only stare. It was a harsh, mocking laugh.

'To charity? *Theos*, how you trot out your lies. Ann—' his eyes skewered her '—no one, *no one,* gives away that kind of money. No one gives a million pounds to charity when they're living in a squalid dump.'

Her mouth thinned to a white line. Wordlessly, she yanked out a folder from under her travel documents, thrusting it at him.

'Read that—*read it!* And don't you *dare* tell me what I did or didn't do with all that money!'

He took it, the sneer still on his face, the savage anger still in his eyes. But as he opened the folder, stared at the contents, she saw them drain away, leaving his face blank, his expression empty. He stared down at what she had thrust at him. Stared at the colourful leaflet lying on top of the other papers. He said something in Greek. She didn't know what it was, but she could hear the tone. Disbelieving. More than that. Shocked.

His eyes lifted. Stared at her. There was nothing in them. Then, as if every word were costing him, he spoke.

'You built an orphanage with the money?'

'Yes.'

The tips of his fingers were on the printed leaflet, which showed rows of dark, smiling children outside two substantial buildings, with a smaller one in between and one further on a little way away, all set amongst trees in a garden, with the hot

African sun beating down and a white picket fence all around. Around the entrance to each of the two larger buildings was lettering in bright colours. His finger traced the lettering.

'Andreas' House. Carla's House.' There was no expression in his voice, none, as he read out the names.

Nor in hers as she answered, 'One house for the boys, one for the girls. And a schoolhouse in between. The other building is a clinic, because so many of the children there are AIDS orphans and carry HIV. They need medicine and treatment. It serves the local community as well. The money you gave stretched to all of that.' She swallowed. 'It's where I went after I'd given up Ari. The charity I work for has more orphanages across southern Africa. There are so many children in need of care. The money your mother has so generously given can build another one, and run it too. She's been wonderfully, wonderfully kind—'

Her voice broke off. Nikos' eyes were resting on her.

'You told her? About the charity? Your involvement?'

Ann bit her lip. 'She asked me what I did and I told her. Why shouldn't I have? But I never asked her for money, Nikos! I told you—I didn't even know about this money until I got back to London. She wrote such a kind letter with the cheque—as kind as the one she wrote persuading me to give Ari up to her.'

'I thought my money had persuaded you.' There was something odd about his voice.

She shook her head. 'If I hadn't known—because of your mother's letter—how much Ari would be loved, cherished, how desperately she hoped he would help assuage the grief of losing your brother, I would never have willingly let go of Ari! But I was already working for the charity at its London office before Carla arrived, pregnant, and I was planning on going to work out in Africa anyway. Giving up Ari to your mother, giving your money to the charity, all seemed to fit together. And it helped me too—seeing those children there, orphans like Ari, but with no one to look after them. It…comforted me.'

She met his eyes, but they were veiled, shuttered.

'You told my mother—why didn't you tell me?' Again, there was something odd about his voice.

She gave a sigh. 'You didn't ask, Nikos. And you'd been so foul to me, I didn't see why I should try and justify myself to you. It's just as well, isn't it?' She looked at him with the faintest trace of bitterness in her eyes. 'You'd have just said I was lying to you…'

His mouth tightened, but not with anger.

'In Paris you could have told me. When I told you I understood why you'd been so tempted to take the money.'

'I was going to. But—' she looked away and swallowed '—I got distracted.'

'Not sufficiently distracted to stay with me when I asked you to.' There was more than tightness in his voice. Then, abruptly, it changed. 'But I had no right to ask you to stay with me. I can see that now. And I can see—'

His voice broke off. A deep, ragged breath was inhaled. His eyes went down to the leaflet in his hand.

'Andreas' House, Carla's House,' he intoned again, his voice stranger than ever.

'I asked for the houses to be called after your brother and my sister in their memory,' said Ann quietly.

His eyes lifted again, going to hers, and in them was an emotion she had never seen before.

'I thought so ill of you for so long,' he said slowly, as if the words were being prised from him. 'And you have shamed me, Ann. Shamed me as I have never felt shame before.' His face was heavy, stark. 'I came here full of self-righteous rage at you, and now—' He broke off again. His eyes went as if of their own accord to her passport. 'When do you go back to Africa?' His voice was blank, very neutral.

She answered in the same tone. All she could manage, despite the tumult raging through her. Not because she had finally told Nikos where his money had gone, but because…because seeing him standing there, so close and yet an impossible, unbridgeable distance from her, was agony. Agony….

'Tomorrow. I'd only come home on leave when I…when I saw you in that toy store. The charity was very understanding when I requested an extension to go to Sospiris. Besides—' she took a breath '—they were getting a huge donation in exchange. Worth a lot more to them than a few weeks of my time!' Her expression deepened. 'It's not so much extra helpers they need as funding. There's a never-ending need—the situation is so bad in so many parts of the region, even in the countries that are politically stable, let alone those with civil war or repressive governments. We do what we can, take in as many children as we can, but there are always more. Some are injured from landmines, and of course as well as AIDS there are other terrible tropical diseases afflicting them, so…'

She was rambling, she knew, but she was driven to talk. Driven to do anything other than face the fact that Nikos was here, in front of her, a hand's breadth away from her. All she'd have to do was just reach out to touch him, kiss him, go into his arms…

But she mustn't! She mustn't! He would be gone at any moment, all over again. Walking out of the door, away from her. Because what difference did it make, him knowing about her work. What she'd done with his precious money? Even if her pride and her anger at him had kept her silent, deliberately, knowingly, refusing to justify her acceptance of his money— because why should she care tuppence about being in Nikos Theakis' good graces after all the venom he'd spouted about her, about Carla? She'd let him call her names all the while knowing she could make him eat every one of them—and anyway having him look at her with such contempt had kept her safe from him, safe from doing what she had so, so wanted to do. What she had, in the end done despite all her best intentions and warnings.

She'd gone and done it anyway—fallen into his bed, and fallen in love with him... And it didn't matter, that her heart felt as if it were being sheared into pieces, torn up and minced and mangled and shredded, because nothing was going to change that—even if he did know now that she hadn't spent every last penny of his on herself, from luxury holidays to designer clothes, instead wearing Carla's—even if they were four years out of date, as Elena Constantis had spotted instantly, and even if they had only made Nikos think she'd spent his money on them.

Thoughts, emotions, words—all ran raggedly, crazily through her mind. And she let them run on because anything was a distraction from what was going to happen any moment now. Any moment now, Nikos was going to walk out of the door, and walk away...

Taking her heart with him...

And she couldn't bear it—she couldn't bear it. Not all over again. Seeing him again so briefly, so excruciatingly, and now he was going to go again. She would not see him for months and months, and when she did...when she did she would just be history—ancient history. An old flame, an ex—nothing more, nothing ever again...

She heard his voice, penetrating her numb anguish.

'Ann—'

She forced herself to herd her wild, desperate thoughts, forced herself to be what she must be now—calm, composed. Glad that he knew finally where his money had gone, that she wasn't the avaricious gold-digger he'd thought her after all. Glad that they could part without anger and contempt.

'Ann—' There seemed to be something strange about his face, his voice. Something almost...hesitant. But hesitation and Nikos Theakis were not words that went together.

But hesitant was, indeed, what his manner seemed to be. His eyes were still veiled, shuttered. Wary. There seemed to be tension visible in every line of his body.

'Ann,' he said again, 'once before I paid you for your time—insulting you grievously as I did so. But…but now that I know why you took my money, what your life actually is instead of my ugly assumptions, I…I wonder whether… whether you would consider…reconsider…your decision?' He took a deep breath. 'In Paris you said you had a life of your own to lead, and I respect that now entirely—indeed shamingly, for it shames me to think how you have dedicated your life to children who have so little. But if…if what you just said is true…that what is most valuable to those children is money, not western aid workers…then supposing I…I…gave enough money to…to make it unnecessary for you to go back, to hire someone in your place—?'

He stopped. Said something briefly, pungently in Greek, then reverted to English. 'I am saying this all wrong!' Frustration was in his voice. 'I am making it sound like I am trying to buy you out! But I don't mean it like that, Ann—I am simply trying to say that if my wealth would make it easier for you not to feel you had to go back to Africa yourself—if you could instead stay—come to Sospiris. To Ari.' He took another breath. 'To me.'

Suddenly out of nowhere his eyes were unveiled, unshuttered, a new expression blazing from them. She felt emotion leap in her—impossible to crush, impossible to deny. She couldn't move. She was rooted to the spot. Rooted as he stepped forward, took her face in his hands. And the touch of his fingers cradling her skull made her weak, and faint, and the closeness of his face, the heat of his gaze, the overpowering *thereness* of his body towering over her, so strong, so powerful, so *Nikos*…

'These days without you have been agony, Ann! I've been

impossible—impossible to live with! Angry and ill-tempered and short-fused and *hurting,* Ann—just hurting without you. Because I want you so much! I just want you back—back with me again. Because of what we had—what we've always had— even when I hated myself for wanting you, when I thought you were little better than your own sister, whom I thought then the lowest of the low. Even that could not stop me wanting you day and night. I was driven insane with not having you—until, thank God, my mother came up with her scheme for Ari's holiday in Paris. And then—even more thanks to God—I came to my senses over you and realised that you could not, *could not* be the person I had despised for four years. Having you respond to me was everything I'd been aching for, and I don't want to lose it. I want so much for you to come back to Sospiris with me now, and not go to Africa. Ari's missing you so much, and I...I am desperate for you, Ann!'

Her heart was cracking open. She could hear it. Feel, too, the agony in her muscles as she drew away from him.

'I can't, Nikos,' she whispered. 'I just can't.'

His hands dropped to his sides. 'Does your work mean so much to you?' There was emptiness in his voice.

She shut her eyes, her throat almost closing. Then she forced her eyes to open, to look at him.

'No,' she said. Then she said it. 'But you do.' She swallowed, never taking her eyes from his. 'You do, Nikos. And I know you didn't mean it—didn't even think about it. Because why should you? What we had in Paris was an affair—I knew that, knew that's all it could be. And that if I came back to Sospiris that was all it would be still. An affair. And one fine morning you'd decide you'd had enough of me, and the affair would be over. For you. But not—' her breath caught like a scalpel '—not for me. And I couldn't bear it, Nikos—living on Sospiris, helping to bring up Ari, and having to see you arrive with other women, see you choose, one day, one of them to be your wife, and knowing I was nothing more than yesterday's affair...'

He was looking at her. Looking at her with the strangest expression on his face. Words sounded in his head. His mother's voice. *But perhaps, my darling, I am not the only one making such assumptions.*

He'd thought she'd meant *him.* But she hadn't. Not in the least.

'Theos mou,' he breathed. 'You thought that? That I wanted you to come back to Sospiris because I wanted to continue an affair with you?'

Two flags of colour stained her cheeks. 'It's what you wanted before. When you offered me that diamond necklace. A clandestine affair in your mother's villa.'

A hand slashed violently, making her jump.

'God Almighty, Ann, that was then! When I still thought you as bad as I'd been painting you for four years! When my entire scheme was to slake my desire for you and remove you from my mother's house by seducing you! I was going to take you away from Sospiris—keep you as my mistress for as long as it took to make it impossible for my mother to invite you to Sospiris again! But how, *how,* after what we had in Paris, could you possibly think I only wanted an affair with you? I wanted—*want still,* desperately, with all my being—you to come back to me, to make a home for Ari, and for us to be *together.* You and me—a *family* for Ari and for us!' He took a hectic breath. 'It was hearing Ari's artless remark the morning he found us in bed together, saying that mummies and daddies slept together, that made it dawn on me that that was exactly what I wanted! For you and me to stay together.' He looked at her. 'To marry,' he said.

Shock was hollowing through her. Shock and other emotions even more powerful.

'To marry?' she echoed, as if she were uttering an alien language. 'Because then we could bring up Ari together?'

'Yes.'

'Because—' she swallowed '—we're good in bed together.'

'More than good, Ann,' he said dryly.

She dropped her eyes. She couldn't meet his, suddenly. Not without colour flaming in her cheeks at the way he was looking at her. And that wasn't what was needed—not now. Not now when she had to say the worst thing of all.

The hardest, cruellest thing.

'So a marriage for Ari, and for good sex?'

'Great sex,' he corrected her. 'And, of course, for one other reason.'

Slowly, as if they were weighted with lead, she made herself lift her eyes to him.

'What…what other reason?' Her voice was faint—as faint as she felt.

'Love, Ann,' he said.

She swayed. He caught her. Drew her to him. Not to kiss, but to hold, as lightly as swansdown. He smoothed her hair.

'Love, Ann,' he said again. 'I didn't know it until you left me. And now—now it's etched in stone upon my heart. Your name. For ever. And you love me, don't you, Ann? You said as much just now. So why not tell me, as I have told you?'

She shut her eyes and said it. 'I love you.' It was a breath of air, no more than that.

And then he folded her to him properly, wrapping his arms around her and she laid her head against his chest. At home. At rest.

'Nikos.' She breathed his name, resting against him. For a long, long while he simply held her. Then, easing back her head, he gazed down at her. Everything she could ever dream of was in his eyes.

And then in his lips.

EPILOGUE

IT WAS THE second wedding on Sospiris in as many months, and even more lavish than Tina's had been. She and Sam were both there, and this time it was Tina's turn to cry buckets—but she had come well prepared, as well prepared as Nikos's mother and Cousin Eupheme, with handkerchiefs to spare. Ari gazed bemused at them, and tugged his grand-mother's sleeve.

'But it's a *happy* day, Ya-ya,' he explained to her. 'Auntie Annie's going to live here for ever and ever now. And sleep in Uncle Nikki's bed, just like in Paris. And I can wake them up—but not too early, Uncle Nikki says.'

Sophia Theakis laughed and stroked his head. Her cousin turned to her. 'It took them *such* a time, Sophia,' she sighed.

Nikos' mother nodded. 'The young are so blind, Eupheme. But it was obvious right from the first moment I saw them together that dear Ann, with not a mercenary bone in her body, would be ideal for Nikos. Spoilt by female adoration, he needed a good dose of animosity to challenge him. And, of course,' she added dryly, 'to be made to win her.'

'Oh, the sparks flew between the pair of them—they cer-tainly flew.' Her cousin nodded.

'So much that they were blinding themselves to what was happening! When I saw them waltzing at Tina's wedding I thought they were seeing sense at last. But even that wasn't quite enough. I had to pack them off to Paris together.'

'Ah, Paris…' Eupheme sighed romantically.

'Indeed—and then the idiotic boy came back here alone. Goodness knows what he said or did to drive her away. But he obviously mismanaged the whole thing! So—' she sighed heavily '—I had to think of something else. It was as plain as day that Ann hadn't told him about the orphanage to commemorate my adored Andreas and Ari's poor dead mother, and I thought perhaps it was that that had come between them. It dawned on me that Nikki was bound to notice if I made a large donation myself, and it would send him back to her to find out why. Thank heavens it finally worked!'

'Yes,' said her cousin dryly, 'or you'd have had to develop a sudden urge to visit South Africa, Sophia…'

'I'm sure they have some very good cardiologists there,' replied Nikos's mother, even more dryly. 'And the climate would be excellent for my health too…'

They laughed together, and then the music was swelling, and Nikos and Ann were walking down between the congregation. Her hand was being held so tightly she doubted there could be any blood left in her fingers—but what did she care for that when her whole heart was singing, her eyes shining like stars? She turned her head to look at Nikos, and he gazed down at her, love in his eyes.

'My most beautiful bride,' he said.

'My irresistible husband,' she answered.

He dropped a swift kiss upon her mouth. 'That's the right answer,' he told her. 'Never leave me, Ann, and I will love you for ever!'

She laughed up at him. 'Oh, well, then you've got me for life, Nikos Theakis!'

Long dark lashes swept over glinting eyes. 'That's the

right answer too,' he said. 'And you have me, my own love, for all our lives together—and beyond—into eternity itself.'

Her breath caught, she was breathless with happiness, and then they were stepping out into the sunshine, man and wife, and Ari was running up to them.

Nikos scooped him up with a hug.

'Uncle Nikki.' Ari beamed, then turned to hold out his arms to his uncle's bride. 'Auntie Annie,' he said. She bent to kiss him heartily. 'And me,' he said. Satisfaction was in his voice.

'Family,' said Nikos.

And they were.

THE GREEK MILLIONAIRE'S SECRET CHILD

CATHERINE SPENCER

Catherine Spencer, once an English teacher, fell into writing through eavesdropping on a conversation about romances. Within two months she changed careers and sold her first book to Mills & Boon in 1984. She moved to Canada from England thirty years ago and lives in Vancouver. She is married to a Canadian and has four grown children—two daughters and two sons (and now eight grandchildren)—plus two dogs. In her spare time she plays the piano, collects antiques and grows tropical shrubs.

You can visit Catherine Spencer's website at www.catherinespencer.com

CHAPTER ONE

EMILY singled him out immediately, not because his father had described him so well that she couldn't miss him, but because even though he stood well back from everyone else, he dominated the throng waiting to meet passengers newly arrived at Athens's Venizelos Airport. At more than six feet of lean, toned masculinity blessed with the face of a fallen angel, he could hardly help it. One look at him was enough to tell her he was the kind of man other men envied, and women fought over.

As if on cue, his gaze locked with hers. Locked and lingered a small eternity, long enough for her insides to roll over in fascinated trepidation. Every instinct of self-preservation told her he was bad news; that she'd live to rue the day she met him. Then he nodded, as though he knew exactly the effect he'd had on her, and cutting a swath through the crowd, strode forward.

Given her first unobstructed view, she noted how his jeans emphasized his narrow hips and long legs, the way his black leather bomber jacket rode smoothly over his powerful shoulders, and the startling contrast of his throat rising strong and tanned against the open collar of his white shirt. As he drew closer, she saw, too, that his mouth and his jaw, the latter firm and faintly dusted with new beard shadow, betrayed the stubbornness his father had spoken of.

When he reached them, he asked in a voice as sinfully seductive as the rest of him, "So you beat the odds and made it back in one piece. How was the flight?"

"Long," Pavlos replied, sounding every bit as worn and weary as he surely must feel. Not even painkillers and the luxury of first-class air travel had been enough to cushion his discomfort. "Very long. But as you can see, I have my guardian angel at my side." He reached over his shoulder, groped for her hand and squeezed it affectionately. "Emily, my dear, I am pleased to introduce my son, Nikolaos. And this, Niko, is my nurse, Emily Tyler. What I would have done without her, I cannot imagine."

Again, Nikolaos Leonidas's gaze lingered, touring the length of her in insolent appraisal. Behind his chiseled good looks lurked a certain arrogance. He was not a man to be crossed, she thought. "*Yiasu,* Emily Tyler," he said.

Even though her sweater and slacks pretty much covered all of her, she felt naked under that sweeping regard. His eyes were the problem, she thought dizzily. Not brown like his father's, as she'd expected, but a deep green reminiscent of fine jade, they added an arresting final touch to a face already possessed of more than its rightful share of dark beauty.

Swallowing, she managed an answering, "*Yiasu.*"

"You speak a little Greek?"

"A very little," she said. "I just exhausted my entire vocabulary."

"That's what I thought."

The comment might have stung if he hadn't tempered it with a smile that assaulted her with such charm, it was all she could do not to buckle at the knees. For heaven's sake, what was the matter with her? She was twenty-seven, and if not exactly the most sexually experienced woman in the world, hardly in the first flush of innocent youth, either. She knew well enough that appearances counted for little. It was the person inside that mattered, and from everything she'd been told, Niko Leonidas fell sadly short in that respect.

His manner as he turned his attention again to Pavlos did nothing to persuade her otherwise. He made no effort to embrace his father, to reassure him with a touch to the shoulder or hand that the old man could count on his son for whatever support he might need during his convalescence. Instead he commandeered a porter to take care of the loaded luggage cart one of the flight attendants had brought, and with a terse, "Well, since we seem to have exhausted the formalities, let's get out of here," marched toward the exit, leaving Emily to follow with Pavlos.

Only when they arrived at the waiting Mercedes did he betray a hint of compassion. "Don't," he ordered, when she went to help her patient out of the wheelchair and with surprising tenderness, scooped his father into his arms, laid him carefully on the car's roomy back seat and draped a blanket over his legs. "You didn't have to do that," Pavlos snapped, trying unsuccessfully to mask a grimace of pain.

Noticing, Niko said, "Apparently I did. Or would you have preferred I stand idly by and watch you fall on your face?"

"I would prefer to be standing on my own two feet without needing assistance of any kind."

"Then you should have taken better care of yourself when you were away—or else had the good sense to stay home in the first place, instead of deciding you had to see Alaska before you die."

Emily was tempted to kick the man, hard, but made do with a glare. "Accidents happen, Mr. Leonidas."

"Especially to globe-trotting eighty-six-year-old men."

"It was hardly his fault that the cruise ship ran aground, nor was he the only passenger on board who was injured. All things considered, and given his age, your father's done amazingly well. In time, and with adequate follow-up physical therapy, he should make a reasonably good recovery."

"And if he doesn't?"

"Then I guess you're going to have to step up to the plate and start acting like a proper son."

He favored her with a slow blink made all the more disturbing by the sweep of his lashes, which were indecently long and silky. "Nurse and family counselor all rolled into one," he drawled. "How lucky is that?"

"Well, you did ask."

"And you told me." He tipped the porter, left him to return the airport's borrowed wheelchair, then slammed closed the car trunk and opened the front passenger door with a flourish. "Climb in. We can continue this conversation later."

As she might have expected, he drove with flair and expertise. Within half an hour of leaving the airport, they were cruising the leafy green streets of Vouliagmeni, the exclusive Athens suburb overlooking the Saronic Gulf on the east coast of the Attic Peninsula, which Pavlos had described to her so vividly. Soon after, at the end of a quiet road running parallel to the beach, Niko steered the car through a pair of ornate wrought-iron gates, which opened at the touch of a remote control button on the dash.

Emily had gathered Pavlos was a man of considerable wealth, but was hardly prepared for the rather frightening opulence confronting her as the Mercedes wound its way up a long curving driveway, and she caught her first sight of…what? His house? Villa? Mansion?

Set in spacious, exquisitely landscaped grounds and screened from local traffic by a stand of pines, the place defied such mundane description. Stucco walls, blindingly white, rose in elegant proportions to a tiled roof as blue as she'd always imagined the skies to be in Athens, even though, this late September afternoon, an approaching storm left them gray and threatening. Long windows opened to wide terraces shaded by pergolas draped in flowering vines. A huge fountain splashed in a central forecourt, peacocks preened and screeched on the lawns, and from somewhere on the seaward side of the property, a dog barked.

She had little time to marvel, though, because barely had the car come to a stop outside a set of double front doors than they opened, and a man in his late fifties or early sixties appeared with a wheelchair light years removed from the spartan model offered by the airport.

The devoted butler, Georgios, she presumed. Pavlos had spoken of him often and with great fondness. Behind him came a younger man, little more than a boy really, who went about unloading the luggage while

Niko and the butler lifted Pavlos from the car to the chair. By the time they were done, he was gray in the face and the grooves paralleling his mouth carved more deeply than usual.

Even Niko seemed concerned. "What can you do for him?" he muttered, cornering Emily near the front entrance as Georgios whisked his employer away down a wide, marble-floored hall.

"Give him something to manage the pain, and let him rest," she said. "The journey was very hard on him."

"He doesn't look to me as if he was fit to travel in the first place."

"He wasn't. Given his age and the severity of his osteoporosis, he really ought to have remained in the hospital another week, but he insisted on coming home, and when your father makes up his mind, there's no changing it."

"Tell me something I don't already know." Niko scowled and shucked off his jacket. "Shall I send for his doctor?"

"In the morning, yes. He'll need more medication than what I was able to bring with us. But I have enough to see him through tonight." Struggling to preserve a professional front despite the fact that Niko stood close enough for the warmth of his body to reach out and touch hers, she sidled past him and took her travel bag from the pile of luggage accumulating inside the front door. "If you'd show me to his room, I really should attend to him now."

He stepped away and led her to the back of the villa, to a large, sun-filled apartment on the main floor. Consisting of a sitting room and bedroom, both with

French doors that opened onto a low-walled patio, it overlooked the gardens and sea. Still in the wheelchair, stationed next to the window in the sitting room, Pavlos leaned forward, drinking in the view which, even swathed in floating mist as the storm closed in, held him transfixed.

"He had this part of the house converted into his private suite a few years ago when the stairs proved too much for him," Niko said in a low voice.

Glancing through to the bedroom, Emily asked, "And the hospital bed?"

"I had it brought in yesterday. He'll probably give me hell for removing the one he's used to, but this one seemed more practical, at least for now."

"You did the right thing. He'll be more comfortable in it, even if he won't be spending much time there except at night."

"Why not?"

"The more mobile he is, the better his chances of eventually walking again, although…"

Picking up on the reservation in her voice, Niko pounced on it. "Although what? You said earlier you expect him to make a reasonable recovery. Are you changing your mind now?"

"No, but…" Again, she hesitated, bound by patient confidentiality, yet aware that as his son, Niko had the right to some information, especially if her withholding it might have an adverse effect on Pavlos's future well-being. "How much do you know about your father's general health?"

"Only what he chooses to tell me, which isn't very much."

She should have guessed he'd say that. *There's no need to contact my son*, Pavlos had decreed, when the hospital had insisted on listing his next of kin. *He minds his business, and I mind mine.*

Niko pinned her in that unnerving green stare. "What aren't you telling me, Emily? Is he dying?"

"Aren't we all, to one extent or another?"

"Don't play mind games with me. I asked you a straightforward question. I'd like a straightforward answer."

"Okay. His age is against him. Although he'd never admit it, he's very frail. It wouldn't take much for him to suffer a relapse."

"I can pretty much figure that out for myself, so what else are you holding back?"

Pavlos spared her having to reply. "What the devil are the pair of you whispering about?" he inquired irascibly.

Casting Niko an apologetic glance, she said, "Your son was just explaining that you might not care for the new bed he ordered. He's afraid you'll think he was interfering."

"He was. I broke my hip, not my brain. I'll decide what I do and don't need."

"Not as long as I'm in charge."

"Don't boss me around, girl. I won't put up with it."

"Yes, you will," she said equably. "That's why you hired me."

"I can fire you just as easily, and have you on a flight back to Vancouver as early as tomorrow."

Recognizing the empty threat for what it really was, she hid a smile. Exhaustion and pain had taken their toll, but by morning he'd be in a better frame of mind. "Yes, sir,

Mr. Leonidas," she returned smartly, and swung the wheelchair toward the bedroom. "Until then, let me do my job."

Niko had seized the first opportunity to vacate the
premises, she noticed, and could have slapped herself
for the pang of disappointment that sprouted despite her
best efforts to quell it. The faithful Georgios, however,
remained on the scene, anxious and willing to help
wherever he could. Even so, by the time Pavlos had
managed a light meal and was settled comfortably for
the night, darkness had fallen.

Damaris, the housekeeper, showed Emily upstairs to
the suite prepared for her. Decorated in subtle shades of
ivory and slate-blue, it reminded her of her bedroom at
home, although the furnishings here were far grander
than anything she could afford. Marble floors, a
Savonnerie rug and fine antiques polished to a soft
gleam exemplified wealth, good taste and comfort.

A lady's writing desk occupied the space between
double French doors leading to a balcony. In front of a
small blue-tiled fireplace was a fainting couch, its
brocade upholstery worn to satin softness, its once-
vibrant colors faded by time. A glass-shaded lamp
spilled mellow light, and a vase of lilies on a table filled
the room with fragrance.

Most inviting of all, though, was the four-poster bed,
dressed in finest linens. Almost ten thousand kilometers,
and over sixteen hours of travel with its inevitable
delays, plus the added stress of her patient's condition,
had made serous inroads on her energy, and she wanted
nothing more than to lay her head against those snowy-
white pillows, pull the soft coverlet over her body and
sleep through to morning.

A quick glance around showed that her luggage had been unpacked, her toiletries arranged in the bathroom and her robe and nightshirt laid out on the bench in front of the vanity. But so, to her dismay, was a change of underwear, and a freshly ironed cotton dress, one of the few she'd brought with her, hung in the dressing room connecting bathroom and bedroom. And if they weren't indication enough that the early night she craved was not to be, Damaris's parting remark drove home the point in no uncertain terms.

"I have drawn a bath for you, Despinis Tyler. Dinner will be served in the garden room at nine."

Clearly daily protocol in the Leonidas residence was as elegantly formal as the villa itself, and the sandwich in her room, which Emily had been about to request, clearly wasn't on the menu.

The main floor was deserted when she made her way downstairs just a few minutes past nine, but the faint sound of music and a sliver of golden light spilling from an open door halfway down the central hall indicated where she might find the garden room.

What she didn't expect when she stepped over the threshold was to find that she wouldn't be dining alone.

A round glass-topped table, tastefully set for two, stood in the middle of the floor. A silver ice bucket and two cut-crystal champagne flutes glinted in the almost ethereal glow of dozens, if not hundreds, of miniature white lights laced among the potted shrubs lining the perimeter of the area.

And the final touch? Niko Leonidas, disgracefully gorgeous in pale gray trousers and matching shirt, which together probably cost more than six months' mortgage payments on her town house, leaned against an ornately carved credenza.

She was sadly out of her element, and surely looked it. She supposed she should be grateful her dinner companion wasn't decked out in black tie.

"I wasn't aware you were joining me for dinner," she blurted out, the inner turmoil she thought she'd conquered raging all over again at the sight of him.

He plucked an open bottle of champagne from the ice bucket, filled the crystal flutes and handed one to her. "I wasn't aware I needed an invitation to sit at my father's table."

"I'm not suggesting you do. You have every right—"

"How kind of you to say so."

He'd perfected the art of withering pleasantries, she decided, desperately trying to rein in her swimming senses. The smile accompanying his reply hovered somewhere between derision and scorn, and left her feeling as gauche as she no doubt sounded. "I didn't mean to be rude, Mr. Leonidas," she said, her discomfiture increasing in direct proportion to his suave assurance. "I'm surprised, that's all. I assumed you'd left the house. I understand you have your own place in downtown Athens."

"I do—and we Greeks, by the way, aren't big on honorifics. Call me Niko. Everyone else does."

She didn't care what everyone else did. Finding herself alone with him left her barely able to string two words together without putting her foot in her mouth. Resort to calling him Niko, and she'd probably manage to stuff the other one in next to it.

"At a loss for words, Emily?" he inquired, evil

laughter shimmering in his beautiful green eyes. "Or is it the prospect of sharing a meal with me that has you so perturbed?"

"I'm not perturbed," she said with as much dignity as she could bring to bear. "Just curious about why you'd choose to be here, instead of in your own home. From all accounts, you and Pavlos don't usually spend much time together."

"Nevertheless, I *am* his son, and the last I heard, my choosing to spend an evening under his roof doesn't amount to trespassing. Indeed, given the present circumstances, I consider it my duty to make myself more available. Do you have a problem with that?"

Hardly about to admit that she found him a distraction she wasn't sure she could handle, she said, "Not at all, as long as you don't interfere with my reasons for being here."

"And exactly what are those reasons?"

She stared at him. His eyes weren't glimmering with laughter now; they were as cold and hard as bottle-green glass. "What kind of question is that? You know why I'm here."

"I know that my father has become extremely dependent on you. I know, too, that he's a very vulnerable old man who happens also to be very rich."

She sucked in an outraged breath at the implication in his words. "Are you suggesting I'm after his money?"

"Are you?"

"Certainly not," she snapped. "But that's why you're hanging around here, isn't it? Not because you're worried about your father, but to keep an eye on me and make sure I don't get my hooks into him or his bank account."

"Not quite. I'm 'hanging around' as you so delicately put it, to look out for my father because, in his present condition, he's in no shape to look out for himself. If you find my concern offensive—"

"I do!"

"Then that's a pity," he replied, with a singular lack of remorse. "But try looking at it from my point of view. My father arrives home with a very beautiful woman who happens to be a complete stranger and whom he appears to trust with his life. Not only that, she's come from half a world away and signed on to see him through what promises to be a long and arduous convalescence, even though there's no shortage of nurses here in Athens well qualified to undertake the job. So tell me this: if our situation was reversed, wouldn't you be a little suspicious?"

"No," she shot back heatedly. "Before I leaped to unwarranted conclusions or cast aspersions on her professional integrity, I'd ask to see the stranger's references, and if they didn't satisfy me, I'd contact her previous employers directly to verify that she's everything she purports to be."

"Well, no need to foam at the mouth, sweet thing. Your point is well taken and that being the case, I'm prepared to shelve my suspicions and propose we call a truce and enjoy this very fine champagne I filched from my father's cellar. It'd be a shame to waste it."

She plunked her glass on the table so abruptly that its contents surged over the rim with an indignation that almost matched her own. "If you think I'm about to share a drink with you, let alone a meal, think again! I'd rather starve."

She spun on her heel, bent on making as rapid an exit as possible, but had taken no more than two or three steps toward the door before he caught up with her and slammed it closed with the flat of his hand. "I regret that, in looking out for my father's best interests, I have offended you," he said smoothly. "Trust me, I take no pleasure in having done so."

"Really?" She flung him a glare designed to strip paint off a wall. "You could have fooled me. I'm not used to being treated like a petty criminal."

He shrugged. "If I've insulted you, I apologize, but better I err on the side of caution."

"Meaning what, exactly?"

"That my father's been targeted before by people interested only in taking advantage of him."

"He might not be quite so susceptible to outsiders if he felt more secure in his relationship with you."

"Possibly not, but ours has never been a typical father-son relationship."

"So I've been given to understand, but I suggest the time's come for you to bury your differences and stop butting heads. He needs to know you care."

"I wouldn't be here now, if I didn't care."

"Would it kill you to tell him that?"

He gave a snort of subdued laughter. "No, but the shock of hearing me say so might kill *him*."

What was it about the two of them, that they held each other at such a distance, she wondered. "Do either of you have the first idea of the pain that comes from waiting until it's too late to say 'I love you?' Because I do. More often than I care to remember, I've witnessed the grief and regret that tears families apart because time ran out on them before they said the things that needed to be said."

He paced to the windows at the other end of the aptly named garden room whose exotic flowering plants set in Chinese jardinieres must give it the feel of high summer even in the depths of winter. "We're not other people," he said.

"You're not immortal, either." She hesitated, conflicted once again by how much she could say, then decided to plunge in and disclose what she knew, because she wasn't sure she could live with herself if she didn't. "Look, Niko, he'll probably have my head for telling you this, but your father's not just battling a broken hip. His heart's not in very good shape, either."

"I'm not surprised. That's what comes from years of smoking and hard living, but nothing his doctor said was enough to make him change his ways. He's a stubborn old goat."

That much she knew to be true. Pavlos had discharged himself from Vancouver General against medical advice, and insisted on flying back to Greece even crippled as he was, because he refused to put up with the nursing staff's constant monitoring. *They don't let a man breathe,* he'd complained, when Emily tried to talk him into postponing the journey. *I'll be carried out feetfirst if I let them keep me here any longer.*

"Well, the apple doesn't fall far from the tree, Niko. Where this family's concerned, you're both pretty pigheaded."

He swung around and surveyed her across the width of the room; another long, searching gaze so thorough that a quiver shafted through her. He probed too deeply beneath the surface. Saw things she wasn't ready to acknowledge to herself. "Perhaps before *you* start leaping to unwarranted conclusions," he purred, advancing toward her with the lethal grace of a hunter preparing to move in for the kill, "you should hear my side of the story."

"You're not my patient, your father is," she said, backing away and almost hyperventilating at the determined gleam in his eye.

"But isn't modern medicine all about the holistic approach—curing the spirit in order to heal the body, and such? And isn't that exactly what you've been advocating ever since you walked into this room?"

"I suppose so, yes."

"How do you expect to do that, if you have only half the equation to work with? More to the point, what do you stand to lose by letting me fill in the blanks?"

My soul, and everything I am, she thought, filled with the terrible foreboding that unless she extricated herself now from the web of attraction threatening to engulf her, destiny in the shape of Nikolaos Leonidas would take control of her life, and never give it back again. Yet to scurry away like a frightened rabbit was as alien to her nature as taking advantage of Pavlos. So she stood her ground, pushed the irrational presentiment out of her thoughts and said with deceptive calm, "Absolutely nothing."

"Really?" He leaned toward her, dropped his voice another half octave and latched his fingers around her wrist. "Then why are you so afraid?"

She swallowed and ran her tongue over her dry lips. "I'm not," she said.

CHAPTER TWO

SHE was lying. The evidence was there in her hunted gaze, in her racing pulse, so easily and unobtrusively detected when he took her wrist. And he intended to find out why, because for all that he thought he'd remain unmoved by whatever he discovered when he went to meet their flight, the sight of the old man, so brittle and somehow diminished, had hit him with the force of a hammer blow to the heart. They spent little time together, had long ago agreed to disagree and shared nothing in common. But Pavlos was still his father, and Niko would be damned before he'd let some hot little foreign number take him to the cleaners.

Oh, she'd been full of righteous indignation at his suggestion that she wasn't quite the selfless angel of mercy she presented herself to be. He'd hardly expected otherwise. But he'd also seen how indispensable she'd made herself to Pavlos; how successfully she'd wormed her way into his affections. His father had never been a demonstrative man, at least not that Niko could remember. Which had made the way he'd clung to Emily's hand at the airport all the more telling.

If his assessment of her was correct, redirecting her attention would be simple enough. After all, a millionaire in his vigorous prime was surely preferable to one in his dotage. And if he was wrong…well, a harmless flirtation would hurt no one. Of course, when his father figured out what he was up to, he wouldn't like it, but when was the last time he'd approved of anything Niko did?

"You're very quiet suddenly," she said, interrupting the flow of his thoughts.

He looked deep into her dark blue eyes. "Because I'm beginning to think I've judged you too hastily," he answered, doing his utmost to sound convincingly repentant. "But I'm not entirely without conscience. Therefore, if one of us must leave, let me be the one to go."

Ignoring her whimper of protest, he released her, opened the door to leave the room and found himself face-to-face with Damaris. He could not have orchestrated a better exit. Timing, as he well knew in his line of work, was everything. "*Kali oreksi*, Emily," he said, standing back to allow Damaris to carry in a platter loaded with olives, calamari, dolmades, tzatziki and pita bread. "Enjoy your meal."

He was over the threshold before she burst out, "Oh, don't be so ridiculous!"

Suppressing a smile, he swung around. "There is a problem?"

"If having enough food to feed an army is a problem, then yes."

He shrugged. "What can I say? Greeks love to eat."

"Well, I can't possibly do justice to all this, and since I have no wish to offend your father's housekeeper when she's obviously gone to a great deal of trouble…"

"Yes, Emily?"

She grimaced, as if her next words gave her indigestion. "You might as well stay and help me eat it."

He stroked his jaw and made a show of weighing his options. "It would be a pity to let it go to waste," he eventually conceded, "especially as this is but the first of several courses."

For a moment, he thought he'd overplayed his hand. Skewering him with a glance that would have stopped the gods of Olympus in their tracks, she waited until Damaris mopped up her spilled drink, then took a seat at the table and said, "Try not to gloat, Niko. It's so unattractive."

He wasn't accustomed to female criticism. The women he associated with were so anxious to please, they'd have swallowed their own tongues before issuing such a blunt assessment of his shortcomings. That she suffered no such hesitation appealed to him in ways she couldn't begin to imagine. He devoted his entire life to challenging unfavorable odds. And took enormous pleasure in defeating them.

Collecting the wine bottle as he passed, he joined her and topped up their flutes. Nothing like dim lights and good champagne to set the scene for seduction. Raising his glass, he said, "Here's to getting to know one another all over again."

She responded with the merest tilt of one shoulder, took a dainty sip, then helped herself to a little tzatziki and bread.

"Have more," he urged, pushing the tray of mezedes closer.

She selected an olive, but ignored her champagne.

"You don't care for Greek food?"

"I'm not very familiar with it."

"There are no Greek restaurants in Vancouver?"

"Hundreds, and I'm told they're very good. I just don't eat out very often."

"Why is that? And please don't tell me you lack opportunity. Suitors must be lined up at your door, wanting to wine and dine you."

"I'm afraid not. Shift work tends to put a crimp in a nurse's social life."

Right. And you're such a dedicated professional that you never take a night off!

He shook his head in feigned mystification. "What's wrong with Canadian men, to be so easily discouraged? Are they all eunuchs?"

She almost choked on her olive. "Not as far as I know," she spluttered. "But then, I haven't bothered to ask."

"What about your colleagues? As I understand it, hospitals are a hotbed of romance between doctors and nurses."

"The idea that all nurses end up marrying doctors is a myth," she informed him starchily. "For a start, half the doctors these days are women, and even if they weren't, finding a husband isn't particularly high on my list of priorities."

"Why not? Don't most women want to settle down and have children? Or are you telling me you're the exception?"

"No." She nibbled a sliver of pita bread. "I'd love to get married and have children someday, but only if the right man comes along. I'm not willing to settle for just anyone."

"Define 'the right man,'" he said—a shade too abruptly, if her response was anything to go by.

She dropped her bread and stared at him. "I beg your pardon?"

"By what standards do you judge a prospective husband?"

She reached for her glass and took a sip while she considered the question. "He has to be decent and honorable," she finally declared.

"Tall, dark and handsome, too?"

"Not necessarily." She gave another delicate shrug, just enough to cause her dress to shift gently over her rather lovely breasts.

He wished he didn't find it so alluring. "Rich and successful, then?"

"Gainfully employed, certainly. If we had children, I'd want to be a stay-at-home mom."

"If you had to choose just one quality in this ideal man, what would it be?"

"The capacity to love," she said dreamily, her blue eyes soft, her sweet mouth curved in a smile. Outside, the wind tore at the palm trees with unusual strength for September. "I'd want love more than anything else, because a marriage without it is no marriage at all."

Annoyed to find his thoughts drifting dangerously far from their set course, he said flatly, "I disagree. I'd never let my heart get the better of my head."

"Why not? Don't you believe in love?"

"I might have once, very briefly, many years ago, but then she died of a blood clot to the brain. I was three months old at the time."

"You mean your *mother*?" She clapped a distressed hand to her cheek. Her eyes glistened suspiciously. "Oh, Niko, how very sad for you. I'm so sorry."

He wanted neither her sympathy nor her pity, and crushed both with brutal efficiency. "Don't be. It's not as if she was around long enough for me to miss her."

The way she cringed at his answer left him ashamed. "She gave you life," she said.

"And lost hers doing it, something I've been paying for ever since."

"Why? Her death wasn't your fault."

"According to my father, it was." Her glass remained almost untouched, but his was empty. Needing something to deaden a pain he seldom allowed to surface, he refilled it so hurriedly, the wine foamed up to the brim. "She was forty-one, and giving birth at her age to an infant weighing a strapping five kilos put her in her grave."

"A lot of women wait until their forties to have children."

"They don't all die because of it."

"True. But that's still no reason for you to think Pavlos holds you responsible for the tragedy that befell her. After all, she gave him a son and that's not a legacy any man takes lightly."

"You might be a hell of a fine nurse, Emily Tyler, but you're no spin doctor."

Puzzled, she said, "What do you mean?"

"That nothing you can say changes the fact that my father didn't care if he never had a child. All he ever wanted was my mother, and as far as he's concerned, I took her away from him."

"Then he should have seen to it he didn't get her pregnant in the first place—or are you to blame for that, as well?"

"After twenty-one years of marriage without any sign

of a baby, he probably didn't think precautions were necessary. Finish your wine, woman. I don't care to drink alone. It's a nasty habit to fall into."

She took another cautious sip. "I still can't believe that, once his initial grief subsided, having you didn't bring Pavlos some measure of comfort."

"Then you obviously don't know much about dysfunctional families. My father and I have never liked one another. He has always resented me, not just because I cost him his one true love, but because I remained wilfully unimpressed by his wealth and social status."

"I'd have thought he'd find that commendable."

"Don't let misplaced pity for the poor motherless baby cloud your judgment, my dear," Niko said wryly. "I rebelled every step of the way as a child, took great pleasure in embarrassing him by getting into trouble as a teenager and flat-out refused to be bought by his millions when I finally grew up. I was not a 'nice' boy, and I'm not a 'nice' man."

"That much, at least, I do believe," she shot back, leveling a scornful glance his way. "The only part I question is that you ever grew up. You strike me more as someone with a bad case of defiantly delayed adolescence."

This wasn't playing out the way he'd intended. She was supposed to be all willing, female compliance by now, ready to fall into his arms, if not his bed, not beating him at his own game. And his glass was empty again, damn it! "When you've walked in my shoes," he replied caustically, "feel free to criticize. Until then—"

"But I have," she interrupted. "Walked in your shoes, I mean. Except mine were twice as hard to wear.

Because, you see, I lost *both* my parents in a car accident when I was nine, and unlike you, I remember them enough to miss them very deeply. I remember what it was like to be loved unconditionally, then have that love snatched away in the blink of an eye. I remember the sound of their voices and their laughter—the scent of my mother's perfume and my father's Cuban cigars. And I know very well how it feels to be tolerated by relatives who make no secret of the fact that they've been saddled with a child they never wanted."

Flushed and more animated than Niko had yet seen her, she stopped to draw an irate breath before continuing, "I also learned what it's like to have to work for every cent, and to think twice before frittering away a dollar." She eyed his shirt and watch disdainfully. "You, on the other hand, obviously wouldn't know the meaning of deprivation if it jumped up and bit you in the face, and I don't for a moment buy the idea that your father never wanted you. So all in all, I'd say I come out the uncontested winner in this spontaneous pity party."

He let a beat of silence hang heavy in the air before he spoke again, then, "It's not often someone spells out my many shortcomings so succinctly," he said, "but you've managed to do it admirably. Is there anything else you'd like to tell me about myself before I slither behind the wheel of my car and disappear into the night?"

"Yes," she said. "Eat something. You've had too much to drink and are in no condition to drive. In fact, you should be spending the night here."

"Why, Emily, is that an invitation?"

"No," she said crushingly. "It's an order, and should

you be foolish enough to decide otherwise, I'll kick you where it'll hurt the most."

She probably weighed no more than fifty-four kilos to his eighty-five, but what she lacked in size, she more than made up for in spirit. He had no doubt that, given her knowledge of male anatomy, she was more than capable of inflicting serious injury. Which should have deterred him. Instead the thought of fending her off left him so suddenly and painfully aroused that, for the first time, he questioned the wisdom of his plan of attack. *She* was the one supposed to be at *his* mercy, not the other way around, but so far, she remained utterly indifferent to his charms. He, on the other hand, was anything but impervious to hers.

Damaris came back just then to serve spinach-stuffed breast of chicken and ziti, a welcome diversion, which allowed him to wrestle his wayward hormones into submission and redirect his energy into more productive channels. "Why did you allow my father to coerce you into letting him travel, when he's clearly not up to it?" he inquired casually, once they were alone again.

"I did my best to dissuade him," Emily said. "We all did. But the only thing he cared about was coming home to Greece, and nothing anyone said could convince him to wait. I think it's because he was afraid."

"Of dying?"

"No. Of *not* dying in Greece."

That Niko could well believe. Pavlos had always been fanatically patriotic. "So you volunteered to see him safely home?"

"It was more that he chose me. We got to know one another quite well during his hospital stay."

An hour ago, he'd have rated that little morsel of information as yet another sign of her ulterior motives. Now, he didn't have quite the same enthusiasm for the task. Emily the woman was proving a lot more intriguing than Emily the fortune hunter.

To buy himself enough time to reestablish his priorities, he switched to another subject. "What happened to you after your parents were killed?"

"I was sent to live with my father's sister. He was thirty-six when he died, and Aunt Alicia was eleven years older. She and Uncle Warren didn't have children, but they were the only family I had left, so they were more or less stuck with me. It wasn't a happy arrangement on either side."

"They mistreated you?"

"Not in the way you probably mean, but they never let me forget they'd done 'the right thing' by taking me in and would, I think, have found a reason to refuse if they hadn't been afraid it would reflect badly on them. Of course, the insurance settlement I brought with me sweetened the deal by defraying the cost of putting a roof over my head and keeping me fed and clothed for the next nine years."

"What happened then?"

"The summer I graduated high school, I applied to the faculty of nursing, was accepted and moved into a dorm on the university campus at the end of August. I never went 'home' again."

"But at least there was enough insurance settlement left to pay your tuition fees and other expenses."

She shook her head. "I scraped by on scholarships and student loans."

Caught in a swell of indignation he never saw coming, he stared at her. Whatever else his father's sins, he'd never tampered with Niko's inheritance from his mother. "Are you telling me they spent money on themselves, when it should have been held in trust for your education?"

"No, they were scrupulously honest." She started to add something else, then seemed to think better of it and made do with, "The settlement just wasn't very large to begin with, that's all."

Something about *that* answer didn't sit right, either. Wasn't the whole point of insurance to provide adequate recompense to beneficiaries, especially minors? But although the subject bore investigation, he decided now was not the time to pursue it and asked instead, "Do you keep in touch with your aunt and uncle?"

"A card at Christmas about covers it."

"So they have no idea you're here now?"

"No one has," she said. "My arrangement with Pavlos was strictly between the two of us. If my employer knew what I'd done, I'd probably be fired."

Which wouldn't matter one iota, if Niko's first impression of her was correct and she'd set her sights on a much more rewarding prize. What she earned in a year as a nurse wouldn't amount to pocket change if she married his father.

Wondering if she had any idea how potentially damaging her revelation was, he said, "Then why take the risk?"

"Because your father was alone in a foreign country without friends or family to look after him when he was released."

"He had a son. If you'd thought to contact me, I could have been there within twenty-four hours."

"Maybe," she said gently, "he didn't want to bother you."

"So he bothered a perfect stranger instead, even though doing so might end up costing her her job. Tell me, Emily, how do you propose to explain your absence from the hospital?"

"I won't have to. I took a three-month leave of absence and scheduled it to coincide with his discharge."

"A noble gesture on your part, giving up your holiday to look after my father."

"Well, why not? I had nothing else planned."

Except setting aside an hour a day to polish your halo! Struggling to hide his skepticism, Niko said, "All work and no play hardly seems fair. We'll have to see what we can do to change that."

A sudden gust of wind rattled the French doors, making her jump. "Just being here is change enough. If the weather ever clears up, I'm sure Pavlos won't begrudge me the odd day off to see the sights."

"Count on both," he said, recognizing opportunity when it presented itself. "And on my making myself available to act as tour guide."

"That's nice of you, Niko."

No, it's not, he could have told her. Because whatever *her* motives, *his* were anything but pure. And because he'd meant it when he said he wasn't a nice man.

They passed the remainder of the meal in idle conversation, interrupted only by intermittent bursts of rain at the windows, but before coffee was served, she'd run out of things to say and was wilting visibly. Even he, unscrupulous bastard though he undoubtedly was, felt sorry for her. The long transatlantic flight would have been tiring enough, without the added strain of looking after his father. So when she set aside her napkin and begged to be excused, he made no attempt to stop her, but left the table himself and walked her to the foot of the stairs.

"Good night," she murmured.

"Kali nikhta," he returned. "Sleep well."

She was perhaps halfway to the upper landing when a brilliant flash of lightning arrowed through the night. Almost immediately, the electricity failed and plunged the house into darkness.

He heard her startled exclamation and the click of her high heel hitting the edge of the marble step as she stumbled to a halt. "Stay put," he ordered, well aware how treacherous the staircase could be to the unwary. Once, when he was still a boy, a new housemaid had slipped and broken her arm—and that had been in broad daylight. But he'd grown up in the villa; could quite literally have found his way blindfolded anywhere within its walls, and was at Emily's side before she, too, missed her footing.

Just as he reached her, a second bolt of lightning ripped through the night, bleaching her face of color, turning her hair to silver and her eyes into pools as huge and dark as those found in undersea caverns. "What happened?" she whispered, clutching the bannister with one hand as she teetered on the edge of the stair.

Instinctively he pulled her close with an arm around her shoulders. They felt slender, almost childlike to the touch, but the rest of her, pinned warm and sweet against him, was unmistakably all woman. "The lights went out," he said, resorting to the absurdly obvious in an attempt to deflect her attention from the fact that his body had responded to hers with elemental, albeit untimely vigor.

She choked on a laugh. "I pretty much figured that out for myself."

"I expect a power pole was struck."

"Oh," she said faintly, aware as she had to be of her effect on him. Blatant arousal was difficult to hide at such close quarters. "Does it happen often?"

Were they talking about the same thing, he wondered, as his mind fought a losing battle with his nether regions. "No, especially not at this time of year."

"I ought to make sure your father's all right."

"No need," he said, hearing footsteps and noticing the shadow of candle flames flickering over the walls at the rear of the downstairs hall. "Georgios is already on the job. But if it'll ease your mind any, I'll see you as far as your suite, then go check on him myself. Do you know which one you're in?"

"Only that it's blue and cream, with some gorgeous antique furniture, including a four-poster bed."

He nodded, recognizing her description, and keeping one arm looped around her waist, steered her the rest of the way up the stairs, turned right along the landing and felt his way along the wall on his left until he made contact with her door. Pushing it wide, he directed her inside.

The logs in the fireplace had burned down, but enough of a glow remained to fill the room with dim orange light. Enough that when she looked at him, their gazes locked, held prisoner by the sexual awareness, which had simmered between them from the moment they'd first set eyes on each other.

He hadn't meant to kiss her this early in the game, had planned a much more subtle attack, but when she turned within the circle of his arms and lifted her face to his, it was the most natural thing in the world for him to tighten his hold until she was once again pressed against him. The most natural thing in the world to bend his head and find her mouth with his.

CHAPTER THREE

EMILY had been kissed before, many times, but always with some part of her brain able to rate the experience objectively: too slobbery, too bland, too aggressive, too many teeth, too much heavy breathing, not enough tenderness. More often than not, kissing, she'd concluded, was a vastly overrated prelude to romance. Until Niko Leonidas came on the scene, that was, and felled her with a single blow.

Except "blow" was no more the right word to define his effect on her than "kiss" adequately described his action. What he did with his mouth transcended the ordinary and surpassed the divine. Cool and firm, it yet seared her with its heat. Though undemanding, it somehow stripped her of everything—her independence, her focus, her moral compass, even her sense of survival.

Apart from one rash, distinctly forgettable experience, she'd chosen to remain celibate because sex for its own sake held no appeal, and she'd never come close to being in love. But she'd have let him take her there on the floor, if only he'd asked. Would have let him hike up the skirt of her dress and touch her as no other man ever had. For as long as his kiss held her in its spell, she would have let him have his way with her however he wished.

Obviously he did not wish for a fraction of what she was willing to give. Because releasing her, he stepped back and said, rather hoarsely to be sure, "I'll go look in on my father and see about getting some candles up here."

Weak as water, she clutched the back of a nearby chair and nodded. She couldn't have spoken if her life depended on it. Although he'd put a respectable distance between them, she remained trapped in his aura. Her body still hummed. Her breasts ached. Moisture, warm and heavy, seeped between her thighs.

When he turned away, she wanted to cry out that she didn't need candles, she only needed him. But the words remained dammed in her throat and he was gone before she could free them. Dazed, she lowered herself to the chair and waited for him to return.

A brass carriage clock on the mantelpiece marked the passing minutes. Gradually its measured pace restored her racing pulse to near-normal and brought a sort of order to her scattered thoughts. What kind of madness had possessed her, that she'd been ready to give herself to someone she'd known less than a day? He spelled nothing but trouble.

I won't let him in when he comes back, she resolved. I'm out of my league with such a man and don't need the heartbreak an affair with him would bring.

But when a discreet tap at her door signaled his return, all logic fled. Heat shot through her, giving rise to a single exquisite throb of anticipation that electrified her. She couldn't get to him fast enough.

Pulling open the door, she began, "I was beginning to think you'd abandoned—!" then lapsed into mortified silence at the sight of Georgios standing there, a lighted silver candelabra in one hand, and a battery operated lantern in the other.

"Niko asked me to bring these, *thespinis*," he informed her politely, "and to tell you that Kirie Pavlos is sleeping soundly."

Rallying her pride, she stood back to let him pass into the room, and mumbled, "Thank you."

"*Parakalo.*" He placed the candelabra on the dresser and handed her the lantern. "I am also to tell you that he has been called away."

"At this hour of the night?" She made no attempt to hide her disbelief.

He nodded. "*Ne, thespinis.* He received an urgent phone call and will most likely be gone for several days."

Oh, the louse! The cowardly, unmitigated rat! Swallowing the anger and humiliation threatening to choke her, she said scathingly, "It must have been some emergency to drag him out in the middle of a storm like this."

Georgios stopped on his way to the door and shrugged. "I cannot say. He did not explain the reasons."

"Never mind. It's not important." *He* wasn't important. She was there to look after the father, not chase after the son.

"Thank you for the candles and flashlight, Georgios. Good night."

"*Kalispera, thespinis.* Sleep well."

Surprisingly she did, and awoke the next day to clear skies and sunshine. Last night's storm was as much a part of the past as last night's kiss.

Pavlos was already up and dressed when she went

downstairs. He sat on the veranda outside his sitting room, gazing out at the garden. A small empty coffee cup and a phone sat on a table at his side. A pair of binoculars rested on his lap.

Catching sight of her, he pressed a finger to his lips, and gestured for her to join him. "Look," he whispered, pointing to a pair of fairly large birds. Pretty, with bluish-gray heads, pearly-pink breasts and brown wings mottled with black, they pecked at the ground some distance away. "Do you know what they are?"

"Pigeons?" she ventured.

He grunted disdainfully. "Turtle doves, girl! Timid and scarce, these days, but they come to my garden because they know they're safe. And those over there at the feeder are golden orioles. Didn't know I was a bird fancier, did you?"

"No," she said, noting the spark in his dark eyes and his improved color. "But I do know you look much better this morning. You must have had a good night."

"Nothing like being on his home turf to cure a man of whatever ails him. Not that that son of mine would agree. Where do you suppose he is, by the way? I thought he might at least stay over, my first night back."

"No. He was called away on some sort of emergency."

"Gone already, eh?" He squared his shoulders, and lifted his chin, a formidable old warrior not about to admit to weakness of any kind. "Off on another harebrained escapade, I suppose. Doesn't surprise me. Never really expected he'd stick around. Ah well, good riddance, I say. You had breakfast yet, girl?"

"No," she said, aching for him. He could protest all he liked, but she saw past his proud facade to the lonely parent underneath. "I wanted to see how you were doing, first."

"I'm hungry. Now that you're here, we'll eat together." He picked up the phone, pressed a button and spoke briefly with whoever answered. Shortly after, Georgios wheeled in a drop-leaf table set for breakfast for two, and equipped with everything required for what she soon realized was the almost sacred ritual of making coffee. It was prepared with great ceremony over an open flame, in a little copper pot called a briki, and immediately served in thick white demitasses with a glass of cold water on the side.

"No Greek worthy of the name would dream of starting the day without a *flitzani* of good *kafes*," Pavlos declared.

Possibly not, and she had to admit the aroma was heavenly, but the strong beverage with its layer of foam and residue of grounds took some getting used to. She found the fruit and yogurt salad topped with almonds and drizzled with honey and a sprinkling of cinnamon much more enjoyable.

In the days that followed, she also found out that Pavlos had little faith in doctors, rated physiotherapists as next to useless and had no qualms about saying so to their faces. He could be fractious as a child when forced to suffer through the regimen of exercises prescribed to strengthen his hip, and sweet as peach pie if he thought Emily was working too hard.

While he napped in the afternoons, she swam in the pool, walked along the beach or explored the neighborhood, taking particular pleasure in the shops. In the evenings, she played gin rummy or poker with him, even though he cheated at both.

One morning, she was wheeling him along the

terrace after his physiotherapy session when he asked, "Do you miss home?"

She looked out at the flowers in brilliant bloom, at the peacocks strutting across the lawns, the blue arc of the sky and the stunning turquoise sea. Soon the rainy season would come to Vancouver, its chilly southeasterly gales stripping the trees of leaves. People would be scurrying about under a forest of umbrellas where, just few weeks before, they'd been lying on the beaches taking in the last of summer's sunshine. "No," she said. "I'm happy to be here."

"Good. Then you have no excuse for wanting to leave early."

She thought not, either, until the beginning of her second week there, when Niko reappeared as suddenly as he'd left.

"So this is where you're hiding," he said, coming upon her as she sat reading in a wicker love seat on the patio—except they called it a veranda in Greece. "I've been looking everywhere for you."

Though startled, she managed to hang on to her composure enough to meet his glance coolly and reply with commendable indifference, "Why? What do you want?"

Uninvited, he sat down beside her on the sun-warmed cushions. "To ask you to have dinner with me tonight."

The nerve of him! "I don't think so," she said, projecting what she hoped was an air of cool amusement. "You're likely to take off at the last minute and leave me to foot the bill."

"The way I did the other night, you mean?" He grimaced. "Look, I'm sorry about that but—"

"Forget it, Niko. I have."

"No, you haven't. I haven't, either, and nor do I want to. Spend the evening with me, and I'll try to explain myself."

"Whatever makes you think I'm interested in anything you have to say?"

"Because if you weren't, you wouldn't be so ticked off with me. Come on, Emily," he wheedled, inching closer. "Be fair, and at least hear me out before you decide I'm not worth your time."

"I usually play cards with Pavlos in the evening."

"Then we'll make it a late dinner. How is my father, by the way? I stopped by his suite before I came to find you, but he was sleeping."

"He still tires easily, but he's better since he started physiotherapy."

"I'm glad he's on the mend." He glanced at her from beneath his outrageous lashes, stroked his finger down her arm and left a trail of shimmering sensation in its wake. "So what do you say, sweet thing? Do we have a date?"

Resisting him was like trying to trap mist between her hands. "If that's what it takes for you to leave me to read in peace now, I suppose we do. But I won't be free much before ten, after your father's settled for the night."

He edged closer still, a long, lean specimen of masculine grace, handsome as sin, dangerous as hell, and kissed her cheek. "I can wait that long," he said, "but I'm not saying it will be easy."

He took her to a restaurant on the water, about a fifteen-minute drive from the villa. She'd pinned up her hair in a sleek chignon, and wore a black dress she'd bought on sale in a boutique just a few days earlier, and high-heeled black sandals. Simple but beautifully cut, the dress had a narrow draped skirt, strapless bodice, and a shawl lushly embroidered with silver thread. Her only accessory was a pair of dangling vintage silver earrings studded with crystals.

All in all, a good choice, she decided, glancing at her surroundings. Unlike the bougainvillea-draped tavernas she'd seen in the neighborhood, with their paper table-cloths and simple, sometimes crudely constructed fur-niture, this place gave new meaning to the term stylish sophistication. Crisp linens, a single perfect gardenia at every place setting, deep, comfortable leather chairs, a small dance floor and soft music combined to create an ambience at once elegant and romantic.

They were shown to a window table overlooking a yacht basin. Tall masts rose black and slender against the night sky. Beyond the breakwater, moonlight carved an icy path across the sea to the horizon, but inside the room, candles cast a warm glow over the stark white walls.

Once they'd been served drinks and he'd chosen their meal—noting no prices were listed on the menu, she'd left him to decide what to order—Niko leaned back in his chair and remarked, "You look very lovely tonight, Emily. More like a fashion model than a nurse."

"Thank you. You look rather nice yourself."

Which had to be, she thought, mentally rolling her eyes, the understatement of the century. The superb fit of his charcoal-gray suit spoke of Italian tailoring at its best, and never mind the gorgeous body inside it.

He inclined his head and smiled. "I like your earrings."

"They were my mother's. She loved jewelry and pretty clothes." She touched her fingertip to one crystal pendant, memories of her mother, all dressed up for an evening out, as clear in her mind as if they'd taken place just yesterday. "I still have all her things—her dinner gowns and shoes and beaded handbags."

"Do you use them?"

"Not often. I don't have occasion to."

His gaze scoured her face, meandered down her throat to her shoulders, and it took all her self-control not to shrink into the concealing folds of her shawl. "What a waste," he murmured. "A woman as beautiful as you should always wear beautiful things."

"My mother was the beauty, not I."

"You think?"

"I know," she said, nodding thanks to the waiter as he presented a tray of appetizers. *Mezedes*, she'd learned, were as integral to the evening meal as the main course itself. "And my father was incredibly handsome. They made such a glamorous couple."

"Tell me about them," he said, resting his elbow on the arm of his chair, wineglass in hand. "What were they like—beyond their good looks, that is?"

"Crazy about one another. Happy."

"Socialites?"

"I suppose they were," she admitted, remembering the many times she'd watched, entranced, as her mother prepared for a gala evening on the town.

"What else?"

She stared out at the yachts rocking gently at their moorings. "They wrung every drop of enjoyment from life. They'd dance in the sitting room after dinner, go swimming at midnight in English Bay, dress up in fabulous costumes for Hallowe'en, decorate the biggest tree they could find at Christmas. They were on everyone's guest list, and everyone wanted to be on theirs. And they died much too soon."

Detecting the sadness infecting her memories, he framed his next question in quiet sympathy. "How did it happen?"

"They were on their way home from a party, driving along a road infamous for its hairpin bends. It was raining heavily, the visibility was poor. They were involved in a head-on collision and killed instantly."

Again, his voice grazed her with compassion. "Ah, Emily, I'm sorry."

Aware her emotions swam dangerously close to the surface, she gave herself a mental shake, sat a little straighter in her seat and firmly changed the subject. "Thank you, but it all happened a long time ago, and we're here to talk about you, not me. So tell me, Niko, exactly what frightened you off after that impulsive kiss last week? And please don't say you were too busy checking the main fuse box to find the cause of the power failure, because Georgios already told me you left after receiving a phone call. Had you forgotten you had a previous date, or was I so inept compared to the other women you know that you couldn't wait to escape me?"

"Neither," he said. "I had to go to work."

"You *work*?"

"Well, yes, Emily," he said, laughing. "Don't most men my age?"

"Yes, but you don't seem the corporate type."

"I'm not."

"And it was the middle of the night."

"Right, again."

"So?"

"So I had to prepare to leave Athens at first light, the next day."

"To go where?"

"Overseas."

"How tactfully vague. You'll be telling me next you're involved in smuggling."

"Sometimes I am."

It was neither the answer she was expecting nor one she wanted to hear. Tired of his stonewalling, she threw down her napkin, pushed back her chair and stood up. "If this is your idea of explaining yourself, I've had enough."

"Okay," he said, grabbing her hand before she could bolt, "I delivered some urgently needed supplies to a medical outpost in Africa."

Abruptly she sat down again, her annoyance fading as the implication of his reply hit home. "Are you talking about Doctors Without Borders?"

"In this particular case, yes."

Their waiter came back just then to whisk away the remains of the mezedes and deliver their main course. A dozen questions crowding her mind, she waited impatiently as he made a big production of serving grilled calamari and prawns on a bed of rice. "How did you get there?" she asked, when they were alone again.

"I flew," Niko said.

"Well, I didn't think you walked!"

His mouth twitched with amusement at her acerbic response. "I happen to own a small fleet of aircraft. It comes in handy on occasion."

"Are you telling me you piloted your own plane?"

"In a word, yes."

"Going into places like that can be dangerous, Niko."

He shrugged. "Perhaps, but someone has to do it."

She stared at him, her every preconceived notion of what he was all about undergoing a drastic change. "Where did you learn to fly?"

"After finishing my National Service, I spent five years as a Career Officer with the HAF—Hellenic Air Force. That's when I first became involved in rescue missions. It irked my father no end, of course, that I chose the military over seconding myself to him and his empire."

"Is that why you did it?"

"Not entirely. I loved the freedom of flying. And providing humanitarian aid wherever it's needed struck me as a more worthwhile undertaking than amassing more wealth. How's your calamari, Emily?"

"Delicious," she said, though in truth she'd hardly tasted it. What she was learning about him was far more interesting. "You said a while ago that you own a fleet of aircraft, which I assume means you have more than one."

"Ten in total, and a staff of fifteen. We're a private outfit, on call twenty-four hours a day, seven days a week, and go wherever we're needed, providing whatever kind of help is required. Last month, we joined forces with the Red Cross after an earthquake in northern Turkey left hundreds homeless. The month before, Oxfam International called on us."

"Well, if you care so little for money, how are you able to afford all that? Does Pavlos support you?"

"You ought to know better than to ask such a question," he scoffed. "Even if he'd offered, I'd have starved before I took a single euro from him. And for the record, I never said I didn't care about money. It's a very useful commodity. I just don't care about his."

"Then I don't understand."

"I inherited a sizable fortune from my mother which, to give credit where it's due, Pavlos invested for me. By the time I had access to it at twenty-one, it had grown to the point that I could do pretty much anything I wanted, without having to rely on sponsors. And I chose to use it benefiting those most in need of help." He glanced up and caught her staring. Again. "Why do you keep looking so surprised?"

"Because you told me last week that you're not a nice man, and I believed you. Now I realize nothing could be further from the truth."

"Don't get carried away, Emily," he warned. "Just because I'm not immune to human suffering doesn't make me a saint."

"But you are, I begin to think, a very good man."

Irritably he pushed aside his plate, most of the food untouched. "The wine must have gone to your head. Let's dance, before you say something you live to regret."

She'd have refused if he'd been in any mood to take no for an answer—and if the prospect of finding herself once more in his arms hadn't been more temptation than she could withstand. "All right," she said, and followed him onto the dance floor.

Weaving a path through the others already swaying to the music, he waited for her to catch up with him and extended his hands in invitation. "Come here, sweet thing," he said, and she went.

Whatever resentment she'd harbored toward him had melted away, and left her completely vulnerable to him, all over again. Who could blame her, when the plain fact of the matter was that with a single touch, a glance from those dark green bedroom eyes, he could make a woman forget everything she'd ever learned about self-preservation? That he also turned out to be so thoroughly *decent* merely added to his appeal and made him that much more irresistible.

CHAPTER FOUR

IT FELT good to hold a woman whose curves hadn't been ravaged by malnutrition. Whose bones, though delicate and fine, were not so brittle that he was afraid they'd break at his touch. Whose breasts hadn't withered from bearing too many children she hadn't been able to nourish properly. Who didn't shrink in fear when a man touched her. Who smelled of flowers, not poverty.

"Stop it," he said, inhaling the sweet fragrance of her hair.

"Stop what?"

"Thinking. I can hear your brain working overtime."

"Well, I can't help wondering—"

He pulled her closer, enough for her warmth to melt the block of ice he carried inside, and make him whole again. Whenever he returned from a particularly harrowing assignment, a woman's soothing voice and generous, vital body always helped erase the hopeless misery he never got used to witnessing; the wasted lives, the terror, the shocking evidence of man's inhumanity to man. "Don't wonder, Emily," he said, glad she'd left her shawl at the table, and loving the ivory smoothness of her skin above the top of her strapless dress. "Don't ask any more questions. Forget everything and just be with me in the moment."

"Not easy to do, Niko. You're not who I thought you were."

Sliding his hand down her spine to cup her hip, he pressed her closer still. "I know," he said.

He was worse. Much worse. Not at all the high-minded hero she was painting him to be, but a man on a mission that was far from laudable where she was concerned. Blatantly deceiving her as to his true motives for dating her, at the same time that he used her to assuage his personal torment.

She stirred in his arms and lifted her face so that her cheek rested against his. The whisper of silk against those parts of her he couldn't see or feel inflamed him. "I'm sorry I jumped to all the wrong conclusions about you."

"You didn't," he muttered, fire racing through his belly. "I'm every bit as bad as you first assumed."

"I don't believe you."

They weren't dancing anymore. Hadn't been for some time. While other couples dipped and glided around them in a slow foxtrot, they stood in the middle of the floor, bodies welded so close together that even if she weren't a nurse well acquainted with male anatomy, she had to know the state he was in.

"What I don't understand," she continued, so intent on her thoughts that nothing he said or did seemed able to derail them, "is how you can show such compassion toward strangers, and spare so little for your father."

"I didn't bring you here to talk about my father."

Her hips nudged against him, a fleeting touch that

stoked his arousal to disastrous heights. "And I wouldn't be here at all, were it not for him."

"Thanks for the reminder," he ground out, dancing her back to their table sedately enough for his rampant flesh to subside. "With that in mind, I'd better get you home if you're to be on the job bright and early in the morning."

"Actually I usually don't start work until nine. Pavlos prefers to have Georgios help him bathe and dress, and I join him for breakfast after that."

He picked up her shawl and flung it around her shoulders. The less he could see of her, the better. "Even so, it's growing late."

She nodded sympathetically. "And you're tired."

"Among other things," he replied ambiguously, gesturing to the waiter for the bill.

Outside, the temperature still hovered around twenty degrees Celsius, warm enough for the top to remain down on the BMW. "Rather than having to drive all the way back to Athens after you drop me off, why don't you stay at your father's house tonight?" she suggested, pulling the shawl more snugly around her as he started along the shore road to the villa.

"No," he said, surprising himself because, at the start of the evening, he'd planned to do exactly that. Had had every intention of seducing her; of using her soft loveliness to erase the heart-rending images he'd brought back with him from Africa and, at the same time, prove his original theory that she would sell herself to the highest bidder. After all, she now knew he had money to burn.

But much though he still desired her, he'd lost his taste for using her. And if she was as duplicitous as he'd first suspected, he was no longer sure he wanted to know.

* * *

It was well after one o'clock in the morning. Within its walls, the villa lay smothered in the thick silence of a household at sleep. Except for Emily, who should have been exhausted, but was instead wide-awake and so disappointed she could have cried.

Pacing to the French windows in her suite, she stepped out on the balcony and promptly wished she hadn't. The classical marble statuary in the garden, gleaming white under the moon, was too reminiscent of Niko's stern profile as he'd driven her home; the cool whisper of night air on her skin, too much a reminder of his lips brushing her cheek as he kissed her good-night.

What had happened, that the evening was covered with stardust promise one moment, and over the next? They'd been so close, so attuned to one another when they were dancing. She'd known how aroused he was, had felt an answering tug of desire for him.

She'd thought, when he announced they should leave the restaurant, that after the way he'd held her, he'd at least end the evening on a high note with a kiss to rival the one from the week before. She'd wanted him to, quite desperately in fact, and why not? He'd redeemed himself so completely in her eyes, she was willing to fan the spark of attraction between them and let it take them to the next level. But rather than setting her on fire as she'd hoped, he'd brought her straight back to the villa and walked her to his father's front door.

"Thank you for a lovely evening," she'd said woodenly, hardly able to contain her disappointment.

"My pleasure," he'd replied. "I'm glad you enjoyed it."

Then he'd bestowed that pale imitation of a kiss on her cheek, muttered, "Good night," and raced back to his idling car as if he was afraid, if he lingered, she might drag him into the shrubbery and insist he ravish her.

What a contradiction in terms he was, she decided, turning back into her room. On the one hand, he was all cool suspicion laced with lethal charm and passion when it suited him, and on the other side of the personality coin, a reluctant hero and considerate escort more concerned about keeping her out past her bedtime than catering to his own base needs. Either that, or he took masochistic pleasure in keeping the women he dated off balance. And if that was the case, she was better off without him. One temperamental Leonidas at a time was enough.

"Out on the town till all hours of the night with that no-good son of mine, were you?" Pavlos inquired, glaring at her across the breakfast table when she joined him the next morning. "What if I'd needed you?"

"If you had, Georgios knew how to reach me."

"That's beside the point."

"And exactly what point are you making, Pavlos? That I'm under house arrest and not allowed to leave the premises without your permission?"

Ignoring her sarcasm, he said baldly, "You're asking for trouble, getting involved with Niko. Women are nothing but toys to him, created solely for his entertainment and pleasure. He'll play with you for as long as you amuse him, then drop you for the next one who catches his fancy. He'll break your heart without a second thought and leave you to pick up the pieces, just like all the others who came before you."

Not about to admit she'd pretty much reached the

same conclusion herself, she said, "I'm a grown woman. I know how to take care of myself."

He scowled. "Not with a man like him, you don't. He's bad news, no matter how you look at it. Take my advice, girl. Stay away from him."

A shadow fell across the floor. "Talking about me again, old man?" Niko stepped through the open French doors.

No custom-tailored Italian suit this morning, she noted, but blue jeans again, and a short-sleeved blue shirt revealing strong, tanned forearms. Not that the packaging counted for much. It was the man inside and his sexy, hypnotic voice that set her heart to palpitating.

Annoyed that he so easily snagged her in his spell, Emily averted her gaze, but his father continued to look him straight in the eye and said, "Know anyone else who fits the description?"

"Can't think of a soul," Niko replied evenly.

"There you have it then." Pavlos thumped his coffee cup down on the table. "Why are you here anyway?"

"To have a word with Emily, and to see how you're coming along."

"You needn't have bothered."

"Obviously not. You're as cantankerous as ever, which I take to be a very good sign that you're recovering nicely."

"And Emily doesn't want to see you."

"Why don't you let her tell me that for herself? Or does the fact that you're paying her to be your nurse entitle you to act as her mouthpiece, as well?"

"Just stop it, both of you!" Emily cut in. "Pavlos, finish your toast and stop behaving badly. Niko, the physiotherapist should be here soon, and I'll be free to talk to you then."

He shook his head. "Afraid I can't wait that long. I have a meeting in the city—"

"Then don't let us keep you," his father growled, snapping open the morning paper and feigning great interest in the headlines. "And whatever you do, don't hurry back."

Niko's face closed, and spinning on his heel, he strode off down the hall. But not before Emily caught the flicker of pain in his eyes that he couldn't quite disguise.

"That," she told Pavlos, "was both cruel and unnecessary."

"Then chase after him and kiss him better."

"An excellent suggestion," she said, pushing away from the table. "Thank you for thinking of it."

Niko had already reached his car when she yanked open the villa's front door. "Niko, wait," she called, running across the forecourt.

He turned at the sound of her voice, but made no move toward her. "If you're here to apologize for my father, save your breath," he informed her curtly. "I'm used to him."

"Well, I'm not," she said. "Look, I don't know why he's in such a foul mood this morning, but for what it's worth, I want you to know that I don't let other people dictate whom I should or should not associate with."

"In this case, you might be better off if you did," he said, once again turning to get into the car. "After all, he's known me all my life which makes him some sort of expert on what I'm all about."

Stepping closer, she stopped him with a hand on his

arm. Although his skin felt warm, the flesh beneath was unresponsive as stone to her touch. Undeterred, she said, "Perhaps I'd have believed that yesterday at this time, but I know better now and it'll take more than your father's say-so to convince me otherwise. So if you're using the scene back there in the house as an excuse to end our friendship, it's not going to happen. Now, what did you want to talk to me about?"

He regarded her broodingly a moment. "Your time off," he eventually admitted.

"Why do you want to know?"

"Why do you think, Emily? I want to see more of you."

Again, the tell-tale lurch of her heart warned her how susceptible to him she was. "Then why the mixed messages last night, Niko?" she asked, deciding to lay her misgivings to rest once and for all. "Do you blow hot and cold with all the women you date, or have you singled me out for special attention?"

He didn't bother to dissemble. Was, indeed, shockingly, hilariously blunt in his reply. "In case you didn't notice, my dear, last night when we were dancing, I was sporting an erection that would have done a stallion proud. That ought to have told you something."

Smothering a burst of laughter, she said with equal candor, "At the time, I thought it did. But after hustling me outside, you either decided I wasn't quite your type after all, or else you lost your nerve."

A flush of indignation stained his finely chiseled cheekbones. "I neither lost my nerve, nor anything else."

"Then why the hasty brush-off?"

"There's a time and a place for everything, Emily, especially seduction. I'm not the sex-in-the-backseat-of-the-car type of guy—which isn't to say I didn't want to take you to bed. But you'd given no indication you'd have welcomed such an overture. Just the opposite, in fact. You never stopped talking."

"If you'd bothered to ask," she said, "I could have told you we weren't as far apart in our thinking as you seem to suppose. I just did a better job of hiding it."

He blinked. "Are you sure you know what you're saying?"

"Very sure. I realized the moment I set eyes on you that the chemistry between us could easily become explosive."

"This isn't the first time you've left me at a loss for words," he said, almost stumbling over his reply, "and I have a sneaking suspicion it won't be the last."

"Well, don't misunderstand me. I'm not saying I'm ready to jump into bed with you, but…"

"But you won't turn me down if I ask you out again?"

"I'll be disappointed if you don't."

He slid his arm around her waist and pulled her to him. "When's the next time you have a few hours off?"

"Later this afternoon, from about three until seven."

"I'll pick you up at three-thirty. Wear something casual—slacks and a light sweater in case you get cold, and bring a camera if you have one. Today, we play at being tourists in the city."

Then he kissed her. Hard and sweet. On the mouth. And made it last long enough that when he finally released her, she had to clutch the top of the car door to keep herself upright.

She'd read the travel brochures and thought she knew what to expect of Athens. Traffic congestion and noise and smog. Ancient, crumbling ruins sitting cheek by jowl with towering new apartment buildings. And overshadowing them all, the Acropolis and the Parthenon. But brochures didn't come close to preparing her for the real thing.

Niko showed up not in the BMW but on a candy-apple-red motor scooter. Helping her onto the passenger seat, he plunked a bright red helmet on her head, fastened the strap, then climbed aboard himself and said, "Hang on tight."

On that note, they were off, zooming through the outskirts of the city, weaving in and out of traffic, zipping up steep hills, along narrow streets and through tiny squares, until suddenly the famous landmarks were everywhere she looked. She should have been terrified at the speed with which they traveled. With anyone else, she undoubtedly would have been. But seated behind him, her front sandwiched against his spine, her arms wrapped around his waist, she felt fearless, confident.

She loved the wind in her face, the aromas drifting from the tavernas, the energy buzzing in the air. Loved the feel of him, all sleek muscle beneath his short-sleeved shirt, and the scent of his sun-kissed skin.

Finally he parked and locked the scooter, then led her through a pedestrian avenue lined with restaurants and cafés, and along a marble path to the top of the Acropolis. Up close, the sheer size and majesty of the Parthenon overwhelmed her. "I can't believe I'm really here, and seeing it for myself," she breathed. "It's amazing, Niko. Magnificent! And the view…!"

She lapsed into silence, at a loss for words. Athens

lay at her feet, a sprawling mass of concrete occasionally interspersed with the green of pine-covered hills.

"Gives a pretty good idea of the layout of the city," Niko agreed, "but if ever my father decides he can get through an evening without you, we'll come back another time, at sunset. Enjoying a bottle of wine and watching the lights come on is equally impressive."

"What surprises me is that it's not nearly as crowded as I thought it would be."

"Because most tourists have gone home and left Athens to those of us who choose to live here. The smart ones, though, know that October is one of the best times to visit."

They spent an idyllic few hours wandering among the ruins, stopping on the way down the hill for iced coffee at a sidewalk café, and visiting a beautiful little church tucked in a quiet square. But although everything she saw left Emily awestruck, it was what Niko brought to the afternoon that left the most indelible impression.

His lazy smile caressed her, hinting at untold pleasures to come. His voice reciting the history of the temples held her mesmerized. The way he took every opportunity to touch her—holding her hand to guide her over the uneven ground as if she were the most delicate, precious thing in the world to him, or looping an intimate arm around her shoulders as he pointed out some distant landmark—filled her with shimmering happiness.

With a casual endearment, a glance, he inspired in her an unsuspected passion and yearning. The blood seethed in her veins. She had never felt more alive; never known such an uprush of emotion.

Too soon it was six o'clock and time to head back to Vouliagmeni. The setting sun slanted across the lawns and the front door stood open when they arrived at the villa. "Are you coming in?" she asked, as he propped the scooter on its kickstand and swung her to the ground.

He shook his head. "No, *karthula*. Why spoil a perfect afternoon?"

"I wish it didn't have to be like that," she said, removing her helmet.

He took it from her, slung it over the handlebars and cupped her face between his hands. "It is what it is, Emily, and what it's always been."

"Well, I find it very sad. It's not—"

He silenced her with a lingering kiss that emptied her mind of everything but the heady delight of his mouth on hers. "Oh," she breathed, when at last it ended.

He lifted his head and stared past her, then, "I think we should try that again," he murmured, and drawing her to him, kissed her a second time at even greater length.

An exclamation—most likely an expletive, judging by its irate tone—shattered the moment, and spinning around, Emily found Pavlos leaning on his walker, silhouetted in the open doorway.

"Wouldn't you know it?" Niko said cheerfully, releasing her. "Caught in the act by my disapproving *patera*. I'd better make myself scarce before he comes after me with a shotgun. I'll call you, Emily. Soon."

A moment later, he was gone, disappearing down the long driveway in a candy-apple-red blur of speed, and taking with him all the joy the afternoon had brought. Because she knew without a shadow of doubt that the reason he'd kissed her a second time had nothing to do with her. He'd done it for the pure pleasure of stirring his father to anger.

Unbidden, and decidedly unwelcome, Pavlos's earlier warning came back to haunt her. *Women are nothing but toys to him, created solely for his entertainment. He'll break your heart and leave you to pick up the pieces, just like all the others who came before you....*

CHAPTER FIVE

Pavlos wore such an unmistakable told-you-so expression that Emily knew she looked as let down as she felt. Shuffling along beside her as she stalked into the house, he crowed, "Lived down to my expectations, didn't he?"

"You don't know what you're talking about, Pavlos," she informed him curtly, rallying her pride. "I had a fabulous afternoon."

"And I ran a marathon while you were gone!" He elbowed her in the ribs. "Admit it, Emily. He disappointed you."

"If you must know, you both disappoint me. Father and son—grown men at that—taking potshots at each other isn't my idea of adult entertainment. Have you had dinner?"

"No. I waited for you."

"I'm not hungry."

"Ah, girl! Don't let him do this to you. He's not worth it."

The edge of compassion softening his tone caused serious inroads on her composure, and that he happened also to be right didn't make the advice any easier to swallow. "He's not 'doing' anything," she insisted.

Except play fast and loose with her emotions, which she wasn't about to admit to his father.

That night when he was preparing for bed, Pavlos slipped on the marble tiles in his bathroom and split his forehead open on the edge of the sink. Striving to maintain calm in the face of chaos—Georgios panicked at the sight of blood, was sure his beloved master was dying and blamed himself for the accident—Emily directed him to call for an ambulance while she attended to Pavlos who lay sprawled on the floor. Although somewhat disoriented, he swore irritably and smacked her hand away when she tried to prevent him from struggling to his feet.

Leaning against the tub, he scoffed, "I'm not dead yet, woman! It'll take more than a cracked skull to finish me off."

"It's not your head I'm worried about, it's your hip," she said, applying a folded facecloth to the superficial cut on his brow. In fact, the sink had broken his fall and that he was able to sit on the floor without showing much evidence of pain was a good sign, but she wanted more scientific proof that he was as fine as he claimed.

The paramedics arrived shortly after and transferred him to the hospital for X-rays. Fortunately he'd incurred no further damage to his hip, required only a couple of sutures to his cut and vetoed any recommendation that he stay there overnight. "I didn't bring you all this way to look after me so you could turn the job over to someone else," he reminded Emily.

By the next morning, he sported a black eye but was otherwise his usual self. "No reason to," he snapped, when she suggested letting his son know what had happened.

But, "He has a right to be kept informed," she insisted, and left a brief message on Niko's voice mail.

He didn't acknowledge it until three days later when he again showed up unannounced as they were finishing lunch. "Very colorful," he remarked, inspecting Pavlos's black eye which by then had taken on a distinctly greenish hue. "Tell me, old man, do you plan to make a habit of abusing your body?"

"Accidents happen," his father shot back. "You're living proof of that."

Emily winced, appalled by the stunning cruelty of his reply, but realized that although he'd rather die than admit it, Pavlos was hurt that Niko hadn't bothered to stop by sooner.

"We all have our crosses to bear, *Patero*," Niko said scornfully. "Yours isn't any heavier than mine."

"Don't call me *patero*. You're no more a son to me than a dog on the street."

After their last confrontation, Emily had made up her mind she was never again getting caught in the middle when these two went at each other, but the insults flying back and forth were more than she could tolerate. "How do you the pair of you live with yourselves?" she asked sharply.

"By having as little to do with each other as possible," Niko said, addressing her directly for the first time since he'd entered the room. "*Yiasu*, Emily. How have you been?"

"Very well, thank you. The same can't be said of your father, but I guess that didn't much matter to you, seeing that you waited three days to visit him after his accident."

"Don't waste your breath appealing to his sense of decency," Pavlos advised her. "He doesn't have one."

Niko regarded him with weary disdain. "Unlike you in your prime, my career involves more than sitting behind a desk while my minions do all the work. I was away on assignment and didn't get back to Athens until this morning."

"Racing off on another mercy mission to save the world, were you?" Pavlos sneered.

"As to *thialo, yarro!*"

"You hear that, Emily?" Pavlos flung her an injured glare. "He told me to go to hell!"

Emily glanced from one to the other. At the father, his iron-gray hair still thick and his eyes piercingly alive, but his once-powerful body decaying, its bones so brittle it was a miracle they hadn't crumbled when he fell. At the son, a modern-day Adonis, tall, strong and indomitable. And both so proud, they'd have walked barefoot through fire rather than admit they cared about each other.

"I can't imagine why he bothered," she said witheringly. "The way I see it, he's already there, and so are you."

On that note, she left them. They might be determined to tear one another apart, but she'd be damned if she'd stay around to pick up the pieces.

Exiting through the French doors, she marched along the terrace and around the side of the villa to the lodge behind the garages. The widowed gardener, Theo, and his son, Mihalis, whom she'd met the day she arrived, lived there. Snoozing on the step outside the back door was their dog, Zephyr, a big friendly creature of indeterminate breed who, when she approached, wriggled over to make room for her to sit beside him and planted his head on her lap.

Niko found her there a few minutes later. "Is there space down there for me, too?"

"No," she said. "I prefer civilized company and you don't qualify."

"But the dog does?"

"Definitely. I'll take him over you any day of the week."

He shoved his hands in the back pockets of his jeans and regarded her moodily. "For what it's worth, Emily, I take no pleasure in constantly doing battle with my father."

"Then why don't you put an end to it?"

"What would you have me do? Stand by and let him use me as a verbal punching bag?"

"If that's what it takes…"

"Sorry, *karthula*, I'm not the subservient type. And I'm not here now to carry on with you where I left off with him."

"Why are you here, then?"

"To ask if you'll have dinner with me again."

"What for? So you can flaunt me in your father's face, the way you did the other day?"

Ignoring Zephyr's warning growl, he hunkered down on the few inches of sun-warmed step beside her. "Would you believe because I can't stay away from you, though heaven knows I wish I could?"

"Why? Because you blame me for your father's accident?"

"Don't be absurd," he said. "Of course I don't."

"Perhaps you should. I'm supposed to be nursing him back to health, not exposing him to further injury.

It's a miracle he didn't do more damage to himself when he fell."

"The point is, he didn't, and I knew it within hours of the accident."

"How is that possible if, as you claim, you arrived back in town only this morning?"

"This might come as a surprise, Emily, but I'm not completely heartless. I admit I'm away more often than I'm here, but I maintain regular contact with Georgios or Damaris, and know practically to the minute if a problem arises. Judging from their glowing reports, not only are you a dedicated and skilled professional who's taking excellent care of Pavlos, but you're earmarked for sainthood when you die—which, I hasten to add, I hope won't be anytime soon."

"If you care enough about him to phone them for an update on how he's doing, would it hurt you to tell him so?"

"Why would I bother when he makes it patently clear it's not something he wants to hear?"

"He might surprise you."

"You're the only one to surprise me, Emily, and I can't say I'm enjoying the experience. I've got enough on my mind, without that."

At his gloomy tone, she ventured a glance at him. Noticed the grim set of his mouth, the frown puckering his brow and felt an unwelcome stab of sympathy. "You ran into problems when you were away?"

"Nothing unusual about that," he said, shrugging. "My business is all about solving problems, as long as they're other people's. But I learned a long time ago that the only way to deal effectively with them is to draw a firm line between my work and my personal life, the latter of which I make a point of keeping complication free." He paused, sketched a groove in the dust with the toe of his shoe as if to illustrate his point and laced his fingers through hers. "But somehow, you've become just that, Emily. A complication. One I can't ignore."

"I don't see how."

"I know you don't. That's half the trouble."

"Try explaining it, then."

"I can't," he said morosely. "That's the other half."

She sighed, exasperated, and pulled her fingers free. "I'm not a big fan of riddles, Niko, and you don't appear exactly overjoyed to be involved with me, so let me put us both out of our misery. Thanks, but no thanks. I don't want to have dinner with you again."

Bathing her in a molten-green gaze, he inched closer. Slid his hand around her nape. "Liar," he murmured, the tip of his tongue dallying insolently with the outer curve of her ear.

The last time a man had tried that, she'd barely managed to suppress a revolted *Eeuw!* before she shoved him away. What was so different about Niko Leonidas, that his every touch, every glance, left her panting for more?

"Just because I refuse to let you play games with me doesn't make me a liar," she insisted weakly, almost paralyzed by the throb of tension unwinding inside her to affect body parts she was beginning to wish she didn't have.

"It doesn't make you any easier to resist, either."

"Then I guess we've reached an impasse."

For a long moment, he stared at her as if trying to fathom the solution to a dilemma only he could resolve.

Then with a shrug that plainly said, *Ah, to hell with it,* he rose to his feet with indolent grace. "I guess we have," he replied, and sauntered away.

"Good riddance!" she muttered, crushing the wave of disappointment threatening to engulf her. "Other women might trip over themselves in their eagerness to fall in with your every whim and wish, but I'm made of sterner stuff."

She repeated her little mantra several times during the rest of the afternoon, because it was all that stood between her and the urge to call him and say she'd changed her mind about spending the evening with him. To make quite sure she didn't weaken at the last minute, she went for a long walk on the beach, and ate dinner at a taverna. Upon her return to the villa, she played checkers with Pavlos for an hour, then pleading a headache, escaped to her suite.

Night had long since fallen, and closing the door behind her, she surveyed her sanctuary with a mixture of relief and pleasure. Damaris had turned back the bedcovers and made a fire against the chill of mid-October. Flames danced in the hearth and cast burnished-gold reflections over the polished antique furniture. The pleasant scent of burning olive wood filled the air.

Yes, she'd definitely made the right decision, Emily thought, tossing her sweater on the foot of the bed and kicking off her shoes. Although she couldn't deny the magnetic attraction between her and Niko, she couldn't ignore her feminine intuition, either. From the start, it had warned her that giving in to her attraction to him would invite nothing but trouble. If she didn't step back now, she'd find herself hopelessly, helplessly entangled with a man so far out of her league that she'd be guaranteed nothing but misery. After all, he'd made it graphically clear that his interest in her was purely sexual, and realistically, what else could she expect? He had no room in his life for a serious relationship, and even if he had, her future lay half a world away.

Warding off the unavoidable but depressing truth of the matter, she went into the bathroom and while the whirlpool tub filled, stripped off the rest of her clothes, pinned up her hair and lit a scented candle. Solitude was preferable to heartache any day of the week, she told herself bracingly, as she sank up to her chin in the hot water and let the air jets massage the day's tension into oblivion.

With the candle finally burned down to nothing, she dried herself with a towel from the heated rack, applied a generous dollop of body lotion to her water-wrinkled skin and pulled on a clean nightshirt. Then feeling limp as cooked spaghetti and so relaxed it was all she could do to stand upright, she tottered back to her bedroom.

Surprisingly the fire still burned brightly as if it had recently been replenished. And her shoes stood neatly aligned next to the armchair which, she noticed in appalled disbelief, was occupied. By Niko.

"I was beginning to think you'd drowned," he remarked conversationally.

Horribly aware that she wore nothing but a nightshirt whose hem came only midway down her thighs, she tried ineffectually to tug it lower. A huge mistake because, when she let it go, it sprang up with alarming vigor and revealed heaven only knew what of her anatomy. "Don't look!" she squeaked, shock rendering her incapable of a more quelling response.

"If you insist," he said, and very politely turned his head aside.

"How did you get in here?"

"Through the door, Emily. It seemed the most logical route to take."

If she had an ounce of backbone, she'd have matched his sarcasm and told him to leave the same way, but curiosity got the better of her. "Why?"

"I decided I owe you an explanation. Again!"

Wishing the sight of him didn't fill her with such desperate yearning that she was practically melting inside, she said, "You don't owe me anything, Niko. And you have no business being in my room."

"But I'm here regardless, and I'm staying until I've had my say."

"It seems to me we've been through this routine before and it got us precisely nowhere."

"Please, Emily."

She gave a long suffering sigh. "Then make it quick. I'm tired and I want to go to bed."

He slewed an audacious glance at her bare legs. "Could you put on something a little less revealing first? I'm only human, and staring at the fire doesn't quite cut it compared to looking at you."

Annoyed at the burst of pleasure his words aroused, she stomped back into the bathroom, grabbed the full length robe hanging on the door and dived into it.

"That's better," he said, vacating the armchair when she returned with only her hands, feet and head open to his inspection. "Why don't you sit here?"

"No, thanks," she informed him starchily. "I don't anticipate this taking very long."

He'd convinced himself this would be easy. All he had to do was reiterate his initial reservations, explain he'd put them to rest and no longer had ulterior motives for pursuing her. But the sight of her when she first came out of the bathroom had wiped his mind clean of anything but the raging desire to touch her all over. To lift that absurd scrap of a nightgown and bury his mouth at the cluster of soft, silver-blond curls she'd so briefly and tantalizingly revealed in her attempt at modesty.

"I'm waiting, Niko," she reminded him, sounding like his high school math teacher.

Would that she looked like her, too—moustache and all! "I want to start afresh with you," he said.

"I'm not sure I understand what that means."

He swallowed, grasping for the words that persisted in eluding him. "We got off on the wrong foot, Emily. You're my father's nurse, and I'm his son...."

"To the best of my knowledge, the status quo hasn't changed. I'm still his nurse. You're still his son."

How could he do it? How cut to the chase and say bluntly, *Despite pretending I no longer believed it, I remained convinced you were out to take him for all he's worth and decided my only choice was to seduce you, but have now decided I was wrong,* and expect her to understand? He wouldn't, if their situation were reversed.

"But something else *has* changed," he said instead.

"What?"

He took a deep breath and plunged in, laundering the

truth in a way that made him cringe inside. "Can we just say I'm tired of playing games and leave it at that? I'm not interested in using you to score points off my father, or for any other reason. I want to be close to you not because it'll annoy him to see us together, but because I like you for yourself. So I guess the only questions still to be answered are, do you want the same thing, or have I misread the signs and the attraction I thought existed between us is just a figment of my imagination?"

"It's not a figment of your imagination," she admitted, "but I don't understand why you'd pursue it when you said just this afternoon that I was a complication you didn't need."

"Overanalyzing is second nature to me. It's saved my skin more often than I care to count. But in this case, I took it too far."

She shifted from one foot to the other, clearly weighing his words. "Maybe not," she said judiciously. "Maybe you simply realized there was no future in a relationship with me."

"Never counting on the future is another by-product of my job. The only certainty is the here and now."

He took a step toward her, then another, until he was close enough to inhale the scent of her skin. She'd pinned up her hair, but tendrils had escaped to curl damply against her neck. The robe was at least two sizes too large and gaped at the front, drawing his gaze to the faint swell of her cleavage just visible above the top of her nightshirt.

The urge to kiss her, to hold her, nearly blinded him. "What do you say, Emily?" he asked hoarsely. "Will you take a chance on it with me?"

CHAPTER SIX

THE persistent voice of caution warned her not to fall for his line of reasoning. What was he offering her, after all, but the pleasure of the moment?

On the other hand, what had she gained in the past by pinning all her hopes on a better tomorrow? A degree in nursing, a crippling mortgage on her town house, a secondhand car and a short-lived, disappointing relationship with a medical student. Even her circle of friends had dwindled as more and more of them exchanged the single life for marriage and babies. Not that they completely abandoned her, but their interests no longer coincided as they once had. Her schedule revolved around shift work and case histories; theirs, around spouses and midnight feedings.

"Emily?" Niko's voice flowed over her, sliding inside the bathrobe supposedly shielding her from his potent appeal, to caress every hidden inch of skin, every minute pore.

Why was she holding out for a future that might never dawn, when the man who epitomized her every waking fantasy was offering her the chance to fulfill them? Giving in to her heart instead of her head, she lifted her gaze to meet his and whispered, "Why don't you stop talking and just kiss me?"

He groaned and reached for her. Cupped her face between his hands and swept his lips over her eyelids, her cheekbones, her jaw. And finally, when she was quivering all over with anticipation, he buried his mouth against hers. Not as he had before, with calculated finesse, but in scalding, desperate greed.

For the first time in her life, her natural caution deserted her, annihilated by a yearning so painful, she was filled with the consuming need to satisfy it at any price. Barely aware that she'd anchored her arms around his waist, she tilted her hips so that they nudged boldly against him exactly where he was most evidently aroused. His hard, unabashed virility inflamed her, scorching any remnant of doubt to ashes.

Somehow, her robe fell undone and he was touching her, his clever seeking fingers tracing a path from her collarbone and inside her sleeveless nightshirt to shape the curve of her breast. But she wanted more and tried to tell him so, angling herself so that her nipple surged against his palm, and pleading with him not to stop.

But stop he did. "Not here," he ground out, a sheen of sweat glistening on his brow. "Not in my father's house."

"But I can't leave," she whimpered. "What if he needs me and I'm not here?"

"Emily, *I* need you. I need you now."

Without a twinge of shame, she lifted the hem of her nightshirt and guided his hand between her legs. "You think I don't need you just as badly?"

Chest heaving, he molded his hand against her and pressed, flexing his fingers just so. The ensuing jolt of sensation ricocheted through her body and almost brought her to her knees. Gasping, she sank against him.

Steering her backward, he lowered her to the bed and touched her again, teasing the pivotal nub of flesh at her core that marked the dividing line between cool reason and clamoring ecstasy. And when she tipped over the edge in explosive release, he smothered her high-pitched cry with his mouth and stroked her until the spasms racking her body faded to an echo.

How many languid minutes ticked by before he pushed himself upright and, in a belated attempt to restore her modesty, covered her limbs with the bathrobe? Not nearly enough, and she clung to him. "Stay," she begged.

He shook his head. "I can't."

"Don't you want me, Niko?"

"So badly I can taste it. But not with my father's shadow hanging over us."

"Then how…when…?"

"Tell him you're taking the weekend off. We'll go away to someplace where we can be completely alone."

"What if he won't agree?"

"He doesn't own you, *karthula*," he said. Then, searching her face, asked, "Or does he?"

"Of course not, but he *is* my patient and he *is* paying me to look after him. And whether or not you accept it, he isn't as far along the road to recovery as he'd have you believe. To expect Georgios to assume respon-sibility for him would be unprofessional and negligent on my part."

"All it takes to solve that problem is a phone call to a private nursing agency for someone to replace you.

We're talking three days at the most. He can manage without you for that short a time."

"I suppose," she acknowledged dubiously, not because she wasn't sure she wanted to spend the weekend with him, but because she knew she'd have to fight Pavlos to get it.

A muscle twitched in Niko's jaw. "You know, Emily, if I'm asking too much—"

"You're not!"

"Are you sure?"

"Yes." She pressed her lips together and nodded. For pity's sake, when had she turned into such a wimp? She'd been in Greece over three weeks and more or less at Pavlos's beck and call the entire time. It wasn't unreasonable for her to ask for a break. "I'll work something out, I promise."

He brushed a last kiss over her mouth. "Let me know when it's arranged."

In the hectic two days that followed, she alternated between euphoria and bouts of horror at how shamelessly she'd offered herself to Niko. How would she ever face him again? But her yearning outweighed her chagrin and overriding Pavlos's objections, she booked the weekend off.

"A bikini and lots of sunscreen," Niko said, when she called to tell him she'd be ready to leave on Friday evening at six and asked what she should pack.

"What else?"

She could almost hear his shrug. "Something warm for the evenings, maybe, although the weather's supposed to be good. Shorts, a couple of tops. Not enough to fill a suitcase, by any means. Just throw a few things in a carryall."

"In other words, travel light and keep it casual."

"That about covers it, yes."

Much he knew, she thought, scurrying out to shop late Thursday afternoon while Pavlos napped. The clothes she'd brought with her to Greece were, for the most part, serviceable and basic. She hadn't come on vacation, she'd come to work, and in her profession that meant easily laundered cotton slacks and tunic tops, and comfortable, soft-soled shoes. She certainly didn't have anything designed for a romantic weekend with the sexiest man on the planet.

After dinner that night, she laid out her purchases, setting aside the dark red velour jogging suit and white socks and runners for traveling, but stuffing racy new lingerie, sheer nightgown, sandals and silk caftan, as well as shampoo, toothbrush, cosmetics and all the other items he'd specified, into a canvas tote designed to hold far less. He had said they'd be completely alone, but clearly didn't understand that it wasn't looking the part for strangers that she cared about, it was looking her best for him.

Although Pavlos had allowed a nurse from an agency to fill in for her while she was gone, he'd made it plain he was doing so under duress. To drive home the point, he sulked all Friday morning and ignored Emily all afternoon.

The one thing he hadn't done was inquire where she was going, or with whom, although from his dire mutterings, he'd obviously concluded it somehow involved Niko. So with her replacement up to speed on her duties, and rather than starting the weekend on a sour note with a confrontation, Emily collected her bag and slipped out

of the villa a few minutes before six, to wait for Niko
at the foot of the driveway.

Right on time, he drew up in the BMW. "You made
it," he greeted her, slinging his arm around her shoulders in a brief hug.

"Did you think I wouldn't?"

"Let's just say I wouldn't have been surprised if my
father had thrown himself on the floor and started
foaming at the mouth when you tried to leave. And the
fact that you're lurking here, hidden from view by anyone
in the villa, tells me you pretty much feared the same."

"If I admit you're right, can we agree that the
subject of your father is off-limits for the duration of
the weekend?"

"Gladly." He tossed her bag in the trunk and held
open the passenger door. "Hop in, Emily. I want to get
underway while we still have some daylight left."

"Underway," she discovered was not aboard an
aircraft as she'd half expected, but a fifty-two-foot sloop
moored at a private yacht club in Glyfada, a twenty-five
minute drive north of Vouliagmeni. Sleek and elegant,
with a dark blue hull and the name *Alcyone* painted in
gold across her transom, she was, Niko told Emily,
built for speed. But without any wind to fill her sails
and sunset no more than a crimson memory on the
horizon, he was forced to steer her under diesel power
to the tiny island of Fleves, just off the east coast of the
Attic peninsula.

It was a short trip only, but what made it magical for
Emily was the rising moon, which laid down a path of
silver to mark their passage, and the luminescence
sparkling in their wake like a handful of tiny diamonds.

Niko, in blue jeans and a lightweight cream sweater wasn't too hard to take, either.

After they'd dropped anchor, he set a lantern over the companionway in the center cockpit, told her to stay put and disappeared below, returning a few minutes later with a bottle of chilled white wine, crystal glasses and a small tray of appetizers. "I'd toast you in champagne," he said, taking a seat across from her and pouring the wine, "but it doesn't travel well in a sailboat."

"I don't need champagne," she assured him. "I'm happy just to be here with you."

He tipped the rim of his glass against hers. "Then here's to us, *karthula*."

The wine dancing over her tongue, crisp and cold, lent her courage. "You've called me that before. What does it mean?"

"Sweetheart." He raised one dark brow questioningly. "Do you mind?"

"No," she said, and shivered with pleasure inside her cozy velour jogging suit.

Noticing, he gestured below deck. "Dinner's in the oven and should be ready soon, but we can sit in the cabin where it's warmer, if you like."

"I'd rather not," she said, shying away from the closed intimacy it presented. Now that the rush and excitement of getting away was over and it was at last just the two of them, she was gripped with an almost paralyzing shyness. "It's so peaceful and quiet on deck."

"But you're on edge. Why is that, Emily? Are you wishing you hadn't agreed to spend the weekend with me?"

"Not exactly. I'm just a little…uncomfortable."

He scrutinized her in silence a moment, tracking the conflicting emotions flitting over her face. At last, he said, "About us being here now, or about the other night?"

She blushed so fiercely, it was a miracle her hair didn't catch fire. "Do we have to talk about the other night?"

"Apparently we do," he said.

She fiddled with her glass, twirling it so that the lantern light glimmered over its surface. From the safety of distance, she'd been able to put her conduct on Wednesday down to a temporary madness *he'd* inspired. But now, with no means of escaping his probing gaze, how she'd responded to him left her feeling only shame-fully wanton and pitifully desperate.

What had possessed her to behave so completely out of character? Professionally she was ICU Nurse Tyler, capable, skilled and always in control. Socially, she was good friend Emily, affable, dependable—but again, always in control.

She did not rush headlong into affairs, she did not beg a man to make love to her and she most certainly did not brazenly invite him to explore her private parts. That she had done all three with Niko made her cringe. Yet, here she was, because embarrassed or not, she couldn't stay away from him. And that meant facing up to what had transpired between them.

"You must know how very difficult it was for me to leave you as I did," he said softly, divining so exactly the source of her discomfort that she wondered if she'd actually voiced her thoughts aloud. "I won't pretend I'm not eager to pick up where we left off, but only if you feel the same. We take this at your pace, Emily, or not at all."

She glanced around, at the velvet moonlit night; at the dark hulk of the island rising to her left. She listened to the silence, broken only by the gentle wash of the sea against the boat's hull. Finally she dared to look at the man staring at her so intently. "It's what I want, too," she admitted. "I'm just a little out of my element. This is all very new to me, Niko."

His posture changed from indolent relaxation to sudden vigilance. "Are you trying to tell me you're a virgin?"

She choked on her wine. "No."

"No, that's not what you're trying to tell me, or no, you're not a virgin?"

"That's not what I'm trying to tell you. I was referring to the setting—the boat, the glamour, the exotic location. As for whether or not I'm a virgin, does it really matter?"

"Yes, it does," he said soberly. "Not because I'll judge you one way or the other, but because if I'm your first lover, I want to know beforehand." He leaned across and touched her hand. "So?"

Another blush raced up her neck to stain her face, though she hoped it didn't show in the dim light. "I'm not."

Picking up on her discomfiture anyway, he burst out laughing. "Don't look so mortified," he said. "I'm not, either."

"But it was only once, and not exactly…a howling success. Contrary to the impression I might have given you the other night, I'm not very good at…well…*this*."

"I see," he said, making a visible effort to keep a straight face. "Well, now that you've got that off your chest, what do you say we have dinner and let the rest of the evening take care of itself?"

"I'd like to freshen up first." In reality, she'd like to put her head down the toilet and flush, or better yet, jump over the side of the boat and never resurface.

"Sure," he said easily. "I'll be a couple of minutes getting everything ready, so take your time. Our stuff's in the aft cabin, which has its own bathroom."

It had its own built-in king-size bed, too. Dressed in navy-blue linens, with a wide ledge and window at the head, and brass wall lamps on either side, it set the stage for seduction and sent a tremor of terrified anticipation fluttering in Emily's stomach.

Would she disappoint him? she wondered, unpacking her clothes and laying out her toiletries on the vanity in the bathroom. Make an even bigger fool of herself this time than she had before? Was she being too reckless, too naive, in straying so far out of her usual comfort zone? Or had she finally found the one man in the world who made all the risks of falling in love worthwhile?

Soft lights and music greeted her when she returned to the main cabin. The air was fragrant with the scent of oregano and rosemary. Navy-blue place mats and napkins, crystal, brushed stainless steel cutlery and white bone china graced the table. In the galley, on the counter above the refrigerator, were a basket of bread and a bowl containing olives, and chunks of tomato, cucumber and feta cheese drizzled with olive oil.

Long legs braced against the barely perceptible rise and fall of the boat, Niko stood beside the oven, arranging skewers of roasted lamb, eggplant and peppers over rice. "Not exactly a gourmet spread," he remarked, carrying the platter to the table. "Just plain, simple picnic fare."

"I'd hardly call it plain or simple," she said, thinking of the plastic forks and paper plates, which marked the picnics she usually attended. "How do you keep your dishes and glassware from breaking when you're under sail?"

"I had the boat custom built with cabinetry designed to keep everything safely in place. I'll show you later, if you're interested."

"Interested? Intrigued is more like it. At the risk of repeating myself, you're not at all the playboy I took you to be when I first met you."

Green eyes filled with amusement, he said, "You're an expert on playboys, are you?"

"No, but I'm willing to bet they don't put their lives on the line to help people in distress, and they don't cook."

"Don't let the meal fool you. I had it prepared at a local taverna. All I had to do was heat up the main course, which pretty much sums up my talents in the kitchen."

He brought the bread and salad to the table, poured more wine and clinked his glass against hers. "Here's to us again, *karthula*. Dig in before everything gets cold."

The food was delicious; conversation easy and uncomplicated as they discovered more about each other. They both enjoyed reading and agreed they could live without television as long as they had a supply of good books at hand, although he preferred nonfiction whereas she devoured novels. And neither could live without a daily newspaper.

Niko was an avid scuba diver and had explored a

number of wrecks off the Egyptian coast. The best Emily could manage was snorkeling in a protected lagoon and admitted to being nervous if she was too far away from the shore.

He'd seen parts of the world tourists never visited. She stayed on the safe and beaten track: other parts of Canada, Hawaii, the British Virgin Islands.

When they'd finished eating, she helped him clear the table. Dried the dishes he washed. Stacked the wineglasses in the cunning little rack designed to hold them. And loved the domesticity of it all. A man, a woman, a nest...

As ten o'clock inched toward eleven, he suggested they finish their wine on deck. The moon rode high by then, splashing the boat with cool light, but he took a blanket from a locker and wrapped them both in its fleecy warmth.

"I dream about places like this when I'm away," he said, pulling her into the curve of his arm. "It's what keeps me sane."

"What is it about your work that made you choose it? The thrill, the danger?"

"In part, yes. I'd never find satisfaction playing the corporate mogul sitting behind a mile-wide desk and counting my millions, despite my father's trying to buy my allegiance with more money than I could spend in a century of profligate living. To him, money's the ultimate weapon for bringing a man to heel, and it infuriated him that, in leaving me my own fortune, my mother stripped him of that power over me. It's the one thing she did that he resented."

"But there's another reason you decided on such an unconventional career?"

He shifted slightly, as if he suddenly found the luxuriously padded seat in the cockpit uncomfortable. "This isn't something I'd tell to just anyone, but yes, there's another reason. Using her money to help people in need eases my conscience at having killed her."

Aghast to think he'd carried such a heavy burden of guilt all his life, Emily burst out, "I know I've said this before, but her death was an unforeseen tragedy, Niko, and you're too intelligent a man to go on blaming yourself for something that wasn't your fault. That Pavlos let you grow up believing otherwise—"

"I thought we'd agreed not to talk about my father."

"We did, but you're the one who mentioned him first."

"Well, now I want to forget him, so let's talk about your parents instead, and satisfy my curiosity on a point that's puzzled me ever since you first mentioned it. You said they were killed in a car accident, so how is it that you were left with virtually no financial security? Usually in such cases, there's a substantial settlement, especially when a minor is left orphaned."

If she'd pressured him into confronting his own demons, his question very neatly forced her to address her own. "There was no settlement from the accident," she said. "At least, not in my favor."

"Why the devil not?"

She closed her eyes, as if that might make the facts more palatable. It didn't. It never had. "My father was at fault. He was speeding and he was drunk. Sadly he and my mother weren't the only victims. Four other people died as a result of his actions, and two more were left with crippling injuries. Because of the ensuing lawsuits, I was left with nothing but my mother's personal effects and a small insurance policy she'd taken out when I was born. And you already know how that was spent."

"They had nothing else of value? No stock portfolio or real estate?"

She shook her head. "We never owned a house, or even an apartment. Home was a top floor suite in a posh residential hotel overlooking English Bay in Vancouver. A place where they could entertain their socialite friends and host glamorous parties."

Niko muttered under his breath and she didn't have to understand Greek to know he swore. "So they could afford that, but never thought to provide for their only child's future?"

"They lived for the moment. Every day was an adventure, and money was meant to be spent. And why not? My father was hugely successful in the stock market."

"A pity he wasn't as committed to setting some aside for his daughter's future as he was to spending it on himself."

"He and my mother adored me," she flared. "They made me feel treasured and wanted. I led a charmed life, filled with warmth and laughter and love. You can't put a price on that."

"They were spoiled children playing at being adults," he countered harshly. "Even if they'd left you a fortune, it could never make up for what their fecklessness ended up costing you."

"Stop it!" she cried, not sure what angered her more: that he dared to criticize her family, or that he was right. "Just shut up!"

Throwing off the blanket, she climbed onto the side

deck and went to stand at the bow of the boat. It was the most distance she could put between them.

He came up behind her. Put his arms around her. "Hey," he said. "Listen to me."

"No. You've said enough."

"Not quite. Not until I tell you I'm sorry."

"What is it about 'shut up' that you don't understand? I'm not interested in your apology."

"And I'm not very good at taking orders. Also, I'm the last person qualified to comment on flawed relationships." He nuzzled the side of her neck, his jaw scraping lightly, erotically against her skin. "Forgive me?"

She wanted to refuse. To end things with him while she still could, and save herself more heartache down the road. Because that annoying voice of caution was whispering in her head again, warning her that this was just another in a long list of differences. They disagreed on too many critical issues ever to remain in harmony for very long. He didn't care about family. Didn't believe in love. Wasn't interested in marriage or commitment.

But the starch of her resistance was softening, leaving her body pliant to his touch, her heart susceptible to his seduction. A lot of men said the same things he had—until the right woman came along and changed their minds. Why couldn't she be the one to change his?

"Emily? Please say something. I know I've made you angry, hurt you, but please don't shut me out."

"Yes, I'm angry," she admitted miserably, "because you had no right trying to strip me of my illusions. And I'm hurt, because you succeeded." She spun around, dazzled by tears. "I've spent the last eighteen years wilfully ignoring the truth about the parents I so badly wanted to preserve as perfect in my memory. Thanks to you, I won't be able to do that anymore."

He swore again, so softly it turned into an endearment, and buried her face at his shoulder. She started to cry in earnest then, for lost dreams and fate's cruel indifference to human pain.

"Let me make it better, angel," Niko murmured, stringing kisses over her hair. "Let me love you as you deserve to be loved."

And because she wanted him more than she wanted to stay safe, she lifted her tearstained face to his and surrendered. "Yes," she said.

CHAPTER SEVEN

THE lover's grand romantic gesture—sweeping her into his arms and carrying her to bed—didn't work on a sailboat. Slender though she was, the companionway just wasn't big enough for them both at the same time. The best he could do was precede her into the main cabin and guide her as she backed down the four steps leading below deck.

Not exactly a hardship, he decided, steadying her with a hand on either side of her hips as she descended. She wasn't very tall, a little over one and a half meters, and weighed no more than about forty-six kilos, but as her slim, elegant legs crossed his line of vision, the prospect of laying them bare to his renewed inspection left him hard and aching.

Unfortunately, by the time he'd led her into the aft sleeping quarters, her eyes were enormous in her pale face, she was trembling and hyperventilating. Some men might have interpreted that as an eagerness that matched their own, but he'd seen too many refugees huddled in war zones with bombs exploding around them, to be so easily taken in.

Virgin or not, and for all that she'd seemed willing

enough when he'd asked her to let him make love to her, now that the moment lay at hand, she was afraid. And in his book, that meant ignoring the raging demands of his libido, because the day had yet to dawn that he satisfied his own needs at the expense of a woman's.

Instead he flicked on the wall lamps, and slipped a CD into the built-in sound system. With the soothing sound of a Chopin nocturne filling the silence, he drew her down to sit beside him on the edge of the bed and wiped away the remains of her tears. "You are so incredibly beautiful," he told her.

She managed a shaky laugh. "I doubt it. I never learned to cry daintily. But thank you for saying so. Most men hate it when a woman resorts to tears."

"I'm not most men," he said, running his fingers idly through her hair. It reminded him of cool satin. So did her skin when, grazing his knuckles along her jaw to her throat, he extended his slow exploration. "And you very definitely are not most women."

He touched her mouth next, teasing her lips with his thumb. Not until they parted of their own volition did he lean forward and kiss them softly.

Her eyes fell shut as if the weight of her lashes was too much to bear. She sighed. And when she did, all her pent-up tension escaped, leaving her flexible as a willow against him.

Still he did not try to rush her, but cupped his hand around her nape and touched his mouth to hers again. She tasted of wine and innocence, and only when the subtle flavor of desire entered the mix did he deepen the kiss.

Gradually she grew bolder. Her hands crept under his sweater and up his bare chest, deft and sure. She murmured, little inarticulate pleadings that said the fear was gone and she was ready. More than ready. Her hunger matched his.

Suppressing the urgency threatening his control, he undressed her at leisure, discarding her shoes and socks first, then her jogging suit. A practical outfit and attractive enough in its way, it did not merit lingering attention. But underneath, she wore peach-colored lace; a bra so delicate and fine, her nipples glowed pink through the fabric, and panties so minuscule they defied gravity.

Clinging provocatively to her body, they were so blatantly designed to stir a man to passion that he had to turn away from the sight before he embarrassed himself. Had to rip down the zippered fly of his jeans or suffer permanent injury from their confinement. Kicking them off, he yanked his sweater over his head, flung it across the cabin, and sent his briefs sailing after it.

Misunderstanding his abrupt change of pace, she stroked a tentative hand down his back and whispered, "Are you angry? Did I do something wrong?"

"You're the nurse here," he ground out roughly, spinning around so that there was no way she could miss the state he was in. "Does it look to you as if you did something wrong?"

She blinked. And blushed.

If he hadn't been such a seething mass of sexual hunger that the functioning part of his brain was concerned only with how soon he could satisfy it, he'd have told her how her shy modesty charmed him. But his stamina was nearing its limits and wanting his dwindling endurance to be focused on bringing her pleasure, he drew back the bedcovers and pulled her down to lie next to him.

Willing his obdurate flesh to patience, he undid the clasp of her bra. Slid the outrageous panties down her legs. And when at last she lay naked before him, feasted his eyes on her. Dazzled by her blond perfection, her delicate symmetry of form, and perhaps most of all by the sultry heat in her eyes, he shaped her every curve and hollow with his hands, and followed them with his mouth.

She undulated on the mattress, offering herself to him without reserve. Clutching his shoulders in swift bursts of tactile delight when he found her most sensitive spots. Arching, taut as a high-tension wire, as he brought her to the brink of orgasm. And collapsing in a puddle of heat as she surrendered to it.

That she was so responsive to his seduction gratified him, but it inflamed him, as well. He wasn't made of stone, and knew he couldn't go on indefinitely denying himself the same pleasure he afforded her.

She knew it, too, and reaching down, she closed her hand around him. With another of her engaging little sighs, she traced her fingers over his erection, glorying in its strength, cherishing its vulnerability. Did so with such reverence that she somehow managed to touch him elsewhere, in places he kept separate from other people. In his heart, in his soul.

The emotional onslaught, as singular as it was powerful, blinded him to the encroaching danger. Responsibility, finesse, all the vital prerequisites by which he defined his sexual liaisons, deserted him. He was consumed with the overwhelming need to possess and be possessed. Seeming to sense the latter, she angled her body closer and cradled him snugly between her smooth, beautiful thighs.

Her daring lured him past all caution. The blood pulsed through his loins. He could feel her damp warmth beckoning him, knew of his own near-capitulation, and with only nanoseconds to spare, he dragged himself back from the brink of insanity and sheathed himself in a condom. Then and only then did he bury himself fully within her.

Tilting her hips, she rose up to meet him, caught in his relentless rhythm, absorbing his every urgent thrust. She was sleek, hot, tight. Irresistible. She took his body hostage. Held him fast within her and rendered him mindless to everything but the rampant, inexorable surge of passion rising to a climax that threatened to destroy him.

It caught her in its fury, too. He felt her contract around him. Was dimly conscious of her muffled cries, her nails raking down his back, and then the tide crashed over him. Stripped him of power and tumbled him into helpless submission. With a groan dragged up from the depths of his soul, he flooded free.

Spent, but aware he must be crushing her with his weight, he fought to regain his breath, to regulate his racing heart. Finally, with a mighty effort, he rolled onto his side and took her with him. Glancing down, he found her watching him, her eyes soft, her lovely face flushed. A world removed from the trembling creature she'd been half an hour before.

Curious as to the reason, he said, "You were nervous when I first brought you down here, weren't you?"

"I still am."

It wasn't the answer he expected, but remembering her comment about her previous experience, he thought he knew what prompted it. "If you're thinking you disappointed me as a partner, *karthula*, be assured I could not ask for better."

"It's not that at all," she said. "Before we made love, I was afraid I'd end up liking you too much. Now I'm afraid because I know I was right."

Her admission splintered his heart a little, as if she'd driven a needle into it and caused a tiny wound. He was not accustomed to such quiet honesty from his partners. "Is that such a bad thing?" he asked her.

"Not necessarily bad. I knew making love with you meant taking a risk. I just didn't realize how big a risk."

Then don't think of it as making love, he wanted to tell her. Be like the other women I take to bed, and see it as enjoyable sex. But she was so aglow that he couldn't bring himself to disillusion her. Which, in itself, gave rise to another troubling stab to his hitherto impregnable heart. She brought out a protective tenderness in him that he found as frightening as it was unacceptable.

Reading his thoughts with daunting insight, she said, "Don't worry, Niko. I'm not so naive that I think this weekend is the prelude to a long-term relationship. I'm not expecting it to end with a proposal of marriage or a ring."

Why not?

The question so nearly escaped him that he had to bite his tongue to contain it. "I'm in no position to offer either, even if I wanted to," he said, when he recovered himself. "My career doesn't lend itself to that sort of commitment, and I doubt there are many women who'd put up with a husband who's away more often than he's at home."

"Exactly. Realistically, neither of us is in the market

for anything but a casual fling. I'm just not very good at 'casual.'"

"There's nothing wrong with liking the person you're in bed with, Emily, and if I haven't already made it clear, let me say now that I like you very much. I wouldn't have asked you to come away with me if I didn't."

Her smile turned into a thinly disguised yawn. "That's good," she said. "I'll sleep much better knowing that, but I need to brush my teeth first."

"Of course. I'll use the head—bathroom in nautical terms, in case you're wondering—in the forward cabin."

She slithered off the bed and disappeared, a too-fleeting vision of slender, lamplit femininity that stirred him to fresh arousal. But he had his own rituals to attend to, not the least of which was making sure the anchor was well set for the night. Nothing like having a sailboat run aground to ruin the romantic ambience.

When he rejoined her in the bed some fifteen minutes later, she lay on her side facing away from him and was sound asleep. Just as well, really. She made it too easy for him to forget the rules he'd long ago set for himself. To those he rescued—the orphans, the widows, the elderly—he gave everything of himself because they didn't trespass into his personal life. Those he associated with the rest of the time he'd learned to keep at a safe distance.

Even though he wasn't touching her, he lay close enough that the heat of his body coiled around her. She knew that if she turned, if she made the slightest overture, he'd take her in his arms and they'd make love again. And she couldn't do it. She was too terrified of his power over her. Terrified that as the pleasure he gave her built to an unbearable peak, she might utter the three words guaranteed to put an end to what she had rightly termed a fling.

He might like her very much, but that was light years removed from his wanting to hear her say "I love you." Not that she did love him. In fact, she knew very well that she did not. *Could* not. Because anyone with half a brain knew that blissful, incredible sex didn't equal love.

Men have a one-track mind, she once overheard an embittered nursing colleague say. *They want a woman between the sheets, and they achieve it by making you feel as if they don't want to be anywhere else but with you—until the next day or the next week, when they move on to someone else, and you're left feeling slightly shopworn and incredibly stupid. The only way to gain the upper hand is either to fool them into thinking you don't care if you never see them again, or else swear off sex altogether.*

Apart from her one dismal experience with the third-year medical resident whose ego had surpassed anything else he had to offer, Emily had subscribed to the latter. She would not risk her self-respect or her reputation for the sake of a tawdry one-night stand. What was best, she'd decided in what she now recognized as pathetic naiveté on her part, was to settle for nothing less than complete commitment before leaping into intimacy with a man. But that prudent argument was before Niko Leonidas swept into her life, and swept out all her pre-conceived notions of what was best.

Sharing the same bed with him now, and so graphi-cally conscious of him that her skin vibrated with awareness, she forced herself to remain completely still as she waited for his breathing to settle into the deep, even rhythm that signaled sleep.

Seconds passed. Spun into long, painful minutes. Nothing broke the silence but the whisper of the sea and the equally subdued sound of his breathing. He was a very quiet sleeper, unlike his father who snored lustily when he nodded off.

Cautiously she shifted her foot; tucked her hand beneath her pillow. And waited for a sign that he was as wide-awake as she was. He did not stir. Convinced it was now safe to do so, she stopped pretending, opened her eyes and admitted to the moon-splashed night the awful truth.

She *was* in love with him. She had been for days. She'd committed the ultimate folly and laid on the line everything she had to give, in exchange for what she'd always known could never be more than a passing affair. And now she was paying the price.

The painful enormity of what she'd allowed to happen overwhelmed her. Tears seeped onto her pillow and silent sobs shook her body. All at once she was a child again, left with a heart full of love and no one to give it to. She wanted Niko to look at her as her father used to look at her mother, as if she was the most beautiful, fascinating creature ever to grace the earth. She wanted the magic and passion and permanence they'd known. She wanted it all, and she wanted it with Niko.

In short, she wanted what he couldn't give her.

"Emily?" His voice swam softly out of the gloom. "Are you asleep?"

"No," she muttered thickly, "but I thought you were."

She heard the rustle of the bed linen, felt his hand glide over her silky nightgown and come to rest at her hip. "Anything but," he said, his voice sinking to a husky growl. "I'm lying here thinking about you…and wanting you again."

He inched the hem of her gown up past her knees. Past her waist. His hand ventured, warm and possessive, between her thighs. "Emily?" he said again.

Any woman with an ounce of self-preservation to her name would have slapped his hand away, but not Emily Anne Tyler. No, she melted at his touch. Rolled onto her back, let her legs fall slackly apart and advertised the fact that she was more than willing to accommodate him. Well, why not, some distant part of her brain rationalized. At this point, she had nothing left to lose and might as well hoard as many precious memories as possible of this brief enchanted interlude.

He kissed the side of her neck. Murmured in her ear all the words men were supposed to murmur to a woman they planned to seduce. Words calculated to break down her resistance, to make her compliant to his every wish. Eventually he lowered himself on top of her and, pulling her legs up around his waist, eased himself smoothly inside her. As if, she thought, struggling to retain a grip on reality, God had designed them specifically for each other.

He loved her slowly this time, transporting her in leisurely increments of sensual delight until she could hold back no longer, then supporting himself on his forearms to watch her as she climaxed. When he came, she watched him, too. Saw the grim line of his mouth as he fought a battle he hadn't a hope of winning. Saw how, at the last moment, he closed his eyes and groaned as his body shuddered in helpless surrender. The unguarded honesty of it all made her cry again.

"What is it?" he asked, clearly appalled. "Did I hurt you? Tell me, *mana mou*."

"No," she said, because confessing the truth—that with every touch, every word, every glance, he made her love him all the more—wasn't an option. "Making love again was so beautiful, that's all."

A weak excuse, but thankfully he accepted it. Cradling her so that her head rested on his shoulder and his arm kept her close, he said, "It was magnificent. It will be the next time, too."

She was able to fall asleep on that promise, comforted by the steady beat of his heart beneath her hand and lulled by the gentle rise and fall of the sea beneath the boat.

They didn't wake up until almost nine o'clock. After a simple breakfast of yogurt and fruit, they took their coffee up on deck. Although summer's intense heat was long past, it was still a shorts-and-tank-top kind of day.

"By noon," he told Emily, pulling her into the curve of his arm, "you'll be lying on the foredeck, stripped down to your bikini."

"Mmm." She lifted her face to the sun. "Lolling in a bikini on a sailboat in October. Not too tough to take, I have to admit."

"Happy you decided to come away with me?"

"Who wouldn't be? It's lovely here."

Right answer, but it didn't quite ring true. Something was bothering her. "Are you sure?"

"Of course," she said, and promptly changed the

subject. "Will the water be too cold for swimming, do you think?"

"We can find out later, if you like, but it's a bit too early yet. Emily, is there something—?"

"Early! Heavens, Niko, it's after ten already. Do you always sleep in so late?"

"Only when I'm away on the boat. It's my one, sure outlet of escape from the everyday routine." He didn't add that the constant danger inherent in his work, the risks involved, took a toll. He left that part of his life behind the second he cast off from the yacht club and took to the sea.

"Burn-out, you mean? I know what that's like. It's one reason I agreed to come to Greece and nurse Pavlos back to health. I needed a change of scene."

"And the other reason?"

She chewed her lip thoughtfully. "I'd grown very fond of him during the time he was hospitalized. In a way, we'd become more like father and daughter than nurse and patient, and I didn't feel I could abandon him."

"More like grandfather and granddaughter, surely?"

"When you don't have any other family, you don't quibble about little things like that."

A month ago, he'd have taken that remark and found any number of hidden messages in it. Now, he took it at face value.

"Even after all these years, you still miss your parents, don't you?"

"Yes. Very much."

"And I made it worse with my comments last night," he muttered, cursing himself. "I tarnished your perfect memories of them."

"Not really, because nobody's perfect, not even my parents, for all that I tried so hard to idealize them. The truth is, I've sometimes thought it was as well they died young and together. They wouldn't have dealt well with old age or being alone. And I would never have filled the emptiness left behind if only one of them had been killed in the accident."

She captivated him with her honesty, which was pretty ironic considering his first impression of her had been that she wasn't to be trusted. "They might not have been perfect, Emily, but they came close to it when they made you. I'm sure they loved you very much."

"Oh, they loved me," she said, moving away from him and gazing mistily at the blue horizon, "but they never really needed me. If you must know, that's why I decided to become a nurse. I wanted to be needed. You don't, though, do you?"

Her question threw him. "Why else do you think I put my life on the line to help other people?"

"Because they're strangers who invade your professional life for just a little while. But your personal life…well, that's different. It's off-limits. A person only has to look at your relationship with your father, to see that."

She saw too much, and he wouldn't sink so low as to deny it. "Having him join the party isn't my idea of a good time, Emily."

She made a face. "My fault. I'm the one who mentioned him."

"Then I suggest we make a concerted effort to get rid of him. What do you say we take the dinghy ashore and go for a walk on the island?"

"I'd love to," she said with alacrity. "Let me get my camera."

Her relief was palpable. Because she didn't want his father hanging around, either, Niko wondered, or because she wanted to put distance between the two of them?

He shouldn't have cared, one way or the other. Annoyingly he did.

CHAPTER EIGHT

A GREAT suggestion, Emily concluded, watching as Niko tilted the outboard engine clear of the water and the bottom of the dinghy scraped onto the narrow strip of gravelly beach edging the island. Luxuriously comfortable though it might be, the yacht's big drawback was that it offered no means of escape when the conversation got out of hand. And it had, dangerously so, straying close to disastrous when she foolishly brought up the business of wanting to be needed. Another few minutes and her feelings for Niko, which she was so desperately trying to suppress, would have spilled out.

Hiding behind her camera gave her the chance to regroup. She took pictures of flowers enjoying a riotous last bloom before winter: wild geraniums and gaudy poppies; daisies and ice plant in shades of mauve and white. She snapped the yacht riding peacefully at anchor in the sheltered bay. And when he least expected it, she captured images of Niko; of his dazzling smile, his chiseled profile, his lashes lowered to half-mast as he squinted against the brightness of the sparkling sea.

The atmosphere on the island was different, she realized. Freer, less soberly intense. Here, she could breathe and not have to worry about keeping up her guard. If necessary, she could put distance between her and Niko. Contrarily, because she could, she felt no need to do so.

Sensing her change of mood, he matched it with a lighthearted teasing of his own. "If you didn't have a camera slung around your wrist, you'd be up to your neck in trouble," he growled with mock ferocity, grabbing her before she could escape after she'd caught him unaware at the water's edge and splashed him.

That kind of trouble she could handle. "I wish I could say I'm sorry, and mean it," she returned cheekily, and splashed him again.

Suddenly his laughter faded and twining her hands in his, he regarded her searchingly. "*I* wish I could take you away for a month, instead of a weekend," he said. "Being around you is good for me, Emily. You remind me that there's more to living than burying myself in work. I'm a happy man when I'm with you."

Her spirit soared at that. Could he possibly be falling for her, too?

Well, why not? Wasn't she forever telling her patients and their families that they should never give up hope? And hadn't she seen for herself, time and time again, that miracles did happen? Why couldn't one come her way for a change?

"Keep looking at me like that," he went on, his voice lowering to a thrilling purr, "and I won't be held liable for what I might do, which would be a mistake on two counts. This beach isn't designed for comfortable seduction, and even if it were, I didn't bring a contraceptive with me."

Flirting shamelessly, she glanced up at him in her

best imitation of a siren bent on luring him to destruction. "Then why don't we go back to the yacht?"

His eyes darkened, turned a deep forest-green. "Race you to the dinghy, angel."

Love in the afternoon was different, she discovered. Sunlight pouring through the window above the bed and casting dancing reflections of the sea on the cabin ceiling brought an openness to intimacy that, at first, dismayed her because it left her with no place to hide.

He soon put paid to that nonsense. He examined her all over, from the soles of her feet to the top of her head. He found the tiny scar on her bottom where she'd fallen on broken glass at the beach when she was little, and he kissed it as if it were new and still hurting.

He paid attention to every inch of her, sometimes with his hands, sometimes with his mouth and tongue, pausing every now and then to murmur, "Do you like it when I do this?"

Like? She'd never before felt such slow, rolling awareness of herself as a woman. He made her quiver with anticipation. He brought her body to electrifying life and made it yearn and ache and throb. He made her scream softly and beg for more.

Until him, she'd never climaxed. With him, she came so quickly and with such fury that she couldn't catch her breath.

His touch sent her flying so high, she could almost touch the heavens, and he knew it because he watched her the entire time. Knew to the second when she hovered on the brink, and tipped her over the edge into a glorious, sparkling free-fall she wished might never end.

Then, when she was dazed with exhausted pleasure and sure she didn't have the strength to lift a finger, let alone peak again, he buried himself in her hot, sleek folds and taught her otherwise. Caught in his urgent, driving rhythm, she swooped and soared with him again to a magnificent crashing finale.

At two in the afternoon or thereabouts, they put together a snack of fruit and cheese and ate it in the shade of the canvas bimini in the cockpit. They drank a little wine, and they talked, mostly about Niko as it turned out, which inevitably meant Pavlos crept back into the conversation, too.

"Was he cruel to you?" Emily asked, when Niko spoke briefly of his unhappy childhood.

"Not in the way you're thinking," he said. "Far from it. I never lacked for a thing. Clothes, toys, tutors, whatever I needed, he provided. When it came to my later education, there was no limit to how far he'd go to make sure I had the best. He sent me to the most prestigious boarding school in Europe—more than one in fact, since I managed to get myself kicked out of several."

"Then why the estrangement?"

"He didn't understand that there was more to being a father than spending money."

"Or else he didn't understand that you were crying out for his love."

"It was never about love with him. It was about power. And from his point of view, money and power are one and the same. Which is another bone of contention between us because to me, money's merely the means to an end. If I end up without any, I'll find a way to make more, but I'll never let it rule my life the way it rules his."

"Why do you think he sets such store by it?"

"Probably because he grew up without any. He was the by-product of an affair between a housemaid and the son of her millionaire employer who abandoned her when he learned she was pregnant. If you asked him what his most driving ambition had been when he was a boy, I guarantee he'd say it was to end up one of the wealthiest men in Greece, able to pick and choose his friends, his associates and, eventually, his wife."

"He appears to have succeeded."

Niko inclined his head in agreement. "Yes, but it took him years. He didn't marry my mother until he was thirty-one which, back then, was considered pretty old. She was just twenty, and the only daughter of one of his biggest business rivals."

"Is that why he married her—to score points over her father?"

"No," he said. "He really loved her. I have to give him credit for that much."

"What a shame he could never see you as her most lasting legacy to him."

"I was too much the rebel, refusing to toe the Leonidas line, determined to go my own way and to hell with anyone who tried to stop me."

He'd never been so open with her before. Was it the lazy afternoon heat or their lovemaking that made it easier for him to share his life story with her now? Whatever the reason, Emily was hungry to know everything about him and prepared to listen for as long as he was willing to talk. "Did he want you to go to university?"

"In the worst way, and was pretty convinced he could make it happen since I wouldn't have any money of my own until I turned twenty-one. He saw a business degree as the next logical step to my joining his empire. But I got out from under his control when I joined the air force, and there wasn't a damned thing he could do about it. After I left the service, I spent a year in England with a former UN pilot who taught me everything he knew about mercy missions, and introduced me to the finer points of the English language. After that, I came back to Greece, took over my inheritance and set up my own operation."

"And the rest, as they say, is history?"

He stood up and stretched. "*Ne*—and pretty dull at that, if you ask me, not to mention a criminal waste of a beautiful afternoon. What do you say to a swim?"

He was finished baring his soul and, for now at least, she realized she'd gain nothing by pressing for more. "Okay, if you're sure the water's warm enough."

"Only one way to find out, Emily," he said, dragging her to her feet. "You coming in of your own free will, or do I throw you in?"

"At least let me change into my bikini."

"What for?" He dropped his shorts and briefs, pulled off his T-shirt and climbed onto the swim grid in all his beautiful naked glory. "Nothing like going au naturel, as they say in polite society, especially as neither of us has anything to show that the other hasn't already seen."

"Once a rebel, always a rebel," she muttered self-consciously as she peeled off her clothes.

He favored her with a lascivious grin. "I hardly expected a nurse to be so modest, my dear. Even your bottom's blushing."

There was only one response to that remark and she

wasted no time delivering it. Bracing both hands against his chest, she shoved him into the water. He landed with a mighty splash and she followed suit before he had the chance to climb back on board and exact his revenge.

After the first chilling shock, the sea was deliciously refreshing. Heaven had never seemed so close, Emily decided, floating on her back with her hair streaming out behind her and the big blue bowl of the sky arcing overhead.

Niko, whom she'd last seen swimming in a powerful crawl toward the mouth of the bay, suddenly bobbed to the surface next to her. "You look like a mermaid," he said. "A particularly delectable mermaid."

And he looked like a sea god, she thought, her heart turning over at the sight of his broad, tanned shoulders, his brilliant smile and the thick lashes spiking in clumps around his remarkable green eyes. Small wonder she'd fallen in love with him. What woman in her right mind could resist him?

They climbed back on board and lay down on the foredeck to dry in the sun's benign warmth. He'd swum farther than he intended, a strenuous workout that left him pleasantly tired and happy just to lie next to her, his limbs touching hers, his fingers brushing lightly against her arm. Not moving, not speaking, just looking into her dark blue eyes and letting utter contentment sweep over him.

Was he falling in love?

He couldn't be. It was completely out of the question. A misguided romantic fantasy brought on by brain fatigue or some other disorder of the mind, because he absolutely refused to entertain the possibility that it might have something to do with his heart. Yet if it was so impossible, why did he suddenly hate the man who'd taken her virginity? She belonged to no one but him, and should have waited until he found her.

"What dark thoughts are chasing through your mind?" she murmured drowsily, peering at him from half-closed eyes.

The unpalatable truth rose in his throat, bitter as bile. Scowling, he said, "I have a confession to make. More than one, in fact."

"Oh?" A shadow flitted over her face. "Such as?"

"For a start, I'm jealous of my predecessor."

Clearly at a loss, she said, "What are you talking about?"

"I'm jealous of whoever it was that you slept with before you met me."

"I see." She pushed herself up on one elbow, propped her head on her hand and regarded him thoughtfully. "Should I be flattered?"

"I don't know. I've never found myself in this kind of situation before."

And that, he thought, was the whole problem in a nutshell.

Before he met her, sex had been all about mutual pleasure with no strings attached. He never lied to his willing partners, never made promises he couldn't keep, was never intentionally cruel. But sometimes he hurt them anyway because they wanted more than he could give.

Until now. Until Emily, when his initial plan had somehow gone terribly wrong and he found himself in danger of wanting to give much more than he could ever afford.

"That doesn't sit well with you, does it?" she said.

"No. I prefer to stick to the rules."

"What rules?"

"Those I've set for myself."

"And you're breaking them with me?"

"Yes," he said grimly, uncertain whether it was self-preservation or self-destruction that drove him to bare his soul so brutally. "When I first started seeing you, all I ever intended was to act as a decoy."

"A decoy?"

He heard the wariness in her voice edging closer to outright dismay, and wished he'd kept his mouth shut. But palming her off with half-truths left him feeling dirty and unworthy of her. And even if it didn't, he'd said too much to stop now. "Yes," he said. "To keep you away from my father. There being no fool like an old fool, I decided to step in and save him from himself—and you—by diverting your attention from an ailing old man to one who could better please you."

Dazed, she glanced away and focused her attention on the boat, appearing fascinated by its sleek lines, gleaming fiberglass deck and oiled teak. "So this weekend is all about proving a point?"

"No. That's the trouble. Now it's about you and me, and feelings I never bargained for. I tried to tell you this the other night, but I lost my nerve."

She wasn't listening. Instead she was scrambling to her feet and swinging her head wildly from side to side, a wounded creature desperate to escape her tormentor.

Springing to her side, he trapped her in his arms. She

lashed out at him, catching him a glancing blow on the jaw. "Let me go!" she spat. "Don't ever touch me again!"

"You're not hearing me, Emily," he told her urgently. "Everything's different now."

"Sure it is." She was sobbing. The sound drove splinters through his heart. "You've finally shown your true colors."

"No, Emily. I made a stupid mistake."

"So you decided to make it up to me by giving me a weekend to remember? How tedious you must have found it, pretending you wanted to have sex with me."

"I wasn't pretending! For God's sake, Emily, you of all people know a man can't pretend."

"So how did you manage? By closing your eyes and imagining I was someone else?"

He crushed her to him, shocked. "Never. It was always you. Only you, right from the start. I just didn't realize it at the time."

"And here I thought we'd put to rest that whole ludicrous notion that I was some sort of fortune hunter out to fleece your poor father." She wasn't crying now. She was encased in ice.

"We have," he protested. "You are what you've always been, as beautiful on the inside as you are on the surface."

"I don't feel beautiful," she said tonelessly. "I feel stupid and pathetic, because I let myself fall in love with you."

"Then I guess we're both stupid and pathetic, because that's what I'm trying to say. I'm falling in love with you, too, and the damnable thing is, I don't know what the hell to do about it."

"Then I'll tell you," she said. "You get over it. We both do."

* * *

The look on his face told her it wasn't the answer he wanted to hear. "Why should we?" he whispered against her mouth.

But the damage was done and nothing he said or did could put things right again. "Because there's no future in it for either of us." She pulled away just far enough to look him in the eye, then added pointedly, "Is there?"

"If you're asking me to predict what might happen tomorrow, I can't, Emily. All any of us ever has is today. Can't you let that be enough?"

Temporary bliss, in exchange for long-term misery? Not a chance! She was in enough pain already, and prolonging the inevitable would merely increase the agony. "No. I made up my mind long before I met you that relationships heading nowhere are a waste of time."

"I could change your mind, if you'd let me."

She was terribly afraid that he could, and knew she had to get away from him before he succeeded. He was kissing her eyes, her hair, her throat. Stroking his hands down her arms and up her bare back with killing tenderness. Sabotaging her with caresses when words failed to get him what he wanted, and already her resistance was dissolving under the attack.

"I don't want to be here with you anymore," she said, clinging to her vanishing resolve with the desperation of a drowning woman. "Take me back to the mainland."

"I will," he murmured. "Tomorrow."

"Tonight."

"*Ohi*...no." He lifted her off her feet and set her down in the cockpit. Traced his lips over her cheek and brought his mouth to hers and kissed her softly.

He made her legs shake, her insides quiver. He made her heart yearn. "Please," she whimpered helplessly.

"Give me one last night, my Emily."

"I can't."

He touched her fleetingly between the legs. "Tell me why not, when I know you want me as much as I want you."

She shuddered, caught in the clenching grip of rising passion. "Tell me why I'm inexplicably drawn to a man who isn't at all my kind of man," she countered.

"And what kind of man is that?"

"The kind who's not afraid of love. Who's happy with a nine-to-five job and a mortgage," she said, grasping at a truth she'd refused to acknowledge until now. "The safe kind who doesn't need to flirt with danger all the time in order to find fulfillment."

"Then you're right. I'm definitely not your kind of man."

But he pulled her closer, and the way her body tilted to meet his, welcoming the questing nudge of his erection, proclaimed otherwise. As if she'd finally found what she'd always been looking for. As if he was exactly her kind of man.

She was lost, and she knew it. The irrepressible pulse of his flesh against hers enthralled her. Lured her into forgetting how he had deceived and used her. Nothing mattered except to know again the pleasure only he could give. If, the next day or the next week, he reneged on his protestations of love, at least she'd have this weekend to remember him by.

The hunger, rapacious, insatiable, spiraled to unbearable heights. Casting aside all pretense at dignity, she sprawled on the cockpit cushions. At once, he was on top of her. Thrusting inside her, hot, heavy, demanding.

Perfectly attuned, they rose and sank together, pausing at just the right moment to drown in each other's gaze. There was no need for words to justify a decision that went against everything they'd just said to each other. They had come together because they could not stay apart. It was as simple as that.

CHAPTER NINE

WHEN they finally stirred and she mentioned that she'd like to freshen up, Niko ran a critical hand over his jaw, said he could use a shower and shave himself and told her not to rush. "We have all the time in the world," he said. "We'll have mezedes and wine and watch the moon rise, then eat dinner when the mood takes us."

So she indulged herself in a leisurely bath, and shampooed the saltwater out of her hair. After toweling herself dry, she massaged lotion into her sun-kissed skin, spritzed a little cologne at her elbows and behind her knees and put on the silk caftan, glad she'd had the good sense to smuggle it aboard. He'd said he was in love with her, but she sensed he'd made the admission reluctantly, and pinned little hope on his feeling the same way in the morning. If so, and if this turned out to be their last night together, she intended it to be one neither of them would soon forget.

Nor did they, but not for the reasons she'd supposed. The very second she joined him in the main cabin, she knew their plans had changed. He'd showered—his damp hair attested to that—but he hadn't shaved. There was no sign of the appetizers he'd mentioned, no tempting aromas drifting from the oven, no wine chilling. All that lay on the table was his cell phone, and one look at his face told her it had been the bearer of bad news. "Something's happened," she said, a sinking feeling in the pit of her stomach.

"Yes. I'm afraid we have to head back right away."

"Is it Pavlos?"

He shook his head. "I just got word from my director of operations that we've lost contact with one of our pilots in north Africa. He was scheduled to pick up an injured Red Cross worker from a refugee camp. He never showed up."

"What can you do about it?"

He stared at her as if she wasn't in command of all her faculties. "Go find him. What did you think—that I'd sit back and leave him stranded in the desert?"

"No, of course not." She swallowed, stung by his brusque tone. "Is there any way that I can help?"

"Change into something warmer, for a start. That thing you've got on won't do. Quite a stiff onshore breeze has sprung up. It'll be a chilly trip back to the mainland."

She must have looked as forlorn as she felt because when he spoke again, his voice softened. "I know you're disappointed, Emily. I am, too. This isn't how I'd fore-seen the evening playing out. But when situations like this come up, I'm afraid everything else has to go on hold. A man's life could be at stake."

"I understand," she said. And she did. Completely. But what about *his* life? How safe would he be, rushing off to the rescue without knowing the danger he might be facing? "Will it be risky, your going looking for him?"

"It's possible, but so what? Risks come with the job. You get used to it."

You, maybe, but not me, she thought, the harsh reality of his vocation hitting home with a vengeance for the first time and filling her with apprehension. "How will you know where to start looking for him?"

"If he's turned on his epurb—electronic positioning beacon, that is—it'll lead me straight to him. If not, I'm familiar with the area, I know where he was headed and his coordinates before he lost contact."

"What if you still don't find him?"

"That's not an option," he said flatly. "He's just a kid of twenty-three, the eldest of four children and the only son of a widow. It's my job to locate him and bring him home to his family. They need him."

"But what if—?"

He silenced her with a swift, hard kiss. "No 'what ifs.' It's not the first time I've had to do this, and it won't be the last. I'll be back before you know it—by tomorrow night at the latest, but we really need to get going now if I'm to be ready to set out at first light in the morning."

Set out to where? Some vast arid region miles from civilization? Some rebel stronghold where human life didn't count for a thing? "Then I'd better get organized," she said, and turned away before he saw the desolation in her eyes.

"At least my father will be glad to have you back earlier than expected."

"I suppose."

He came up behind her and wound his arms around

her waist. "Did I mention how lovely you look, Emily?" he said softly against her hair.

On the outside, maybe. But inside, she was falling apart.

The nurse who'd replaced her was so happy to be relieved of her job, she practically flew out of the villa before Emily stepped in. "Is impossible!" she screeched, indignation fracturing her English almost past recognition. "He die, then *me niazi*! I do not care. One day more, I break his neck. *Adio*. Please not call me again. *Apokliete!*"

"Have a nice night," Emily said wearily, as the front door slammed shut in her face.

Pavlos didn't even pretend to hide his glee when she appeared at breakfast the next morning. "Didn't take you long to come to your senses, did it, girl?" he crowed.

"Try to behave yourself for a change, Pavlos," she snapped. "I'm in no mood for your shenanigans."

He smirked into his coffee cup. "That bad, was it? Could have told you it would be."

"For your information, I had a wonderful time. The only reason I came back early is that your son has gone searching for a young pilot lost somewhere over the Sahara."

His derision faded into something approaching concern, but he covered it quickly. "Damned fool! Serve him right if he got himself killed."

"I'll pretend I didn't hear you say that."

"Why not?" he retorted. "Ignoring the facts isn't going to change them. Wherever the latest hotbed of unrest shows up, you can bet he'll be there, and one of these days he'll push his luck too far."

Ill-timed though it might be, the truth of his answer could not be denied, and how she got through the rest of the day she didn't know. The minutes dragged, the hours lasted a small eternity. Morning became afternoon, then evening and, all too soon, night. Every time the phone rang, her heart plummeted. And sank lower still when the call brought no news of Niko.

"Better get used to this if you plan on sticking with him," Pavlos advised her, as the dinner hour came and went without any word.

"The same way you have?" she shot back. "You talk a good line, Pavlos, but you're as worried about him as I am."

"Not me," he huffed, but there was no real conviction in his tone and his gaze wandered to the clock on the wall every bit as often as hers did. "Where did you say he'd gone?"

"North Africa—the desert—I'm not sure exactly."

"Hmm." He drummed his arthritic old fingers on the edge of the table. "That's a lot of ground for one man to cover."

She closed her eyes. Fear beat a tattoo in her blood.

"Go to bed, Emily," Pavlos said with uncommon gentleness. "I'll wait up and let you know if we hear anything."

As if she could sleep! "I'm not tired. You should rest, though."

But neither made any move. Anxiety thick as molasses held them paralyzed.

Just after eleven o'clock, the phone shrieked into the silence one last time. Hands shaking, she grabbed it on the first ring. "Niko?"

She heard his smile. "Who else were you expecting at this hour?"

"No one…you…but it grew so late and you hadn't called—"

"You're going to have to learn to believe what I tell you, Emily," he said. "I promised I'd be back today, and I am."

"Yes." Giddy with relief, she reached for Pavlos's hand and squeezed it. "Where are you now?"

"At the office. I'll be heading home as soon as I've filed my report."

"And the man you went to find?"

"Had a fire in his control panel that knocked out his communications system. He made an emergency landing on a deserted Second World War airstrip. There are dozens of them, hundreds even, all over the Sahara. The one he chose lay nearly two hundred kilometers from where he was supposed to be, but his epurb was still working and led me straight to him."

"And he's okay?"

"He's fine, though I wish I could say the same for the aircraft. But the good news is, we picked up the man he was supposed to bring back and got him to a hospital, albeit twenty-four hours later than expected."

"You've put in a long day and must be exhausted."

"Nothing an early night won't fix. I'll see you tomorrow?"

"I can't wait," she said. "I missed you."

"Same here, *karthula*." His yawn echoed down the line. "I'd come over now, but—"

"Don't even think about it. Go home and catch up on your sleep."

"Will do. *Kali nikhta*, my sweet Emily."

"Kali nikhta," she replied. "Good night."

* * *

In the days following, she should have been completely happy. Although he vetoed any suggestion that he should terminate her employment, Pavlos was on the road to recovery and didn't need her as he once had. Accepting that she and his son were an item, he compromised by letting her take the weekends off.

She lived for the sheer heaven of those two days and nights. Niko's spacious penthouse in Kolonaki was their retreat. The living and dining rooms and en suite guest room opened onto a terrace. A small library and starkly modern kitchen comprised the rest of the main floor, with a gorgeous master suite upstairs. The decor was as spare and elegant as he himself, lacking any of the usual personal touches like photographs, but the huge collection of books and CDs told her much about his tastes and hinted at a man content with his own company.

He did his best to please her during their time together; to make it seem they were like any other couple in love. Working around his erratic schedule, they explored the countryside, going by scooter if the weather allowed but, with the cooler temperatures of November, more often by car.

They hiked in the pine-covered hills behind the town, took a picnic hamper and sailed down the coast of the Attic peninsula. Sometimes, they drove to out-of-the-way villages where they sampled wonderful local dishes in quaint, unpretentious tavernas whose walls were lined with wine barrels. Other times, they went into Athens and dined in fine style on the best the city had to offer. They danced cheek to cheek in the Grande Bretagne Hotel; made passionate love in his king-size bed.

If he had to break a date—and he did, often—he sent

her flowers, or texted messages to her in the night so that she found them on waking. In return, she tried to keep her anxiety under control when he was away, but never knew a moment's real peace until he returned. She couldn't sleep and walked the floor half the night. She couldn't eat because anxiety robbed her of her appetite. Noticing, Pavlos never missed the chance to tell her she was making the biggest mistake of her life.

She learned to live with all of it because the alternative—to put an end to it—was unthinkable.

Once, when Niko discovered he'd left his cell phone on his desk at work and had to go back to get it, he took her with him and showed her around the private airfield that served as his base of operations. The flat-roofed office building had only four rooms but was equipped with the latest in electronic equipment. Probably the aircraft sitting on the tarmac were, too, but when Emily first saw them, what struck her most forcibly was how flimsy they seemed.

"Are they what you use to fly overseas?" she asked, trying to mask her dismay.

Discerning it anyway, Niko laughed and said, "Were you expecting hot air balloons, my darling?"

"No, but these things are so small and…old-fashioned."

"Old-fashioned?" He regarded her in mock horror over the top of his aviator sunglasses.

"Well, yes. They've each got two sets of those spider-leg propellor things stuck on the front."

"I know," he said dryly. "They're what get them off the ground and keep them in the air."

"But why wouldn't you use jets? Surely they're faster?"

"Faster, but not nearly as versatile or fuel-efficient.

Twin-engine piston aircraft like these don't require nearly as long a runway as a jet, can land just about anywhere and fly at a much lower altitude." He eyed her mischievously. "Would you like me to take you up in one and show you what it can do?"

"No, thanks," she said hurriedly. "I'll take your word for it."

As they were leaving, they ran into Dinos Melettis, Niko's second-in-command. "Bring her to dinner," he insisted, after the introductions were made. "Come today. We have nothing on the board until later in the week, which makes it a good night to relax with friends, and Toula would love to meet the lady in your life. Toula," he added to Emily in an aside, "is my wife."

They accepted the invitation and had a delightful evening. "Never before has Niko brought a ladyfriend to our home," Toula confided to Emily in her careful English. "He is very enamored of you, I think."

The way he pressed his knee against hers under cover of the table and muttered between courses that he couldn't wait to get her alone again, Emily thought so, too. Yet for all that the passion between them burned brighter by the day, not once in all those weeks did they talk about the future. To do so would have shattered a present made forever uncertain by the demands of his job.

Although Emily did her best to live with that, what she couldn't get over, what terrified her, was the nature of the work that took him away from her, and the fact he always assigned himself to the most dangerous missions.

When she dared to ask him why, he said, "Because I have the most experience and the least to lose."

"But what about Vassili?" she pressed, referring to another colleague they'd bumped into one day at a kafenion in Athens. "You told me he's one of the most skilled pilots you've ever come across."

"He also has a wife and two-year-old son at home," Niko replied.

His answer and all it implied chilled her to the bone.

One Sunday evening in mid November, they stood on the terrace outside his penthouse, sipping cognac and admiring the night view of Athens spread out below. But even though Niko appeared perfectly relaxed and content, a shimmering tension emanated from him, one Emily now recognized all too well, and she braced herself for what she knew was coming.

He didn't leave her in suspense very long. "I'm off again tomorrow," he said, as deceptively casual as if he were planning to play golf, but then added guardedly, "I might be gone a bit longer than usual."

In other words, this undertaking was riskier than most. "How much longer?"

"Three days, possibly four, but you can count on my being home by the weekend."

"Where to this time?"

"Africa again."

A typically ambiguous reply. He never elaborated about his exact itinerary, was always deliberately vague about why he had to go. *Delivering food and clothing to an orphanage…survival kits to a village cut off by a landslide…a medivac rescue…supplies to a field hospital,* he'd say offhandedly when she questioned him, then quickly change the subject.

But she knew it was never as straightforward or simple as he made it sound. If it were, he wouldn't come back looking so drawn. He wouldn't wake up bathed in sweat from a nightmare he refused to talk about. He wouldn't reach for her in the night as if she was all that stood between him and an abyss of utter despair.

"Where in Africa?" she persisted now.

"Does it matter?"

"Yes, it matters."

He hesitated and she hung on tenterhooks, waiting for his answer. When he told her, it was so much worse than anything she'd let herself contemplate, was such a hellhole of violence, devastation and peril, that she felt sick to her stomach.

She knew how she was supposed to respond. Calmly. With acceptance. And she couldn't do it. Not this time. Instead she started to cry.

"Ah, Emily," he murmured and held her close. "Don't do this. We still have tonight."

But she'd broken the rules and commited the cardinal sin of wanting tomorrow, and tonight was no longer enough.

Her tears caught him off guard. Angry with himself for distressing her, and with her, too, because she'd known from the first the career he'd chosen for himself, he said, "This is why, until now, I've avoided serious involvement with a woman. When I take off on assignment, my attention has to focus on people whose lives, for one reason or another, are in jeopardy. Worrying about you is a distraction I neither need nor can afford."

"I know." She swiped at her tears and attempted a valiant smile. "I'm being selfish and unreasonable. Sorry. I don't know what came over me. I'm not usually so emotional."

She hadn't been during the early days of their affair, he had to admit. Lately, though, the smallest thing seemed to upset her. Just last week, he'd gone to pick her up at the villa and found her all teary-eyed over a bird that had flown into a window and broken its neck. He wasn't very happy about the poor thing's untimely end, either, but she knew every bit as well as he did that death was part of life and didn't differentiate between old and young, guilty or innocent.

"If this is harder than you thought it would be and want out," he said now, "just say so. I'll understand."

She closed her eyes against another bright gleam of tears and shook her head. "More than anything else, I want you."

"Even with all the baggage I bring with me?"

"Even then."

He wanted her, too. Enough that he'd willfully overstepped the limitations he'd imposed on his personal life prior to knowing her. And at that moment, with her body haloed in the nimbus of light from the city, and her beautiful face upturned to his in vulnerable despair, he had never wanted her more. "Then come with me now," he whispered, drawing her inside and up the spiral staircase to the bedroom. "Let's not waste the few hours remaining before I have to leave you."

That night, unlike some when his desire for her overrode any attempt at finesse, he loved her at leisure. Caring only about pleasing her and driving the demons of fear from her mind, he kissed her all over. He seduced her with his hands, with his tongue. He hoarded the scent and texture of her skin. He watched the slow, hot flush of passion steal over her, tasted the honeyed warmth between her thighs. He commited to memory the tight rosy buds of her nipples and the little cry she made when she came.

When at last he entered her, he did so slowly. Wished he could remain forever locked within her tight, silken warmth. And when his body betrayed him, as it always did, he surrendered all that he was or ever wanted to be. *"S'agapo, chrisi mou kardhia,"* he groaned. "I love you, Emily."

He awoke just after dawn, left the bed quietly and in order not to disturb her, took his clothes and went to the guest bathroom to shower and prepare for the day ahead. When he was done, he returned to the master suite and stood a moment, watching her sleep.

Early sunlight caught the sweep of her eyelashes. Cast a pearly shadow along the line of her collarbone. Her hair fell in captivating disorder over the pillow. Her arm reached across to his side of the bed as if seeking him.

He wanted to touch her. Put his mouth on hers and whisper her name. And knew he could not, because doing so would make it impossible for him to leave her.

Turning away, he picked up his bag and quietly let himself out of the penthouse.

CHAPTER TEN

COMPULSIVE worry took over her life and gnawed at it until it was full of holes. Holes that tormented her every waking hour and haunted her dreams.

Niko had willingly flown into an area where none of the rules of the civilized world applied. Every day, news reports of unspeakable atrocities made the headlines. Murder, banditry and torture were commonplace; starvation and disease had reached epic proportions.

Intellectually Emily recognized that helpless men, women and children desperately needed the kind of humanitarian relief people like Niko dedicated themselves to providing. But the Geneva Convention had no meaning for the perpetrators of the crimes being committed, and those trying to help were finding themselves subjected to increasing violence, some of it so extreme they were being evacuated for their own safety. Others had lost their lives for the principles they believed in.

What if he became one of them?

Self-fulfilling prophecies were dangerous in themselves, she realized, and in an effort to divert her mind into other channels, she turned to anger. Why had he left without saying goodbye? To spare them both the pain of a farewell, or because he cared more about strangers than he did about her?

But that line of reasoning merely shamed her. How could any thinking person, let alone a woman who'd made caring for those unable to care for themselves her vocation, be so blindly selfish? His compassion for others was one of the main reasons she loved him so desperately.

She then turned to optimism, telling herself that he was the best at what he did. He'd never lost a pilot and to make sure he never did, insisted every man involved in his operation, himself included, constantly hone his skills to remain at the top of his game. "Emergencies aren't the exception," he'd once told her, "they're the rule, and we're always prepared."

How could she not support such heroic measures? How could she resent his taking a few days away from her to make a difference in the lives of those so much less fortunate? By Saturday, she'd be in his arms again and the nightmare would have passed.

But the weekend came and went with no word from him. By Monday morning she couldn't hold herself together any longer and broke down in front of Pavlos. "I'm worried sick about him," she sobbed.

"That's what happens when you get involved with a man like him."

"You make it sound as if I had a choice about falling in love with him, but that's not how it works. It happened despite my better judgment."

"What can I say? I tried to warn you, girl, but you wouldn't listen and now you're caught in a trap with no way out."

"You're not helping," she wailed, swabbing at her tears.

He looked at her sadly. "Because I can't help. I learned a long time ago that where my son is concerned, worrying's a waste of time. He's going to do what he wants to do, and to hell with anyone or anything that stands in his way."

"How do you sleep at night, Pavlos?" she cried bitterly. "How do you turn your back on your only child and not give a damn whether he lives or dies?"

"Years of practice at being unpleasant, girl. The way I see it, if I make him dislike me enough, he'll survive just to annoy me. My advice to you is the same as it's always been: forget you ever met him. You're better off not knowing what he's up to."

But she'd passed that point of no return weeks ago, and the uncertainty of not knowing was killing her. Another endless night of pacing the floor, and she'd lose her mind, so that afternoon while Pavlos napped, she took a taxi to the airfield. Better to learn the worst than be held hostage to the horrors her imagination so willingly conjured up.

The big hangar stood empty and only five aircraft waited on the tarmac, but several cars were parked outside the flat-roofed office. Not bothering to knock, she opened the door and stepped inside.

Huddled around a chart spread out on the desk in the reception area, three men and a woman talked quietly. She recognized Dinos and Toula; the other two were strangers. On hearing the door open, all four looked up and at the sight of her, their conversation subsided into a ghastly silence that fairly screamed of disaster.

"Emily." Dinos came forward with a smile. But it was a poor, pitiful effort that soon faded.

"You know something," she said, every fear she'd entertained over the last week crystalizing into certainty. "Tell me."

He didn't pretend not to understand what she was talking about. "We know nothing," he told her quietly. "We are waiting—"

"Waiting for what? To learn he's been taken captive? That he's dead?"

"There is no reason to assume either. He is a little overdue, that is all."

"Overdue?" She heard the shrill edge of hysteria climbing in her voice and could do nothing to control it. "He's *missing*, Dinos!"

At that, Toula came forward and grasped her hands. *"Ohi.* Do not distress yourself, Emily. He will return. He always does."

"How do you know that? When was the last time anyone heard from him?"

Again that awful silence descended, so thick it caused a tightness in her chest. She'd experienced the same suffocating sensation once before, the day she learned her parents had been killed.

"Thursday," Dinos finally said. "But in itself, that is not necessarily significant. Sometimes it is safer to remain incommunicado in hostile territory than risk giving away one's whereabouts."

He was lying and doing it badly. "You don't have the foggiest idea where he is or what's happened to him, do you?"

His gaze faltered and he shrugged miserably. "No."

She felt the tears pressing hot behind her eyes and fought to control them. "When were you planning to tell me? Or aren't I entitled to be kept informed?"

"Today I come to you," Toula interrupted. "That is why I am here first. To learn what is latest news and hope it will be good."

Hollow with despair, Emily said, "How do you do it, Toula? If Dinos doesn't show up when he's supposed to, how do hold on to your sanity?"

"I believe," she said, her dark eyes filled with pity. "I pray to God, and I wait. It is all I can do. It is what you must do also. You must not lose faith."

"Toula's right, Emily." Dinos touched her shoulder gently. "You must believe that whatever has happened, Niko will find his way back to you."

"*Neh*…yes." The other two men nodded vigorously.

"There is nothing you can do here," Dinos continued, guiding her to the door. "Go back to the villa and wait for him there. I will call you the very second I have anything to report. Where did you leave your car?"

"I came by taxi."

"Then Toula will drive you home."

Dinos didn't call. No one did. Instead as she was passing through the foyer late on Tuesday afternoon, she heard the sound of a vehicle departing down the driveway. A moment later, the doorbell rang. Fearing the worst, she rushed to answer and came face-to-face with Niko.

Bathed in the orange glow cast by the setting sun, he leaned against the wall, his left arm held close to his chest. "I hear you've been inquiring about me," he said.

She'd prayed for just such a miracle so often in the

last few days. Had rehearsed exactly what she'd say, what she'd do. But now that it had come to pass, she was at a loss for words and simply stared at him.

In one respect, he looked much as he had that long-ago day they'd met at the airport. Same blue jeans, open-necked shirt and black leather bomber jacket. Same rangy height, black hair and mesmerizing green eyes. But that man had been the picture of health. So strong and invincible, he could have taken on the world single-handed and emerged victorious. Had picked up his father as if Pavlos weighed no more than an infant.

This one looked ill. Gaunt, hollow-eyed and barely able to support his own weight, let alone anyone else's. The sight paralyzed Emily. Left her speechless with dismay.

"Well, Emily?"

Collecting herself with a mighty effort, she said, "You haven't shaved in days."

The ghost of a smile touched his mouth. "Somehow, I'd expected a warmer welcome. Perhaps I should have stayed away longer."

"Perhaps you should have," she said, shock giving way to irrational anger. "Perhaps you shouldn't have come back at all."

His gaze drifted over her and came to rest on her face that she knew was ravaged with pent-up misery. "Emily, *karthula*," he murmured, a wealth of regret in his tone.

Her insides sagged. Melted into tears that flooded her eyes and washed her aching heart clean of everything but the burning need to touch him. To feel the tensile strength of muscle and bone beneath his clothing, the steady beat of the pulse at the corner of his jaw. To prove once and for all that she wasn't dreaming and he wasn't a ghost, he was real. "I didn't mean that," she cried, launching herself at him.

He grimaced and fended her off with an involuntary grunt of pain, reinforcing her initial impression that something was terribly wrong. His eyes, she noticed belatedly, held a feverish glint and a film of sweat beaded his upper lip.

"What happened to you?" she whispered.

His careless shrug turned into a flinch. "Just a minor scratch to my shoulder. Nothing to get excited about."

"I'll be the judge of that," she said, drawing him over the threshold.

He stepped inside, but staggered against a table just inside the door, sending it and the vase of flowers it held crashing to the marble floor. The noise brought Damaris and Giorgios running from the kitchen.

"I need a hand here," Emily panted, buckling under Niko's weight as she struggled to hold him upright. "Help me get him upstairs to a bed."

From the rear of the house, Pavlos spoke. "My room is closer. Bring him this way."

Between the three of them, they half-led, half-dragged Niko the length of the central hall and into the suite. As they eased him onto the bed, the front of his jacket fell open to reveal a spreading bloodstain on the upper left corner of his shirt.

The housekeeper gasped faintly but Emily immediately went into professional mode. "Pass me my scissors, Damaris," she ordered calmly, peeling off his jacket. "I'll have to cut away his shirt. Giorgios, I need clean towels, disinfectant and hot water."

Under the shirt she found a blood-soaked dressing covering a ragged puncture wound slightly to the right of his shoulder joint and just below his collarbone. "I'd say being shot amounts to a bit more than a minor scratch, Niko," she said, hoping nothing of her inner panic showed in her voice.

"What makes you think I've been shot?"

"I'm a nurse. I know a bullet injury when I see it, and this one's infected. A doctor needs to look at it."

"A doctor already has. Who do you think patched me up?"

"Someone in too much of a hurry from the looks of it. I'm taking you to the hospital."

He closed his eyes, weariness etched in every line of his face. "You'll do nothing of the sort. If I wanted to spend another night in a hospital, I wouldn't have had Dinos bring me here."

"I'm not Dinos, and I'm not taking any chances with your health."

"And I'm not a child."

"Then stop behaving like one and do as I ask."

"Forget it. I didn't just escape one hell to be thrown into another."

She looked for support from Pavlos who stood impassively at the foot of the bed, his gnarled old fingers gripping its rail. "For heaven's sake, will you talk some sense into your son, Pavlos?"

He shook his head. "No point trying, girl. His mind's made up."

Frustrated, she swung her attention back to Niko. "Fine. Have it your way. But don't blame me if you end up dead."

He opened his eyes a slit. "As if you'd let that happen, *karthula*. You're my angel of mercy."

"Let's see if you still think so after I'm finished with you."

She put on a pair of surgical gloves and began her task. As far as she could tell, he'd sustained no permanent damage. She found no sign of an exit point when she rolled him over on his side, which meant the bullet had lodged in his flesh and hopefully been removed by the doctor who'd treated him.

"Yeah," he mumbled, when she asked. "I told him he could hang it on his key chain."

He'd been lucky. As gunshot injuries went, she'd seen much worse, with major organs and bones damaged beyond repair. Nonetheless, the point where the bullet had entered his shoulder was ugly, with swelling around the sutures and angry red lines radiating from the wound site. And therein lay the reason for her alarm. "When did this happen, Niko?"

"A few days ago."

Typical vague answer, she thought, exasperated. "Were you hospitalized?"

"Overnight."

"Did you receive a tetanus shot?"

"*Neh.* In my other arm."

"Are you sure?"

"I was shot in the shoulder, Emily, not the brain. Yes, I'm sure. I can still feel where they shoved the needle in."

One piece of good news at least. "You'll be feeling this, as well," she warned, knowing she was going to hurt him. But he'd left her no choice. Bits of debris from the dressing and heaven only knew what else were adhered to his sutures and had to be removed. "It isn't going to be pleasant."

"Do what you have to do and get it over with," he ground out.

Brave words and nothing less than she'd expect from a man who refused to admit to any sort of weakness, but as she probed at the raw edges of his wound with surgical tweezers, then irrigated the area with warm water, the tendons on his neck stood out like cords.

Finally, with a clean dressing in place, she said, "That's about it for now."

"Good. Hand me my jacket and I'll be on my way."

He struggled to sit up, turned gray in the face and toppled back against the pillows.

Her patience snapped at that. "Try not to be a bigger fool than you already are, Niko Leonidas! The only place you're going is to bed, and you won't need your jacket for that."

He eyed her malevolently. "*Ade apo tho re,* Emily. You're beginning to annoy me."

"Not half as much as you're annoying me. Giorgios, grab his good arm and help me get him upstairs. We'll put him in the room adjoining mine—and I suggest," she added sweetly, addressing Niko again, "that you don't fight me on this. You've suffered enough pain for one night."

Although his glower was black as thunder, he offered no further resistance except to mutter, "Your bedside manner could use improvement, woman. Escaping rebel forces was a walk in the park compared to this."

But by the time they got him upstairs and into the bed Damaris had rushed to prepare, he had no fight left in him. "Clean sheets," he murmured on a ragged sigh. "Never thought they'd feel so good."

A moment later, he was asleep.

Emily left the connecting door between their rooms open and checked on him frequently during the remainder of the night, concerned as much about his rising temperature as the injury causing it. At one point, he opened his eyes and stared at her in the dim light as if he didn't know who she was. Another time, she heard him muttering her name deliriously and, placing the back of her hand against his cheek, realized he was burning up. Without knowing the extent of any vessel damage, she daren't give him aspirin and had to settle for sponging him down with tepid water. It helped temporarily, but never managed to subdue the fever completely.

From the outset, she'd known that what she could do for him would be, at best, a stopgap measure, and had hoped the new day would make him more amenable to accepting the kind of treatment only a physician could provide. But when, despite her efforts, his temperature spiked dangerously just before dawn, she knew she couldn't afford to wait for his permission, and phoned Pavlos's family physician.

She and the doctor had developed a strong mutual respect in the months since she'd come to Greece, and he brushed aside her apologies for disturbing him at such an ungodly hour. "I'll come at once," he said, after listening without interruption as she related the situation.

He arrived just as the sun was rising, subjected Niko

to a thorough examination, treated the infected gunshot wound and wrote out a prescription for topical and oral antibiotics. "Be glad you have a first-class nurse in residence, young man," he told Niko, when he was done. "You'd be hospitalized otherwise, whether or not you like it."

Then turning to Emily before he left, he added quietly, "Change his dressing regularly, and make sure he takes in plenty of fluids to replace what he's lost. If you're at all concerned that he's not getting enough, don't hesitate to call and we'll rehydrate him intravenously. Other than that, bed rest and medication should do the trick. Unless I hear from you sooner, I'll stop by again in the morning."

For two days, Emily was unconditionally happy. She had her man safe, close by and on the road to recovery. Although he slept a good part of the time, he always sensed when she was near. "Hey, angel," he'd murmur drowsily, fumbling for her hand, and her heart would swell with love.

The reprieve was short-lived. By the Thursday, he was chafing at being confined to bed and insisted that moving around was the best way to regain his strength. On Friday, he made it downstairs for breakfast, which was all it took for hostilities to resume between him and his father. And as usual, she found herself caught in the middle.

"What are you doing down here?" Pavlos demanded testily when he saw him.

"I have better things to do than lie around in bed all day, old man."

"Such as what?" Emily put in, horribly afraid she knew the answer.

"Unfinished business," he replied cryptically.

"If by that you mean going back to Africa and getting shot again, forget it."

"Don't tell me what to do, Emily. You're not my keeper."

"No, I'm the woman who loves you."

"More fool you," Pavlos chipped in, "because you have a jealous rival, my dear, and it's called death. He flirts with it constantly and has done for years."

"*Pre sto diavolo*—go to the devil, old man!" Niko retorted irascibly. "You know nothing about what motivates me, and even less about my relationship with Emily."

"I know she deserves a man willing to give her more than you ever will."

"Someone like you, I suppose?"

"At least she wouldn't be pacing the floor wondering where I am half the time."

"Because you can barely make it as far as the front door under your own steam."

They were like two lions fighting over the day's kill, the older one battling for dominance over a younger, more powerful adversary, and it sickened her.

"I could strangle the pair of you!" she exploded. "You're both so full of Greek pride, you can't see past it to what you're doing to one another. Or maybe you can, and you don't care."

"Stay out of it, Emily," Niko warned her. "This is between him and me."

"I won't!" she said, so angry she almost stamped her foot. "Pavlos is your father, for pity's sake, and you're his only child. You're all the family either of you has left and it's past time you put this senseless feud aside and made peace with one another. I know I would, were I in your place."

"But you're not," Niko said, so coldly that she shivered, "so can we agree to disagree and leave it at that? What you and I do in the bedroom is one thing, but you don't hear me interfering in your life the rest of the time. I'd appreciate it if you'd afford me the same sort of courtesy."

If he'd slapped her, she couldn't have been more shocked. "I thought we were about more than what happened in the bedroom."

He looked almost as shattered as she felt. "We are," he muttered, raking a furious hand through his hair. "I love you, you know that."

She'd once believed those three words were all it took for a man and a woman to make their relationship work, but she'd been wrong. They meant nothing if they came wrapped in resentment and soured what was once beautiful.

"Maybe you do," she said dully, "but not nearly enough."

CHAPTER ELEVEN

BEFORE he could respond to her accusation, let alone refute it, she was gone from the room. Seconds later, the front door slammed, drowning out the sound of her racing footsteps.

"That went well." Pavlos sneered. "Have anything planned for an encore?"

"Butt out," he growled, and turned to go after her.

"Do her a favor." The old man's voice followed him down the hall. "Let her alone. She's better off without you."

Maybe she was, but it wasn't in Niko's nature to give up without a fight. He'd be dead by now, if it were. And they'd invested too much of themselves in each other for it to end like this, over careless words spoken in the heat of the moment.

Wrenching open the door with his good hand, he stood on the step and shaded his eyes against the late morning sun. She'd already cleared the circular parking area and was swerving past an outraged peacock, which happened to be obstructing her path as she fled across the south lawn.

Intent on stopping her, Niko gave chase. Another dumb

move, he soon realized. Every bone in his body crunched as he hit the ground running. He covered no more than about forty meters before he was gasping for breath, and his shoulder was throbbing almost as badly as it had when he'd first been shot. He hadn't a hope of catching anything that moved, let alone a woman bent on putting as much distance between him and her as she was. And if that wasn't indignity enough, his father was now standing in the open doorway, watching the whole debacle.

"Emily!" The effort of raising his voice almost brought Niko to his knees.

She swung back to face him. *"What?"*

He couldn't answer. His lungs were bursting and black dots danced before his eyes. Humiliated by his weakness, not to mention his audience, he bent over, his chest heaving.

Seeing the shape he was in, she made her slow way back to him. "I already know how cruel you can be," she said, "but I had no idea you were stupid, too. You've probably made your wound bleed again and undone all the progress you made. Keep it up and you'll wind up in hospital, whether or not it's where you want to be."

"I want to be with you," he wheezed.

"Whatever for? We have nothing in common outside the bedroom, remember?"

"We both know that's not true."

"Then why did you say it?"

"Because I was—*am* frustrated as hell. I can no more tolerate not being in charge of my life than I can abide being on the receiving end of my father's grudging hospitality. The sooner I move back to the penthouse, the better for everyone."

"You're in no condition to go back to the penthouse," she informed him flatly.

"Too bad. I'm going anyway. Pavlos and I bring out the worst in each other. We always have." He grabbed at her hand. "Come with me, angel. It's Friday and we have the whole weekend ahead. Let's spend it together, making up for lost time."

"I don't know about that. Given your recent history, I doubt you're going to be feeling very...energetic."

"My upper torso might not be quite up to par, but below the waist everything's working just fine," he assured her. "Fully recovered or not, I want you so badly it hurts. More than that, I need you."

"You're only saying that to get your own way."

Annoyed, he snapped, "I thought you knew me better than that, Emily, but since you apparently don't, let me make one thing clear. I've yet to resort to lying in order to get a woman to sleep with me, and if you think that's what I'm doing now, then perhaps you should just keep running in the other direction and not look back." He released her hand and took a step away. "There, you're free. Off you go."

She bit her lip. A lone tear drizzled down her cheek. "I can't. I love you."

"Then why are we standing here arguing?"

"I don't know," she said and, closing the distance between them, buried her face against his neck.

"Go with him," Pavlos said, when she told him Niko was set on returning to the penthouse after lunch, then surprised her by adding, "and don't worry about being back here on Monday. Stay a week, or however long it takes to get him back on his feet. Judging from what I just saw, he's not quite the iron man he'd like to think he is."

"But you hired me to look after you," she protested, although they both knew he hadn't needed a resident nurse in days.

"Right now, he needs you a lot more than I do."

"I'm afraid you're right."

"Then pack a bag and be on your way. How are you getting into the city?"

"By taxi."

"No need. Giorgios will take you in the Mercedes. It'll be more comfortable for superhero."

She dropped a kiss on his cheek. "Thank you, Pavlos. You're an old softie under all that grump."

He swatted her away with rough affection. "Watch your mouth, girl, and don't be so quick with the gratitude. My son's about as cussed an individual as you could ask to meet, and I don't expect you'll have an easy time with him."

But she didn't care if she didn't have easy, as long as she had time.

They'd no sooner arrived at the penthouse than it started to pour with rain. Huge drops danced wildly on the terrace. Veils of cloud swirled outside the floor-to-ceiling windows, bringing an early dusk to the afternoon and obscuring the outside world. They didn't care. Wrapped in splendid isolation and with days of being together stretching before them, they didn't need sunshine. All they needed was each other.

That night, they sent out for dinner, ate it by candle-light and retired early. Knowing the day had wearied him, Emily didn't anticipate they'd make love, nor did she mind. She was happy simply to lie beside Niko in his big bed and feel the steady beat of his heart beneath her hand because, a week ago, she'd been afraid she'd never do so again. But he was alive, they were together, and that was all that mattered.

Proximity, though, was a powerful aphrodisiac and desire stole over them in quiet waves, with none of the tempestuous urgency they were used to. He turned on his side and his leg brushed hers, hair-roughened skin against smooth, warm thigh. His hand whispered over her hips to the hem of her short nightie and drew it up past her bottom. His mouth searched out hers and he uttered her name in muted invitation when she reached down and found him already hard.

All silken, pulsing heat, he positioned himself between her legs and slid inside her. They moved together in a slow, sweet symphony, adoring one another with soft murmurs of love. They climaxed in unison, the passion unspooling between them, lazy as waves rolling ashore. They fell asleep locked in each other's arms, sated with pleasure, and awoke to a morning washed clean and sparkling with sunshine.

So began a week she knew she would remember for the rest of her life. Sometimes they slept late. Other times, they went grocery shopping, arriving early at the markets to choose from a bewildering selection of food, and coming home loaded with goodies. Succulent lamb for souvlaki, or ground beef for moussaka. Fresh prawns and squid, cheese and olives for mezedes.

Ignoring Niko, who laughed and reminded her they were buying for two, not an army, she lingered at the fruit and vegetable stands, choosing jewel-toned egg-plant, vivid green peppers and bright red tomatoes, as well as lemons, tangerines and melons. She went to the bakery for bread still warm from the oven, and a quaint little shop at the entrance to the Plaka that sold honey, coffee, yogurt and nuts.

She learned to make tzaziki and saganaki. Even tried her hand at baklava. Although he had a housekeeper who usually came in every couple of days when he was in residence, Emily sent her away, preferring to change the bed linens and take care of the laundry herself, while Niko caught up by phone with what was happening at the airfield.

They took walks around the city. Visited museums and ancient churches. Explored art galleries and antique shops. Sometimes they'd go out for a meal. Mostly they stayed home, preferring to be alone.

. They made love whenever and wherever the mood took them. Suddenly, urgently, in the late afternoon, on the rug in front of the fire in the living room, with the scent of burning apple wood filling the air. Sleepily, in the middle of the night, spurred by heaven only knew what dreams might have woken them. Wildly, hilariously, on the desk in his study, while he tried to conduct a serious phone conversation with Dinos at the office.

They lazed on the big overstuffed couch in the living room and read or listened to music, taking unhurried pleasure in simply being in the same room together.

It was like being married, except marriage was one subject they never discussed. To do so would have meant talking about the future which, in turn, would have brought that other world into focus. The one that took him away from her. Better to live in a fool's paradise.

But that dreaded other world intruded anyway, evidenced by a restlessness in him that increased as he regained his strength. Phone calls to the office weren't enough to satisfy him. He started spending time at the airfield again, an hour or two at first until, by the middle of the second week, he was back at work pretty much full-time. Domesticity had palled, even if his desire for her hadn't. He was raring for something more challenging than building fires or checking the firmness of tomatoes in the marketplace.

"I'm the boss," he said when she remonstrated with him. "Bosses are supposed to lead, not sit at home and let others do the job for them."

Matters came to a head on the third Sunday. All day, he'd been on edge. Finally, with evening closing in and Christmas carols playing on the stereo, he poured them each a glass of wine and came to sit next to her on the couch. "I have something to tell you, *karthula*," he began.

She knew what it was, without his having to elaborate. "You're leaving again."

"Yes."

"When?"

"Tomorrow."

"With so little advance notice?"

"Not exactly. I've known for a couple of days now that I'd be going."

"Where to this time?"

He looked at the fire, at the red roses she'd arranged in a vase on a side table, at the book lying facedown on the arm of the couch. He looked anywhere but at her, and her stomach turned over in a sickening lurch of prescience. "Oh, no," she whispered on a trembling breath. "Please tell me you're not going back to that horrendous place."

"I must," he said.

"Why? To get shot again, fatally this time?"

"People there are in terrible straits and they need help. And I need you to understand that I can't turn my back on them."

Anger welled up in her and she struck out at him, slamming her fist against his right arm. "What about what *I* need, Niko, or doesn't that matter to you?"

"I have given you all of myself."

"No. You give me what's left over after you take care of other people."

"Not so. You're what keeps me sane when the world around me erupts into madness. Before we met, I didn't care if I never came home. Now, I live for the time that we can be together again."

"Sure you do," she said, tears clogging her voice. "I'm the warm body that makes you forget the horrors you left behind, but it doesn't change the fact that you care more about strangers than you'll ever care about me."

"I don't deserve that, Emily."

"I don't deserve to be left waiting and wondering if you'll come back to me in one piece or a body bag."

"No, you don't," he said, setting down his wine and going to stand at the glass doors leading to the terrace, "which is why I never promised you forever. I've always known I couldn't give it to you."

So there it was, the end of the affair, delivered with the

uncompromising honesty that was his trademark. They'd finally run out of borrowed time and the tomorrow she'd tried so hard to postpone stood on the doorstep.

Hollow with pain, she said, "We were never a good fit, were we?"

"Never," he admitted, after a horrible, tension-filled pause.

"Always a ships-passing-in-the-night sort of thing."

"That about covers it."

But his voice was all rusty, as if he'd choked on a peanut. And she…she was perilously close to sobbing. She had followed in her parents' footsteps and gambled everything for the pleasure of living in the moment. And in doing so had lost everything. Their biggest mistake had become hers, too.

"So…o…o." She drew out the word on a long, quivering sigh. "I guess this is goodbye."

"I guess it is."

"It's for the best."

"Probably."

She dug her fingernails into her palms; bit the inside of her lip until she tasted blood. "I'll collect my stuff and get out of here. You must have a lot to do and don't need me underfoot."

He didn't argue, just straightened his shoulders and turned back to confront her, his face unreadable. "Fine. I'll drive you back to the villa."

And subject them both to more suffering? "No," she said. "There's a taxi stand right outside your building. I'll take a cab."

She left her untouched wineglass next to his and went upstairs to the bedroom to throw clothes, shoes and toiletries haphazardly into her suitcases. She had to get away quickly, before she fell down on her knees and begged him not to leave her.

At last she was ready. All that remained to be done was walking away from him. If there'd been a back entrance to the penthouse, she'd have taken it and spared them both the agony of a last goodbye, but he remained in the living room which opened off the long hall leading to the foyer.

"I think I've got everything," she said, staring straight ahead because, if she looked into his jade-green eyes one more time, she'd lose it completely.

"Anything you've forgotten, I'll send to the villa."

"Thanks." She swallowed painfully. "Take care of yourself."

"You, too."

She tried to open the door. Fumbled with a latch, which refused to budge. Was dimly aware of movement in the room behind her and renewed her efforts, not wanting him to come and help.

She could not look at him, or speak to him, or let him come near her again. She could not.

Eyes streaming, she made one last effort. The blasted latch clicked, but still the door refused to budge because, she realized, staring blurrily through her tears, he was holding it shut. Over the tormented thud of her heart she heard his voice so close behind her that his breath wafted warm and damp over her nape. "Emily, don't go," he begged. "It doesn't have to end like this."

She wilted, empty of pride and so full of hurt that she had no fight left in her. Dropping her luggage, she turned in his arms and clung to him, accepting that she was as helpless to refuse him as she was to change the course he'd set himself long before he met her. "I'm so afraid for you," she sobbed.

"I know, sweetheart," he said, kissing her eyes, her tears. "I know."

Hounded by the remorseless hunger, which had held them in thrall from the first, they sought the only comfort left to them and went at each other like mad things, giving the lie to any notion that being apart was better than being together. She clawed at him, desperate in her need, raking her hands down his shirt-front to tear open the buttons. He pinned her against the door, yanked up her skirt and ripped off her panties. Freeing himself from his jeans, he hoisted her off her feet, pulled her legs around his waist, and drove into her as if she was all that stood between him and damnation.

After that, there was no question of her leaving. Instead they tried to do what they'd done so successfully for over two weeks. They tried to play house.

He sorted the clothes he'd take with him in the morning. She folded them, the way a good wife would, and put them neatly in the canvas carryall that held enough to see him through as many days as he'd be gone. Too many, she noticed, counting three pairs of jeans, eight shirts and as many changes of undershorts and socks.

They tried to talk about anything except where he'd be tomorrow night at that time, but the conversation stalled at every turn and they'd subside into stricken silence before making another valiant attempt at normality.

They sat down to dinner, but abandoned the table when neither of them could eat. Their gazes met and held, and broke apart again when the emotion in their depths threatened to overwhelm them.

"Let's stop this," he finally said. "Come to bed, *khriso mou*. Let me hold you in my arms and love you one last time before I go."

She tried, fusing her body with his in a desperate, hopeless attempt to stop time. Amassing his every word, his every touch, and hoarding them against an empty future. She wished she could shut down her mind and simply listen to her body. But the specter of his flying off into the teeth of danger, of death, haunted her. It left her drained, deprived of everything that gave her life meaning. "Please don't go," she finally beseeched him. "If you love me at all, please stay and keep me with you."

"I can't," he said.

And she couldn't, either. He was an adventurer, at heart as much a rebel as those he fought against, albeit for different reasons. Risking life and limb gave him a rush she'd never understand. She needed stability—a real home, a husband, children—and she couldn't live suspended indefinitely on the fine edge of sanity, wanting what he couldn't give her.

Light from the en suite bathroom filtered into the room, crowding the corners with shadows but providing enough illumination for her to watch him sleeping. With the hours racing by much too fast, she committed to memory the curve of his mouth, the clean line of his jaw and cheekbones, his lashes, so long and thick he could sweep a street with them.

Beyond the windows, the sky grew imperceptibly lighter, precursor of a new and hellish dawn shouting that today was their last day. She did not want to hear or see it, and closing her eyes, she pressed her body close to his, inhaling through every pore the very essence of all that he was.

6:30 a.m.

Time to make a move.

Deactivating the alarm clock before it disturbed the silence, Niko took a moment to savor the warmth of her body next to his. Feigning sleep himself, he'd listened to her crying softly throughout the night. It had taken every last milligram of self-control for him not to reach for her and tell her what he knew she wanted to hear.

I'll send someone else in my place, and stay with you. We'll get married, make a home together, raise a family.

Exhaustion had claimed her before temptation got the better of him. Now she slept, with strands of her pale blond hair spread over his shoulder as if to bind him to her. She looked young, beautiful. Defenseless as a child, and unutterably sad.

He had done that to her. What had started out to be no more than a harmless flirtation designed to show Pavlos that his trust in her was misplaced, had blossomed out of control. Niko had seen it coming, but had done nothing to put an end to it. She had captivated him like no other woman he'd ever met, and he'd made the fatal mistake of falling in love with her.

Worse, selfish bastard that he was, he'd let her fall in love with him. And now he had to leave her because he knew that happy-ever-after wasn't in the cards. Of his fifteen employees, ten were pilots. The youngest was single and still living at home. Five of the remaining nine were divorced, victims of a career that demanded too much of the women who'd once loved them enough to take their names and bear their children.

He did not want that for her, for them. He'd rather lose her now, with the good memories still intact, than wait until all the joy and passion had turned bitter with resentment.

6:31 a.m.

Stealthily he eased himself off the bed, collected his clothes and, as he'd done before, went downstairs to shower and dress in the guest suite. As a rule, he stood under the jets an indecently long time because there was no telling when he'd next have access to hot water or clean towels. But that morning he made quick work of preparing for the day ahead.

6:49 a.m.

Ready to go. A better man than he'd ever be would have picked up his bag and left. He couldn't go without a last farewell, and went to the library to find pen and paper.

I love you enough to set you free to live the kind of life you're looking for, he wrote. *The man who can give it to you will be lucky indeed. Be happy, Emily.*

Then stopping by the living room, he plucked a rose from the bouquet she'd arranged, and stole back upstairs.

She lay exactly as he'd left her. He ached to kiss her. To whisper her name. To taste her mouth one more time.

For once, he did the right thing. He placed the note and the rose on his pillow and left her.

CHAPTER TWELVE

"He's gone again," Pavlos said, his wise old eyes absorbing everything in a single glance. "He's left you."

Too awash in misery to put a brave face on things, Emily collapsed into the chair next to his. "Yes."

"So what now?"

"I think I must go, too, Pavlos. There's nothing more for me here." Except a rose already wilting, a note that put a final end to hope and a heart in shreds.

"There's me."

She shook her head sadly. "I've taken advantage of your generosity too long already."

"Rubbish! You nursed me back to health, put up with my bad temper and—"

"And now you're well again." Or as well as he'd ever be. His hip had healed to a degree, but his eighty-six-year-old body was worn-out, and there wasn't a thing she or anyone else could do about it.

"You gave me a reason to get out of the bed in the morning," he insisted. "I've grown fond of you. You're like a daughter to me and will always have a place in my home."

For a moment, she was tempted. To be needed,

wanted; to be part of a family, however small...hadn't she longed for just such peace of mind and heart ever since she was nine? But common sense told her she'd find neither in this house. She'd never hear the doorbell without hoping it was Niko come to tell her he'd changed his mind, that he wanted forever after all, and he wanted it with her.

If Pavlos had been truly alone, it might have been different, but he had the devoted Giorgios and Damaris to take care of his daily needs, and a family doctor who visited three times a week. She'd be leaving him in good hands.

"I'm fond of you, too, and I'll never forget your kindness," she told him gently, "but my life is in Vancouver. I have a house there. Friends, a career, financial and professional obligations to honor."

"And I'm not enough to make you turn your back on them." He sighed and nodded acceptance. "Will you keep in touch?"

"Of course."

"I don't suppose I have to tell you that my son is a fool."

"No more than I was, Pavlos."

"I tried to warn you, girl."

"I know you did."

The trouble was, his warning had come too late. It had been too late from the moment she and Niko had set eyes on each other. The attraction between them had blazed out of control, instantaneous combustion bent on destroying anything that stood in its path. The fear that she might live to regret giving in to it had dissolved in the lilting excitement, the sheer *aliveness* of being in love. Nothing compared to it.

What she hadn't known was that when it ended, it

took more than it had ever bestowed. Without Niko she was empty, incomplete. She had known him less than three months and in that time he had turned her life upside down, stolen everything she had to give, and left her with nothing.

Or so she believed when she said goodbye to Pavlos. And perhaps, if she'd chosen a different career, she might have ascribed the mood swings and exhaustion she brought home with her to the unavoidable emotional fall-out of a love affair gone wrong. But nursing school had taught her well. She was attuned to her body and as the old year came to an end, she hardly needed a home pregnancy test to confirm the cause of the fatigue and faint but undeniable nausea that hounded her every waking hour.

The future Niko had insisted no one could predict was staring her in the face with a certainty that eliminated any possibility that she might one day come to forget him. He would be with her always in the shape of his child.

The realization shattered the blessed numbness, which had cushioned her since the day he'd left. She was a twenty-seven-year-old, highly trained medical professional, for pity's sake! Of all people, she should have known how to protect herself from an unplanned pregnancy. How could she have been so careless?

Except she hadn't been, nor had Niko. Even at their most spontaneous they'd taken precautions, to the point that he'd joked about buying condoms in bulk, to cut down on the number of trips to the drugstore! But there'd been a few times during their last two weeks together that they'd almost left it too late to be safe. Idiot that she was to have exposed herself to such risks, she must have conceived then.

Her doctor, whom she went to see in late January, soon put paid to that theory. "You're well into your second trimester, Emily. About sixteen weeks along, I'd say."

"I can't be." Unless…had they cut things too fine on the boat? Been too carried away by the newness of their affair to be as responsible as they should have been?

"Are you sure you last menstruated at the end of October?"

"Pretty sure," she said, vaguely recalling her period had been lighter than usual. Nothing more than spotting, but she hadn't paid much attention at the time. She'd been too busy falling in love.

"What about the father?"

"What about him?"

"Are you going to tell him?"

"No."

"Why not?"

"Because we're not together anymore. He's not into parenthood, at least with me."

That night, she lay in bed, surrounded by all the comforting things that spelled home. The blue and white toile de jouy wallpaper she'd hung herself. The handmade wedding ring quilt she'd bought at auction, three years ago. Her reproduction four-poster bed and matching rosewood bombe chest of drawers. The silver-framed photograph of her parents and two small oil paintings she'd found at an estate sale, the summer she'd graduated from nursing school.

They were proof she didn't need a man around, she

told herself. Closer to her due date she'd put a rocking chair in the alcove near the window, where she'd nurse her baby, and a white bassinet next to her bed. When he grew too big for that, she'd turn the second bedroom into a nursery. Paint clouds on the ceiling. Stencil unicorns and pixies on the walls—oh, and a guardian angel, because every child had to have a guardian angel, even if he couldn't have a father.

A father…Niko…

Memories of him rushed to the forefront of her mind. Of his warm breath tickling her neck when he leaned over to kiss her good morning. His mouth against hers, his voice in her ear.

Of his long, strong body and olive skin. The planes of his chest, the swell of muscle over his shoulder, the lean, taut curve of his buttocks.

Of his beautiful face, and his mesmerizing eyes and the way they turned dark when the passion he tried so hard to contain rode roughshod over him.

Of his laughter, his wicked sense of humor… *You've left me with an erection that would do a stallion proud, Emily….*

Oh, to hear him laugh again! To see him, to hold him!

As winter turned to spring, she struggled to put the past behind her, but it wasn't easy with his baby growing inside her. Wouldn't have been even if she wasn't pregnant.

Any mention of humanitarian aid brought him vividly alive in her mind. A melody they'd listened to together, the scent of aftershave on another man, a stranger, when it belonged only to him, were enough to turn a good day bad. He was in her heart, in her soul.

But in every other respect, she was alone. Alone and

pregnant, because although he'd paid lip service to loving her, when put to the test, the father of her unborn child chose to risk life and limb in some benighted corner of the world, rather than risk his heart to her.

Well, let him, she'd tell herself, furious at her own weakness. She'd had her fill of reluctant charity, growing up as she had in her aunt's house where she'd never been welcome. If Niko couldn't commit to her without reservation, she didn't want him at all.

Anger was so much easier to bear than grief, even if they did both boil down to the same thing in the end.

"Will you be able to manage financially?" her friends asked when they heard she was about to become a single parent.

"Yes," she said, the irony not escaping her that her baby's grandfather was responsible for the substantial savings she'd amassed. "I have it all planned out. I can work for another five months, then after the birth, take a year's maternity leave, and when that ends, hire a live-in nanny to look after the baby."

But her calculations misfired. On the twelfth of May when she was only thirty-three weeks into her pregnancy, and contrary to anything she or her doctors had reason to expect, she gave birth to a three pound, eleven ounce daughter.

As a nurse, she knew that a mildly preterm baby's chances of surviving without lasting complications were excellent. As a mother, she wore herself to a shadow fretting over the tiny, delicate creature who had taken her heart by storm from the second she entered the world.

She named her Helen and brought her home when

she weighed five pounds. "At least she looks all there," the well-meaning woman next door remarked, stopping by the next day to inspect the new arrival. "For a preemie, that is."

Emily's friends were somewhat more encouraging. "She's adorable, so petite and feminine," they agreed, flocking around the bassinet.

To Emily, she was the most beautiful baby ever born. She brought light to a life which, since the day Niko left, had been too often filled with darkness. Sitting in the rocking chair, with her baby at her breast and the dogwood trees blooming outside the window, Emily found a measure of peace that had eluded her for much too long.

Spring melded into summer. If it wasn't too hot, Emily would tuck Helen into her stroller and take her for walks in the park or along the seawall. She'd nurse her in the shade of a sun umbrella on the patio.

She'd kept her promise to stay in touch with Pavlos, and at first they'd exchanged frequent e-mails but, as the months came and went, they'd written to each other less often. He never mentioned Niko, had little to say about anything really, and she decided against telling him about her pregnancy. What was the point in upsetting him?

After Helen was born, she wasn't so sure she'd made the right decision. Would learning he was a grandfather bring a little joy into Pavlos's life, or merely create an even deeper rift between father and son? More to the point, could he keep it a secret from Niko?

She had no doubt that, should he find out she'd had his baby, Niko would feel obligated to do the honorable thing and marry her. And that, she knew, would merely invite long-term misery for everyone. He would never

settle happily for domesticity, and she wouldn't—
couldn't live with his career choice. No child needed a
daredevil for a father. Better to have no father at all than
one who, as Pavlos had once pointed out, flirted with
death every time he went to work.

As summer advanced, Helen continued to thrive.
Although still small for her age, she gained weight
steadily, clocking in at over six and a half pounds when
she was three months old.

One morning, Emily had put her down for her
morning nap and was folding laundry at the kitchen
counter when she received a distraught phone call from
Giorgios. Pavlos had taken a turn for the worse and was
not expected to recover. He had refused to be admitted
to hospital and was asking for her.

"What about his son?" she said. "Has he been con-
tacted?"

"We have tried, but he is far away."

Typical! she thought. Why stick close to home and
your ailing father, when you could be somewhere else
giving your all to strangers?

"Will you come, Emily?"

How could she refuse? Pavlos needed her. "Yes, but
it'll take me a little time to make the arrangements."

"I am afraid he does not have much time left."
Giorgios's voice broke. "He is tired of fighting to live,
Emily. Many times, he asks me, 'What for do I wake up
each morning to an empty house?'"

"You tell him he has to hold on," she said fiercely.
"Don't you dare let him die before I get there."

* * *

She and Helen arrived at the villa by taxi two days later. Obtaining a passport for her baby at such short notice had taken some doing, but Emily had appealed to a sympathetic government official who, when he'd heard her situation, had cut through the bureaucratic red tape in record time.

As the cab rounded the last curve in the driveway and the villa came into view, nothing seemed to have changed. The palm trees rose tall against the deep blue sky. The flower beds blazed with color under the sun. Proud as ever, the peacocks strutted over the immaculate lawns.

Inside, the house told a different story. The atmosphere was somber, oppressive, although her showing up with a baby caused something of a stir.

"Yes, she's mine," Emily said to a stunned Damaris. Then, to Giorgios, "Am I in time?"

"*Neh.* When he heard you were coming, he found new strength. He is awake and just a few minutes ago asked how soon you would be here."

Lifting Helen from her infant seat, she said, "Then let's not keep him waiting any longer."

She had witnessed death in all its guises many times in her career, but even though she thought herself prepared, she was shocked when she saw Pavlos. He lay against his pillows, so frail and shrunken that a stiff breeze could have blown him away. His face was the color of parchment, his eyes closed, and had it not been for the shallow rise and fall of his chest, he might have already been dead.

"Hold her for me for a second, will you?" she whispered, passing Helen to Damaris, and approached his bed. "Hello, darling," she said softly.

He opened his eyes. "You came," he said, his voice a pale imitation of what it once had been.

"Of course."

"You're a good girl."

Stifling a rush of grief, she took Helen from Damaris and laid her in his arms. "I've brought someone with me," she said. "Say hello to your grand-daughter, Pavlos."

He gazed at Helen who stared up at him from big blue eyes. Almost inaudibly, he whispered, "She is Niko's child?"

"Yes."

Tears trickled down his face. "I never thought to see the day. *Yiasu, kali egoni.* Hello, my little one."

"Her name's Helen."

"A good Greek name." The breath rattled in his belea-guered lungs. "A beautiful name for a beautiful child."

"I thought you'd approve."

He tore his eyes away from Helen. "How could I not? She is of my blood and has you for her mother. Tell me all about her."

"Tomorrow," she said, seeing that he was tiring fast. "For now, Pavlos, try to get some sleep."

He groped for her hand. "Sleep will come soon enough, girl, and we both know it is not one from which I will awake. Talk to me while there is still time. I want to know everything."

"Stay with him," Damaris murmured, scooping Helen into her arms again. "I will look after the little one."

"Take Giorgios with you when you go," Pavlos

wheezed. "His mournful face and death bed vigil weary me."

"Poor man," Emily said, when they were alone. "He loves you so much, Pavlos, and all this…" She indicated the oxygen tank and other hospital paraphernalia in the room. "It probably scares him."

"I know, and it hurts me that he is so overwrought. I would spare him seeing me like this, if I could. He has been more of a son to me than Niko ever was."

"Niko loves you, too."

"Save me the platitudes, girl! I am dying. If he cares about me at all, why is he the only one not here now?"

Footsteps crossing the adjoining sitting room came to a halt in the open doorway. "But I *am* here," Niko said. "I came as soon as I heard."

CHAPTER THIRTEEN

HORRIFIED, Emily froze, battered by panic and such a welter of conflicting emotions that her instinct was to run as far and as fast as she could to escape him. Anything to suppress the surge of longing aroused by the sound of his voice, the craving to touch him again. Anything to prevent his finding out about Helen. But what if he'd already seen her and recognized her as his? And even if he hadn't, how could she justify leaving Pavlos when he was clutching her hand so desperately?

Reining in her emotions, she drew on the control which had served her so well as a critical care nurse. With deceptive calm, she swiveled in the chair and in one sweeping glace took in everything about him from the top of his head to his dusty flight boots.

He looked like hell. Fatigue smudged his eyes, he hadn't shaved in days and he needed a haircut. Judging by their appearance, he must have slept in his jeans and shirt longer than was good for them or him, and the crystal was cracked on his flight computer watch. But more than all else, he looked unutterably sad.

"I'll leave the pair of you alone together," she muttered, rising to her feet.

"No," Pavlos wheezed, his eyes beseeching her.

Niko crossed the room and pressed her down on the chair again. "Please stay, angel," he said. "What I have to say is as much for you as for my father."

"Don't you dare upset him."

"I won't."

He pulled a chair close on the far side of the bed and took his father's other hand. The contrast between them, the one so big and strong and deeply tanned, the other so weak, with every vein showing through the paper-thin skin, was painfully moving to behold.

"If you're here to dance on my grave," Pavlos said, the faintest spark of the old hostility charging his words, "you needn't have rushed. I'm not dead yet."

"And I thank God for that, *Patera*, because I want to tell you I'm sorry I've made such a poor job of being your son."

"An *epiphaneia* at this late date?" Pavlos let out a croak of feeble laughter. "What brought that on?"

"I have just come back from a hell where political corruption and genocide rule the day. I've witnessed mothers ripped away from their newborn infants, fathers murdered before their children's eyes and been powerless to prevent either. I've met thousands of orphans infected by diseases, which will kill them before they grow to be adults. I have buried a dead baby and wept over his grave because there was no one else to mourn him."

Momentarily overcome, he cleared his throat and rubbed his thumb lightly over the back of his father's hand. "In the end, the devastation and ruin defeated me. What was I doing, trying to mend broken families in a foreign country when my own was falling apart at home? By what right had I held you at a distance, *Patera*, when your greatest sin was wanting to give me a better life than you had when you were young?"

"You're my son," Pavlos said. "Stubborn and proud and hell set on making your own way in the world, just as I was at your age. And you wanted to make that world a better place."

"Yes, I did. But I neglected you in the process. Have I left it too late to ask your forgiveness?"

With great effort, Pavlos lifted his other hand and laid it alongside Niko's stubble-covered jaw. "Ah, my foolish boy," he said hoarsely. "Don't you know it's never too late for a father to welcome his son home again?"

Niko started to cry then, harsh, horrible, rasping sobs that tore through his body. Emily couldn't bear it. Springing up from her chair, she stumbled to the French doors in the sitting room and ran out to the terrace.

At the far end, a path led away from the villa and wound through the gardens to a marble bench set in a shady arbor screened from the house by a grove of lemon trees. Reaching it, she sank down on the seat's cool, hard surface and wrestled with the demons plaguing her.

She had fought so hard to get over Niko. To shut herself off from dreams of him vivid enough that she awoke with the scent of his skin, the silken touch of his intimate flesh, taunting her. She'd struggled to find a foothold in a world without him. To build a safe, secure, contented life around her baby.

And for what? To fall for him all over again in less time than it took to blink, swayed by tears she'd never thought to see him shed, and words she'd never believed she'd hear him utter? Casting aside his indomitable pride, he'd revealed his innermost heart and in so doing, had walked right back into hers.

She could not allow it. Could not risk being dragged back into the morass of misery where loving him had landed her before. She had a child to protect now. Helen needed a mother who was whole, not half a woman pining for what she couldn't have. If she acted quickly and discreetly, she could leave the villa without anyone being the wiser. It was the best thing, the only thing to do.

Mind made up, she went around the side of the house to let herself in the front door, and came face-to-face with a harassed Georgios. "I've been looking for you, Emily. Your little one is screaming with hunger and Damaris cannot comfort her."

Right on cue, Emily's breasts started to leak and a quick glance at the clock on the wall showed her it had been over two hours since she'd last nursed her baby. Leaving would have to be postponed a little longer. "Please ask Damaris to bring her to me in the drawing room. It's cooler in there."

"If you'd rather be upstairs, everything's ready in your suite."

"Thanks, Giorgios," she said, "but now that Niko's arrived, I won't be staying here after all."

"Pavlos will be disappointed."

"I don't think so. We had our time together. Now it's his son's turn."

Niko sat with his father until he drifted off to sleep, then quietly left the bedroom and went in search of Emily. He and Pavlos had made peace at last. Now it was time to mend things with her. He'd hurt her badly. Hurt them both, for reasons which, in retrospect, struck him as unforgivably egotistical on his part. Well, no more. Things would be different from now on.

The house was silent as a tomb. An unfortunate comparison, he thought with a pang. Already the scent of death, indefinable but all too familiar, pervaded the atmosphere. But as he drew level with the pillared entrance to the formal day salon, a place so seldom used that he couldn't remember the last time he'd set foot in it, a soft, dovelike murmur caught his attention.

Thinking a bird might have flown in from the garden, he stepped quietly into the room and instead discovered Emily sitting by the open window, a lightweight shawl of some sort draped over her shoulder, her head bent attentively over the infant at her partially exposed breast.

The shock almost felled him. Yes, he'd urged her to find a man who could give her what he'd thought he never could, but not once in all the months they'd been apart had it occurred to him that she'd take his advice to heart so quickly or so thoroughly.

As though sensing she was being observed, she looked up and caught him staring. Her eyes widened and quickly, almost defiantly, she drew the shawl over the baby—a newborn, from what he'd been able to observe, probably no more than a few weeks old.

"Well," he said, affecting amusement when what he most wanted to do was howl with disappointed outrage, "I hardly expected this."

She tilted one shoulder in a dismissive little shrug. "What can I say? The day's been full of surprises."

He angled a glance at the baby, although all he could

see were its tiny legs and the little red soles of its feet poking out beneath the shawl. "Boy or girl?"

"Girl."

"Does she look like you?"

"Some people think so."

"Lucky her. And you're happy?"

"Deliriously. I have everything I ever wanted."

"Really?" He'd never have guessed. She was fidgety, tense, the picture of uneasiness. Rearranging the shawl needlessly. Looking anywhere but at him.

There was something else not right about the picture of contentment she was trying to present, and watching the nervous fluttering of her fingers, he all at once realized what it was. "In that case," he said, "why aren't you wearing a wedding ring?"

Of all the questions she'd feared he might ask, this one had never crossed her mind, and she briefly considered trying to come up with an inspired lie to throw him off the scent. Since she'd done such a good job of fooling him into thinking she'd found some other man to take his place, why not continue with the charade? But suddenly she'd had enough of the deceit and the subterfuge. She'd tell him the truth, or at least an edited version of it, and if he persisted in leaping to all the wrong conclusions, that was hardly her problem. "Because I'm not married," she said.

"Why not?"

"I rushed into a relationship with the wrong man, we went our separate ways and I'm bringing up my baby alone. Don't look so disapproving. It was my choice, and hardly unique in today's world. Hundreds of women make the same decision every day."

"You're not one of those women, Emily," he said. "You should have held out for the husband you always wanted."

"Well, I didn't. I had a baby instead."

His unforgettable green eyes scoured her face, undermining her resolve to remain coolly disinterested. "It's not too late for you to have both."

"I'm afraid it is. There aren't too many men out there willing to take on another man's child."

"There's me," he said. "If you'll have me, I'll marry you."

She was so unprepared for his answer that she almost dropped Helen. "Don't be ridiculous! The Niko Leonidas I know doesn't invest in marriage."

"That man doesn't exist anymore. He grew up and learned what was important in life."

"He used to believe helping those in need was important."

"He still does."

Bristling, she said, "I'm not in need, Niko. I can manage very well on my own."

"You misunderstand. What I'm saying is that I haven't abandoned the causes I've supported all these years. I still believe in doing my part and I always will. I just don't need to keep proving it by playing Russian roulette with my own life. There are other, more effective ways to make a difference."

"Marrying me isn't one of them," she said. But oh, how she wished it were!

He crossed the room in swift strides and came to where she sat. "Listen to me," he implored. "I love you. Give me a chance to show you how much. Let me make a home for you and your baby. Let me be a father to her. I don't care who else's blood runs in her veins. That she's yours is reason enough for me to love her as if she were my own."

"Oh…!" She pressed her trembling lips together and fought to hold back the tears. "This is so not what I expected when I woke up this morning."

"Me, neither. If you need time to think about it—"

"We both do, Niko. Right now your father needs you more than I do, and you're too emotionally fragile to be making any other major decisions."

"Not to the point that I don't know my own mind. In deference to my father, I won't pressure you to accept my proposal now, but I won't be put off indefinitely."

"There's more at issue here than just you and me, Niko. My situation…well, it's not exactly what you think."

"Do you love me?"

"Yes."

"Are you married?"

"I've already told that I'm not."

"Then there are no issues that can't be worked out."

He ran his hands down his crumpled shirt and dusty jeans. "Look, I'm a mess, inside and out. I'm going home to get cleaned up and pull myself together, but in the event that you're worried my proposal is some spur-of-the-moment impulse on my part—"

"Is it? You are a man who likes to rush to the rescue, after all."

"The person I'm rescuing this time is myself, Emily. It's taken me a long time, but I've finally set my priorities straight. Only a fool discards the treasures that bless his life. I was on my way home to tell my father that even before I heard he was dying. To my lasting regret, I've left it too late to make it up to him for all the wasted years. I won't make the same mistake with you."

He left her then, but not as he had before. Not empty of everything but despair. She'd once read that when it rains in the desert, all the cacti burst into glorious flower. For such a long time her spirit had been arid as a desert, but his words made hope bloom in every corner of her heart and fill it to overflowing.

While he was gone, Giorgios came to tell her Pavlos was awake again. She went to him immediately.

His tired eyes brightened when he saw she'd brought Helen with her and he tried to reach out to hold her, but the effort was too much for him and he sank back against the pillows. His pulse was weak and erratic, his breathing labored as his poor old heart struggled to keep working, and he soon drifted asleep again.

Niko joined her not long after and took up his post on the other side of the bed.

Sensing his presence, Pavlos muttered haltingly, "You here, son?"

"I'm here, *Babas*."

"You'll be a rich man when I go."

"Not as rich as I'd be if you stayed."

"Not enough time left for that, boy. It's up to you and Emily now."

"I know."

"You take good care of her."

"I will."

"And my granddaughter. Be a better father to her than I ever was to you."

Startled, Niko shot Emily a quick glance, but he said only, "I won't let you down, *Babas*."

"Never have, boy," Pavlos said, his voice barely above a whisper. "Always made me proud...should have told you before now."

He never spoke. He subsided into sleep again, deeper this time, his respirations so shallow they barely moved the sheet covering him. Emily busied herself checking the IV solution and oxygen, hoping to avoid the inevitable question about his father's comment, but Niko's attention remained fixed on Pavlos.

An hour passed, and then another. Helen squirmed and scrunched up her face, the prelude, Emily knew, to a very vocal demand for food. "I'll nurse her in the other room so she doesn't disturb him," she told Niko.

"Don't take too long," he said.

Afternoon slipped toward dusk. Giorgios brought tea and sandwiches. Damaris took Helen and put her to bed in a drawer she'd taken from a dresser, which was lined with soft blankets. The doctor paid a call, met Emily's gaze, shook his head regretfully and said he'd be by again in the morning.

Throughout the night, Emily and Niko kept vigil. Lost in their own thoughts of the man who'd made such an indelible impression on them both, they spoke little. At six o'clock the next morning, Pavlos died.

"He's gone, Niko," she said. "It's over."

He nodded, bent his head and gathered his father's frail body in his arms.

Leaving him to make his private farewell, she slipped from the room and went out to the terrace. In the half-light of dawn, the flower beds shone like pale clumps of stars. It was going to be another beautiful late August day. The first of many without Pavlos.

She didn't hear Niko join her until he spoke. "He was rambling, wasn't he, when he said the baby's mine?"

"No," she said, too sad and exhausted to prevaricate. The truth had to come out sooner or later, it might as well be now. "You're her biological father."

"That's impossible. We always used protection."

"We couldn't have been as careful as we thought," she said.

"How old is she? She looks practically newborn."

"She's three months old."

"How much does she weigh?"

"Nearly seven pounds now, but she was less than four at birth. She looks small because she was born seven weeks early."

He almost staggered. "Why didn't you tell me?"

"I tried to when you found me with her yesterday. You wouldn't let me."

"I'm not talking about yesterday afternoon, Emily. I'm talking about the last nine or ten months. I would have married you at once, if I'd known."

"I know you would. I didn't want you on those terms. I still don't."

"I was afraid that might be the reason," he said. "I seem to have a real talent for screwing up the relationship that means the most to me."

And he walked back into the house, a man so bowed down with sorrow that she couldn't bear to watch him.

CHAPTER FOURTEEN

SHE saw little of him in the week that followed. Arranging the funeral and the myriad tasks associated with it kept him occupied. Pavlos had many business associates and the stream of callers coming to the villa to pay their respects was endless.

Emily helped poor Damaris, who was run off her feet providing refreshments, and spent many quiet hours in the gardens with Helen, wondering what the future held. Although he'd made time to get to know his daughter, Niko treated Emily more like a sister than a lover. Had she ruined their chances by keeping their baby a secret? she wondered.

She received her answer when he sought her out as she sat in the shade of an olive tree, on the lawn overlooking the Saronic Gulf. For the last two days, they'd had the villa to themselves again, but it was too lovely an afternoon to spend indoors.

"We've pretty much laid the past to rest, Emily," he announced, dropping down beside her on the blanket she'd spread on the grass. "Now we have to take care of the future. I said I wouldn't rush you for an answer to my proposal, and I've tried to keep my distance, but I'm afraid I've run out of patience."

Her mouth dropped open. "Are you saying you still want to marry me?"

"More than I've ever wanted anything in my life. The question is, do you trust me enough to want to marry me?"

"Why wouldn't I trust you?"

"Well, let's see. I showed myself to be devious and un-scrupulous by trying to expose you as a fraud. I seduced you, then agreed that we weren't a good match and might as well end our relationship. I left you, and you had a baby you didn't dare tell me about because you quite rightly thought I'd make a lousy father. Shall I go on?"

"No. We've laid the past to rest, remember, so let's do as you suggest and talk about the future."

"Okay. Here's what I've decided. Although I'll continue to support the causes I hold dear, I'm retiring as a pilot and sharing management of the company with Dinos. I intend to take an active role in overseeing my father's investments as he always wished me to do. Giorgios and Damaris have been very loyal to my family, so if you and I get married and you're agreeable, I'd like to live here and keep them and the rest of staff on. How am I doing so far?"

"Very well. I couldn't ask for better."

"Is that a yes to my proposal?"

"I'm not sure," she said coyly. "You moved into the villa a week ago and have been sleeping in a room down the hall from mine and your daughter's ever since. Do you plan to keep on doing that?"

"Not if you'll let me sleep in yours."

"Then it's a yes."

He closed his eyes and let out a long, slow breath. "Thank you for that, angel," he said. "I've been a very sad and lonely man since my father died, disappointed in myself on many levels and so afraid I'd blown any chance I might have had with you."

"I've been sad, too, Niko," she said, "but it hasn't changed the way I feel about you. I love you. I always will."

"I love you, too, so much more than you'll ever know. I love our daughter and will protect you both for the rest of my life."

That night, they lay together in bed with Helen between them. After fussing all evening, she'd finally fallen asleep.

"How beautiful she is," Niko whispered, his gaze tracking her face feature by feature. "Her ears are like little shells and look how tiny her nose is."

"She has your dark hair," Emily told him.

"She has your mouth.'

She smiled. "She is *our* baby."

"Yes," he said. "And I think you should put her in the drawer so that we can practice making another just like her, *mana mou*."

They made love, taking slow delight in rediscovering each other. He traced his tongue over the pale blue veins in her swollen breasts. She kissed the scar on his shoulder where he'd been shot. With hands and mouths and whispered words of love, they found the magic they once thought they'd lost and made it new and wonderful again. And when, at last, he entered her, they clung together and let the passion roll over them in sweet, endless waves and carry them to the far shores of ecstasy.

Afterward, Emily curled up in his arms and, hearing Helen whimper in her sleep, murmured drowsily, "We really must buy her a proper crib, don't you think?"

"Tomorrow, my darling," he said, bringing his mouth to hers in a lingering good-night kiss.

He tasted of lemons and sunshine and all things Greek. Of the fabulous turquoise sea, the dazzling mango-tinted sunsets, the ethereal dawns.

He tasted of forever.

THE GREEK'S
LONG-LOST SON

REBECCA WINTERS

Rebecca Winters, whose family of four children has now swelled to include three beautiful grandchildren, lives in Salt Lake City, Utah, in the land of the Rocky Mountains. With canyons and high alpine meadows full of wild flowers, she never runs out of places to explore. They, plus her favourite vacation spots in Europe, often end up as backgrounds for her Mills & Boon® romance novels, because writing is her passion, along with her family and church.

Rebecca loves to hear from her readers. If you wish to e-mail her, please visit her website at: www.rebeccawinters-author.com

A very loyal fan who read one of my Greek romances, *If He Could See Me Now*, urged me to write Stella's story. Stella was a member of the powerful Athas Greek shipping family and a secondary character in the book. How lucky am I to have readers who get hooked on a novel and want to know more?

Stella's story, *The Greek's Long-Lost Son*, is for you, BUFFER, with my gratitude!

CHAPTER ONE

AFTER a hard day's work negotiating prices with their overseas clients, Stella Athas left her office at the Athens headquarters a little after three o'clock in her new white Jaguar XK convertible, the first car she'd ever owned. Until she'd bought it with her own money two months ago, she'd used the old clunker estate car to get around.

Along with her new purchase, it seemed a different hairdo was necessary too. She'd always worn her dark hair long and straight, but all that had changed with the convertible, because the whole point of having the top down was to feel the sun and the breeze. It had only taken one day of whizzing around in it looking like the head of a mop for Stella to go to a beauty salon and get her hair cut in a trendy jaw-length style.

Everyone seemed to approve of her new look. Her colleagues said it emphasized the high cheekbones of her oval face. Her friends insisted it brought out the velvety texture of her midnight-brown eyes.

Her oldest brother, Stasio, teased her that she'd better watch out; she was a great beauty like their deceased mother. All the men, eligible or otherwise, had their eye on her now that she'd been seen around Athens in her flashy new sports car. When was she going to get serious over Keiko and take him for a ride in it? Didn't she know she was breaking his heart?

Stella knew that her brother was hoping she and Keiko Pappas would get together, but she'd been too burned by an experience in her past to get into an intimate relationship with another man. She preferred to remain friends with Keiko or any other guy hoping to get close to her for that matter.

As for today, she didn't want to think about anything but having fun because this marked the beginning of her three-week vacation from work. It was also the end of the school year for her six-year-old son, Ari.

Although she liked the family's town villa in Athens well enough—after all, it had been home to the Athas clan for three generations—she was a beach girl at heart and always looked forward to their holidays on Andros with Stasio and his wife, Rachel.

When Stella had attended college in New York, she'd met an American girl named Rachel Maynard. They had become best friends at a time when Stella had been recovering from what she could only look back on now as a nervous breakdown. When Theo Pantheras had deserted her and their unborn child, she'd allowed it to almost destroy her. Of course, that had been six years ago. She'd long since recovered, but the experience had caused her to lose her faith in men.

Still, with a vacation looming, none of that mattered now. She was eager to join Rachel, who'd married Stasio and who now had two little daughters, Cassie and Zoe, who adored Ari and he them. Everyone was looking forward to being together at the family villa on Andros and at some point her brother Nikos would be arriving from Switzerland with his wife Renate to vacation with them, too.

Nikos's arrival was always a worry for Stella, because he had a nasty temper and could make life difficult when he wanted to. Hopefully, this time he'd be on his best behavior, but she didn't know if it was possible.

Rather than be flown in Stasio's helicopter, Stella planned to drive her and Ari this visit. She wanted the new car at her disposal as she sped around the island and enjoyed the glorious summer. Tomorrow morning they'd leave early and take the ferry from Rafina. Ari loved ships of all kinds and adored being on the water. So did she and couldn't wait to get away from the city. It was starting to get overcrowded with tourists.

Once she'd pulled around the back of the house, she parked away from the trees and birds and hurried through the screened-in back porch where deliveries were left. When she entered the big kitchen, she saw the elderly housekeeper watering a plant at the sink.

"*Yiasas,* Iola. How was your day?"

She turned her gray head to look at Stella. "Busy."

"Cheer up. Ari and I will be leaving in the morning. With Stasio's family out of here, too, you'll have three weeks to take it easy and enjoy yourself." Stella gave her a kiss on the cheek. "I'm going upstairs to get packed."

"Everything has been washed and dried. You want me to bring up the luggage?"

"Thank you, but my suitcase is already in my closet. We don't need to take that much to the beach. Mine will hold both our things."

Grabbing an apple from the basket, she took a big bite and headed for the staircase at the front of the house. When they weren't on Andros, Stasio and Rachel lived at the villa on the third floor with the girls, she and Ari on the second. Nikos's suite was on the first floor next to the pool, but he was rarely here.

Once she entered her suite adjoining Ari's, she got to work. Ari had gone to spend the day with his school friend Dax, and Stella planned to pick him up at his friend's house around four-thirty. That gave her an hour.

While she started gathering tops, shorts and swimsuits for both of them, the house phone rang once. She picked up the receiver at her bedside table. "What is it, Iola?"

"You need to come downstairs. The postman has a registered letter for you that only you can sign."

Stella frowned. "Anything legal goes to Stasio's office, but you already know that."

"I told him, but he said this one is for you. He insists he has to deliver it into your hands, no one else's."

The postman could have done that while Stella had still been at the office. "I'll be right down."

What on earth was going on? Stella hung up the phone, eager to straighten out what was obviously a mistake so she could finish her packing. She hurried downstairs to the foyer and entered the front room.

"*Yiasou.*"

The postman nodded. "You are Despinis Estrella Athas?"

"Yes." But no one ever addressed her by her birth name.

He thrust a clipboard at her. "Please sign the card on the bottom line to prove this was delivered to you personally."

"May I ask who sent it?"

"I have no idea."

Despite her irritation, Stella smiled while she wrote down her signature. "Don't shoot the messenger, right?"

But her comment was wasted on the postman, who remained stoic.

He took the clipboard and handed her the letter. "I'll see myself out."

Iola followed him to the front door and shut it behind him. Stella wandered into the foyer, more bemused than anything else by the interruption. "Perhaps I got caught speeding in my new car by one of those traffic cameras. You think?" Stella quipped.

"Aren't you going to open it and find out?"

Stella had waited too long for her vacation to be bothered by anything now. "Maybe after I get back from our trip. After all, if this had been brought to the door tomorrow, I wouldn't have been here."

"But you signed for it today!"

"True. Why don't you open it and tell me what it says while I finish packing." She handed it to Iola before starting up the stairs to make inroads on her packing.

Stella fully expected the housekeeper to come rushing after her with the news, yet no such thing happened. In fact it was eerily quiet. After a few minutes Stella stepped out in the hall and walked to the head of the stairs.

"Iola?"

Total silence.

"Iola?" Stella called in a louder voice.

When nothing was forthcoming she raced down the stairs. No sign of her in the salon. "Iola?" She ran through the house to the kitchen, where she found her sitting on one of the kitchen chairs, her head in her hands. The letter lay open on the table.

As she started to reach for it, Iola grabbed it from her and pressed it to her ample bosom. "No! This is not for your eyes."

The loyal housekeeper had been with their family since Stella had been in elementary school. She knew everything that went on under their roof. Stella had no doubt Iola would defend her to the death if the situation warranted it.

"What's so terrible you don't want me to see it?" Her question was met with quiet sobs. Stella sat down on the chair next to her and put a loving arm around her heaving shoulders. "Iola? Please. Let me see it."

A minute passed before she handed Stella the one-page letter. Her eyes fell on the missive. It was hand-written in bold, decisive strokes that looked faintly familiar. Stella's heart skipped a beat.

Dear Stella:

It's been a long time since the last time we were together. After the letters I sent you came back unopened and I'd exhausted every possibility of finding you, I left for New York to work, but now I'm back in Athens for good.

I saw you walking near your villa with a boy who has Pantheras written all over him. He's my flesh and blood, too.

You and I need to meet.

I can be reached at the phone number on my office letterhead. I've also written my cell phone number here. I'll expect your call tomorrow before the day is out. Don't make me petition the court to secure my right to be with my son. That's the last thing I would want to do to either of you.

Theo.

Stella's cry reverberated against the walls of the kitchen.

As she read the letter again, Theo's name swam

before her eyes. She started to get up from the chair, but her body began to feel icy. Nausea rendered her too weak to stand. There was a ringing in her ears. In the distance she heard Iola cry before she felt herself slump against the housekeeper.

When next she had any cognizance of her surroundings, she discovered she was lying on the kitchen floor. Iola was leaning over her whispering prayers while she patted Stella's cheeks with a cold, wet cloth. As the housekeeper fussed over her, a memory of the letter filled her mind.

After six years Theo Pantheras had reappeared in her life, as if from the dead, wanting to talk to her? The very idea was so staggering Stella could hardly fathom it.

She'd known moments of anger in her life, but no amount of pain compared to the violence of her emotions against Ari's father, the man who'd come close to destroying her.

For him to think for one second she would pick up the phone and call him was too ludicrous to comprehend. The night she'd told him she was pregnant, he'd acted thrilled and told her he would find a way to take care of her and their baby. They would get married immediately despite their families being against it.

They had arranged to meet at the church, and once Theo arrived they would get married in secret, but Theo never came and Stella never saw him again. It was as if he'd simply disappeared off the face of the earth. The pain and the shame of waiting for him pretty well shattered her. Without Stasio's love and support, and of course the love she had for her gorgeous Ari, she probably would have died.

"I'm all right, Iola," she assured her. Sheer negative

adrenaline flowed through her body, driving her to get to her feet. She clung to the chair back while she waited for her head to stop reeling.

"Drink this." Iola handed her a glass of water.

It tasted good and she drank the whole thing. "Thank you."

"Theo Pantheras has obviously been stalking you. That is not good. You must call Stasio at once."

"No," she countered in a quiet voice. "That's the one thing I won't do. I have Ari to think about. This is something I intend to handle myself."

Since her parents' deaths, Stella had relied on her brother for everything. It had almost ruined his life in the process, but she wasn't a helpless teenager anymore. She'd grown into a twenty-four-year-old woman with a responsible position in the company, who'd been raising her son for the last six years.

Stasio had done more for her and her son than any human could expect of another. Her love for her brother bordered on worship. The only way to repay him in some small way was to leave him out of this. He had a wife and children he doted on, and Rachel was expecting for a third time. Stella wasn't about to impose her problems on him or his family. Never again.

She stared at Iola. "Not one word of this to anyone, especially not Nikos or Stasio. It will be our secret. You understand?"

The older woman nodded, but she said another prayer under her breath.

With no time to lose, Stella went upstairs for her purse. While there she phoned Dax's mother and told her she was coming to collect Ari. After telling Iola where she was going, she put the letter in her purse, then left the villa and drove to Dax's house.

As soon as Ari saw her, he ran down the steps of the front porch carrying his backpack and got into the car. She gave him a kiss on the cheek. "How was your last day of school?"

"Okay. We had to bring all our pictures and stuff home. Can we fly to Palaiopolis tonight?" It was the village on Andros where Stasio lived.

"No, honey. I'm planning to drive us tomorrow morning. I'd like my own car while we're on vacation."

"Hooray! I love our new car."

She chuckled. "So do I."

"Stasi says I'll be able to drive a car like this one day."

"Not for years yet, honey."

Whatever Stasio said, that was it. Long ago, when Stasio had told Stella he'd help her raise Ari, Nikos had warned Stella that Ari would always look to Stasio as his father. No other man could hope to compete. Nikos had told Stella that she should put her son up for adoption so he could have a normal life with a mother and father, but Stella wouldn't hear of it. Ari was her life! Since Theo had opted out of all responsibility, a boy could pray to have a surrogate father like Stasio.

While they waited for an old man to cross the street in front of them she glanced at her son. For six years she'd purposely concentrated on his Athas traits, but since receiving the letter from Theo, she was forced to take a second look at him.

Like Stasio, Ari was tall for his age with brown-black hair. He had Nikos's beautiful olive skin and her smile. But if she were honest with herself, his jet-black eyes, the musculature of his lean body, the shape of his hairline with its widow's peak belonged to Theo.

Pain stabbed her heart. Ari was the most adorable six-year-old in the entire world. Theo had no idea what he'd given up when he'd turned his back on the two of them. Why in heaven's name would he be interested in his child now? It didn't make sense.

She moved on. The breeze played with Ari's overly long hair. It had a tendency to curl at the tips, like Theo's…. Sometimes he held his head at an angle while he was looking at something with intensity, and again he reminded her of the man she'd once loved so completely she'd thought she couldn't live without him.

But that man who'd shown her so much love and had made her feel immortal had disappeared from her life. After realizing he was never coming back, she'd thought she was in the middle of a nightmare and would wake up. To her horror, she discovered she'd been awake the whole time. Welcome to the new reality of her life.

Remembered pain still had the power to shake her. She glanced at Ari. "Are you hungry?"

"No. Dax's mom fed us. Do you think Dax could come to Andros for part of our vacation?"

Any other time she would have said yes without thinking about it, but her entire world had been turned upside down this afternoon. She dreaded broaching the subject of his father with Ari, but if she put it off she would become more frantic than she already was. Then he'd know something was terribly wrong.

Ari had a very intuitive nature. Since she'd always been honest with him, she couldn't be any different now. When they pulled around the back of the villa, she didn't immediately get out of the car.

"Ari—before we go inside, there's something I have to tell you."

He looked upset. "Is it about Dax? You don't like him, huh."

She blinked. "Where did you ever get that idea? He's my favorite friend of yours."

"Because you wouldn't let him come with us to Andros last year, either."

Stella let out an anxious sigh. "That wasn't the reason. Dax's parents had other plans for him, remember? They took him to Disneyland. It was a surprise. That's why he couldn't come with us."

"Then how come you haven't said he can come with us this time?" He continued to look at her with those penetrating black eyes while he waited for an answer. Sometimes he could be very adult for his age. It always caught her off guard, probably because he reminded her of the Theo she had once known.

At sixteen Stella had been so shy and unsure of herself, yet he'd been tender and patient with her and he'd slowly built her confidence. When Nikos had been mean to her and made fun of her and her friends, Stella had turned to Theo, whose love and acceptance had made all the hurts go away.

Where had that man gone? After he'd disappeared from her life, she'd wanted to die.

Clearing her throat she turned to Ari and said, "Do you remember when you asked me if I knew where your father lived and I said no?"

All of a sudden she felt Ari go quiet. He nodded.

"It was the truth. I didn't know anything about him. When I asked why you wanted to know, you said there was no reason, but I knew that wasn't true."

He didn't move a muscle.

"I…I'm afraid I haven't made it easy for you to talk about your father," she stammered.

"Stasi said he hurt you so much you got sick."

"He was right. You see, my mommy died before you were born. Then your father went away and I never saw him again. I was so sad I fell apart for a while."

To make the pain even more unbearable, Nikos had been cruel and impossible to live with back then, always siding with their father that Theo came from the wrong kind of people with no background or class and no money. A marriage between them was unthinkable. She should be thankful he was out of her life.

Sensing how traumatic the situation was, how fragile her feelings were, Stasio had taken Stella to New York to have her baby. Six months later their father had suffered a fatal heart attack. After his funeral she and Ari had stayed in New York for the next four years. With Stasio there doing business half of every month, it had worked out well for all of them, and Stella had been able to get her college degree.

Thankfully at the time, Nikos went back and forth from Athens to the family's condo in Chamonix where he skied. She rarely saw him. That was a plus.

"Because of your uncle Stasio's love and kindness, I got better. The point is, that was a long time ago and a lot has changed since then." She moistened her lips nervously. "I found out this afternoon that your father has been living in New York."

His eyes rounded. "Just like *we* did?"

"Yes." That had come as another shock. For four years they'd both lived in the same city and hadn't even known it. Incredible. "However, he's back in Athens now to stay. He…wants to see you."

A long silence ensued. She could see him digesting what she'd just told him, but before he could ask another question, she needed to tell him the rest.

"Because it's been six years and he's never come near us until now, I need to know how you feel about seeing him. You don't have to answer right now. Just think about it. If you decide you'd like to meet him, then we'll call him up, but if you don't feel comfortable, Ari, you just have to say so—okay?"

If he didn't want to meet his father, then Stella would phone him when Ari wasn't aware of it. How she would love to hear Theo's reason for wanting to be with his child after all this time!

She couldn't imagine what Theo could say that would absolve him of what he'd done to her—to them! Stella couldn't comprehend a man walking away like that with no conscience, but it happened to other women all the time.

There were a lot of amoral men in the world, but she didn't want this one to be anywhere near her son. To her horror, Theo had brought up the possibility of getting the court involved if she didn't cooperate. She couldn't bear the thought of it, so she didn't dare ignore his letter.

Ari lowered his head. "I don't want to go and live with my father. I want to stay home with you. But I'd like to see him." He reached for her.

Waves of intense love for her son swept over her. "If that's your decision, then we'll tell him together."

He squinted up at her. "Can he make me go with him? Alex always has to go with his father to his new house and he doesn't like it."

Alex was one of Ari's friends. The situation in their home was very sad since his parents had divorced.

Her heart pounded with sickening intensity. The court could order visitation, but in the letter Theo had said he didn't want to go that route. Right now she was praying he meant it. "Let's not worry about that today."

In an abrupt motion Ari broke away from her and got out of the car with his backpack. "I'm going to call Stasi."

"No, Ari!"

That brought her son to a halt. He turned around, not quite believing her firmness. "Why can't I?"

"Because he's been forced to worry about us for too long as it is."

"But—"

"I said no." She cut him off before getting out of the car herself. "This isn't his business and doesn't involve anyone but you and me. Do you understand? After we go into the house we'll phone Dax's parents. Maybe they'll let him come to Andros with us for a few days. But whatever happens, when we get to the island, I don't want you to say a word about your father to anyone.

"Except for Iola, no one else knows he's back in Greece. You're not to tell the girls or Rachel or Stasio or Nikos. Can you promise me you'll keep quiet about it?"

"Yes." She'd thought the mention of Dax joining them might take the edge off this new worry in his life, but she was a fool to think that. After hearing his father wanted to see him, what little boy could think about anything else?

At this point Ari was horribly confused. So was she, and heartsick for him. His dark eyes filled with tears before he trudged toward the porch, leaving her devastated.

* * *

The resort Theo had built on St. Thomas in the Saronic Islands brought an influx of the elite from the major continents. The manager Theo hired said they were fast becoming the preferred vacation destination in all Greece and had the statistics to back it up.

That was always good news, but after leaving Athens to spend the night here, he'd had other things on his mind. He'd give Stella another hour to respond to his letter before phoning her. There was no telling where she was right now. Probably with her brothers while they planned a way to stop Theo cold. It would do them no good.

There was a reason for that and it lay in front of him. The velvety green of the golf course extending in two directions from the sprawling white hotel represented many lucrative investments that now ensured Theo's wealth. It took this kind of money to be on a par with the Athas dynasty.

Theo had never been a mercenary man. He still wasn't. That was why the medium-size villa he'd had built on Salamis was comfortable without overwhelming Theo's own parents and siblings with a lifestyle foreign to them.

Needing an outlet for his energy, he walked around the resort to the marina. Most of the motorboats and small sailboats were out enjoying the beautiful late afternoon. One morning soon he'd take his boy out on the calm water.

He didn't doubt his son had been exposed to every water sport imaginable, but he'd only been taught by the Athas family. There was a whole side to him he didn't know about yet that only Theo could show him because he was his father.

After chatting with a few of the employees, he

entered the hotel and headed for the manager's office. The other man had arranged for Theo to meet the new head chef and go over the various menus for Theo's approval.

Once their business was concluded, he had the office to himself. Boris, his bodyguard, stood outside the room while Theo walked over to the window that looked out on the blue sea. He pressed the digit for Stella's cell phone he'd programmed into his. Nestor Georgeles, his attorney, had his methods of obtaining information. Theo flicked on the device that blocked his caller ID.

When Stella picked up after four rings, she was still talking to someone else. He could hear another voice in the background.

"Hello?"

It was her voice. Yet it was different. It was the voice of a woman.

"*Kalispera*, Stella."

He heard her sudden intake of breath. "Theo— h-how did you—" She paused. "Never mind. I guess I shouldn't be surprised."

"I have to admit that when I drove past your villa for old-time's sake, *I* was surprised to discover you hadn't aborted our baby after all."

"Aborted?" she cried.

Just then Stella had sounded too aghast at his comment to have faked it. He clutched his phone tighter. Among Nikos Athas's many sins, he'd coldbloodedly lied to Theo about Stella getting rid of the baby.

Sickened by the possibility that she'd really gone through with it and couldn't face him with the truth, Theo had left for New York determined to start a new life and make the kind of money so his family would never know poverty again.

However, now that he was back home and had discovered he had a son, no power was going to keep Theo from him. If Nikos interfered again and tried to do his worst, it wouldn't get him or her brother Stasio anywhere. Theo was more than prepared to fight fire with fire because he intended to be a full-time father to his child.

All these years he'd accused her in his heart of doing the worst thing a mother could do. He should have known she wouldn't have done away with their child. It wasn't in her nature. But for her to keep all knowledge of their son from him wounded him so deeply, he could hardly talk. His eyes smarted.

"What did you name him?"

There was a period of silence before she said, "I...I'm surprised you didn't find that out since you seem to know everything else." After another pause while he waited, she added, "He was christened Ari."

He sucked in his breath. "Is that an Athas family name?"

"No. I just liked it," she murmured.

Now that he knew that, he liked it, too. Very much, in fact. For the moment she was sounding like the old Stella.

In the past they'd been forced to speak quietly over the phone so her family wouldn't know she was making plans with him. She hadn't been allowed to start dating until she was eighteen, but she'd caught his eye before her seventeenth birthday. The thrill of falling in love had made both of them careless.

They'd slipped out at different times to be together. Theo had paid an old fisherman on a regular basis for the use of his wooden rowboat. There had been a protected cove on Salamis and he had always taken her there. They'd swim and then lie on a quilt spread on the sand. Theo knew he shouldn't touch her, but he couldn't help it, not when she begged him to make love to her.

She had been so giving, so utterly sweet and passionate while at the same time being so innocent, he had told her that if they waited until she turned eighteen, they'd get married and have a real church wedding. Though they'd tried to wait, there came a day when neither of them could stand it any longer. Once they'd made love, there was no going back.

He cleared his throat, intent on learning everything about his son. There were six years to catch up on. "If you could tell me the most important thing about him, what would it be?"

"I couldn't pick just one thing." Her voice shook. "He's sweet, loving. I think he's the smartest, kindest little boy in the world."

That described the woman he'd once loved. She'd spoken like a mother who adored her son. Ari sounded the antithesis of his uncle Nikos who years before had caught up to Theo with his first volley of threats. "Stay away from my sister or you'll live to regret it."

Nikos had been watching them at church, following them while they went for walks. When his threats didn't work, he had tried to bribe Theo with money. Theo had thrown it back in his face.

A week later there had been a small fire at his parents' taverna. The police had said it was arson, but they never found the perpetrator. Someone working for Nikos had phoned with more threats, and Theo had been warned there was more to come if he didn't leave Stella alone.

When Theo's brother Spiro had been injured on his

motor scooter by a luxury car driving way too fast for that time of night, Theo realized Nikos was in dead earnest.

The last time he ever saw Stella, she had told him she was pregnant. The news had overjoyed him and suddenly everything made sense. She'd been impregnated by a Pantheras. It was no wonder Nikos had behaved like a madman—Theo had violated his sister and there'd be hell to pay.

That night Theo had told her he wanted to marry her as soon as possible. They would go away and he'd get a good job to support her and the baby. They'd planned everything out and had decided to meet at the church in secret. But on the night in question, Nikos had been waiting for him in the church parking lot. He had told Theo that Stella wouldn't be coming now or ever, that she had aborted their baby and wanted to forget all about Theo.

In shock Theo had lunged for him, but he had been beaten up by hired thugs and left for dead on the island of Salamis. After he had recovered from his injuries he'd looked everywhere for Stella, but no one had seen her. She didn't answer his calls or letters. She'd simply vanished.

Eventually he came to the conclusion that she really didn't want to see him again. It was evident her family had talked her into getting rid of the baby. *His* baby.

He shifted his weight. "I've been waiting all day for your call so we could discuss Ari. When I didn't hear from you, I decided to phone you. Where and how would you like my first meeting with him to take place?"

"I'd rather it never happened in this lifetime or the next."

A nerve throbbed at the corner of his mouth. "Then you're saying you want this handled through the court?'

"No," she blurted in agony. For a moment she reminded him of the vulnerable girl he had once known. "I have to know what you plan to do. Ari keeps a lot of things to himself. Naturally he's frightened about things."

"So am I," his voice grated. "Do you have a sense of how he truly feels?"

A groan escaped her throat. "I wish I could tell you he despises the idea of you and would prefer you didn't exist, but the truth is, I have no idea how he feels deep inside."

In other words, Ari knew his mother hated Theo.

"Today he was probably reacting the way he did to please me. He always tries to please," she explained. "Maybe more than is healthy at times."

He had little doubt that Ari hated the man who'd fathered him and then had promptly rejected him even before he was born. A six-year-old could hate just as vehemently as a fifty- or an eighty year-old. Theo was under no illusion that this would be easy. In this case the hatred would be worse because Ari would have been indoctrinated by his uncles who'd wished Theo dead long ago.

He realized he needed to be prepared for hostility from Ari that might last a lifetime. A lot of factors would enter in, beginning with the atmosphere in which Ari had been raised, the amount of hate built up against Theo on the part of Stella's family. Her parents had been against him from the beginning.

Taking into account that the Athas brothers considered Theo the underbelly of Greek society and had done everything short of killing him to keep him away from Stella, Theo was starting off with an enormous minus handicap.

"Thank you for that much honesty, Stella." He hadn't expected it. "Since I already love him more than life itself and know you do, too, let's meet somewhere this evening to discuss him. A public place or not, whatever you prefer. Can you arrange for someone to watch him while we're together?"

"Of course, but it's not possible. I'm on Andros right now."

In other words, she assumed he was in Athens and that any plans he had for tonight were out of the question. He had news for her. "I can be there in an hour. Just tell me where you'll be exactly."

He counted a full minute while she was forced to realize he had a helicopter at his disposal. That put him in the same league with the way her family moved around. "There's a paddleboat concession on the beach in Batsi. I'll wait for you there in the parking lot at seven-thirty."

She clicked off before he could say thank you, but it didn't matter. Progress had been made. The gods had been with him today.

He checked his watch. It was six-thirty. After phoning the pilot to give him their next destination, he rang the manager to say goodbye, then headed for the helipad with Boris.

Theo had never been to Andros, but Stella had told him so much about it, he felt like he knew its special places by heart. Certainly his son, young as he was, could probably show Theo around and know what he was talking about.

Andros was the home of the legendary Stasio Athas, where some of the most elite Greek families lived. To the people in Theo's family it represented lala land. A smile broke one corner of his mouth. This Pantheras member was about to trespass on ground not meant for untouchables.

Stella's elite family viewed other families like Theo's, who lived close to the poverty line, at the bottom of the food chain. When Theo had refused the money Nikos had thrust at him to stay away from Stella, Nikos had snarled words like *scum* and *untouchable* among the many insults hurled at him. Nice people, Stella's family.

He looked out the window. Summer had come to the Cyclades. As Andros came into view, his breath caught at the lush green island dotted with flowers. No wonder Stella loved it here. St. Thomas was idyllic, but it didn't compare in the same way.

After the helicopter had dropped down over the little port of Batsi, his gaze swerved to a white convertible sports car driving along the road at a clip toward the water. The sight intrigued him. Once the chopper touched ground, he jumped down and started across the wooded area to the car park where it had just pulled to a stop.

To his surprise he saw a well-endowed brunette woman climb out and walk around the area with confidence, as if she were searching for someone. Closer now, he noticed she bore a superficial resemblance to the lovely long-haired teen of Theo's youth.

Stella.

CHAPTER TWO

THE years had turned the only Athas daughter into a gorgeous female, whose classic white dress was cinched with a wide belt, highlighting curves above and below her slender waist. She'd always been beautiful to Theo, but having the baby had caused her to blossom.

Her high cheekbones, combined with the lovely contours of her face and glossy hair made her so striking, he couldn't look anywhere else.

He'd wondered how much she might have changed. What he hadn't expected was to feel his senses ignite by simply looking at her again. That wasn't supposed to happen, not when she'd kept all knowledge of their child from him.

Another step and their eyes met. Those velvety brown eyes he remembered so well stared at him with a mixture of shock and anxiety. After what she'd done, she ought to be terrified of him. She seemed to weave for a minute before she wandered back to her car and held on to the frame as if needing support.

He strolled up to the other side of the car. Deciding they were too much of a target for any observers, he climbed in the passenger side and shut the door. She hesitated before following suit.

The second she sat behind the wheel, her fragrance reached out to him. Again he was stunned because it was the scent he would always associate with her. It took him back to the last time they were together. Everywhere he'd kissed her, she'd tasted delightful, like fresh flowers on a warm spring morning.

Right now it was the last thing he wanted to be reminded of, but trying to blot out certain intimate thoughts was like attempting to hold back a tidal wave.

He turned to her, sliding his arm across part of the seat. She'd averted her eyes. If he wasn't mistaken, she was trembling. On some level it pleased him she wasn't in total control.

"Thank you for meeting me, Stella."

"You didn't leave me a choice." Her words came out jerkily.

"Actually, I did."

"You're talking about court. I can't imagine anything more terrifying for Ari," she cried, sounding desperate.

"Believe it or not, it frightens me even more. Too much time has been lost as it is." It surprised him how much he wanted to reach out and touch her, to see if she was real. "You were always lovely before, but you've turned into a startlingly beautiful woman."

If anything, her features hardened at the compliment.

His gaze drifted beyond her face. "Strange how this little secluded stretch of beach reminds me of—"

"Don't." Her profile looked chiseled. Apparently she'd had the same impression and didn't want to travel down that road of remembered ecstasy. "I agreed to meet you so we could talk about the best way to help Ari deal with this situation."

A situation that had been put in play six years ago

and was never of his choosing, but he didn't voice his thoughts. For the moment Theo was walking on eggshells. "Do you think he'd be more comfortable meeting in Athens than here?"

She kneaded her hands, drawing his attention to her beautifully manicured nails. He grimaced to realize every part of her body looked quite perfect to him. It was impossible to eye her dispassionately. "Ari won't be comfortable anywhere with you, but since we're staying on Andros for a while, it should probably take place here."

"What have you told him about me?"

She sucked in her breath. "Very little."

"Even so, could you spell that out for me?"

Suddenly she jerked her head in his direction. Those gorgeous brown eyes pierced his with laserlike intensity. "You mean the way you spelled it out for me?" she cried. Her hands had gripped the steering wheel with enough force he imagined she could bend it. "I told him the truth, that you didn't love me after all, so we never saw each other again. That was all I knew to tell him. It's all he knows."

Theo studied her features. "Yet you left out half the story. It's time he heard that *you* stopped loving me. I'm sure he has no idea that you never intended to come to the church and go away with me so we could be married and have our baby in peace."

The blood seemed to drain out of her face. "I was there, waiting inside the back of the nave. I waited for hours," her voice throbbed.

Theo was incredulous. "That's an interesting fairy tale. I was attacked before I could make it inside and was told that you got rid of our baby because you didn't want anything to do with me." For now he didn't want to mention Nikos's name and give her something else to fight him about.

"You're lying!" she lashed out. "No one would believe such a monstrous story."

"In the beginning I didn't, either, not until you never, ever tried to make contact with me again. Obviously, this is a case of your word against mine, except I have the scars to prove it."

"What scars?"

"The ones you're looking at. While we've been talking, I've felt your eyes on me. They're traveling over the small cuts, noticing the dents where my face got smashed in and my nose had to be rebuilt. These are nothing compared to what my X-rays show below the neck."

Stella quickly concealed her glance, but not before he glimpsed confusion in those dark brown depths. That was something, at least.

"Whatever happened to you," she finally said in a less-than-assured voice, "don't you think it's stretching it just a little to take six years before showing up?"

"Under ordinary circumstances, yes, but after you were nowhere to be found and all my mail to you came back unopened, I realized I would have to return to Greece and hire a PI to locate you. Unfortunately, I didn't have that luxury at the time, not when I was building a business I couldn't leave."

Her head whipped around. "I don't know what mail you're talking about."

Theo reached in his trouser pocket for the first letter he'd sent to her after he'd gotten out of the hospital. He'd addressed it to Stella at the Athens villa. It had the canceled stamp and date. Across the bottom the words "Addressee Unknown" had been scrawled.

"Take a look." He handed it to her. "If you're ever curious enough to read what's on the inside of the envelope, then you'll know my state of mind at the time. In the meantime, I'm here to claim what's mine—Ari."

She glanced at the front of it before tossing the letter back at him. "Ari's not yours," she said in an icy voice he didn't recognize.

He put the letter back in his pocket. "Let me phrase that a better way. He's both of ours."

She threw her head back, causing those glistening dark strands to splay across her jaw. Combined with her golden skin, she was a miracle of womanhood. "You gave him life, but that's all you did."

"That was all I was allowed to do," he countered. "Since you clearly don't believe me, let's not talk about the past. It's over and done with. I much prefer to discuss Ari's future. Perhaps you could bring him here tomorrow so we can get acquainted. We'll let him choose what he'd like, or not like, to do. How does that sound?"

Her body stirred in agitation. "You can't expect too much, if anything, Theo."

As if he didn't know. "I'm aware of that. What time shall I meet you both?"

She started the car. "Tomorrow's Sunday. We have plans." She was stalling, but he had to be patient if he hoped to get anywhere with her. "The day after would be best. One o'clock."

"I'll be here. Stella, I swear I'll treat him with the greatest consideration possible. I'm not unaware he wouldn't be the marvelous boy he is if you weren't his mother. You were meant to be a mother, Stella. Every child should be so lucky."

Though they weren't touching, he could feel her

trembling. "Y-you can have two hours with him if he's willing," she stammered.

"That's more than I'd hoped for. The Stella I once knew was a giver. Remember that little heart I gave you?" It had been a cheap trinket he'd bought her in the Plaka because it had been all he could afford, but the sentiment had described her. "Love the giver."

She revved the engine, obviously not liking being reminded of anything to do with their past. "Please get out of the car. Ari's waiting for me."

There was a time when she would have begged him not to leave. Of course, back then he wouldn't have gone anywhere because he'd needed one more kiss, one more embrace before wrenching his mouth from hers. Damn if he didn't need her mouth so badly right now he was ready to explode.

Forcing himself to act, he got out of the front seat. "I love your car by the way. With its classic lines, it looks like you. In case you didn't know, that white dress was made for you."

For an answer she backed out and drove off.

Stella only made it two kilometers before she had to stop the car for a minute. She buried her face in her hands. How was it possible Theo could get under her skin like this after the pain she'd undergone at his hands?

Inside of half an hour he'd pushed every button until she'd wanted to scream. But what truly haunted her was the change in his facial features.

As far as the gradation of male beauty was concerned, Theo had been a beautiful man before. If she were honest with herself, he still was. However, one scar pulled at the corner of his mouth a little. His right eyelid didn't open as wide as the other. At some angles it gave him a slightly sinister look. His nose was still noble, but there were several bumps.

Theo hadn't lied about the damage done to him. As he got out of the car, she'd seen the scar below his left earlobe. A thin white line ran down his bronzed neck into the collar of his dark blue shirt.

The rest of his tall body covered by his elegant clothes revealed he'd grown into a powerfully built man. She didn't want to think about the damage beneath the surface he'd referred to, the kind an X-ray could detect.

He had an aura about him that hadn't been obvious six years ago, but that was because he'd needed time to mature. Other men would be intimidated by him now. She bit her lip because she recognized that women would be irresistibly drawn to him.

While deep in torturous thought, she heard his helicopter pass overhead. Embarrassed that he might think she'd had to pull over because of her reaction to him, she started driving through the cobblestone streets of Batsi toward Stasio's villa in Palaiopolis.

En route she picked up some toiletries in the village, proof of the reason she'd had to go out for a little while. She'd left the boys swimming in the pool with Rachel and the girls.

Unless Ari had let something slip to the family by mistake, she felt relatively confident they could keep Theo's presence a secret so they could get through this holiday without anyone being the wiser. On Monday she would tell the family she was going to drive the boys around the island as Dax hadn't been to Andros before.

Stasio worked so hard. Now that he'd taken three weeks off work to enjoy his wife and children, she didn't want her problems to mar their families' precious time together. Hopefully when Nikos arrived, he wouldn't cause trouble.

He'd been wildly against her keeping Ari. In his opinion it wasn't fair to their parents' wishes, nor to Stella, who didn't have a husband and who couldn't give Ari what adoptive parents could. He'd been furious at Stasio for helping her, telling him he should have kept out of things.

She knew Nikos didn't like Ari. Her son knew it, too, thus the reason he clung to Stasio who openly adored him. That Nikos couldn't show Ari affection caused Stella perpetual sadness and made it hard for her to be around him. A long time ago she had decided he didn't have the capacity to be happy, especially after their parents died.

Perhaps it was wicked of her, but a part of her hoped he might decide not to come this holiday. With the advent of Theo in their lives, Ari had enough going on without worrying about Nikos. But maybe she was getting way ahead of herself. It all had to do with Theo, who was well and truly back in Athens, demanding to spend time with her son.

His son, too, her conscience nagged.

No matter what terrible things had happened to Theo, surely it was too late for him to start up a relationship with Ari that should have begun at his birth?

Hot tears rolled down her cheeks. The agony of his rejection and the desolate years that followed could send her over the brink if she allowed herself to dwell on that nightmare. No more.

All she wanted was to be able to provide a wonderful life for Ari. She wasn't about to let Theo suddenly show up and turn their lives into chaos. Did he really think she would believe that the letter he'd shown her was authentic? She wiped the moisture from her cheeks before entering the gate that led up the drive to Stasio's villa.

Apparently she'd arrived in time to join everyone for a motorboat ride followed by dinner further up the coast. It was probably Stasio's idea because he knew Ari liked to steer part of the time, with Stasio's guidance of course. Undoubtedly Dax would get a turn, too. An evening out on the water sounded heavenly to her.

Stasio helped her into the boat with a hug. Her handsome brother looked so happy, she knew her secret was safe for the moment.

Theo flew to Andros on Monday at noon. He'd brought a backpack filled with treats and a few other essential items. Not sure what Ari would like to do, Theo had opted to wear casual trousers with a navy T-shirt and hiking boots. Today he would let Ari make all the decisions.

After grabbing a sandwich and a drink at a nearby taverna with Boris, he strolled over to the concession area to watch for Stella's car. It hardly seemed possible this day had come. He'd been dreaming of it for too long. This morning he'd awakened wired, unable to concentrate on his work.

The beach had filled up with tourists. He would have preferred not to be around a lot of people, but he had to follow Stella's lead if he wanted to gain a modicum of trust. While he tried to imagine his son's thoughts, his heart picked up speed as he spied Stella's car.

Riding with her were two boys of the same age sharing the passenger seat. One dark, the other blond, they pulled into the parking area. Stella had sprung a surprise on him. If she felt there was strength in numbers, that was all right with him. He'd deal with it.

Adjusting his pack to his shoulders, he approached the car. "Hello, Ari," he said, smiling at his son, who had on khaki shorts and a soccer jersey. He was on the lean side with black-brown hair; the kind of handsome child every man dreamed of fathering. The sight of him and his mother caused Theo's breath to catch in his throat.

He studied his son. The only thing that was going to guarantee any success at all was the purity of Ari's spirit and Theo's unqualified love for the child who was part him, part Stella. If their boy had inherited her sweetness, her loving nature, then maybe Theo had a prayer of getting through to him. But he knew it would have to be on Ari's timetable.

"Hi," he responded without enthusiasm, refusing to look at him.

"Who's your friend?"

"Dax."

"Hi, Dax. I'm glad you came. I want to get to know Ari's friends. I think there's a character on the *Star Trek* television series with your name? He has special powers."

Dax blinked. "I already know that. How did *you* know?"

"I love science fiction. Especially UFO stories."

"Me, too. My dad thinks they're stupid though."

"Well, I don't."

"Rachel knows some real ones," Ari said, drawn into their conversation in spite of himself.

"Who's Rachel?"

"My aunt. Her daddy was a pilot in the air force."

Theo's eyes took in Dax, who wore jeans and a tank top. Stella had put on trousers and a white blouse that her figure did wonders for. Considering everyone's attire to be appropriate, he made a decision.

"Your mother told me we would only have two hours today, Ari, but I think it's long enough to go for a hike. What do you say we all go?"

"That sounds cool," Dax responded enthusiastically.

Ari stared at Theo in surprise.

"You mean Mom, too?"

"She and I spent all our time outdoors. We must have walked all over Salamis Island. There's no one I'd rather trudge up a mountain with. In fact, I'd like to see if she can still keep up with me."

Theo moved around the other side of the car and opened the door for Stella, who looked at a total loss for words.

"I...I didn't plan to come with you." Her voice faltered.

"Please, Mom?" Apparently this idea pleased their son. With his mother along, he wouldn't be so afraid. Theo couldn't ask for more than that. She would have trouble refusing.

"I second the motion," Theo murmured. "You know all the secret places around here. I remember you telling me about the deserted lookout on the mountain behind us where you once found an eagle's nest."

Again Ari looked surprised. He stared at Stella. "I've never seen it."

"That's because I've never taken you hiking up there, honey."

Good. This would be a new experience for the four of them. "Let's find out if it's still there, shall we? I've brought enough goodies for all of us."

Everyone was looking at her. She could hardly say no. Stella would walk through fire to protect their son. "Well, all right."

While the boys got out, Theo assisted her. The sight of those long, elegant legs covered in khaki raised his blood pressure. When their arms brushed by accident, it sent a rush of desire through his body so intense he was staggered. To his chagrin, everything about her appealed to him more than ever.

"Ari? I bet you know how to put the top up on the car for your mother." The boy nodded, but Theo could tell Ari hadn't thought of it until it was mentioned. "That's good. We want it to be safe while we're gone. This car's a beauty," he said, eyeing Stella. She looked away.

"Will you let me do it, Mom?"

"I'll help," Dax volunteered.

"Yes. Of course." She'd been outvoted and outmaneuvered. Nothing could have pleased Theo more. He helped the boys and made easy work of it.

Once she'd locked the car with her remote, Theo opened his pack. "Give me your purse." Though he sensed she was fighting him every step of the way, she had to be careful in front of Ari. After she'd handed it to him, he zipped the compartment and eased it onto his shoulders a second time.

"If everyone's ready, there's a footpath beyond that copse of trees running up the side of the valley. Last one to the lookout is a girlie man."

Both boys laughed. Dax asked, "What's that?"

"A phrase I picked up while I was living in New York. It means wimp!"

Ari's smile faded. He stared hard at him as they walked. "Mom and I used to live in New York."

That was where she'd gone? Where she'd been for so long?

It was an astounding piece of news, despite the fact

that he knew Stasio did business there on a regular basis. To think Ari had been living in the same city where Theo had worked… So close? It slayed him. "Did you like it?"

"Yes, but I like Greece better."

"So do I."

"Come on, everyone," Stella urged. "At this pace we'll never get there." Theo wondered what had made her so nervous that she'd been a little short with Ari just now. A tight band constricted his breathing. By the end of their hike he intended to find out.

"I've never been to New York," Dax muttered.

"It's an exciting city."

"I thought you lived in Greece."

"I did until my twenties, Dax, then I moved to New York to earn my living. Now I have an office in Athens and am back to stay." Stella walked ahead of him with Ari, but he suspected she was listening to make sure the conversation didn't touch on things she wanted kept quiet.

"What do you do?"

"I deal in stocks and investments. Some real estate. What does your father do?"

"He owns a bank."

Of course. Dax belonged to the approved sector of Greek society. "Does your mother have a job, too?"

"No. She stays home with my brother and sister and me."

"You're very lucky. Do you know my mother still helps my father run their taverna on Salamis? I can't ever remember when they weren't working. Sometimes I wished my mother could stay home with me and my brothers, but we were too poor. She had to work."

"Is she a cook?"

Theo smiled. "She's a lot of things. The other day I

told her she and papa didn't have to work anymore because I planned to take care of them from now on. Do you know what she said?"

Dax looked up at him. "What?"

"'I've worked all my life, Theo Pantheras. If I didn't have work, I wouldn't know what to do with myself.'"

Ari slowed down and turned around. "Do they know about me?" Stella looked back. The pain in her eyes as she reached for their son tore him apart.

"They know all about you and hope the day will come when you might like to meet them."

To ease the moment, Theo pulled off his pack and opened a compartment. "Let's see. I've got water, oranges, peanuts, hard candy. Who wants what before we race the rest of the way?" The relief on Stella's face needed no explanation.

Once they'd refreshed themselves, Theo stood next to a pine tree. "I'm going to count to twenty while you two guys head up the trail first. Take my binoculars, Ari. If you see something exciting, shout."

The second he started counting in a loud voice, they took off on a run. It was steeper in this section and the trail zigzagged up through the forest. "Twenty!" he called out at last, then eyed Stella. "Are you ready to try catching up to them?"

"Just a minute, Theo."

"What's the matter? Are you about to tell me I've done everything wrong?"

Her chest heaved with the strength of her emotions. "Don't pretend you don't know you've done everything right," her voice shook. "Inviting Dax along made Ari feel comfortable."

"I thought that was why you brought him with Ari."

"No. I was going to take Dax on a little tour of the island while we waited for you, but your idea was much better." She wouldn't make eye contact with him.

"Then you're angry because I got you involved in the hike. When I saw Ari's face stripped of animation, I made an impulsive decision hoping it would help our son."

She wiped the palms of her hands against her womanly hips in a gesture of nervousness he'd seen many times years ago. He would always be touched by her vulnerability.

"Your instincts were dead on," she admitted. "I didn't expect him to have a good time today. Instead I…I have the feeling he won't be averse to seeing you again," she stammered. "That's what I need to talk to you about."

He chewed on some more peanuts. "Go on."

She cleared her throat. "We're here on vacation for two and a half more weeks." After a pause she leveled a guarded brown gaze with its hint of pleading on him. "Before you ask to see him again, would you wait until we're back in Athens?"

Two and half weeks sounded like a lifetime. "Of course I will," he answered in a husky tone without hesitation, "provided you tell me why you're so frightened for any more visits to take place here."

"I'm not frightened." Yet her whole trembling demeanor told him otherwise.

"Yes, you are." Without conscious thought he grasped her cold hands. "I take it your family is here and you haven't told them about me yet." Stella tried to pull away, but he drew her closer. "They're going to find out through Ari or Dax. You can't keep something of this magnitude a secret."

"Maybe not, but I'm hoping to deal with everything after we're back home in the city."

He grimaced. "It's like déjà vu, the two of us sneaking around to see each other without your family knowing what's going on. Nothing's changed has it."

"Please let me go." She tried to get away, but he still had questions.

"It wouldn't be because you're afraid to see me again, would it?"

"Theo—"

"Do my scars repel you so much?"

"Your scars have nothing to do with anything!" Her anger sounded genuine enough to satisfy him on that score.

"Then stay here with me for a little while."

"I can't!"

"That isn't what you used to say to me."

"You mean until you left me waiting at the church?"

"We've already been over this, Stella. I told you I came for you, but I was accosted. When I was able to search for you, you'd disappeared on *me*."

A strange cry escaped her throat.

His hands slid up her arms where he could feel the warmth of her skin through the thin material of her blouse, seducing him. He gave her a gentle shake. "Do you honestly believe I wouldn't have come to the church unless a life-and-death situation had prevented me? You and I talked marriage long before I found out I'd made you pregnant."

Her eyes filled with tears. "I don't want to talk about it. The boys might see us."

"They're at least a kilometer away by now. We *have* to discuss this at some point." He slowly relinquished his hold on her.

She shook her head, backing away from him as if the contact had been too much for her. "I don't know what to believe about anything. If you'll please give me my purse, I'm going back to the car while you join the boys."

He took several deep breaths to calm down while he got it out for her. The fact that she needed to run away from him meant it was possible his logic was getting through to her. His heart leaped. "Will you be all right going back alone?"

"That's an odd question to ask when you haven't been around in years. Please go and catch up to the boys. This is unfamiliar territory to them."

"I'll bring them back safely."

She darted away like a gazelle, leaving him bereft. He watched until he couldn't see her anymore, then he hurried up the mountain filled with new energy.

The Stella he'd loved to distraction was still there beneath her defenses, breathing life back into his psyche. He'd forgotten he could feel like this. In time he would get answers to why she never tried to get in touch with him again. She wasn't going anywhere now. Neither was he.

Before long he discovered the boys at the outlook. Dax had the binoculars trained on something. When he saw Theo, he pointed to an area along the ridge, then handed them over. Theo raised them to his eyes.

"You have a sharp eye, Dax. That's an Elenora falcon having fun with a friend."

They weren't thirty meters away. He handed the field glasses back. "Just like you and Ari."

Dax laughed, but there wasn't a glimmer of a smile from Ari's lips. Theo hadn't expected much positive reaction from his son yet and he wasn't getting it. To make progress he was going to have to practice infinite patience if he hoped Ari would let him into his life, let alone show him love.

Stella had received his promise that he wouldn't try to see Ari again until they were back in Athens. He had to honor it, but he didn't have to like it.

"I hate to break this up, but your mother is waiting for us." He opened his pack. "Finish off whatever's left and we'll go."

The boys needed no urging to eat the snacks. Theo packed the binoculars and they took off down the mountain.

Stella had already put the top back down. She looked as composed and untouched as before. Much to his satisfaction Theo could see the little nerve throbbing madly at the base of her throat, giving him irrefutable proof to the contrary.

When they reached the car, he checked his watch. The outing had taken three hours. More time with his son than he'd expected. He studied Stella's profile while he fastened the boys' seat belts and shut the door. "You guys were great sports today. I had one of the best times I've ever had. Maybe we can do it again some time."

Dax high-fived him. "It was awesome."

Ari squinted at him. "Is that your helicopter over there?"

His son didn't miss much. "Yes."

"Who's that man walking around?"

"My bodyguard. His name is Boris."

A short silence ensued. "Stasi has one, too." And his own hit men who included Nikos, but Ari wouldn't know that. "Are you going back to Athens now?"

Theo thought about his question. Ari probably

couldn't wait to get rid of him. But fool that Theo was, he'd dared hope he detected a forlorn tone in his son's question. Then again it was possible Ari was just being curious. Hell— Theo didn't know what to think.

Ari was his son, a boy he'd only known for three hours. The horror story of the past shouldn't have happened. His pain was starting all over again in a brand new way. "Actually I'm flying to my home on Salamis Island."

"Do you live with your mama and papa?" Ari asked quietly.

They are your grandparents, Ari. "No. They live in Paloukia, upstairs above the taverna." Ari wouldn't know what that would be like to live with so many bodies thrown together in a small space. So little privacy. The walls thin. Hand-me-down clothes. The smells from the kitchen permeating everything. "My house is on the beach about ten minutes away from them."

"Oh."

"Thank you for a fun hike, guys."

"It was cool!" Dax cried with enthusiasm. Nothing from Ari of course. Stella had averted her eyes.

Theo wheeled away from them and strode toward the helicopter. He didn't dare look back or he wouldn't want to leave.

CHAPTER THREE

FOR one crazy minute a sense of loss swept over Stella, the kind she used to feel every time she had to leave Theo and hurry home.

No— This couldn't be starting all over again. She wouldn't allow it.

Like the other day she found herself speeding toward the villa while Theo's helicopter flew overhead. But there was one difference. This time she didn't stop to give in to her emotions or relive feeling Theo's hands on her again. Today he'd caught her off guard. Never again.

"When we get back and anyone asks, remember that we drove around, got some treats and stopped at Batsi to do some paddle boating. Do you guys think you can handle that?"

Dax nodded. Ari didn't say anything, but she knew he'd keep quiet. She wasn't surprised he was in a state of shock. A full dose of Theo Pantheras for three hours would awe any child, especially when the bigger-than-life man was his own father.

Once they reached the villa and the boys hurried to Ari's room to change into their swimsuits, Stella went straight to hers to call Dax's mom and assure her all was going well. This was the boy's first trip away from his parents with her and Ari. It was an experiment of sorts. So far Dax seemed perfectly happy. Theo had made the outing so exciting she doubted the boy had given home a thought.

She sat down on the side of her bed to phone her. As soon as they talked, maybe she'd be able to enjoy the holiday she'd been looking forward to before Theo had burst on the scene like one of those UFOs they'd talked about earlier.

That particular conversation had been a natural ice-breaker in ways Theo couldn't possibly have imagined. For his age Ari showed an interest in science fiction on an adult level. After the talks with his aunt Rachel, he was determined to be an astronomer when he grew up and search for new galaxies with life on them.

All this time Stella had thought he'd picked up this passion from his aunt, but now she was convinced he'd come by it through his Pantheras genes. Ari had several of the *Star Trek* series on DVD. Who could have guessed Theo was a *Star Trek* junkie too? It only showed Stella how little she knew about Theo.

"Stella?"

"Hi, Elani."

"How's it going with my boy?"

"They're having a terrific time. We just got back from a hike, and now they're going to swim."

"No problems yet?"

She smiled. "Not one." For the next few minutes she told her everything they'd been doing, only leaving out the details that Theo had been along. After Stella got back to Athens, she would confide in Elani about him. For now the episode on the mountainside when she'd been alone with Theo would be her secret. That was a mistake she wouldn't be making another time.

"Promise to let me know if there's any trouble with him and we'll come for him."

"So far so good, my friend. I'll make certain he calls you tonight before he goes to bed. I'm sure he'll want to."

"You're an angel, Stella. Talk to you later."

They both hung up.

Stella sat there in a daze, her thoughts on Theo. Though he might have killed her love long ago, the way he'd treated their son today convinced her he didn't want to make any mistakes with Ari.

She went over the day's events in her mind. He hadn't tried to influence Ari unduly or put fear in him with underlying threats of any kind. The truth was, he hadn't done one thing wrong. Not in front of their son.

The other part had been her fault for not telling Ari to go hiking alone with his father. Instead she'd let his apprehension persuade her to join all of them for the hike.

Except that wasn't the whole truth, and this was the part she hated admitting to herself. When Theo conned her into going with them, it hadn't been Ari she was thinking about.

Her curiosity over the man he'd become had been her Achilles' heel. In that moment of weakness she had given in and it had almost cost her her soul all over again. Would she never learn her lesson when it came to Theo?

She jumped up and hurried into the bathroom to put on her bathing suit. Amazing that on the way to meet Theo in Batsi, she'd imagined the outing would end in disaster, but nothing could have been further from the truth.

Stella was in shock. A new Theo had risen from the ashes, yet in all the ways that counted, she found him to be remarkably similar to the younger man. That Theo had stolen her heart before hurling it into the void where it could never be recovered.

Now he was back with a different explanation of what had happened the night she'd waited for him at the church. Wherever the truth lay, it had happened too long ago to do anything about now. The damage had been too pervasive for too many people. You couldn't go back and pick up the pieces. It wasn't possible.

"Mom?" Ari came running into her room.

"I'm in the bathroom changing!" Mortified that Theo was still on her mind, heat stormed her cheeks. "I'll be right there! I had to phone Dax's mother first."

"Aunt Rachel wants to know if you're coming out to the pool."

"Of course!"

"She says Stasi's starving and wants to eat outside now."

When her brother got hungry, it was wise to feed him. "Tell her I'll be right there," she called from the doorway. A second later she walked in the room with her towel and discovered Ari still standing there. Dax had to be downstairs. If Ari didn't want to talk, he would have run back to the pool.

"What is it, honey?"

He stared at her with the most somber expression. "Does my father want to see me again?"

Naturally it was about Theo. "You know he does. That's why he went to all the trouble to take you on a hike today."

"But he didn't say anything before he left in his helicopter, so does that mean he changed his mind about me?"

Was it fear or hope she heard in his question? "Ari, come here." She sat on the end of the bed. He walked over to her. "While we were alone, I told him our family is on vacation right now and asked him if he would wait to plan another visit until we get back to Athens. I hope that eases your mind a little."

By his frown, it appeared her answer didn't satisfy him. She began to realize there was nothing she could say to help him right now.

"Will I have to go with him?"

She sucked in her breath. "I tell you what. If you don't want to be alone with him, I'll go with you again next time." She searched his eyes. "He was nice to you today, wasn't he?" Her son didn't say anything. Stella couldn't tell what was going on in his mind.

Ari stared at his feet. She recognized that look of uncertainty. "Did your father frighten you today in some way I don't know about? You have to be honest and help me understand."

He shook his head. "No."

"But he did upset you, didn't he."

"Yes."

He dashed out of the room leaving her totally desolate. She hurried through the myriad of corridors and down some steps to catch up to him. When she reached the patio he was just jumping in the pool.

"Oh, good!" Rachel called to her. "Stasio! Come on out! We're ready to eat."

Stella found Dax and made sure he filled his plate. She fixed herself some food too and sat on the swing next to him because Ari was still swimming.

Speaking in a hushed tone she said, "Did you really have a good time today?"

He nodded. "It was great!"

"Then could you tell me what Ari's father did that seemed to upset Ari? Do you know anything?"

"No, but he got mad at me."

She frowned. "Mr. Pantheras got mad at you?"

"No. Ari."

"He did? When?"

"When we got back to the house he wouldn't talk to me and started playing with the girls."

That didn't sound like Ari. "I'm sorry, honey. His behavior doesn't have anything to do with you."

"He told me I should go home."

Stella hated hearing that. "He didn't mean it, Dax. Of course your feelings got hurt, but he'll get over what's wrong and apologize. After dinner I'll have a talk with him." *Another one.* "I bet he tells you he's sorry before we finish eating."

Except that Ari didn't do anything typical for him. He stayed in the pool, refused to eat and teased Cassie until she got out of the water and ran to her mother in tears. Even Stasio was aware something was wrong and got in the pool to talk to him.

But Ari wasn't having any of it and left the patio on a run. Stasio sent her a questioning glance. This wasn't good.

"Excuse me for a minute, Dax. I'll be back."

With a pounding heart she chased after her son. When she caught up to him, he was on the verge of locking his bedroom door.

"Ari—" She crushed him in her arms, refusing to let him go.

It didn't take long before the sobs came. In his whole life she'd never seen him convulsed like this.

"Tell me what you're feeling, darling. Let me help," she begged. "I know you're upset over your father."

"I don't want to talk about him."

"Then we won't."

"I'm glad I don't have to see him until after our vacation." He wiped his eyes. "I'm going to go back downstairs now."

"To talk to Stasio?"

"No."

"Then what?"

"Nothing."

"Please wait—" He was about to leave. "Dax said you got mad at him. How come?"

"Because he made me mad while we were hiking."

"I see." Except that she didn't. Dax was a darling boy. They'd always gotten along perfectly. "That happens with friends. You've had a lot of togetherness today. When you go back downstairs, do me a favor and make up with him? He's out on the patio feeling bad. If the shoe were on the other foot, you'd be feeling pretty awful about now."

"I don't want to make up."

"That doesn't sound like you." Stella didn't see her son act this way very often. "You still have to apologize because he's our guest. And while you're at it, how about telling Cassie you're sorry for keeping her beach ball away from her in the pool? She's only four, honey. When a big boy like you takes her stuff, she can't defend herself."

"Sorry."

"Tell *her* that. Okay?"

He nodded, then disappeared.

By the time she reached the patio, Ari had found Dax and had started to eat a lamb shishkabob with him while they talked privately. Pretty soon the boys got in the pool and played nicely with Cassie, letting her have the ball when it was her turn. Stasio flashed her a smile, glad all was well again.

Stella slipped in the deep end and did the backstroke, trying to unwind after a day she'd never forget. Ari might be acting normally right now, but she knew that deep inside, his emotions were in turmoil. So were hers.

Maybe she was wrong to ask Ari not to say anything to Stasio yet, but she wanted to believe they could handle this situation on their own. Stella hated to think she had such a weak character she always turned to her brother for help. How would Ari ever stand on his own two feet if he ran to Stasio every time there was a crisis? It had to stop.

The next day Stella walked into Ari's bedroom with some ice water for him. They'd just come back from a day's sailing. He'd picked up a little too much sun and complained he didn't feel very well. While the rest of the family and Dax played in the pool before dinner, she excused herself to see about him.

He lay on his back on top of the covers with his sun-tanned arm covering his eyes.

She sat down next to him and felt his forehead.

"You're hot. Drink this, honey. I'm going to get my phone and call the doctor."

She raced to her room, then hurried back to him. Relieved to see him drink part of it, she phoned information and got connected to the doctor's office. His receptionist said he was busy. After leaving a message for him to call, she hung up and took the glass from Ari.

"I don't want to see the doctor. I'll be okay."

"Let's let him be the judge of that."

"I wish Dax could go home, but I know he can't."

Dax again.

"Of course he can. All I have to do is call Elani and

she'll come for him." She studied him with an aching heart. He hadn't been the same since the hike with Theo yesterday. "Did you two have trouble again today?"

"Yes."

"Want to tell me about it?"

"No." He turned over so he wouldn't have to look at her.

"We have to talk, honey. Something's very wrong. Don't you know how much I love you?"

"Yes."

On impulse she said, "If you need to talk to your uncle about your father, then I'll ask him to come up here after he's through eating."

"I don't want Stasi." That had to be a first. He rolled off the bed so fast, she knew she'd touched a live wire.

"Why aren't you getting along with Dax?"

"Because he wants to talk about stuff I don't want to talk about."

"You mean like personal things?"

He nodded.

On a burst of inspiration she said, "Has he been asking questions about your father?"

"Yes."

"Like what?"

"He thinks my daddy is cool."

"I take it Dax got along well with him."

"They talked all the time."

She knew she was getting closer to some kind of answer. "Dax's father is an older man and fairly quiet. Dax probably liked Theo's attention."

"He keeps asking me about when I'm going to see him again so we can all do stuff together." His eyes filled with tears. "He's not Dax's daddy!"

"What do you mean?"

He blinked back the tears to keep them from falling. "My daddy liked Dax better than me."

"What?"

"I thought he wanted to be with me, but he was nicer to Dax. I hate both of them."

"Oh, darling!" Stella reached for him and hugged him harder while she tried to comprehend that far from feeling hostility toward his father, Ari was jealous of the attention Theo had paid to his best friend.

In order to feel jealous, it meant you had to care.

This meant Ari had nursed a longing for his birth father all his cognitive life, but it had lain dormant until put to the first test.

Before yesterday she'd assumed Theo would see that it was too late to bond with Ari. She'd been positive her son would never be able to warm up to him. Ari already had a surrogate father in Stasio, the best man in the world. He didn't need or want another one. In the end Theo would find out it was no use, but the surprise had been on Stella.

She had to do something immediately to help Ari, but what? Only one person had the power to make this right. For once it was beyond Stasio's ability to fix, which was a revelation in itself.

While she rocked her son back and forth, her cell phone rang. The last thing she wanted to do was answer it, but it was probably the doctor.

"Let me see who it is." She let go of him long enough to reach for her phone on the dresser.

She recognized the blank caller ID. It was Theo! She almost bit her lip all the way through before answering it. "Hello?"

"Stella?" The sound of his deep voice permeated

through her body to the soles of her feet. "I promised you I wouldn't try to see Ari until after your vacation, but I need to see you tonight. Alone," he added, sending a shock wave through her body. "I'm here in Palaiopolis at a small bistro called Yanni's. I'm seated at a table on the terrace overlooking the water and will wait an hour for you to come."

Stella's pulse sped up. She'd been there once with Rachel, but it was a romantic spot meant for couples so she had never gone to that particular restaurant again. "I-is there something wrong?" she stammered.

"Yes. I'll tell you when you get here."

She shifted her weight nervously. "I don't know if I can come without arousing suspicion."

"It's important." After a slight pause, "While you're thinking about it, I'd like to talk to Ari for a minute and tell him how much our outing meant to me yesterday. With Dax around I couldn't say all the things I wanted to. Do you think he'd be willing to come to the phone or call me back? If he doesn't want to do either, then I'll leave it alone."

Stella couldn't believe the timing of his call or the reasons for it. But she heard something in his voice that sounded like he was anxious. "Just a minute and I'll check."

She put it down on the dresser and walked over to Ari. "It's your father on the phone. He'd like to talk to you for a minute."

That brought Ari's head around. "What does he want?"

Her poor boy had been suffering all last night and today. She'd known it, but she hadn't known about the jealousy.

"He said there are things he wanted to tell you but couldn't because Dax was there. You don't have to talk to him now. He said you could call him anytime or not at all. It's your choice, honey."

He took a long time making up his mind before he walked over to pick it up.

She held her breath as he said a tentative hello.

At first it was a very one-sided conversation with Theo doing most of the talking. She thought it would end fast, but like every assumption she'd made since he'd come back into her life, he surprised her with the unexpected.

In a minute Ari grew more animated. He actually laughed at one point. Before the phone call, she hadn't thought it possible. The call went on another five minutes.

All of a sudden he said, "Mom?"

"Yes?"

"Do I have to wait till our vacation is over to see my father again?"

How utterly incredible! She'd died and come back to life several times since Theo had returned to Athens. "What about Dax?"

"Dad says I can ask him to come with us if I want. It's up to me."

Amazing. Theo had taken the sword out of their son's hand without knowing it. "Then it's fine."

Stella couldn't believe she'd just said that, but after Ari had been honest with her just now, she was thankful tonight's crisis had been abated by the only person who could help their son.

The fact that Theo was the cause of all the trouble in the first place hadn't escaped her, but none of that mattered in light of Ari's pain which seemed to have vanished at the sound of his father's voice. She would call the doctor back and tell him everything was okay after all.

"Mom? Do we have anything planned for tomorrow?"

That soon?

"Nothing special."

More conversation ensued before he walked over with her phone still in his hand. She waited for him to say something.

"Did you make plans?"

He made an affirmative sound in an offhand manner like it was no big deal, but the light in his brown eyes told her it was a very big deal.

"Mind filling me in first?"

"Dad's going to fly us to Meteora at four o'clock. He says that's where the monasteries are. We're going to hike around until it gets dark. He'll bring his telescope so we can look at the stars. Maybe we'll see some UFOs."

Stella could only marvel.

"It's a good thing your aunt Rachel won't know about this or she'd want to go with you."

"Don't worry. He said no women allowed this trip." This trip? Theo was doing everything right. She could find no fault. "I've got to tell Dax."

"Not yet," she cautioned him. "You and I still need to talk for a minute first. Stay here."

"Okay. Dad wants to speak to you again." He handed her the phone.

"Theo?" she asked too breathlessly for her own ears.

"Ari's response was more than I'd hoped for. It's yours I'm counting on now. This time, however, I'm the one waiting for *you* to show up. Let's pray no dark forces will prevent you from arriving."

Before she could say anything, Stella heard the click. It echoed the thud of her heart.

"Mom? Do you think Aunt Rachel would let me borrow her photos of Mars some time? I want him to see them."

"I'm sure she will."

"When do you think I could ask her?"

"Honey? I was hoping we'd keep this from the family until after we go back to Athens. You know, until we've got things a little more settled."

"Okay."

"Ari? Listen to me. Your father's here on Andros."

His eyes lit up. "He is?"

"Yes. He says he has to talk to me about something very important before he flies back to Salamis. I...I told him I would try to meet him, but I need your help because I don't want anyone else to know about it."

"I won't tell."

"I know that, so what I'd like you to do is stay here in your room and get ready for bed. I'll send Dax up to keep you company and you can tell him what your father has planned for tomorrow. In the meantime I'll tell Rachel I need to do an errand and will be right back."

"I wish I could go."

"Not this time, honey. Your father and I have things we need to discuss alone. Can you understand that?" He nodded. "You'll be seeing him tomorrow, right?"

His lips broke into a smile. "Yeah."

Stella kissed him and hurried to her room for her purse. She didn't dare change out of her pants and top she'd worn sailing. It might give her away.

"Rachel?" she said a minute later. Everyone was out by the pool eating. "Ari's resting. I think he got too hot, but he's feeling better now. Anyway, I'm running into town for some things he wants. I'll be back shortly." She turned to Dax. "When you're through eating, Ari hopes you'll come up."

"I'm all finished," he declared before darting away.

Glad everyone was preoccupied with the girls, Stella hurried out to her car and headed into town. On the way she phoned the doctor and told his receptionist that Ari was doing much better so the doctor didn't need to call back.

Due to the tourists, she had to park a street away from Yanni's. It was getting crowded. By the end of the evening, the night life would take over.

She hurried inside the bistro and told the hostess she was meeting someone out on the terrace. There was no sign of Boris, but that didn't mean he wasn't there.

The other woman showed her to Theo's candlelit table on the terrace. With every step, she wished she'd been able to wear an evening dress at least. Especially when she saw him get to his feet wearing an expensive black silk shirt and gray trousers. He stood out from the other males, drawing feminine attention from every direction including that of the sultry hostess.

His black gaze swept over Stella with that old intimacy. When he helped her to be seated, she felt his hands caress her shoulders lightly, as if he couldn't help himself. It took her back to another time when they hadn't been able to keep their hands off each other.

"You picked up a lot of sun today," he whispered against her ear. "Your beauty radiates like a torch. Every man out here envies me."

She tried not to react, but inside she was a quivering mass of emotions. Theo always did have that effect on her. Right now she was in danger of forgetting the chasm of pain separating them.

Once he was seated he said, "Since I knew you couldn't be gone long from the villa, I took the liberty of ordering for us."

Stella could hardly breathe for the way he was devouring her with his eyes. "You're very sure of me, aren't you."

His gaze narrowed on her features. "I'm sure of what we felt for each other before we were tragically prevented from getting married. Nothing since that time has changed for me. I'm operating on the belief that deep down you still have feelings for me."

She looked away while the waiter served them baked shrimp with garlic and onions. Theo remembered. It was one of their favorite dishes, accompanied by bread and a glass of house wine.

After their server had gone, she began to eat, realizing she was hungry. "This is delicious."

"Like the shrimp we used to eat at the Blue Lagoon during our walks on Salamis."

She reached quickly for the wine, wishing he wouldn't remind her. "We don't have much time. Why don't you tell me what's so important you had to see me tonight."

He broke his bread apart. "I asked you here to let you know I want a relationship with you, not just Ari."

The world reeled for a moment.

Theo had always been frank and direct. In that regard he hadn't changed, but life had changed the situation. She had to keep her head. "If you'll take a look around, Theo, there are any number of females who'd like to accommodate you given half a chance."

A sly smile broke one corner of his compelling mouth. "What females? I only see Stella Athas, the girl who ruined all other women for me."

"Theo…" her voice throbbed.

"You did, you know." He cocked his head. "I saw a lot of women in New York and found every single one wanting. I'd hoped to meet someone who would make me forget you, but it never happened. Believe me, if it had, I would have married her and stayed in the States."

His words sent a shiver through her body. After seeing him again, after knowing what he already meant to Ari, the thought of him married to anyone else brought a fierce new pain to her heart.

"How many men have you known since me?" His deep voice had taken on a territorial quality.

"That's none of your business."

"How many, Stella? They must be legion."

She stared at him through veiled eyes. "If you're asking what I think you're asking, the answer is none."

"But not for want of trying?" He lifted the last of the wine to his lips.

"I've been too busy raising Ari."

His jet-black gaze seemed to gleam in the flickering light. "You've done a superb job."

"Thank you." She couldn't handle this conversation any longer. After putting her napkin down, she got up from the table. He didn't make a move to stop her. "I have to buy a few items in town before I return to the villa. If I'm gone any longer, the family will wonder why."

"We can't have that, can we," he drawled.

Theo knew she was worried about her family's reaction to him being in her life again. It made her unable to sustain his glance. "I'll have the boys waiting at four."

"Come with us tomorrow."

"No," she blurted. She was in too deep already. Any more time spent in his company would confuse her even more. "Ari's looking forward to being alone with you. Good night, Theo."

After a few purchases she headed back to Stasio's. On her way, she needed to figure out an excuse why she and the boys would be gone from the villa tomorrow. She couldn't say they'd be going on a drive around the island again.

By afternoon of the next day Stella had finally come up with a plan. She told the family they'd decided to take a long hike in the mountains. Afterward they'd get a big dinner at one of the restaurants in Batsi and see a film, thus the reason they'd be home late.

At four, when she drove into the paddleboat parking area with the boys, Theo was waiting for them in thigh-molding jeans and a creamy cotton crew neck sweater. He looked so striking her pulse ticked right off the charts.

He put his hands on the door frame next to her. She felt his gaze wander over her, missing nothing. The smell of the soap he used had a familiar tang, causing her to tremble. "We'll be back at ten. Will you plan to join us for a light dinner afterward?"

"I don't think so." She looked at Ari who was still sitting next to her. "This is your night with your father."

"But I want you to come, Mom." He leaned closer and gave her a kiss on the cheek. On that note he got out of the car with Dax.

"You may be too tired to eat a meal that late. Why don't we see what happens."

"I'll take that as a yes" came Theo's low, smooth rejoinder before he put an arm around Ari's shoulders.

Stella didn't know her son, who laughed freely before the three of them hurried toward the waiting helicopter. She stared after them. Was that Theo's first physical gesture of affection toward their son? If so, Ari appeared to welcome it.

The two of them seemed to be bonding before her very eyes. If things continued like this, then she had to face the truth. Theo planned to be Ari's father in every sense of the word, something Ari obviously wanted. That meant Stella needed to grow another skin to survive.

Last night he'd told her he wanted them to have a relationship, but she was terrified. Right now the lines were blurred because she had an undeniable fatal attraction to him. Stella feared that given more time, she'd be right back where she'd started—madly in love with Theo.

On a groan, she walked toward the little town of Batsi where she would while away the hours until their return. She heard the helicopter pass overhead. The sound caused her to quicken her pace so she wouldn't think about the excitement she was missing by not being with them.

CHAPTER FOUR

THAT night Theo took the hostess aside and slipped her a tip. "Can you put us in front where the boys can watch the dancing up close?" He'd picked a taverna in Batsi that was tourist friendly regardless of ages.

"If you and your wife will follow me, I'll seat you."

"Thank you."

Stella had to have heard what the other woman said, but she pretended not to notice. Ushering the boys forward they moved through the crowded terrace to a table overlooking the bay. How many years had he dreamed of being with Stella like this, knowing he could take care of her and his own....

Several couples were already on the dance floor moving to the live band. He was aching to get her out there. Once he got the boys started on some snacks, he planned to steal her away where they could keep an eye on them while he held her as close as decency allowed.

Once a waiter came for their orders and the boys had told Stella about their outing, he asked to be excused before grasping her hand.

"Dance with me?"

"Do it, Mommy. I've never seen you dance before."

"She's an expert," Theo murmured. Without waiting for a yes or a no, he drew her out of the chair onto the floor.

Her body was stiff. "I haven't danced in years."

"Neither have I. The last time was at a church dance with you. Do you remember it was in the basement? Everyone was afraid with all the adults watching. I stepped on your foot."

"No, you didn't. I was the one who stepped on yours several times. I was so embarrassed I wanted to die."

He caught her close, pressing his cheek against the hotness of hers. "All I remember was that I was in heaven because Stella Athas, the most desirable girl in the world, had agreed to dance with me. I was the envy of all my friends who laid bets you wouldn't let me get near enough to touch you."

"Was I that impossible?"

"I thought that at first, but soon discovered you were just painfully shy. You presented a challenge I couldn't resist. My biggest fear was that once you found out I was a Pantheras, you would run from me and go to a different church where I couldn't find you."

"When I was a teenager, the last thing I thought about was money."

"I know that now, but everyone whispered you were an Athas who couldn't see the urchins at your feet."

She pulled back, staring at him through wounded eyes. "How awful that people felt that way."

"Not everyone, Stella." Obeying an insatiable need, he brushed his mouth against hers before winding his fingers into the back of her hair. She was so beautiful. She could have no idea how much he'd missed feeling her next to him.

Her eyes closed tightly. "Please keep your distance. We're on a dance floor with the children watching."

Theo couldn't help smiling. "Everyone else is dancing close." He was fast losing control.

"We're not everyone."

"No, we're not, thank heaven. There's only one Stella." He kissed her hair at the temple. "There are things we have to talk about. Expect a call from me before you go to bed tonight." Theo swung her toward their table and held the chair for her to sit down.

"How's the food, guys?"

"Good," Ari said. "The waiter brought us more drinks."

Dax nodded. "He said we could have as many as we wanted."

Feeling euphoric, he eyed his son. "Have you ever danced with your mother before?" He shook his dark head. "Now's your chance."

"I don't know how."

"I do. My mom taught me." Dax got up and went over to Stella.

She smiled. "I'm honored." Without hesitation she took him for a whirl around the floor.

Theo grinned at Ari. "You see? There's nothing to it."

He could tell his son was girding up his courage. A minute later they came back to the table. To Theo's delight, Ari got up and took his turn with Stella. Nothing like a little healthy competition.

Good for him. He had a shy side like his mother. With a little confidence, he was going to grow up to be an outstanding man. Whatever he chose to do, be it astronomy or otherwise, he had the intelligence and perseverance to succeed. Theo wanted to be his father on a twenty-four-hour basis. The way to do that depended on getting through to Stella.

As if she knew what he was thinking, the minute she came back with Ari, she checked her watch. "It's really late. I'm afraid we have to be going."

Theo put some bills on the table and helped Stella to her feet. The four of them left the restaurant and walked out into the warm Greek night. He accompanied them to the car, knowing better than to hug her too tight.

This time he high-fived his son first. "I had one of the best times of my life today."

"Me, too."

"You can call me anytime. When you're back in Athens, check with your mother and we'll make more plans."

Ari's head whipped around to Stella. "Can't we decide now?"

She looked tormented. "We'll talk about this later."

"Your mother's right. It's been a long day." He tousled both boys' hair, then flicked her a glance. "Drive home safely. Your car holds precious cargo."

Their eyes held for an instant before a look of determination to leave altered her features and she started the car. Ari looked back while they drove away and waved.

He raised his hand. Keep it up, Ari. Keep it up.

No sooner did the three of them walk into the villa than Stella heard a voice that always made her uneasy call to her. It was terrible to feel that way about her own brother, but there'd been too much history in the past to pretend his presence didn't affect her.

"Well, well." He scrutinized the three of them. "Who would have imagined you keeping such late hours."

"Hi, Uncle Nikos."

She paused in the entrance hall to give him a kiss on the cheek. He looked lean and dashing in his swim trunks. Her brother was the personification of the Olympic silver medallist who'd won one of the few medals for Greece in the downhill and giant slalom. He was an icon in his own right.

"Hello, Nikos. It's good to see you. Where's Renate?"

"Upstairs unpacking." His glance alighted on Dax. "Who's this?"

"My friend, Dax."

"Haven't seen you around here before."

"Ari invited me."

Knowing Ari felt uncomfortable, Stella put a hand on their shoulders. "Hurry on upstairs and get ready for bed. Don't forget to brush your teeth. I'll be up in a few minutes to say good night."

She gave them each a kiss before sending them off. Without the boys around, it was easier to deal with Nikos. "Is Stasio still up?"

"They're out on the patio. Are you joining us?"

"Not tonight. To be honest, I'm exhausted. Tell Renate I'll see her in the morning."

"How come you let Ari bring someone? This is our family time."

Stella bristled. "I can't believe you just said that. He's not going to be here the whole time, but even if he were, what difference does it make to you? You'll come and go as the mood suits you. As for the girls, they're two and four, hardly company for a six year-old all the time."

He looked taken back. She couldn't remember the last time that had happened.

"Since when did you become so prickly? I hardly know you like this."

"I didn't pick this fight, Nikos. You did by being offensive, not only to me but the boys." Theo had shown more loving kindness to Dax than Nikos had ever shown to Ari.

"Stella?" he called her back, his dark eyes angry. "What's gotten into you?"

"I'm still the same person. I've just decided to speak my mind the way you do. Sometimes it's not pleasant is it? Good night."

She walked up the stairs without looking back. It had felt good to be honest with him. However, there was no deluding herself. For as long as he stayed on Andros with his Austrian skier wife, also an Olympian, Nikos would make her and Ari pay the price.

That was still on her mind when she reached her room and discovered her son waiting on the top of her bed in his pajamas. Somehow it didn't surprise her.

"Hey, honey…why the long face after such a wonderful outing?"

"Mom? Do we have to stay here for our whole vacation?"

Thank you, Nikos!

"It's what we'd planned."

"But I want to be with my daddy. He has all these fun things we can do at his house."

She'd thought this was about Nikos, but it clearly wasn't. Stella took a steadying breath. "Haven't you been enjoying it here?"

He averted his eyes. "Yes."

"But?"

"I like being with him. He's awesome. Dax says so, too."

"I noticed. Is it like being with Uncle Stasio?" He was Ari's hero.

"Kind of, but he's my papa," he said quietly.

His papa…

"I wish we could go home tomorrow."

Knowing he already felt this strongly about his father, she had no doubt this was going to be a permanent situation from now on. But she needed to know a lot more about Theo's agenda. He wouldn't always have this much free time to spend with Ari. Her greatest desire was to protect their son from being hurt.

The fear of history repeating itself was uppermost in her mind, especially when things were moving so fast. Their lives were changing in ways she hadn't thought possible a week ago. Certainly Ari's world had undergone a total transformation.

"Tell you what. Your father will be calling me in a little while and we'll talk. I'll let you know what we decide in the morning."

His crestfallen look spoke volumes. He wanted answers now, but she couldn't give him one. "Okay." He slid off the bed and darted out of her room.

Her mind on Theo, she went into the bathroom to brush her teeth. If he'd flown straight to Paloukia, then he was probably home by now. She decided to get ready for bed first. Maybe by then he would phone her.

Ten minutes later she slid under the covers, still waiting for his call. Deciding to take the initiative, she reached in her purse for his letter and dialed his cell phone number. He picked up on the second ring.

"Ari?" The tender excitement in his voice was a revelation in and of itself.

"No. It's Stella. Is it a bad time for you to talk?"

"It's a perfect time. I just walked into the house and was about to call you."

She'd thought she could do this, but now she wasn't so sure. Too nervous to lie there, she got out of bed and began pacing.

"This is about Ari."

"I presumed as much, but I live in hope the day will come when you and I can have a conversation about the future. Our future."

Her breath caught. "We don't have time to talk about that right now."

"Why not? Did Ari get sick on all those hors d'oeuvres they ate while we were dancing?"

"No." She wished it were that simple. "Since he's been with you, he's a different boy."

"So am I. That's what happens when a father and son get together."

"That's my concern." She crushed the phone in her hand. "For how long?"

"Forever."

Her body started to shake. "Lots of relationships start out on a forever basis, but deteriorate with time."

"Our love didn't die, Stella," he declared in his deep male voice. "We were ambushed by a force neither of us had the power to stop at the time."

"You keep saying that!" she cried.

"Because it's true. If I thought you would take me at my word that I was torn from you, I'd never tell you another thing because I don't want you and Ari to go through any more hurt."

"What hurt? After what happened, how could there possibly be any more? Look, Theo—for Ari's sake I want to believe you because he wants to be with you, but I'm afraid my ability to trust died years ago."

"So, what are you saying?" His voice sounded bleak.

"Th-that I'm going to go on sheer faith and give you free access to him." Tears rolled down her cheeks. "You've got Ari's heart in your hands. If you do anything to disappoint him…" She couldn't talk for a minute.

"I'm here to stay, Stella. My life is totally tied up in him."

This was hard. So hard when those were the things she'd wanted him to say to her years ago.

"I pray you're telling the truth, because tonight he asked if we could cut our vacation short and go back to Athens in the morning. He wants to be available to you."

"What did you tell him?"

"That we'd talk about it in the morning."

"I'm sure that's the last thing you want to do when you love being with your family. They still don't know I've been seeing Ari?"

"No. It's my business. I've preferred keeping things private. They'll find out soon enough. I'll be driving back home in the morning with the boys."

"In that case I'd like to come to see him tomorrow afternoon. The three of us can talk over plans then."

"He'll be thrilled," she murmured.

"Even with all our history, it'll be the first time for me to make it inside your home, Stella."

She realized that. Years ago they'd had to be careful when he brought her back from an outing on his brother's motor scooter. He'd leave her a block away, then wait for her call when he got back home to make sure she was all right. Theo had never failed her. That's why his unprecedented behavior on that horrific night had been too much for her psyche to handle.

"Ari will be overjoyed." But nothing else has been resolved.

"No more than I. Thank you. This means more than you will ever know." His voice sounded thick-toned.

Get off the phone, Stella. "Good night."

"Good night. Drive home safely." She heard the concern in his tone before hanging up. The rest of the night she tossed and turned, hoping she'd made the right decision.

The second Ari came in the next morning, she told him they were leaving. He whooped it up before running to tell Dax to get his stuff together.

Stella packed quickly before going down to Stasio's study. He usually checked in with his secretary in the early mornings, even when he was on vacation. Like Theo, he was tall with arresting male features. There wasn't a mean bone in his body.

"Knock, knock."

"Stella? We missed you last night. Come on in."

"I'm just peeking in to say goodbye for now. Let's hope Rachel's morning sickness improves."

He frowned. "Bad as it is, I'm more concerned about you at the moment. Tell me what's wrong."

"Nothing specific." She hated lying to him, but she wasn't ready to talk about Theo yet. "Ari and Dax are restless. At home they have more friends their own age to do things with."

He studied her through veiled eyes. "You're not telling the truth, but that's your privilege. I've seen a marked difference in both of you since you arrived. Just remember, I'm here if you need me."

Her brother had radar. "I've always known that and I love you for it. Tell Rachel I'll call her later today after I'm back at the house. Say goodbye to Nikos and Renate for me, too."

Stasio came around his desk and gave her a big hug. "I'll walk you to the car."

The boys were already strapped in. It was so unusual for Ari not to seek his uncle out first, Stasio had to know something of great significance was going on.

"See you later, Uncle Stasi. Thanks for a great time."

"I had fun, too. Thanks a lot," Dax said.

"You come again, anytime you like." He gave Ari a hug.

Stella started the car and they took off for the port of Gavrion to catch the ferry.

No sooner had they driven onboard and walked to the promenade deck than a steward approached Stella.

"You are Despinis Athas?"

"Yes?"

"Your room is ready for you."

She blinked. "I didn't reserve one." Depending on weather and wind conditions to Rafina, the cruise only took two to three hours.

He gave her a knowing smile. "Someone else did. This way please."

"Come on, boys. Someone has planned a surprise for us." The blood hammered in her ears. She could only think of one person.

They followed the steward down to the next deck. He led them around a passageway to a row of cabins and opened the third one for her. Stella gasped when she walked in and saw two dozen long-stemmed red roses in a vase on the nightstand between two double beds.

To one side was a table and chairs. She spied a bowl of fruit, another filled with candy and cookies, and half a dozen cans of various juices.

"Are these for *us?*" Ari cried in delight.

"Who else would they be for?" sounded a deep, familiar male voice.

Stella spun around. "Theo—"

"Papa!" Ari ran to hug him. "We didn't know you were coming with us!"

Theo's black eyes found Stella's. They were so alive she could feel his energy. "Work can wait. I decided I wanted to join in the fun."

"Goody!" their son cried while Dax beamed and began loading up on candy.

Stella was happier to see him than she'd thought possible. "The flowers are gorgeous."

He came all the way inside and shut the door before leaning against it with his arms folded. In a tan sport shirt and white shorts, he looked incredible. "Remember the time we took a ferry to Poros? It was so crowded we had to stand the whole way against the railing at the back? I only had one red rose to offer you. In those days I was so poor, I could only afford to give you token presents."

Stella cherished any little thing he ever did for her. "I still have it," she half whispered. "It's pressed in the big dictionary I keep on my bookshelf at home."

"I've seen that," Ari commented. "I didn't know Daddy gave it to you."

Theo's white smile turned her heart over. "Your mother and I liked to give each other little gifts. I still have the bracelet she once bought me."

Ari munched on a cookie. "Where is it now?"

"Right here." Theo lifted his leg. They all stared at the tiny gold chain around his ankle.

"You still wear it?" Stella was in shock.

"I told you that night I would never take it off."

Her face went hot. Before they'd gone swimming, she'd given it to him and he'd made her put it on him. She remembered him crushing her in his arms, telling her they were now joined forever.

"I want to get one."

"Me, too!" Dax chimed in.

Stella laughed. "Maybe when you two are older."

"Speaking of you two…" Theo walked over to the closet and pulled out a couple of junior life preservers. "I want you to put these on and wear them the whole time." He helped them get them on.

"How come?"

He finished tying them. "Because you never know when something could happen and I want you to be safe."

She could see Ari wasn't too happy about it, but she loved Theo for insisting.

"I bet nobody else is wearing one."

"Maybe not, but I want you to do this for me because I love you so much."

"I love you, too, Papa. Now you have to put yours on."

Both Stella and Theo burst into laughter. He pulled two adult jackets from the closet. "What's good for the goose, eh?" He started toward her with a wicked glint in those fabulous black eyes.

Stella would have put it on herself, but Theo insisted on doing the honors. His touch sent curls of delicious warmth through her body. With his back toward the boys, his eyes ignited as he took his time tying the ends near her throat. She wanted him to kiss her so badly she felt pain to the palms of her hands.

Needing something to do before she acted on her desire, she took the other life jacket and helped him put it on. Had he always been so broad-shouldered and powerful? When her hand touched his chest, she heard his sharp intake of breath.

"Can we go play shuffleboard?"

"Yes," Theo answered while she was still fastening his tie. "We'll come up and join you in a minute."

"Okay. Let's go, Dax!" They grabbed some candy and left the cabin.

When the door closed, Theo pulled her closer to him. "Our son just did us a favor. Without this body armor, you wouldn't be safe from me right now. Let's try it out, in case I'm wrong."

Before she knew what had happened, she was engulfed in his arms, unable to move. "I'm going to kiss you whether you want me to or not."

She thought he would start with her mouth, but he began an exploration of her face, slowly inching his way around until she thought she would die if he didn't satisfy the craving building inside her.

A moan escaped her throat, her body's way of begging him to stop torturing her and really kiss her. When it came, she almost fainted from ecstasy.

Somehow, she didn't really know how, they ended up on the bed in a kiss that seemed to have no beginning or end. She lost complete track of time. It was just the two of them communicating in a wine-dark rapture of need escalating out of control.

Suddenly the door opened. "Hey, Mom? Papa? Aren't you going to play with us?"

Theo recovered first. He bit her earlobe gently, then rolled off the bed. "I'm coming up now. Your mom will join us in a few minutes. You guys want some drinks?"

"Yeah. Thanks."

After they left, Stella sat up, but her head was so

woozy from being kissed senseless she had to maneu-
ver carefully so she wouldn't fall over when she stood
up. The life preserver made it difficult.

One look in the mirror over the dresser spoke a
thousand words and needed no translation. It took her
back to her teenage years. After being with Theo, her
lips were always swollen, her face flushed and the hair
he loved to play with was in disarray.

She buried her face in one of the roses. Their scent
filled the room. Whenever she smelled roses in the
future, she would remember this day and treasure it.
Once again Theo had worked his magic.

After brushing her hair and putting on fresh lipstick,
she phoned Elani and told her they were coming home
but were still going to keep Dax if it was okay. With that
accomplished, she went up on deck to find the guys.

They all played shuffleboard, then walked around to
watch the water traffic. Theo entertained the boys. She
mostly listened. Eventually they went back to their
cabin for more treats. While the boys stretched out on
one of the beds, Theo lay on his side behind Stella who
sat on the edge of the bed to talk to them.

He did it on purpose, knowing it would be pure torture
for her not to be able to lie down next to him. Ten minutes
to port her cell phone rang. She checked the caller ID. It
was Rachel. She had to answer and said hello.

"Stella—I had no idea you were going to leave today.
Stasi let me sleep in. I just woke up and found out you'd
gone. Cassie's so upset."

She got up and went outside the cabin so she could
talk in private. "I'm sorry, Rachel. It's just that with
school out, Ari and Dax want to do some things with
their friends."

"I understand, but I have to admit I'm disappointed."

"Forgive us."

"Of course."

"We'll be back again after Dax goes home in a few days."

"I'm counting on it. Take care."

"You, too. I want you to get over your morning sickness."

"It'll pass. Talk to you later."

Stella hung up feeling horrible, but she couldn't change plans now. It was very evident Theo and Ari loved each other and wanted to be together. This was a vital time for them. She couldn't allow anything else to interfere.

Theo seemed to know instinctively how to handle Ari. Suddenly their son was acting more confident and excited about life. Stella had to admit it was wonderful to think Ari had his own real father in his life like his other friends had theirs. She would never have imagined it, but when she saw them together, it was like they'd never been apart.

At one point she would have to let Stasio and Rachel know. The best time to tell them would be when their vacation was over. He already knew something was going on. When he learned the truth, he'd be thrilled for Ari, even with all the bad history.

A boy needed his father. If Theo wanted to fill that role now, Stella had no desire to prevent it. As long as he made Ari happy, then she'd be happy. She was a fool, of course. It was her middle name, otherwise she wouldn't be living for later this afternoon when Theo said he'd be coming to the villa.

After she clicked off, she went back in the cabin.

Theo flicked her a penetrating glance. "Everything all right?"

"Yes. It was Rachel. She was still asleep when we left, so she called to say goodbye."

"We're docking now," Theo murmured. "It's time to walk to the car. Everybody off with their life jackets." Soon they were all put away in the closet.

Ari looked at his father. "Are you going to come with us?"

"I'd like to, but I have a little work to do at the office. The helicopter will fly me into Athens from here and I'll come to the villa later."

"What time?"

"Around four."

Stella walked over to the flowers. "I want to take these with us."

Theo reached for the vase. "I'll empty the water and carry them to the car. Is everybody ready?"

The boys nodded and trooped out first. Stella reached for her purse while Theo brought up the rear. They walked down the passage to the stairs and went below to the next deck. When they reached the car, Theo put the roses in the trunk.

"Looks like you're all set." He came around to Stella's side and squeezed her shoulder. The contact spread fire through every atom of her body. "Drive carefully."

"See you later, Papa."

"See you, Mr. Pantheras."

Stella started the motor and put the car in gear. It was a wrench having to drive away from him. From the sideview mirror she watched him until they'd driven off the ferry.

"Can Dax play at our house when we get home?"

"I've already checked with his mother and it's okay."

"Hooray."

Forty-five minutes later they reached the house. "Aiyee," Iola cried when she saw them enter the kitchen.

Stella was carrying the roses which she took over to the sink. They needed to be put in water again. "We decided to cut our vacation short. Don't worry. Tell the staff I plan to do the cooking and the cleaning around here. You go on doing exactly what you intended to do. We'll try to stay out of your way."

Iola crossed herself. "What's going on?"

Ari gave her a hug. "My papa's coming over this afternoon."

If the housekeeper's eyes grew any bigger, they'd pop. "Your papa?"

"Yup. He's awesome! Come on, Dax. Let's take our stuff upstairs. Do you want me to take up your suitcase, Mom?"

Since when. "Yes. I'd love you to." Wanting to copy his father was a good thing.

"Okay."

Once they disappeared, Stella turned to Iola. "I know what you're thinking. How could I let this happen after that man nearly ruined my life. But this isn't about me."

They walked through the villa to the salon where she set the roses on the coffee table. "Ari has spent quite a bit of time with him and wants to be with him all the time. That's why we're back in Athens so soon."

Iola's hands went to her own cheeks. "I hope you know what you're doing."

"So do I, but you saw Ari just now. There's a new light in his eyes."

"We'll see how long it lasts."

The housekeeper had been through it all with her. Of

course she was fearful. In time she would see what Stella could see right now.

"It's still a secret," she warned her. "No one knows but you and Dax."

"Not Stasio?" She sounded scandalized.

"Not yet. Rachel's nausea has him preoccupied." Though it was true, she knew her brother hadn't been deceived.

Iola shook her head. "He worries over her the way Ari's father should have worried over you!"

"That's in the past, Iola. Ari's happy. I want him to stay that way."

Iola crossed herself again.

CHAPTER FIVE

IT WAS a novel experience for Theo to be allowed onto Athas property. The guard at the gate let his limo pass through to the front of the square, three-story villa. Built along neoclassic lines, it gave the impression of a temple. In ways it was like a sanctuary, one he'd been forbidden to enter.

But not today. It meant her brothers still didn't know what was going on. He would enjoy his entrée into her world until everything hit the fan. Then he would sit back and watch the spectacle.

At quarter after four he alighted from the limo and bounded up the steps, almost breathless to see Stella. After kissing her on the ferry, he was on fire, and nothing would ever put it out because that was the effect she had on him.

He'd barely rung the doorbell when he heard voices and it opened to reveal his son. They smiled at each other. Dax stood behind him. "Hi, Papa...come on in."

Papa... The most wonderful word he'd ever heard.

"Thanks. Who's your friend?"

The boys laughed.

"Hi."

"Hi, yourself, Dax."

"Mom said to bring you into the salon."

He squeezed Ari's shoulder. "Lead the way."

The elegant interior was what he'd expected of a family of their status, but the only thing that mattered was being with the two people he loved.

"Stella." She looked so gorgeous, the air caught in his lungs. "I like you in yellow." Earlier today she'd been in pink.

A flush swept over her as she looked up from a tray of sodas and snacks she'd just put on the table. The sleeveless top with a matching skirt was sensational on her. "Thank you. Why don't you sit down and we'll talk. Dax, if you'll go to the kitchen, Iola has a snack ready for you. Our meeting won't take long."

"Okay."

Once the three of them were alone, she subsided into a chair facing the couch. Theo guided Ari to it and they sat down together. His son made sure he was supplied something to eat and drink.

"Umm. This baklava is excellent. Thank you. I'm always my hungriest about this time every day."

"Me, too," Ari agreed with him. "We always eat dinner early, huh, Mom."

She nodded. "I thought we ought to talk about plans for the rest of the summer."

"If you don't mind my going first, this might make it easier for you," Theo stated.

"Go ahead."

"As you know," he said, eyeing both of them, "I'm back in Greece with only one agenda, to spend as much time as possible with you."

Ari smiled.

"I want to do what every father wants to do—take you to lessons, the dentist, the doctor, meet your teachers for school this coming fall, plan minivacations, play soccer with you and your friends, shop, go to movies, hang out at my house, just be with you."

"Me, too. Can you stay here and watch *Star Trek* with me tonight?"

"I'd love it. Maybe we could get some takeout for dinner and bring it back while we all watch, but before we plan anything, I want to know what's on your mother's mind. Are you working full-time this summer?"

She put down her soda. "Yes, but I still have two weeks of vacation. Once it's over, I've made an arrangement with Keiko. He'll work from nine to five. I'll plan to go in at six-thirty every day so I can be home by two-thirty. I've planned for Ari to do some reading and math at the next session of summer school in the mornings."

"But I don't want to go to school."

"It's a good idea, Ari," Theo backed her up. "You need to keep your mind active. I was thinking we could get ourselves enrolled in a young astronomers program, too."

"What's that?" He jumped off the couch too excited to sit still.

"I'm sure some of the colleges have them. You look through a telescope and they teach you about the stars."

"Could I do that, Mom?"

"Of course."

"If you would bring me your telephone book, we could call around and see what's being offered."

"I'll get it."

After he dashed out of the room Theo sat forward. "Stella? Look at me for a minute." She lifted her head. "I hope you know I'm not trying to usurp your place. I want to help ease the burden of all you have to do. Look on me as your support system, a permanent one. I'll do whatever you'd like. If I'm overwhelming you, tell me."

She got to her feet. "You're not. It's what Ari wants. I can't deny that Ari is a changed boy already. That's all because of you."

"Thank you for saying that."

She held on to the back of the chair. "All his life he's been surrounded by other children who live with a father and mother. However, I didn't think he noticed that much or cared, not with Stasio, who has been wonderful to him."

Only because he and Nikos had stolen Ari from him. The bile rose in Theo's throat.

"You have no conception of how changed he is. Otherwise he would never have begged to leave Andros where he could have Stasio's constant attention. He didn't even say goodbye to his uncle, the man he has always depended on."

Theo liked hearing it, but when Stasio found out what was going on, there was going to be a showdown. This time Theo was ready for whatever the Athas family had to throw at him.

"His need to be with you supercedes all else," Stella confessed. "There's a new confidence about him. That's because he knows his real father loves him. I have to admit I can't be sorry about that. In truth I've always had to help Ari work on his confidence."

Puzzled, Theo got to his feet. "What are you talking about?"

She rubbed her hands together, a sure sign of nervousness. "It's a long story. You need to hear everything so you'll understand Ari's psyche. I'll tell you after he goes to bed tonight."

He had a feeling that whatever she had to say to him was going to turn his guts inside out all over again. Though he wanted to press her, he could hear the boys coming.

"Here's the directory, Papa." Dax came in with him.

"Terrific. Let me make a few calls and we'll see what's available."

Ari eyed him expectantly while he made inquiries. Eventually he hung up and said, "We're in luck. There's a star-gazing program that started this week, but we can join in on Friday evening, so I have an idea.

"Why don't we visit the college in the morning. After we've registered for the session, we'll fly to St. Thomas for the day."

"Hey," Dax piped up. "My parents went there a couple of weeks ago. My dad loves golf. He said the resort has the best golf course he ever played on."

That was nice to hear. "Have either of you ever played?"

Both boys shook their heads.

"How about you, Stella?"

"No."

"Then we'll make up a foursome and do nine holes. How does that sound?"

"Cool." Ari high-fived his friend.

Stella's mouth lifted at the corners. "Ari? Why don't you show your father to the family room upstairs to watch your DVD."

"Okay. Come on, Papa."

His gaze held hers. "Before we do anything, I'll go pick up some food for us. You guys can come if you want to help me choose."

"That's not necessary, Theo. We have plenty of food here. Ari and Dax can carry it up when you get hungry."

"Then bring on the starship *Enterprise,*" he said before tearing his eyes from hers.

The five-hour marathon with the boys entertained him no end. Stella slipped in and out with sandwiches and salad, but he was glad when she finally insisted the boys go to bed. Until she explained what she'd meant earlier, he would have no peace.

As soon as she joined him in the salon, he said, "What's this about Ari not having confidence?"

Once again she sat down opposite him. "Let me give you some background. After what happened at the church, my grief made me ill. There was too much tension in the house. My father was upset that I'd gotten involved with you, and Nikos's attitude made everything so much worse. Stasio had to leave for New York on business and took me with him.

"I lived in his apartment both before and after I had the baby. He hired a Greek couple to help me when he couldn't be home. He also made it possible for me to attend college and get my business degree there."

Nothing she'd just told him added up to what he'd been thinking about Stasio. Had Theo been wrong about him?

"You're an amazing woman." He was proud of what she'd accomplished, but he could hardly hold on to his rage over events he'd been helpless to prevent at the time.

She shook her head. "No. Thousands of women do the same thing every day. Once I'd graduated, I told Stasio I wanted to go back to Greece and get a job. Ari was old enough to attend kindergarten and I could work out my schedule with Iola's help.

"Everything went well except that in returning to Athens, it brought us back into Nikos's orbit. He never accepted Ari and it showed. The last couple of years have been hard on our son.

"Though Ari doesn't understand why, he's aware of the way Nikos feels and goes to great lengths not to antagonize him for fear of being mocked or ridiculed. As a result, he doesn't always show a lot of confidence. That's what I wanted you to understand." Tears prickled against her eyelids. "For him to finally have his own father who champions him is making all the difference."

He got to his feet. "None of this should have happened," he muttered. More and more he was beginning to think the cruelty was all on Nikos's part. "Though there's nothing we can do about the past, I swear to you I'll never let any harm or hurt come to you or Ari again."

"Theo," she cried in abject frustration. "If you want me to believe you, you have to confide in me completely about the past. No lies."

"If you'll do me one favor first, then I promise to tell you details."

When she closed her eyes, tears squeezed out. "What favor?" she whispered.

"Tell your brothers I've returned to Greece and have been seeing you and Ari." There was going to be an explosion, one Stella needed to experience to understand.

A stillness surrounded her before she got up from the chair. "I don't want them to know yet because this is a very precarious time for you and Ari. I've been waiting to see how things would go. Naturally, I plan to tell them."

"But you're afraid to tell them. I can see it in your eyes. I don't blame you. We always had to hide our love from your family, but we were young then. Now we're two mature adults with a six-year-old son. There's nothing to be afraid of. I'm here to protect you. Does

Ari know how you and I used to have to sneak around to be together?"

"No. As I told you before, he knows nothing about my turmoil."

"I'm indebted to you for that. It's the reason he and I have been able to bond so fast. For that very reason he'll think it's strange if you're not straightforward with your family."

"You're right. It's just that—"

"What?" he broke in. "Are you afraid they're going to object?"

She bit her lower lip, the one he wanted to kiss. "You hurt me. I was their younger sister."

"But we were torn from each other in the most cruel way possible. Surely that would make a difference to any sane, rational person." What she couldn't know was that he didn't put Nikos in that category.

"I'm not ready to say anything quite yet. In a couple of weeks Stasio will be back from vacation. Then I'll tell him." She shook her head, causing her dark hair to swish. "I have to tell him at the right time."

Theo realized she was terrified because he would always be a Pantheras in their eyes and she knew her family would never approve. She had every reason to want to put it off.

"Tell them soon, Stella," he urged, afraid it fell on deaf ears. "We don't want Ari hurt by this if he doesn't have to be. I'm leaving now. My limo's waiting. I'll be by for you at ten tomorrow."

He strode out of the house without looking back. She was too much of a temptation for him to be alone with her in the same room any longer.

* * *

The next morning Stella ate breakfast with the boys, aware of an excitement building inside her she couldn't control. After going back and forth, she chose to wear white cargo pants and a sleeveless lime-green top that tied at the shoulders. There was no use pretending she didn't care what Theo thought. She had her pride and wanted to look beautiful for him.

While she was putting on lipstick, her phone rang. Theo? Her heart thudded as she reached for her cell. It turned out to be Dax's mom. She'd be by at dinnertime to pick him up.

They chatted for a minute before Stella hung up to brush her hair. She had an idea Dax wasn't ready to go home yet. He'd been enjoying Theo's company too much. Ari on the other hand would be thrilled to finally get his daddy to himself.

Twenty minutes later he appeared at the villa. Stella stepped outside and got in the limo next to him. She could feel him studying her. While the boys chattered, she and Theo made desultory conversation. After visiting the campus, they headed for Theo's office.

Once they rode the elevator to the roof, they got in the helicopter. Boris was already onboard and everyone got acquainted. Soon they were airborne. She smiled at Ari. "Are you excited about your stargazing class?"

"Yup. It's going to be awesome."

Awesome was a word that covered everything fun or wonderful. The class started at nine o'clock and went three times a week for two more weeks.

"I'm sure it will be fascinating."

Theo sat in the copilot's seat looking at home there with

headgear on. "As soon as we land, are you guys ready for golf or do you want to play on the water slide first?"

"I didn't know it had one of those." Dax sounded euphoric.

"It's guaranteed to curl your hair."

Everyone laughed. Even Stella. She could trust Theo, couldn't she? Ari did, wholeheartedly. For the rest of the day she was determined to put all doubts behind her and just enjoy the moment.

As soon as she made that decision, her body started to relax, enabling her to entertain feelings she'd been forced to suppress since she'd first seen him at the paddleboat concession.

He had the kind of hard-muscled body that looked good in anything. Today he'd worn a magenta sport shirt and cream-colored trousers that rode low on his hips. Theo was unaware of his masculine charisma. She, on the other hand, had trouble keeping her eyes off him.

Years ago every girl at church had woven a fantasy about him. Stella hadn't been able to believe it when he'd sit behind her in Sunday school and whisper things to her while the priest gave a lesson. When they went into mass, he'd sit in the same row and lean forward so he could smile at her.

Whatever activity, he came and made certain they were together in some capacity. Her friends thought he was sexy and told her how lucky she was. Stella knew it, but with her family looking on, she had to be careful they didn't find out what was happening.

When the church had put on a festival to raise money, he had chosen her as his partner to perform a folk dance. There were practices and they had to wear costumes. The thrill of those moments while they got ready for the big night still set her pulse racing. He'd dance too close and kiss her hair. Theo drove her crazy with all his attention. She loved him with a passion that broke down her inhibitions.

Their son, Ari, sitting next to her was proof that she'd loved Theo body and soul. She hadn't been able to hold back her desire. That period had been filled with the greatest ecstasy imaginable. Then it had ended so abruptly in one night, something in her had died.

She realized she'd been dead for years. Now suddenly he was back. Despite the things she didn't know, something inside her had leaped to life again, portending something bigger and brighter than before. Yesterday in the cabin on the ferry, she'd forgotten everything in the sheer joy of being in his arms again.

"Stella?" The voice infiltrating her body jerked her from her intimate thoughts.

"What is it?"

"We've landed." So they had. "The boys have run ahead to set up our golf game." She noticed that the pilot and Boris had already exited, too. "Do you need help?"

He looked as if he was going to come back and start removing the straps one kiss at a time. Her cheeks grew warm at the direction of her thoughts. If someone saw them... "No, thank you. I can manage."

After unstrapping herself, she moved to the entrance where he swung her to the ground. He did it slowly, causing her body to slide down his, creating delicious heat between them. Yesterday they'd had the life jackets between them, but no longer. She quickly hurried ahead of him, but her legs felt like mush.

As they got closer, she saw the boys come out the doors of the clubhouse with two bags of clubs, but they weren't alone. A shudder rocked her body. To her shock it was Nikos with his longtime Swiss ski buddy Fritz walking behind them. Her secret was out now to the one person she hadn't wanted to know anything!

Who would have thought she'd bump into her brother here? Except that it wasn't a complete surprise. Nikos loved golf when he wasn't skiing. He said the mental game kept him sharp. Was Renate with him, or had he left her on Andros for the day?

She watched him take Ari aside and engage him in conversation. Even as far apart as they still were, she could tell her son was being vetted. Dax stood by Fritz. She'd have given anything if things hadn't happened this way, but there was no help for it now.

Fritz came forward and gave her a kiss on both cheeks. "Stella Athas. It's been a few years. Nikos didn't tell me you'd grown into such a raving beauty."

She'd never cared for his brash manner and didn't like the way he was checking her out. "How are you, Fritz? Let me introduce you to Ari's father, Theo Pantheras. Theo? Fritz here took the bronze for Switzerland in the slalom a few years ago."

"Hello." Theo shook his hand without saying anything else. Most people fawned over Fritz and Nikos, but she knew Theo wasn't as easily impressed.

Ari walked over to stand next to Theo who put his arms around him and hugged him close in a protective gesture. It thrilled Stella. Her son now had his own dad, thank heaven. Nikos couldn't say or do anything about it.

Her brother trained his eyes on her and came closer. They glittered in that icy way they did when his anger was truly kindled. "Well, well, well. A day of golf for my little sister."

Nikos didn't even pretend to acknowledge Theo. Six years had done nothing to teach her brother a thing about human decency. His behavior now reminded her of one time in New York when he'd humiliated Rachel so thoroughly, Stella had thought she'd lost her best friend for good. He'd called her a fat, orange-haired, American military brat in her hearing. Stella had never forgiven him for hurting her friend.

"Who would have imagined finding you on the world's newest and most celebrated golf course?"

"I was about to say the same thing," she said, daring to speak her mind again. It was cathartic to be able to. "Where's Renate?"

"With Rachel," he muttered. "Since you left Andros so fast, I think it's time you and I had a little talk to catch up. If the rest of you will excuse us for a few minutes."

"Maybe another time," Theo interjected smoothly. "We don't want to be late for our tee-off time."

Nothing would have enraged Nikos more than to be snubbed in front of Fritz like that, by Theo no less. She could feel her brother seething. Theo on the other hand seemed to care less.

He put his other arm around Stella's shoulders. "Come on, everyone—Dax—" he urged the boy hauling the other golf bag. Together the four of them headed for the first tee.

"Stella? I'm waiting." Nikos said coldly.

In order to prevent a contretemps, she decided to talk to him, but Theo stopped her from moving. "I'm afraid you'll be waiting a long time. It appears the two of you will have to have one of your family chats another time. She and the boys are with me and we're busy."

Her brother came closer. "I could have you thrown

off this resort for talking to me that way," he snarled at Theo. "One word to the owner from me and that's that."

"Stop it, Nikos," Stella muttered, mortified and infuriated by his behavior. He was out of control. Even with the boys around, he didn't care what they thought of him.

"I will, after we've had our talk." He wouldn't let this go. It was unbelievable.

She felt Theo remove his arm and pull out his cell phone. Whatever he said was short and to the point. Almost immediately she saw Theo's bodyguard and another man coming toward them from the clubhouse at full speed.

"Boris? If you would see that these two gentlemen leave the course, we'd be grateful."

Nikos was a skier, not a body builder. The two men could take care of him with no problem. Part of her was thrilled to see him thwarted, but another part grieved for him. He was her brother and she loved him, but it had been years since she'd liked him. She had to search back in her memory when he was a preteen to remember anything good.

"Who in the hell do you think you are?" Nikos demanded.

"Nikos," Stella cried, "what's the matter with you?"

"It's all right," Theo assured her. "He's just surprised to see me with you again after all these years, aren't you, Nikos. Better get used to it since the blood of our two families runs through Ari's veins.

"If you can learn to behave yourself, you're welcome to golf here again another time when you've cooled down. My treat. I'm the owner. Now we really have to get cracking, don't we Ari."

Her son smiled. "Yes. See ya, Uncle Nikos." When

they'd walked a little distance, Ari looked up at him. "I didn't know you owned this place."

"There's a lot you don't know about me, or me you. That's why it's so great we're planning to spend as much time together as possible, don't you think?"

"Yes." He was beaming. "Mom? I've never seen Uncle Nikos so mad."

She was still shivering. It was truth time. "Unfortunately I've seen him worse, honey. We'll just stay away from him for a while until he apologizes."

"He doesn't like me."

That was the first time Ari had admitted it aloud. All because of his father, who'd given him new confidence.

"It's *me* he doesn't like, Ari," Theo said softly.

"How come?"

"I come from a very poor family. Your uncle didn't like me being with your mother or having anything to do with her."

"That's stupid."

"I agree, but a lot of wealthy people like your uncle feel that way."

"Uncle Nikos isn't wealthy. Uncle Stasi has to give him money when he runs out."

A gasp escaped Stella's lips. Ari knew too much for his own good.

"Well, let's forget it and have ourselves a fun game. Who wants to go first?"

"I do," Stella volunteered. After the awful scene with Nikos, she needed to do something physical to channel all that negative energy in a different direction.

"This is going to be an adventure," Theo whispered against her neck. All her anxiety flew out the window as other sensations took over.

He'd already put his arms around her to demonstrate how to do a golf swing. The weight of his hard body cocooning hers caused her to forget what she was doing. She felt him nibble her sun-warmed shoulder where the tie had slipped a little. It made her breathless.

"How soon is it going to be our turn?" Ari stood next to Dax, resigned it might be a long wait.

He'd asked it so seriously, she and Theo burst out laughing at the same time. It suddenly occurred to her she hadn't been this happy in years. He'd brought joy to his son's life. He'd slain a dragon for her today. A week ago she couldn't have imagined any of it.

Please, God. Don't let the darkness come again. Make this happiness last.

CHAPTER SIX

AT SIX that evening, Stella walked Dax out to his parents' car. Ari and Theo followed with his suitcase and the games and stuff he'd brought with him. Everyone hugged. Dax gave Theo a super-duper hug.

In front of Dax's parents, Theo invited Ari's friend to come to Salamis Island in a couple of weekends for a sleepover. The other man nodded his agreement of the idea. They chatted about the golf course for a few minutes.

"I love you guys," Dax said to Stella before giving her a hug. "I had an awesome time."

"It was a treat for us, too, honey," she told him. With Theo around it couldn't have been anything else.

Elani stared at Theo before flashing Stella a private message. She could hear her friend asking where *he'd* come from. Not even Elani was immune. Dax would fill her in on some of the details. The rest would have to wait until Stella phoned her friend and confided in her.

When the three of them went back into the house, Ari turned to her. "Now that Dax has gone home, can papa sleep in my room tonight? Please?"

Stella should have seen it coming, but the thought of Theo staying over made her heart skip a couple of beats.

"What do you say, Stella?" Theo teased gently.

He probably sensed how much she wanted him to stay. Maybe it would be a good thing. Maybe they could really talk after Ari went to bed. She was finally in a mood to listen. "It's all right with me, but only if you don't tell UFO stories and keep each other awake all night."

Ari launched himself at her. "Thanks, Mom." His eyes looked suspiciously bright in the foyer light. "I love you."

"I love you, too, honey."

"This was the best day of my life!"

He said that every time he'd been with Theo. She believed it.

His father grabbed him. "And it's not over yet!"

"Come on upstairs, Papa."

Stella nodded to him. "I'll be up in a minute to bring you a few things." While she was at it she'd find one of Stasio's robes for Theo to wear. He was a tall, powerfully built man like Theo. They'd be hanging in Stasio's closet.

"Hurry," he whispered with urgency in his voice before racing Ari up the stairs two at a time. They whooped it up like two kids. Their laughter floated down and followed her to the kitchen.

Iola came rushing in. "What's going on? I thought Dax went home."

She gathered some fruit and chips for them. "He did, but now we have another guest."

"Who?"

"Ari's father."

She crossed herself. "Aiyee—"

Stella chuckled. "It's all right. I'm glad they're together. A boy should be with his father."

"That isn't what you thought last week."

"A lot has changed since then. He's come back to stay, Iola."

"You have forgiven him?'

She sucked in her breath. "Yes." *Until I know differently.*

"What if he disappears again?"

"He won't." She knew that in her heart even if she didn't know all of it. Theo had convinced her that Ari meant everything to him. She had to believe him. She would go on believing it.

"How long is he going to stay here?"

"I don't really know yet. He and Ari have a lot of stuff to catch up on."

"And you, too?"

"Maybe."

"Just don't get hurt again."

If it was going to happen, the advice had come too late. "Don't fuss about anything, Iola. We'll just be lazing around here for a few days." Ari needed a taste of what it was like to be around his father all the time.

"But what if your brothers come home for some reason?"

"It doesn't matter." Now that Nikos had seen them together, it wouldn't be long before he told Stasio. In a way it was just as well. With the word out, both brothers would have time to get used to the idea. Once she told Stasio how happy Ari was, he'd be his loving, understanding self.

She had this dream that one day Theo and Stasio would become good friends in their own right, and not just because of Ari, whom they both adored. Though the two men were almost ten years apart, they had the strongest work ethic she'd ever seen. Best of all, they were both intrinsically kind and loved Ari.

"Good night, Iola."

Stella darted off to her room. She was pretty sure there was an extra toothbrush in the bathroom cupboard. She also had some throwaway razors Theo could have if he wanted.

Once she'd found everything and made a detour to Stasio's room, she hurried to Ari's room.

"Hi, Mom. I'm showing papa my scrapbooks so he can see what I looked like when I was a baby." They sat on the bed side by side, poring over everything.

She laid things down on the end of the other queen-size bed. "Those are precious photos."

"Amen." Theo's voice grated with deep emotion. She knew why. He hadn't been there for any of it. He patted the side of the bed next to him so she'd join them. "Ari's been telling me about the couple who lived with you in New York. I want to meet them."

"They're marvelous people."

"They were really nice, Papa."

"And lucky," Theo added. "They got to hold you all the time, change your diapers, tell you stories and kiss you when you cried. I'm jealous."

It wrenched Stella's heart that Theo had missed out on all of it. She felt his hand slide around her waist and squeeze her hip. "I'll be eternally grateful to them for helping your mom when I couldn't. One day we'll fly to New York so I can meet them."

"Could we?" Ari cried.

"We'll do a lot of things."

Stella was curious to know what kinds of things he had in mind, but she would have to ask him later. "I think it's time you got ready for bed," she reminded Ari.

"Okay."

"Theo, I brought you a robe and a couple of other items. You can use Ari's bathroom to change."

"Thank you." His eyes captured hers. "This is what I call living!" He got up from the bed and disappeared into the bathroom.

Ari slipped on his pajamas in record time. "Mom? Can Papa stay with us all the time?"

"I'm afraid not, honey."

"How come?"

Floundering, she said, "Because he has his own house. Like you, I'm getting used to having him in my life again."

His eyes shone. "But you like him."

"You know I do."

"I love him."

"I kind of figured that out."

"I'm so glad he came back."

"I'm glad, too," she admitted. Her son was a different person. "Good night, honey."

She kissed his forehead, then rushed to her own room to get ready for bed. Stella couldn't imagine how she would get to sleep knowing Theo was next door. The knowledge that they'd be spending tomorrow together made her even more excited.

After slipping on a nightgown, she went into the bathroom to brush her teeth. Once she'd turned off the light, she had every intention of going to bed. However, she heard their voices carry because she shared a bathroom with Ari. Though she hated herself for eavesdropping, she couldn't resist listening at the door for a second.

"...because I felt inferior to my brother. Hektor was the oldest in my family and had a calling for the priesthood. My parents loved him so much, I thought they didn't love me."

"Did it make you cry?"

"A lot when I was really young."

"I love you, Papa."

"I know you do. I love you, too. More than anything on earth."

"Did your other brothers feel bad, too?"

"I think so, but I never talked to them about it. When
he left our house for good, it was very hard on me. I'd lost
my big brother. About that time I made plans to go away
with your mother and marry her, but the night we were
going to meet at the church, some mean guys beat me up."

"How come, Papa?" he cried in a tear-filled voice.
"Why did they do that?"

"Because they didn't like me and wanted to keep me
and your mother apart. They got their wish."

Stella felt bile rise in her throat. Who was responsible
for such a crime? Who would have cared to that degree?

"When I got better, I looked everywhere for your
mother. My friends and family helped me. I made phone
calls and sent her letters, but no one had seen her and I
realized I'd really lost her."

"She went to New York with Stasi."

"I know that now, but at the time it was like she'd
never existed. Suffice it to say that when I lost her, I lost
my very best friend."

Tears gushed down her cheeks. *You were mine, too,
Theo.*

"And because I lost her, I lost you."

"I'm here now, Papa."

"Don't I know it. Unfortunately back then, I was in
a very bad way. That's when I decided to leave home
and start working on a career, but it was the most
painful time in my life. I never thought I'd see her

again, but then I drove by your house last week and saw both of you walking. I couldn't believe it! It made me so happy, I wrote your mother a letter and asked her to call me."

"But Mommy thought you didn't love her anymore."

"I realize that now, but it wasn't true. I loved your mommy so much I would have done anything for her. But I had to make money so I could pay someone to help me find her."

"Because you were poor, huh."

"Yes, because I'm a Pantheras from the poor part of Salamis and Stella was an Athas from the best part of Athens."

"I'm a Pantheras, too!" Ari declared.

"Yes you are, half me, half your mom, and none of it matters as long as we're all together."

She couldn't take any more and went back to her room. Theo had told her there were things she still didn't know that could hurt her and Ari. Had her father been so against her marrying Theo, *he* was the one behind the attack?

Stella's father had been a very stern man who'd risen to prominence in the Greek government. He was very proper, old-fashioned. His pride had always made it difficult for her to approach him about her personal life.

When she thought about it, he had many influential friends in high places. Had he arranged things behind the scenes, never expecting Theo to come back and fight for his son? Deep down, had he been a corrupt man?

If so, and Nikos knew about it, then it would explain why her brother had been so obnoxious at the golf course. It was almost as if he were carrying on where her father had left off, but he was blatantly open about it. Stasio would have been kept in the dark. She knew for a fact he would never have sanctioned anything cruel or criminal. It wasn't in his nature.

Was that why Theo was afraid to tell her, because he didn't want her to hate her father?

For the rest of the night her mind ran in circles, driving her crazy with more questions until she knew no more. By morning she was worn out. When Ari came to her room and begged her to let his daddy stay at their house through the weekend, she couldn't say no. They were all on vacation and her brothers were on Andros.

Every day Ari spent with his father in their house, she could see that he was becoming more secure. Between walks around Athens and their star-gazing class, there was plenty to do that was all new to him. Theo had opened up a different world for him, and her son was having the time of his life.

Before bed on Saturday night, Stella sought out Iola. "Tell cook we'll be wanting a big breakfast in the morning before we go to church."

Stella dashed upstairs and discovered Ari and his father watching a DVD about the day the earth stood still. A smile broke out on her face. "Hi, guys. Considering our plans for tomorrow, you'd better get to bed soon. In the meantime, I need to check and make sure your suit is ready for church, Ari."

She went to his room and walked inside his closet. The pants of his navy three-piece could use a pressing. She pulled them out. The jacket looked fine. After an inspection she discovered both dress shirts had been washed and ironed.

"I like the blue-and-white stripe the best," Theo murmured right behind her. A little cry of surprise broke from her throat. Except for the day he'd helped her with her golf swing, he hadn't made any kind of overture toward her. When he slid his arms around her, bringing her back up tight against his chest, it took her totally by surprise. He'd already changed into his robe.

For quite a while now she'd been so aware of him physically, it had become painful to be near him. With a sense of wonder she felt him kiss her nape, sending little fingers of delight inching their way through her body. She grew weak with those old, breathtaking feelings of desire.

"What a wonderful place to find you," he whispered in a husky voice. In the next instant he'd turned her around so their faces were mere centimeters apart. "I don't know about you, but if I can't have this right now, I'm not going to survive the night."

His dark head descended, covering her mouth with his own. Surrounded by clothes that muffled sounds, he kissed her with a hunger that brought a moan to her throat.

Back and forth they returned each other's kisses, setting off waves of desire. He smelled wonderfully male, intoxicating her. As her hands slid up his chest, she came in contact with a smattering of black hair.

The feel of his skin electrified her, bringing back memories she couldn't afford to entertain with Ari just outside the door. This was crazy. Insane. She wrenched her lips from his. "We can't do this."

His deep chuckle thrilled her. "It appears we are." He kissed her again, long and deep until she was a throbbing mass of needs. He undid one of the ties to kiss her shoulder. Rapture exploded inside her, but she knew where this was leading and finally backed out of the closet, gasping for air.

"Did you forget these?" He dangled Ari's pants in

front of her while she retied her blouse on top of her shoulder. His wolfish grin was the last straw. She took the pants and threw them at him. Ari roared with laughter.

Theo ducked, then swiped them from the floor. "You better watch out, little girl. You're playing with a big boy now."

She screamed and ran away from him. Ari was jumping on top of the bed with a huge smile while he watched them. Stella backed up against the wall. Theo came closer, twirling the pants in the air. He looked dark and dangerous and capable of doing anything.

"Wh-what are you going to do?" She stumbled over the words.

His eyes narrowed. "What you'd like me to do."

"Get her and tickle her, Papa. She hates to be tickled."

"Traitor!"

"Thanks for the tip, son." Except that Theo already knew about her ticklish side.

"No, Theo… Please."

He came at her anyway with a frightening growl. While she tried to dodge him, Iola came to the door with an anxious look. "Is everything all right?"

"No." Stella grinned. "I'm getting tickled to death."

The housekeeper's frown actually turned into a smile. Stella couldn't remember the last time she'd seen one of those from her.

"Good night, but keep the noise down so people around here can sleep!"

"Sorry, Iola," Theo called out. Ari echoed him.

Stella turned to the men. "I'll say good night, too."

"Don't go yet," Theo whispered, but she didn't dare linger. Quick as lightning she grabbed the pants before closing the door. Tomorrow she'd press them.

After giving Iola a hug, she went to her room but couldn't imagine how she would get to sleep after being thoroughly kissed in Theo's arms. The knowledge that they'd be spending tomorrow together caused her body to ache with longing. And trepidation, too.

They were going to church tomorrow to meet Theo's family, and the only reason she was going to be introduced to them after all these years was because of Ari. His parents had never approved of his association with Stella. Knowing that, Theo had never taken her home to meet them. It was all very sad.

She could only hope they would learn to tolerate her for Ari's sake. No matter what Theo might have told them, Stella was the reason Theo had left Greece in the first place. That wouldn't exactly have endeared her to them, but Ari would win them over.

When Theo had returned to Greece, he'd received a blessing from his oldest brother, who was one of the priests at the church in the Plaka near the cathedral. To Theos mind, Hektor had never looked more impressive than in his vestments.

Their reunion had been a heartwarming one. They had spent part of the day together catching up on each other's lives. There was laughter and weeping followed by a serious talk about Stella and Ari. Theo promised his brother that when and if he could, he would bring them both to the church to meet him.

That day had come.

Following the mass, his brother had invited Theo's family into his private study in the old house next to the church. He shared it with two other priests who had apartments there.

"Come in here."

Theo was the last to enter the room with Stella and Ari. He was proud to be able to introduce them. Like his son, he'd dressed in a navy suit that went with the sobriety of the occasion. Stella looked a vision in a summery two-piece hyacinth suit, elegantly tailored. Her coloring added to the picture of classy femininity.

He ushered them over to the couch where the family had congregated. Theo's parents couldn't take their eyes off Stella and Ari. His brothers and their families were equally dazzled.

"As you can all see, I brought a surprise today," Theo began. "Stella? Ari? I'd like you to meet my family starting with my mother, Ariadne, and my father, Gregory."

His mother beamed at both of them. "I've wanted to meet you for a long time."

"I have, too," Stella responded quietly.

Her gaze rested on her grandson. "You and I have the same name."

"I know." Ari smiled as he moved around the room with Stella to shake everyone's hand.

Theo's father studied him. "You look so much like my Theo, I think I'm seeing things."

"We have the same peak," Ari said, pointing to his hair. Everyone laughed.

"This is my brother Dymas, his wife Lina and their children, Calli, Dori and Spiro."

Ari eyed his older cousins. "Hi."

"Hi," they all said in turn.

"This is my brother Spiro, his wife, Minta, and their children Phyllis, Roxane and Leandros."

Ari looked at Theo before he said, "He's the one my age, huh."

"Right. You're both six going on a hundred."

Everyone laughed again.

"Last but not least, my oldest brother Hektor, Father Matthias."

Ari walked up to him and shook his hand. "Papa said he misses you a lot."

Hektor seemed moved. "I'm not supposed to admit it, but I miss all of my family, too."

"Do you like being a priest?"

He smiled. "Very much. I'm so happy you and your father have been united. He didn't know he had a son. What a wonderful present to come home to. He loves you very much."

"I love him, too!"

"If you don't mind, I'd like to give you a blessing. Is that all right with you?"

Ari nodded.

It was a short blessing, sweet and it brought a lump to Theo's throat. He eyed Stella out of the corner of his eye. Her head was bowed. He could tell the words had touched her, too.

After a few more minutes they all said goodbye and climbed into two limos Theo had provided for the family. He and Stella rode with his parents and Ari. They headed to Salamis. During the drive everyone got a little better acquainted. His father laughed more than he'd heard him in a long time.

By the time they ate dinner at the *taverna,* spirits were high. Theo could tell Stella and Ari were enjoying themselves. His son went off with Leandros for a little while, breaking the ice even more.

Stella chatted with his sisters-in-law about their children. The subject was something they could all relate to. As far as he could tell, there were no uncomfortable moments.

"It was a good beginning, don't you think?" Theo asked Stella during their trip back to Athens via the linking road from Perama to the mainland. She was seated across from him next to Ari.

"We had a wonderful time." With Ari along, she couldn't ask Theo how his parents really felt.

"Yeah, but I wish I didn't have to wear this suit all day long."

Theo threw his head back and laughed. "You're so much like me it hurts. I promise you won't have to wear one until we go to church again."

He eyed Theo soberly. "Do you like church?"

Stella glanced at him, waiting to hear his answer.

"Honestly?"

Ari nodded.

"I don't exactly like it, but I always feel better after I've gone."

"Is that how you feel, too, Mom?"

Now the shoe was on the other foot. He grinned while she decided what to say.

"Yes."

"But how did you feel when you were my age?"

She chuckled. "I didn't like it all that much."

"You see why I loved your mother so much, Ari? We think alike."

"I bet you wouldn't tell Hektor that."

"He knew how I felt when I was little because I squirmed all the time. I didn't have to say anything."

"He was nice. So are my grandparents."

"I'm glad you feel that way because they're crazy about you."

"They want me to come and see them next week. Grandma said I could help them in the kitchen."

"Would you like that?"

"I'd love it!"

"Then we'll definitely go over. While your mom and I have dinner, you can serve us before we have to leave for our class."

"That would be awesome. Leandros wishes he could come with us."

"Maybe sometime we can arrange it. We'll have to check with the staff at the college. Does he like UFO stuff?"

"Yeah. He's pretty cool."

High praise. Theo's cup was running over tonight.

"Can you sleep at our house again tonight, Papa?" They'd just driven up in front of the villa.

Without looking at Stella he said, "I have a much better idea. Since your mother still has ten days of vacation left, why don't the three of us take our own vacation on St. Thomas? I haven't been on a real one in years. I can promise you we'll never run out of things to do."

Ari looked like he was going to burst with joy. "Could we, Mom?"

Theo could tell he'd surprised Stella with his suggestion, but knowing she would have to think about it, he would give her the time because it had been a perfect day and he refused to ruin it.

"Tell you what, Ari. I have some business to do and will probably work at my office until I pick you up for our class tomorrow. Afterward, we'll fly to St. Thomas, that is if your mother approves."

"Can we, Mom? Please?"

"I…I think that sounds exciting," her voice faltered.

Until she'd said the words, Theo hadn't realized he'd been holding his breath. "While you guys pack, I'll get my work out of the way so I can concentrate on you for the next ten days."

"I can't wait, but I wish I could come to your office and see what you do."

"Another time and you can. We've got the rest of our lives, Ari."

"Your father's right," Stella interjected. "He's a busy man and you have to respect that."

"What are you going to do tomorrow, Mom?"

"Lots of errands to get ready for our trip."

"I'd rather go with you in our new car."

As she laughed, her eyes happened to meet Theo's. For the first time he felt they were communicating like they once did, sharing the same joy. It was a moment he wanted to freeze.

If he weren't afraid of losing the ground he'd gained, he would take her and Ari to St. Thomas in the morning, but he didn't want to push Stella. Though his work could wait, he pretended otherwise and kept silent, endeavoring to avoid Ari's pleading look. Nothing would please him more than to keep Ari at his office with him, but again, Stella needed time to get used to Theo being in her life again.

Once he'd undone his seat belt, he got out to help them to the front door. "Good night, son." He gave Ari a bear hug.

"Sleep well, Stella." He darted her a penetrating glance before getting back in the limo. After the day they'd spent together, he didn't dare touch her.

CHAPTER SEVEN

WHILE Stella got ready for bed, her mind was on Theo. Today had been a great highlight for her meeting his family, going to church with them. But when he'd brought her and Ari home, she'd sensed a certain reticence on his part to linger. It was impossible to know what was going on inside him. She was afraid, but didn't know of what exactly.

Yes she did. Deep down she knew he didn't want to tell her about her father. Theo was afraid that when he shared that with her, it would devastate her. Maybe it would when confronted with the irrefutable proof, but her austere father had passed on. What was important was Ari's relationship with Theo. No one could hurt that now.

Before she slipped under the covers, she reached for her phone to check any messages. Afraid it would ring while they were in church, she'd turned it off and had forgotten about it. When she looked now, she noticed three from Rachel. Each one begged her to call immediately, no matter how late.

Fearing this had to do with her pregnancy, Stella phoned. Rachel answered right away. "Thank you for calling!" she cried anxiously.

She clutched the phone tighter. "Is there something wrong with the baby?"

"No. Stella—why didn't you tell us about Theo while you were here? When Nikos flew back from St. Thomas the other night, it was all he could talk about."

A band constricted her lungs. "It's exactly for that reason I didn't want anyone to know anything."

"Know what?"

Rachel was Stella's oldest, closest friend. She trusted her with her life. Without preamble she told her everything. When she'd finished, the silence on the other end was deafening.

"Rachel? Are you still there?"

"Yes. Oh, Stella—"

"I know what you're thinking, but...I trust him. He was beaten up. You can see the damage. I think my father had something to do with it."

"You're kidding—"

"No. I've had time to think it all out. At the right moment, I'll get the truth from Theo. In the meantime, don't tell Stasio my suspicions. He revered father so much, it could really hurt him." In fact, the truth would hurt him a lot more than it was hurting Stella right now.

"You honestly believe Theo, don't you."

"Yes, Rachel. You'd have to see him with Ari to understand."

"Well if it's good enough for you, then it is for me, too."

Tears welled up. "Thank you, dear friend. You couldn't possibly know what that means to me."

"Your happiness is everything. Stasio feels the same way. Unfortunately, Nikos keeps talking about your parents and how upset they would be if they knew you'd been seeing him again. He blames your father's heart attack on your association with Theo. Maybe Nikos was in your father's confidence."

"I'm thinking the same thing," she whispered. "The point is, it happened a long time ago. With father gone, this is no longer any of Nikos's business. Not that it ever was, but if father told Nikos how he felt about Theo, then it makes a sick kind of sense."

"I agree. Is it true Theo owns that new resort on St. Thomas?"

"Yes."

"You might as well hear the rest, then. Nikos told Stasio he believes Theo is tied to underworld crime, otherwise he couldn't possibly have made that kind of money, not when he didn't have a drachma to his name."

Outraged, Stella cried, "Where did he come up with such a ludicrous accusation?"

"I don't know."

Stella rubbed her temple where she felt an ache. "Theo has been out of the country for six years working his head off to build a successful career. Nikos is only making wild accusations because his own business plans didn't turn out to be successful."

"I'm sure jealousy enters into it. Stasio's been trying to reason with him, but Nikos insists he's going to have Theo investigated."

"What? That's crazy."

"You're right. Poor Renate has no influence over him right now. She wants to go back to Switzerland, but he won't hear of it. He won't even talk to me, but then he never did like me so that's no news."

Nikos had never approved of Rachel, though he'd had to pretend to get along with her because she was Stasio's wife. At this point Stella feared the worst. "Nikos isn't behaving rationally right now. You should have seen him. He didn't care that Ari and Dax were watching."

"How awful. Listen…when Stasio comes up to bed, I'll tell him you're waiting for his call. He'll be relieved you're available to talk."

"Okay. Love you, Rachel. Take care of yourself."

"Ditto."

They hung up before she realized she hadn't even asked her sister-in-law about her nausea. She eased herself down under the covers and waited for Stasio's call, but he didn't phone for another half hour. It was after midnight when she finally said hello to him.

"I'm so sorry you had to find out about Theo through Nikos. I wanted to handle this myself before I told you."

"I understand. My whole concern is for you."

"I know that. The point is, Theo is back in Greece and he wants to be a father to Ari. He's not asking for anything else. I have to tell you he's done nothing but be wonderful to Ari and me. As I told Rachel, he said he'd been accosted before he could meet me at the church that night, and then he could never find me again.

"He sent me a letter that was sent back to him saying addressee unknown. I saw it with my own eyes. According to him someone tried to destroy our love. I…I believe him, Stasio, even though he hasn't told me everything."

"Did you read what the letter said?"

She shivered. "No. I was too angry at the time, but while I'm on St. Thomas, I'll ask him to let me see it."

"When are you going there again?"

"Tomorrow. I'll stay in touch with you while we're gone. As for Nikos, please don't tell him where I am." Stella had made a decision. "After our vacation I'm going to find a new place to live. As long as Nikos continues to stay at the villa when he comes to Athens, it's not a place I want to be."

After they got back from their vacation, if her brother ever came near her or Ari or Theo again with threats of any kind, then she'd call Costas, their family attorney, and have a restraining order put on him.

"Stella…you have every right to be upset. Before things go any further, let's meet in the morning on Andros to talk."

"You mean with Nikos?"

"Yes. It can't hurt anything. If you include him, he'll see you've forgiven him for his outburst on St. Thomas. When he learns that Theo wants to be a father to his son, he'll settle down enough to be more reasonable."

"No he won't, Stasio. He's never fully accepted Ari. Knowing Theo is back in Ari's life is only going to make him more unpleasant to be around. I won't let him hurt my son."

"I'll try to reason with him one more time."

"Thank you for that. I love you, Stasio."

"I love you, too. If Theo is all the things you believe he is and he can make Ari happy, then I couldn't ask more for you. When you never developed an interest in another man, I prayed Theo might come back to you."

Her eyes smarted. The kisses they'd exchanged over the last few days might have rocked her to the foundations, but these were still early days in their tentative relationship. "I…I'm not sure about that, but I do know he wants to father Ari from now on."

"Six years is a long time to be out of his life," Stasio murmured, "but it's never too late. A boy needs his own father if he's lucky enough to have him."

Stasio was talking about their father of course. Her brother was a saint. To have his blessing was all that mattered to Stella. Now that he knew everything, she felt free and couldn't wait to see Theo tomorrow.

"Kyrie Pantheras?"

Theo was on an overseas call. "What is it?" he asked his secretary.

"There's a courier from the court here with a summons. You have to sign for it."

He'd been expecting it. Nikos Athas hadn't wasted any time. "Send him in."

Theo made his excuses to the other man on the phone and hung up. In a minute the courier entered his office. Theo walked over to him. "I understand you have a summons for me?"

"Yes. If you'll sign and date it, please."

After he'd written his signature, he was given the envelope. Theo closed the door and walked over to the window to open the document.

Pantheras *vs* Athas.

Now that Nikos was back in the picture, Theo had tripled the security on himself, his family, not to mention Stella and Ari. Nikos had tried to destroy them once before. It could happen again. He wouldn't put anything past him and wasn't about to take any chances.

Plaintiff Nikos Athas seeks a restraining order against Defendant Theo Pantheras who has proved to be a threat to Plaintiff's sister, Stella Athas, and her son, Ari. You are hereby summoned to appear before the court at nine a.m., Wednesday, June 15, to answer to charges of manipulation and coercion with intent to harm. Failure to comply will result in your arrest.

Nikos must have been born with a twisted mind.

This summons was what the six years of hard work, sacrifice and preparation had all been about. Theo was more than ready to take on Stella's brother. Since being with her again, heaven knew he hadn't wanted it to come to this, but after bumping into Nikos on St. Thomas, their chance meeting had escalated the situation to a white-hot point.

Theo tapped the paper against his cheek. Stasio Athas's name wasn't on the suit. At this point he began to think he'd been totally wrong about Stella's oldest brother. Stasio had been the one to take her to New York and look after her. He'd been the one to come to Ari's rescue when he and Rachel had been kidnapped. Stella loved Stasio.

He moved over to his desk and phoned Nestor. "I just received a summons from Nikos Athas out of Costas Paulos's office. Who is he?"

"The Athas family attorney. Read me what it says."

After Theo complied, Nestor grunted. "I'll answer it and be in touch with you."

"Thank you. As you know, I don't want a court fight. Do everything you can to prevent it."

"That may not be possible. Costas is one of the best there is and could hold sway over the judge."

"When I made inquiries, I was told you were one of the best, but whatever happens, keep me posted. I'll be on vacation for the next ten days."

"Enjoy yourself. You deserve it."

"Thanks, Nestor."

With that out of the way, Theo couldn't wait to leave the office. He had plans for the three of them, plans he was praying would change his entire life.

* * *

The resort's swimming pool resembled an aqua-blue lake. At one end was the giant slide Theo had told the boys about. Ari had been going down it all afternoon. Stella had taken quite a few turns herself and was worn-out. The hike to the top of the slide provided a work out all its own.

Theo never seemed to tire. He and Ari had thought up a dozen different ways to descend. Her boy was in heaven. If she didn't miss her guess, Theo was, too.

Ari ran over to the stairs. "I'm coming down on my stomach next time, Papa!"

Theo grinned. "Be sure and keep your head up. I'm waiting for you!"

"This is the last one for today, honey," Stella called to him from the sun lounger. "You and your father have your star-gazing class tonight. You need to eat dinner before you go."

"Oh, yeah. I forgot."

As he scrambled up the steps, Stella's gaze drifted to Theo who stood at the bottom of the serpentine slide to watch for him. Every female in the vicinity had their eyes on him, but Theo appeared oblivious. He and Ari were having too much fun.

Stella had brought out a book to read, but she kept looking at the same page over and over again because all she'd done was stare at the dark-haired male no other man compared to. One day Ari would grow up to be every bit as gorgeous and arresting. It gave her a thrill to know she was with Theo, that Ari was their son.

Several females cast her an envious glance. One woman who'd walked over to this part of the pool in a minuscule bikini made a play for him, engaging him in conversation. Stella felt so territorial she wanted to push her into the water, but of course she didn't do it. For one thing, Theo would know without a doubt her attraction to him had reached a dangerously strong level.

Close your eyes, Stella. Don't look at him.

Ari's life had become complete with the advent of his father's vital presence. His unqualified show of love for their son should be enough for Stella. Theo's private life was something else again.

They'd been here four days already. Once this vacation was over, she would get an apartment in the same neighborhood and life would get back to a new kind of normalcy. She'd go back to her work. So would he. Theo had talked about wanting a relationship with her, but they needed to go slowly.

In the meantime she had to put up with other women eyeing him. His kind of charisma brought the females running, just like the one with the tanned body and flowing blond hair still talking to him while he watched for Ari.

Since Theo seemed to be enjoying the attention, Stella decided she'd watched the spectacle long enough. After putting the book in her bag, she slipped on her beach coverup and headed inside the hotel where she wouldn't have to undergo more torture.

Certain things had changed since six years ago when Theo had never done anything to make her jealous. But that was when they'd been young lovers hiding from their families in order to be together. Everything was different now.

As she let herself in the room adjoining Theo's penthouse suite, a shaft of pain robbed her of breath because a part of her didn't want things to be different. In her heart of hearts she longed to be in his arms again. She ached for that fulfillment he'd brought to her life while they'd shut out the rest of the world.

But you could never go back. She didn't want to revisit all the pain that followed after he'd disappeared. Somehow she had to learn to survive with him back in Ari's life, but maybe not hers! Much to Ari's chagrin this special time with him on St. Thomas wouldn't last much longer, but it would be the very best antidote for the illness slowly killing her.

With tears threatening, she hurried into her room with the intention of showering, but all of a sudden Theo burst in through the adjoining door. Ari ran in behind him and disappeared into the bathroom.

"How come you didn't wait for us?" was the first question out of his mouth.

Stella was surprised he'd even noticed. "You two were having such a great time, I didn't know how long you'd be."

She heard him curse before he said, "You and I need to talk." He sounded angry.

"What's wrong?"

"How would you have felt if you'd turned around and discovered I was missing."

"It's not the same thing, Theo. You were talking to that woman. I didn't know if it was about business or not so I decided not to disturb you."

"That woman was a total stranger to me. When she invited me to a party, I told her I was married and my wife was right over there. Except that you weren't anywhere in sight."

"I'm sorry. I don't know what else to say."

"It upset Ari, too."

By now her heart was thundering unmercifully. "I had no idea."

"Next time give me a thought before you bolt." In the next breath he was gone.

"Mom?"

She swung around to see Ari with a towel wrapped around him. "Yes?"

"I thought you liked daddy."

Stella reeled. "You *know* I do. I've already told you that."

"But you don't love him like you used to, huh?"

His question trapped her. No matter how she answered it, Ari would internalize it and eventually tell Theo. "For now, why don't we concentrate on you and your father."

"I wish we could stay here forever."

Unable to resist, she kissed his cheek. "I've never seen you have so much fun before."

His dark eyes shone. "I love him."

"He loves you."

"I know. He's going to take us sailing tomorrow. We're going to stay out overnight and the next day we're going to fish."

"That'll be exciting for you."

"But you'll be with us."

"I don't think so, honey. Your father wants some private time with you. Think of all the years you've both missed."

His cute face crumpled. "Daddy says we won't go if you don't come."

Was Theo worried that Ari might get frightened without her there? If he could have heard his son just now, he'd know the bond between them was so strong, he had nothing to fear in that regard. After they came back from class she would ask Theo about it and reassure him if necessary.

"I'll talk to him later."

"We're going to eat dinner in his room. Come on. You can talk to him right now."

"Not yet. I have to shower first."

A few minutes later Stella rushed back into the bedroom and dressed in a pair of tan slacks and a print top in various shades of earth tones. She'd picked up a darker tan over the past few days. The new lipstick she'd purchased accentuated it. For the first time in years she felt as if she was on a real vacation with nothing to do but eat, sleep and play. She never wanted it to end.

In the past they'd always had to hide from everyone. Yet even after he'd disappeared, she'd never felt free. There was a gloom Nikos brought with him that had always darkened her world, but with Theo she felt free to be herself and Ari was a totally different child.

The more she thought about it, the more she was determined that as soon as they returned to Athens, she would start looking for another place to live. Stasio and his family preferred living on Andros. That left Nikos who could take over the family villa where he'd grown up. It would make him feel in charge. Maybe that's what he needed.

When she walked into Theo's suite, he captured her gaze. They both studied each other. "You look beautiful."

"Thank you."

"In truth you're the most beautiful woman at this resort. I can't believe how lucky I am."

She tried to stifle her gasp of surprise, but she couldn't suppress the surge of pleasure that curled through her body. Since it was Theo, he'd already noticed the signs, like the fact that right now her breathing had grown shallow just being this close to him.

He could read all the little clues that meant she was so aware of him, she was jittery. Of course she wasn't fooling anyone, especially not him, but it was a game she had to play for self-preservation.

"I'm lucky to be with two such handsome men."

"Am I handsome?" Ari wanted to know.

"Yes, just like your father," she blurted before realizing what she'd just said. Theo simply smiled at her.

Stella looked away. "Um, this looks good." She sat down next to Ari where Theo served them a light dinner from the cart sent up from the kitchen. So far they'd been eating all their meals in his room. She loved the intimacy, like they were a real family.

Theo eyed her for a long moment, seeming to assess her until she felt exposed. Her heart did a little kick she couldn't control. "Did Ari tell you my plans for the next few days?"

"Yes. We were just talking about it." If they all went sailing overnight, they'd be away from her brother's long reach a little longer. Without hesitation she said, "I can't think of anything I'd rather do."

"Hooray!" Ari cried.

There was a look in Theo's dark eyes that told her he was pleasantly surprised. "In that case I'd like to leave early in the morning."

"We'll be ready. While you're at class, I'll pack."

"I'll see the galley is stocked with food. That was a luxury I couldn't provide when we used to go rowing. Remember?"

"I didn't know you went rowing with Daddy."

Stella almost choked on the lamb she was eating. "Sometimes we did." Ari had been conceived on one of those outings.

"Was it fun?"

Theo's jet-black gaze shot to hers. "How would *you* describe it?" he asked her in his deep voice.

She couldn't meet his eyes. "As I recall, it was a lot of hard work."

"But the end justified the means every time."

Theo...

Unable to sit there any longer, she got up from the table. "I think I'll get started on that packing. Enjoy your class and come back safely."

Stella couldn't get out of his room fast enough.

Two nights later Stella stood at the bow of the sailboat, gazing at the view.

"That's a sunset you don't see very often." Theo had come up behind her.

"It's glorious." She'd been marveling over a golden orange sky slowly fading into pink. He ran his hands up her arms, kissing the side of her neck. "Wh-where's Ari?" When Theo came up on her like that, she couldn't even talk clearly.

"In the galley finishing his ice cream. Why do you think I stole up here for a moment?" His hands caressed her shoulders.

"No, Theo," she cried, "this isn't the time—" But he wasn't listening to her.

"You're wrong. It's the perfect time. Before I went away, you were my whole life." He turned her around to face him. "Since I've been back, I've discovered you still are. *Agape mou,*" he whispered, finding her mouth, avidly kissing her lips apart. "I need to taste your sweetness again."

His hunger for her made her forget everything else. All she knew was that his mouth set her on fire and she couldn't stop what was happening. As his passion grew, she was engulfed in his arms, craving his touch. There was no one in the world who could make her feel the way Theo did. Her need to merge with him was overpowering.

He finally lifted his head enough to look into her eyes. "I can't believe that when I flew to New York, you were there, too, having our baby. I should have been there for you." She heard tears in his voice. "We were robbed of our lives for a long time. Now that we're back together, I need this more than ever. Tell me you feel the same way…."

For a dizzying moment she felt their bodies meld. The chemistry between them had always been volatile. Right now it was as if they'd never been apart. "Obviously I'm not immune to you, Theo," she confessed on a little moan of surrender, "but having told you that, it changes nothing. We're not young kids anymore."

"No. We're a man and woman who've never been able to stay away from each other."

She searched his eyes. "There are things we have to talk about."

"I agree, but let's enjoy the rest of our trip first. This is heaven for me. I want to make it last as long as possible. Don't you?"

"Of course," she admitted, "but—"

"Do you trust me?"

She felt him probing deep into her soul. "Yes. Otherwise I wouldn't be here."

"That's all I needed to hear."

Once again his mouth fused with hers. This was ecstasy. His lips roved over her face, capturing each feature. As she sought his mouth helplessly, she heard a sound behind them.

"What kind of fish do you think we'll catch tomorrow?"

While she tore her lips away and eased out of Theo's arms, he turned to Ari. "Probably some sea bass. It's very tasty. If they're not biting, then we'll do some snorkeling."

"Will we see a lot of things?"

"I'll take us to a spot where the water's so clean and pure, you won't believe what's swimming underneath."

"Will it be scary?"

"Not where we're going. Besides, your mom and I will be right there with you."

"Yeah."

"Now that we've dropped anchor for the night, come on and help me put the boat to bed."

"A boat doesn't go to bed, Papa."

"Sure it does. It's tired after working hard all day." Ari giggled. No one was more exciting to be with than Theo. "We have to clean up any messes, fasten down anything loose, turn out lights. There's a lot of stuff."

"Will we be able to fish as soon as we wake up?"

"Yes, but it'll be foggy so we'll throw out our lines and see what we can catch until the sun burns it off."

"How did you learn to fish?"

"My father taught me and my brothers. We had to go out very early to catch enough for my mother to cook."

"You mean for breakfast?"

"No. She used fish to make the food we sold at the taverna."

"But what if you didn't catch any?"

"That happened a lot."

"Then what did you do?"

"We had to go to the meat shops and wait for them to sell us the meat parts for a cheap price nobody wanted."

"You mean like brains and liver and stuff?"

"That's right."

"Did we eat brains at the taverna the other day?"

Theo roared with laughter. "No. For you she prepared the very best food."

"It was yummy."

Stella's heart swelled with emotion as she gathered Ari's damp towels and sandals and listened to them talk. For one six-year-old boy, he left a lot of items around, but she didn't care. Theo was telling her son things she hadn't known, not during all the time she'd spent with him.

"Papa? I'd like to live on this sailboat."

She chuckled along with Theo. Ari loved everything they did because he was with his father.

"Shall we do it? Shall we just sail off to wherever we want?"

"Could we?"

"Yes, but I think you'd start to miss your friends and school."

"Did you like school?"

"For the most part."

"I like recess the best."

"So did I. You must be my son."

"I am!" At that remark, Theo threw back his head and laughed that deep, rich laugh Stella loved to hear. "I wish Mom and I could live with you."

"I'd love it," Theo answered without hesitation. His narrowed gaze captured hers. "How about *you*, Stella?"

Her heart thudded in her chest. He didn't play fair

asking her a loaded question like that in front of their son. "Are you being serious?" She'd decided it was his turn to be put on the spot.

There was a strange tension between them. He finally said, "So serious that I'd like to discuss it further after we turn in."

Staggered by his response, Stella left the deck and hurried below. She needed to gather her wits and headed straight to the galley to finish cleaning up. The two of them followed a few minutes later.

There were two bedrooms, one with a double bed and another with two bunk beds. She would have slept with Ari, but Theo insisted she have the big bed because the men were on an adventure.

After kissing Ari good-night, Stella brushed her teeth and changed into a pair of navy-blue tailored pajamas. Turning on the reading lamp, she sat up in bed and pulled out the book she'd tried to read at the pool. It was a spy novel written by an author she liked.

To her dismay she couldn't get into it tonight, either. When Theo entered the room dressed in a pair of sweats and a T-shirt, her heart thumped so hard, it hurt. In the semidarkness his striking masculine features stood out. Disturbed at the appealing sight of him, she pretended to keep reading.

In the next instant he came to sit down beside her and plucked it out of her hands. Then he got on the bed and stretched out next to her with one elbow propped. She felt his eyes study her with toe-curling intimacy. "You could have no comprehension of how gorgeous you look tonight."

She could hardly swallow. "Thank you."

"After I went to New York, there were nights when

I thought I'd die if I couldn't have you. I couldn't fathom that you'd stopped loving me."

Stella averted her eyes. "Then you have some comprehension of how I felt. It took raising Ari to help me deal with the pain."

He took a shuddering breath. "I threw myself into work. I had three jobs, one with a well-to-do Greek café owner who was a boyhood friend of my grandfather's. He told me that if I wanted to make real money, I should study the real estate listings. There were properties I could buy without a down payment. The trick was to fix one up and then sell it for as much as I could.

"I thought he was crazy, but I took his advice. You wouldn't believe how fast I started making money. He told me where to put it. Some of it went to high-risk investments that paid off. I sent money home and started planning my return. One of my goals was to find you and make you tell me face-to-face what happened."

She stirred restlessly on the bed before flicking him a glance. "I was the opposite. It was such a nightmare, I hoped I'd never see you again."

Theo grimaced. "My letter must have come as a shock."

"I fainted, but Iola caught me so I didn't crack my head open on the floor." The compassion in his eyes was too much. She looked away again.

"I'm sorry, Stella. After driving past the villa and seeing you, I didn't know how else to make contact."

She moistened her lips. "No matter how it was done, it was like finding out you'd come back from the dead."

"I was told you'd gotten rid of our child."

"Theo—"

"To see Ari skipping along with you almost sent me

into cardiac arrest. To think the whole time in New York, I believed—"

"That I'd ended my pregnancy?" she cut in on him. "How you must have despised me."

His body stiffened with remembered pain. "I was riddled with rage until I saw Ari. Then I was plunged into another kind of fury because you'd kept him from me."

After taking a deep breath she said, "Who did this to us?"

"It doesn't matter anymore." He leaned over her. "In the beginning I tried to despise you, but I couldn't. I fell in love with you a long time ago, Stella. That's never going to change. Marry me, sweetheart. I can't go on without you."

She let out a little moan as he began kissing her, sweeping her away. "I never stopped loving you, either. You're my whole life!"

"Did you just say yes?"

"You *know* I did," she cried. "I love you, I love you, Theo. I want to be your wife as soon as possible."

"Stella—" came his exultant cry. "Let me love you tonight. Really love you."

The feel of his mouth brought her such rapture, she'd become a trembling mass of need. Over and over she cried out his name. His powerful legs entwined with hers, reminding her of those other times when they'd given in to their desire.

"Papa?"

They both groaned.

"When are you coming back to bed?"

"Don't tell him yet," she whispered. "Let's wait until we know all our plans."

"Agreed." Theo kissed her throat before rolling away from her. "I thought you were asleep, sport."

"I had a nightmare."

"Oh, honey," Stella said. "Come on up here." Ari scrambled on the bed between them. "What was it about?"

"A shark. It was trying to catch me."

"Well, you stay right here with us. We'll keep you safe."

She felt Theo's fingers creep into her hair, tantalizing her. He'd expected her to urge Ari back to bed so they could take up where they'd left off, but it wouldn't be a good idea for several reasons. The main one was snuggled up against them happy as a new puppy, his nightmare forgotten.

"Good night, everyone."

"Good night, Mom. Good night, Papa."

Theo squeezed her shoulder. "Good night, Mom. Good night, son."

"Mommy's not your mom."

More deep laughter reverberated in the room. It was the last thing she remembered before falling asleep.

By the time their vacation was over, Stella felt like they were a family. She could have stayed there forever playing with and loving the two men she adored. The thought of going back to work made her groan. That was how transported she'd been.

"What was that sigh all about?" Theo was so tuned in to her feelings, they could read each other's minds.

"How much I don't want this to be over." The three of them were carrying their bags to the helicopter.

He caught her around the waist. "It's not going to be. You and I need more time together. Hire a temp to help Keiko for another week. Someone in the office will want the opportunity."

Another week with Theo? She almost stumbled in her excitement. "I'll see what I can arrange."

Before long they flew back to civilization. When the helicopter landed on top of his office building, Stella rebelled. For a moment she had the premonition that now he'd asked her to marry him, this fragile new world they'd been building was going to explode by an unseen force and they'd never be able to pick up the pieces.

As Theo helped her out of the helicopter she whispered, "Do you still have that letter? I'm ready to read it."

His black eyes ignited like hot coals. He pressed a hungry kiss to her mouth. "It's in my office."

"Will you get it for me before you drive me and Ari home?"

"I'll do it right now and join you at the limo." He ruffled Ari's hair. "See you in a minute."

CHAPTER EIGHT

THEO made a detour to his suite. There was a message waiting for him. Nestor had talked to the judge, but there was no budging him. The show-cause hearing was going ahead as planned for the day after tomorrow.

He closed his eyes tightly, imagining Stella's reaction. After asking her to marry him, he'd do anything to protect her from being hurt, but it was all going to come out, and he was terrified what it would do to her.

The letter was in his drawer. He put it in his pocket and left his office, catching up to them out in front of the building. The second he climbed in the back next to Stella, Ari said, "I wish we didn't have to go home. I love fishing."

"So do I, son. After our astronomy class has ended, we'll do it again. I know a place in the mountains where we can camp out and fish the stream. Leandros and his papa love to fish, too. Maybe the four of us could go. Would you like that?"

"I'd love it."

That was one of the things he loved most about Ari. His constant enthusiasm. Stella had been right. Their son was the brightest, sweetest boy in the world. They were both his life!

Too soon the limo drove up in front of the villa, bringing their trip to an end.

"See you tomorrow, Papa." Ari gave him a big kiss and climbed out first. Taking advantage of the moment, Theo drew the letter from his pocket and put it in her purse lying next to her on the seat.

He reached for her hand and kissed the palm. "Call Keiko and make those arrangements. I have more plans for us."

She nodded. "I'll let you know tomorrow."

"Stella—" He cupped her face to kiss her one more time. It wasn't long enough or deep enough.

"Come on, Mom."

Theo reluctantly let her go.

"Good night." She got out of the car, leaving him with an ache that was never going to go away.

He watched her rush up the steps to join Ari. Once they were safely inside, he told the chauffeur to take him back to the office. Theo knew he wouldn't be able to sleep, so he might as well get some work done.

A time bomb was ticking. Before long it was going to go off. There had to be a way to help Stella when the time came, but his greatest fear was that she would go into shock. When he thought about one of his own brothers having the capacity to betray him to that degree, he couldn't imagine it.

One thing and one thing only was helping him to hold on to his sanity tonight. To his everlasting gratitude, he had Ari, his greatest ally and link to Stella. Ari always pulled through for him.

What a wonderful son. His joy. That's because he had a mother like Stella. On this trip Theo found out he needed them like he needed air to breathe. If the crisis that was coming was too much for her, he might never be able to reach her again in the same way.

This trip had drawn them so close together, the thought of anything destroying what they had now was killing him. He buried his face in his hands.

Iola took one look at Ari and threw up her hands. "You've turned into a lobster!"

"Lobster…" Ari roared with laughter. "Guess what? I caught two sea bass!"

"How big were they?"

"This long." He demonstrated.

"Good for you! Did you eat them?"

"Yes. Papa's the best cook just like my grandma. The fish was yummy, wasn't it, Mommy."

"Delicious." On their trip she'd discovered Theo had many hidden skills.

"Are you hungry now?"

"No. We're ready for bed," Stella declared. "If he's going to play with Dax in the morning, he needs his sleep. Run on up, honey, and get your bath. I'll be there in a minute to tuck you in."

"Okay."

As he darted up the stairs, she turned to Iola. "How are you?"

"I'm fine now that you've come home so happy. You're in love again."

Stella nodded. "Theo's even more wonderful than he was before."

"He's a man."

"Yes. He's my life and Ari's." She kissed Iola's cheek. "See you in the morning."

Once in her room, she couldn't wait to read the letter.

Her hands trembled as she got it out of her purse. When he'd given it to her on Andros, she'd thrown it back at him. At the time, her state of mind wouldn't allow him inside her head. Now he filled her whole heart and soul.

She sank down on the side of her bed, dying to find out what he'd written. Taking as much care as possible, she opened the sealed envelope and pulled out the short, one-page letter.

Agape Mou,
Something terrible has happened to me. That's why I couldn't come inside the church to get you. I'm in Salamis Hospital, room 434W. Spiro is writing this letter for me because I can't use my hands yet.

Find a way to leave the villa and come to me as fast as you can, sweetheart. My family's going to let you stay with us until I'm better, then we'll get married and find a place of our own.

I love you, Stella. I love our baby.
Come soon. I need you.
Theo.

Stella moaned.

"Kyrie Pantheras?"
"Yes?"
"Stella Athas is here to see you."
Excitement charged his body. "Tell her to come in." He threw down his pen and hurried around the desk to greet her. This morning she was wearing a stunning cocoa-colored silk blouse with pleated pants in a café-au-lait tone.

She looked good enough to eat. Her velvety brown

eyes sought his with a new eagerness. She must have read his letter or she wouldn't have that expectant look on her face.

"Am I disturbing you?"

"Yes," he whispered in a husky tone and reached for her, sliding his hands up and down her arms. "In all the ways only you can do." He could tell she was out of breath. "Did you work things out with Keiko?"

She nodded.

"Anything else you want to tell me?"

"Yes. It's about us. Weeks ago you asked me to accept you on faith. Last night on the boat you asked me to marry you. It's what I want, what Ari wants. That's what I've come here to say and I want us to tell Ari today."

"Stella," he cried. "I prayed that was why you'd come. Now that you're here, I don't intend to waste another second."

He lowered his mouth to the lush moistness of hers, leaving her no escape. They began devouring each other with a fervency that transported both of them back in time to halcyon days when nothing mattered but to be together communicating like this.

His body trembled with desire while they clung in such a tight embrace, there was no space between them. He couldn't believe it. She was giving him everything. It was as if a light had been turned on. Theo couldn't get enough of her as their kisses grew more breathless and sensual.

"I'm in love with you, Stella," he cried into her hair.

Her gasp of ecstasy thrilled him. She burrowed her face in his neck. "I'll love you forever, Theo. I couldn't get through life without you now."

To hear those words caused the blood to sing in his ears. "Do you think I could?" His euphoria made him forget everything except the wonder of holding and kissing her until he was delirious with longings that needed assuagement soon. They were already in deep trouble.

"Kyrie Pantheras? You asked me to buzz you when it was ten to twelve."

Stella's moan of protest was as loud as his.

"Thank you."

He drank from her mouth one more time before putting her away from. Her eyes were glazed from desire. She swayed in place.

"Only Ari could force me to let you go at a time like this."

She kissed his hands. "Let's go pick him up together. I can't wait to tell him our news. He'll be so happy." Her gaze played over him with so much love he felt like he was drowning.

Theo pressed his lips to her palms. "Neither of you could want it as much as I do. After we get him, I'm taking you both to my house on Salamis. While we have lunch there, we'll tell him it will be our home. I want to marry you right away. Will you mind living on the island?"

Her brows formed a delicate frown line. "How can you ask me that?"

"Because you've lived in the heart of Athens all your life."

"As long as I'm with you, I don't care where I live. We used to talk about the house we would have right on the beach one day. It was my dream. Have you forgotten?"

He caught her face between his hands. "There isn't one second of our lives I haven't lived over and over until it has driven me mad. I'm hardly going to forget the plans we made." After kissing her with refined savagery, he wheeled away from her to gather his suit jacket and the phone.

Together they rode the private elevator to the car park where his limo was waiting. En route to Dax's house he held her on his lap and kissed her senseless. For a little while he felt like a teenager again, crazy in love with Stella Athas, the most gorgeous girl in the world.

"We've got to stop doing this before we get there, Theo. Ari's going to know what we've been up to."

He chuckled. "Our son knows exactly what's been going on with us from day one." She slid off his lap and sat across from him to brush her hair. "I love the taste of your lipstick by the way. You can lay it on me anytime."

"Behave, Theo."

"I don't want to. Besides, you don't want me to."

"That's beside the point," she said while she applied a fresh coat to her lips.

"Are you as happy as I am?"

She shot him a glance that enveloped him in love. "I'm so happy I'm in pain. The kind that's never going to go away."

"We can be married in three weeks, Stella. I'll arrange it with Hektor."

Three weeks without being married sounded like an eternity. While Stella was wondering how she would last until then, the limo turned into Dax's driveway. The boys were out in front throwing a ball. Ari waved goodbye to his friend and ran toward them.

"Mom!" He climbed inside next to Theo. "I didn't know you were coming with Papa. This is great!"

"Your mother and I have a plan. I'll tell the driver to run us to your house. Both of you grab some clothes for a sleepover and we'll spend the night at my house. Though you've seen it, your mother hasn't."

"Goody! Will we go to class from there?"

Theo nodded. "Tell me what you and Dax did this morning."

Stella scarcely listened. Too much excitement over the news they had to tell Ari made her restless. Not only that, she couldn't wait to see Theo's house.

While they were at class, she had a wedding to plan. Rachel would help her. She'd include Elani, too. In fact she'd call them both tonight. It would be a joyous time for all of them.

"Stella?" Theo whispered. "What's going on inside that lovely head of yours?" She blinked to realize they were in front of the villa.

"Ari's gone in to get his things."

"I need to get mine, too."

"Just a minute." He pressed a deep kiss to her mouth. "Tell me you're not having second thoughts. I couldn't handle it."

"Hush, Theo." She kissed him back passionately. "Actually I was thinking of Rachel and how excited she'll be to help me plan our wedding."

"I'm looking forward to meeting her."

"You'll love her."

He kissed her temple. "Do you want me to come in while you get your things?"

"No. It'll only take me a minute."

"Hurry!"

"I promise."

He helped her out. She passed Ari in the foyer with his backpack. "I'll be right out, honey." All she needed were some toiletries, a change of clothes and a nightgown.

While she was putting everything in her overnight bag, Iola came in her bedroom. "Where are you going?"

She closed the lid. "To Theo's. I'm not sure when we'll be home. It might be a few days."

"Are you sure you know what you're doing?"

"Absolutely. Iola, you might as well know first. We're back together for good. In fact we're getting married in three weeks."

Her eyes filled with tears before she broke down with happy sobs. Stella gave her a hug. "You'll have to help me with the wedding plans."

Iola finally pulled herself together. "Before I forget, Rachel wants you to call her right away. She says it's an emergency."

"Thanks for telling me. I'll phone her."

"Good."

After she walked out, Stella reached for her phone. She'd purposely turned off the ringer while she'd gone to Theo's office. Much as she'd like to put off this call, she couldn't, but with Ari and Theo outside waiting for her, she'd make this fast.

It barely started to ring when Rachel answered. "Stella?"

"Hi. What's wrong?"

"If you have to ask me that question, then you don't know."

Her heart picked up speed. "Know what?"

After a silence. "I hope you're sitting down."

Stella stood there unable to move. "If this is about Theo, I don't want to hear it."

"You have to hear it, Stella." She heard tears in Rachel's voice.

"Then tell me."

"Nikos has brought a full-blown lawsuit against Theo for misrepresenting who he is and taking advantage of you. The case is set for tomorrow morning. He expects the family to be there for support. I told him I wouldn't have anything to do with it. Stasio's in shock that Nikos has carried it this far."

"I am, too," she murmured. It meant Theo had been aware of the court date for some time now, but he'd never let on.

"Stella?"

"I have to go now."

"Are you all right?" Rachel sounded frantic.

"No. I have to talk to Theo. Tell Stasio I'll call him later."

She hung up feeling so ill she didn't know if she'd survive another second. For her brother to do this at the height of her happiness made him sound unbalanced. In a panic, she rushed downstairs and out the front entrance to the car.

Theo opened the limo door and gave her a squeeze around the waist. "We thought you were never coming."

Avoiding his eyes she said, "I had a phone call that detained me. Before we go anywhere, I need to talk to you alone."

She lowered her head to look at Ari. "Honey? There's something I have to discuss with your father in private. It will only take a minute. Would you mind running inside the house? I'll let you know when we're finished."

He could tell she was serious. His happy expression faded. "Okay." He slid out of the limo leaving his pack behind and raced up the porch steps into the house.

Stella climbed inside and sat opposite Theo. He sat

back, studying her features. She saw nothing but love in those dark eyes.

"Rachel just phoned me. I've been told Nikos has brought a lawsuit against you and you have to appear in court tomorrow. Is it true?"

She thought he paled. "Yes."

"Why didn't you tell me?"

"Because I wanted to put the past behind us."

"I don't understand my brother. There's something really wrong with him."

"Let me worry about it."

"How can you be so calm? Were you planning to go to court without me?"

"Yes. I don't want you there."

"I've just told you I'll marry you. You think I'd let you walk into a courtroom alone after what we've been through in the last six years?"

"You can't come, Stella. I won't let you. The court session shouldn't take long. I'll be back soon enough."

Stella decided not to argue with him. After he left for court, she'd take Ari to Dax's house and slip into the courtroom. Theo wouldn't be able to do anything about it then.

"All right."

He kissed her hard on the mouth. "I'll go in and get Ari now."

"Third district court is now in session. The Most Honorable Judge Antonias Christopheles presiding."

"You may be seated," the judge said, looking out at the crowd assembled.

Besides Theo's entire family, including Hecktor, half of the closed-session courtroom was filled with witnesses Nestor had lined up. The other half of the room was conspicuously empty. Nikos sat at the table with his attorney, but just as the judge began to speak, Stella slipped inside the back and sat down next to Stasio.

Theo hadn't wanted her anywhere near here, but there wasn't anything he could do about it now.

"There are several charges laid before the court this Wednesday, the eighteenth of June by Nikos Athas against Theo Pantheras for unduly manipulating and coercing Stella Athas against her will. Mr. Pantheras, in turn, has laid countercharges against Nikos Athas.

"The first is to ascertain if Nikos Athas intended to murder Theo Pantheras on July 6, six years ago.

"The second is to discover if he set fire to the Pantheras Taverna in Paloukia on the night of July 1.

"The third is to discover if he caused an accident to Spiro Pantheras while he was riding his motor scooter the night of June 27.

"The fourth is to learn if he threatened the lives of the Pantheras family on repeated occasions by telephone calls from June 2 until July 6."

"The fifth is to learn if he tried to bribe Theo Pantheras with ten thousand dollars to leave his sister alone."

With each count, Theo watched Stella's head drop a little lower. He'd warned her not to come. This part was going to devastate her.

"Mr. Paulos, if you'll make your opening statement, please."

Theo watched the burly-looking attorney take the floor. "Thank you, Your Honor. My client has been forced to respond to these totally false allegations without having been given adequate preparation time."

"I'm aware of that. However, may I remind you this

is only a show-cause hearing to determine if this case warrants a full jury trial. Please go ahead."

"Thank you." He cleared his throat. "Athas Shipping Lines is one of Greece's greatest resources. I don't need to tell the court of Nikos Athas's extraordinary talents as one of our Olympians. Their father filled one of the highest positions in our government.

"To think Nikos could perpetrate such crimes is beyond the imagination of this counsel and I dare say this country. I consider it a crime to waste this court's time, Your Honor. If opposing counsel can produce one shred of evidence to the contrary, then let him speak."

The judge nodded. "Mr. Georgeles? If you'll approach the bench."

Nestor patted Theo's arm before getting to his feet. "If Your Honor will look at Exhibit A, I'll ask the physician, Dr. Vlasius, who attended Mr. Pantheras in the E.R. at Salamis Hospital on the night of July 6 to explain. He's on the board there now."

"Step forward, Doctor, and be sworn in."

Once that was accomplished, Nestor began. "Dr. Vlasius, would you tell us about these X-rays, please."

"Certainly. These show the injuries to Mr. Theo Pantheras, the nineteen-year-old man brought in by his friends. When he was beaten up on his way home and left for dead, it revealed that the bones in his lower legs, arms and hands had been broken by a pipe. The type of weapon used has been corroborated by the police. His face was smashed in. He resided in the hospital six weeks while his bones healed and reconstructive surgery was done on his face and nose."

A feminine cry came from across the aisle. Stella's.

"Thank you, Dr. Vlasius. If you'd be seated, I'd like

to call on Damon Arabos, Theo's closest friend who brought him in to the hospital."

Again Theo could tell Stella was stunned to see him walk to the bench. He'd been Theo's sidekick through high school. He was a tease who'd made everyone laugh.

As soon as he was sworn in, Nestor began. "Did you witness this attack on him?"

"Only at the end."

"Did you recognize who did it?"

"There were five men bent over him. I got some of our friends and we started to attack them. They ran away and got in a van. One of our friends took down the license plate. The police traced it to a man who works at the docks for Athas Shipping Lines named Yanni Souvalis, but he suddenly didn't show up for work anymore."

"Thank you, Mr. Arabos. You may be seated. Now I'd like to call Alena Callas to the bench to be sworn in. She works at the telephone company in their records department and has gathered some evidence useful to this case which I've submitted under Exhibit B."

This was the part Theo had been waiting for. It was the paper trails that would bring Nikos down.

"Mrs. Callas, would you tell the court the nature of Exhibit B."

"Yes. These represent the phone logs of the dates between June 2 and July 6. Nine phone calls in all. They originated from the private phone of Mr. Nikos Athas. All calls were made to the Pantheras Taverna on Salamis Island."

"Were they long phone calls?"

"Each one was different, but none of them were longer than forty-five seconds."

"Thank you. You can be seated. I'd like to call Mr. Bion as my next witness."

"I object, Your Honor!" Mr. Paulos blurted.

"Objection overruled. I'm here to listen to the evidence. Please make it short, Mr. Georgeles."

"Yes, Your Honor."

Theo couldn't see Nikos's face. He was huddled behind the desk with his attorney.

"Mr. Bion? Please tell the court who you are."

"I'm the battalion commander for the Paloukia Fire Department."

"Were you witness to a fire at the Pantheras Taverna on the night of July 1?"

"Yes, sir. Of course, then I had just joined the department."

"Tell us what you discovered at the fire?"

"It was an arson case. A chemical was used that the police traced to Athas Shipping Lines. Only a few companies use it."

"So it could have come from another shipping line?"

"Not at that time, no."

"Thank you. You can be seated. I'd now like to call Mr. Spiro Pantheras to the stand."

Spiro winked at Theo on his way to the bench.

"Tell the court who you are, please."

"I'm Spiro Pantheras, Theo's older brother."

"I understand you met with an accident on your motor scooter on the night of June 27 near the taverna."

"That's correct."

"Can you tell us what happened."

"I was on my way home from the store when I heard a car rev behind me. I moved to the right to get out of the way, but it followed me and sideswiped me, knocking me off my scooter."

"Did you see the car?"

"Only the tail end of it before it rounded the corner. It was the latest model black Ferrari with local license plates."

"Were you hospitalized?"

"No, but because of the threatening phone calls to my parents at the *taverna,* I called the police to report it. You have a copy of the police case."

"Did anything happen as a result?"

"No."

"Thank you very much. You may step down." Nestor turned to the judge. "Your Honor? If you'll look at Exhibit C, I've provided a list of every new Ferrari sold within that twelve-month period in Athens. Two could be accounted for. One belonged to the deputy prime minister, the other to Nikos Athas. For my final witness today, I call Theo Pantheras to the stand."

This was it, but Theo felt no joy having to expose her brother this way in front of her. After he was sworn in, Nestor said, "Mr. Pantheras, please tell the court in your own words the happenings during that month leading to your hospitalization."

He took a deep breath and leveled his gaze on Stella. "I committed the crime of falling in love with Stella Athas when she was sixteen and I, eighteen. Her family didn't approve of me and we both knew it, so we had to be creative how we could be together.

"I knew Nikos Athas didn't like me, but I didn't realize he'd go so far as to harass me and my family so I'd stay away from her. One night he followed me home from church. On the way he offered me ten thousand dollars to get out of Stella's life and stay out.

"I told him what he could do with his money and took off. Later that week we received threatening phone calls from him, then the *taverna* was set on fire. After Spiro's accident I realized Nikos was serious. On the last phone call I received from him, he said that if I didn't break up with Stella, he would injure my parents until I didn't recognize them.

"I had to believe him, so I called Stella and told her we were getting married. I'd meet her at the church, but I was beaten up outside in the car park. It was clear Nikos wasn't about to let the Pantheras family merge with his on any level, not even to letting me claim my rights as a father.

"After I got out of the hospital, I left for New York to begin carving out a career for myself. Since then I've returned to Greece and have been with Stella and my son Ari."

Nestor smiled at Theo. "Thank you, Mr. Pantheras. You may step down." Theo went back to his seat behind the desk. "Your Honor, I turn the time back over to Mr. Paulos."

"Mr. Paulos?" the judge asked. "Do you wish to cross-examine?"

"Not at this time, Your Honor."

"What can he say?" Nestor whispered to Theo. "There is no rebuttal to the case we just presented. His case has fallen apart."

Theo agreed. Nikos had already hung himself.

"After hearing the proceedings of this case, I plan for this to go to a full jury trial which is set for September 13. Bail on Nikos Athas is set at ten million dollars. You will not be allowed to leave the country."

Nikos exploded. "You can't keep me here! I live in Switzerland!"

"One more outburst, Mr. Athas, and I'll have the sergeant-at-arms restrain you. This session is dismissed until September 13 at 9:00 a.m." He pounded his gavel and left the courtroom.

The family swarmed around Theo. This was a day they'd needed for closure. Everyone wept. When Theo eventually stood up to find Stella, he discovered she had gone. The emptiness in his heart threatened to swallow him whole. Charging her brother with attempted murder wasn't something easy to forgive. He would treasure the memories of the last few weeks with her and Ari, but they might be all he'd ever have.

CHAPTER NINE

STELLA left the courtroom and raced to the villa ahead of everyone. "Iola?" she cried out the second she entered the house.

"I'm here." The housekeeper came running. "What's wrong?"

"Wait right here." She dashed up the stairs to get the letter Theo had sent her. When she came down again she said, "I'm going to show you something. I want you to think back very hard to the time when Theo didn't come to the church for me."

The older woman frowned. "I'll never forget it as long as I live."

No one would forget. "I want you to take a look at this envelope. Read everything on the front. The date is from six years ago." She handed it to her.

Iola studied it for an overly long moment without lifting her eyes.

Pure revelation flowed through Stella. "You recognize it, don't you."

Still no response.

"Is that your handwriting at the bottom that says addressee unknown?"

She shook her head violently.

"Do you know whose it is? This is important, Iola. I have to know the truth."

"I can't tell you."

"Why?"

"Because I will lose my job."

"What? That's impossible! You're a part of this family." Stella reached out and hugged her. "This is your home. Who told you that?"

She kept her head bowed. "Please don't make me tell you. I'm afraid."

"I can see that."

Stella put a hand over her own mouth, absolutely devastated to think Nikos had blackmailed her into keeping quiet about this. "Did more letters like this come to the house I don't know about?"

"I don't know," she muttered. In the next breath she handed Stella the letter before running down the hall toward the back of the villa.

Stella slowly walked into the salon and waited for the rest of the family to arrive. She'd arranged for Ari to stay with Dax until she came for him.

In a minute she heard footsteps in the foyer. Stasio's pained expression left nothing to the imagination as he entered the salon with Nikos, who'd gone somewhere mentally where she couldn't reach him.

His year-round tan had turned a sickly white. He'd been Stella's nemesis for years. Every truly unhappy moment in her life she could lay at his feet. Her own brother.

Poor Stasio. He'd been just as wounded by him, maybe more, because he was the big brother Nikos hated to love and loved to hate.

On impulse she reached for Nikos's hand. "I have something important to tell you, Nikos. Despite what you've done, I know in my heart Theo doesn't want to send you to prison. That wasn't his focus.

"When he came back to Greece and discovered he had a son, all he wanted was to fight for him and ultimately for me." Never had a woman had more evidence of a man's love.

She squeezed Nikos's hand to get a reaction from him. "Listen to me—I know he'll drop all the charges against you provided you do something for me."

He looked at her in torment.

"If he still wants me after this, we're going to be married. All he would like is peace from my family. He would like to be able to come and go with me and Ari and be treated kindly and fairly. That's all."

Stasio's eyes glistened with tears.

"But that's not all I want. Once upon a time you were a sweet boy, but something happened when you grew up. You'll have to promise me and Stasio that you'll get psychiatric help. You've needed it for years. It'll save your marriage. Renate really loves you, but she can't do it alone."

"It's too late for me," Nikos whispered in a tortured breath.

"No." Stasio sat forward. "It's never to late to change."

Stella patted his hand. "Look at Theo. He's back after six years ready to take up where we left off. He didn't think it was too late."

He shook his head. "I told the guys to rough him up, not kill him."

"I believe you. So does he."

"He has every right to hate my guts forever."

"Theo's not like that." Her voice trembled. "He has so much goodness in him you can't imagine."

The sobs started coming. Suddenly he got up from the couch and left the room. They could hear his anguish all the way to his suite down the hall.

Stasio moved over to sit by her. He put his big arms around her and rocked her against him. "Stella…" She heard every ounce of pain and love in his heart. They'd been through it all together. "When you and Theo work everything out, I want to have a long talk with him. He's a man like few others. No wonder no other guy ever measured up."

"I love him so terribly."

"I know. He's a lucky man to be loved by you. Go to him and put him out of his misery. He deserves every bit of happiness you can find together."

Since returning from court, Theo's family had sequestered him above the taverna. The women got food ready while he sat at the dining room table with his father and brothers. They'd closed the taverna for the day. It was like a holiday with the kids milling around, but the last thing he felt like doing was celebrating.

He kept reliving the court scene in his mind. With each damaging piece of evidence, Stella seemed to have shrunken inside herself a little more. No matter how he went over it in his mind, there hadn't been another way to do it.

If he'd called her on the phone after returning to Athens, and told her the truth right off, she would have hung up on him. There wouldn't have been a discussion. He would never have been able to meet Ari.

"Theo?" Dymas poured him a little wine. "She's going to forgive you."

Spiro nodded. "Give it time. You said she's always had to be careful around Nikos. When it sinks in and she realizes there wasn't any other way for you to handle things, she'll get in touch with you."

He sat back in the chair with his arms crossed. "I'd like to believe you, but I saw anguish on her face today. She has loved her family a lot longer than she has loved me. You know what they say. Blood is thicker than water." His gaze flicked to his family.

"Thank you all for being there for me today."

"As if we'd have been anywhere else." His father patted his arm. "You've suffered long enough. Today we saw justice done. I'm very proud of the great man you've become."

For his father to tell Theo that was something. He'd never said those words to him before. "Thank you, Papa, but I don't feel great. To destroy the woman I love in order to be with her and my son has brought me no joy."

"Nikos Athas destroyed himself without anyone's help, my boy."

"It's too bad the jury trial can't be sooner so this can all be over with."

"There isn't going to be one, Spiro." Theo shoved himself away from the table and got to his feet.

All three of them stared at him, waiting for an explanation.

"Tomorrow I'll tell Nestor I'm dropping the charges."

Dymas looked shocked. "After all you've done to get ready for it?"

"Yes. It's over."

"Nikos could still be dangerous."

"I've thought about that, Dymas. Nevertheless, today's court session is as far as I go. He's been exposed. Enough damage was done for Stella to know the true reason for what happened."

His father got to his feet and walked over to him. "How much does Ari know about any of this?"

"As far as I know, nothing. But today everything exploded. No doubt he'll learn all about it and totally despise me."

"No, Theo. You've won his love. He'll figure it out. Like Spiro said, give this time."

"You mean like another six years? Maybe then my son will be mature enough to acknowledge me again?" Theo was dying inside. "Papa? Will you tell Mama I couldn't stay. I have to leave."

He patted Theo's shoulder. "I understand. Where are you going to go?"

"I don't know. I need to be alone."

"Do you want to take a drive with me?"

"No, thank you, Papa. I have to be on my own." He felt like running until he dropped and the pain went away.

They walked to the top of the stairs. "I love you, Theo."

"I love you, too, Papa." He kissed his cheek before descending the steps leading to the restaurant below. He let himself out of the back of the *taverna* and locked the door before he started running in the direction of the beach.

Stella showered and changed into the white dress with the wide belt Theo seemed to like so much. Wherever he was, when she caught up to him she wanted to look her most beautiful for him.

After talking to Ari on the phone at Dax's house, she found out he hadn't heard from his father all day. It was

after four right now. This had to be the first time Theo
hadn't checked in with their son.

She grew even more apprehensive because they had
their star-gazing class tonight. Theo could have gone
anywhere after court. She wanted to believe he was with
his family, but after what he'd lived through today, he
was probably out of his mind in pain. Somehow she had
to get through this and find him without alarming Ari.

Once she was ready, she said good-night to Stasio
and slipped out the back door to her car. She'd told Ari
to be waiting for her. When she eventually drove up to
Dax's house, he came flying out the front door and
jumped in the car.

"Where's Papa?"

She smothered the moan rising in her throat. "I think
he's at the taverna with his family. I thought we'd drive
there for dinner before you guys leave for class."

"He'll be glad. Papa's afraid you don't like his family."

Stella glanced at her son. "That's not true. I like them
very much."

"He talks about you all the time and told me what you
were like when he first met you. He said you were really
shy. What does that mean?"

"That I didn't speak up and kind of hung back."

"Papa said that was his favorite thing about you. All
the other girls…well, you know. They wanted to be
with him, but he said that once he met you, that was it."

She was certain there'd been other women while he'd
been in New York. He was too attractive and had too much
drive to live like a monk, but he'd come back for her. It
proved that whatever had gone on in his past, it hadn't kept
him in the States. That was all that mattered to her.

"It's nice to hear."

"He wanted to know if you'd had boyfriends."

"What did you tell him?"

"That there'd been some, but you never let any of them come up to the family room or sleep over. Papa was pretty happy to hear that."

In spite of her fear that they wouldn't be able to find him, she chuckled. "I'm afraid when I met him, I never really looked at another man again."

"You love him like crazy, huh."

Her throat practically closed up with emotion. "Yes. How can you tell?"

"Because you're always smiling now."

"So are you. Let's go find him right now and surprise him."

They'd crossed over to Salamis Island. The traffic was horrendous with tourists and people driving home from work.

Be there, Theo, she cried. But when they came in sight of the taverna, she couldn't see his car. That didn't necessarily have to mean anything, but it still made her stomach clench.

She pulled up in front. Ari jumped right out. "I'll get him, Mom."

It was just as well he went inside alone. She didn't feel up to facing his family, not after what they'd all been through this morning in court.

Stella's brother had been the cause of all the pain their family had suffered. Nothing she could ever say or do would make up for what they'd had to endure. Whenever her mind remembered what the doctor had said in court about Theo's injuries, her heart broke all over again.

When Ari came back out, she had to dash the moisture off her cheeks so he wouldn't suspect anything was wrong.

"Grandpa said he was there earlier, but he left to go home."

"Then, that's where we'll go. Do you know where his house is from here? I've never seen it."

"Yeah. I'll show you how to get there. Take that road over there and follow it to the coast road."

Once they reached the other road, everything started to look familiar to her. With each kilometer she realized Ari was directing her toward a favorite area she hadn't seen in six years.

Before long Ari told her to turn into the driveway around the next curve. A gasp of surprise escaped her lips to see a lovely white villa on the stretch of beach where Theo used to take her in the rowboat.

"*This* is your father's house?"

"Yeah. It's so cool. It has a gym and an indoor pool. I can walk right out on the beach from my bedroom. We've set up the telescope on the porch and look at the stars. Dax wishes he lived here."

"I'll bet he does," her voice trembled.

They both got out of the car and walked past the flowering shrubs to the front entrance. "Papa gave me a key. Come on." He opened the door for them. She stepped inside a new, modern world of white with splashes of color on the walls and floors. So much light from the arched windows thrilled her to death.

"Papa?" he called out. "Mom and I are here! Where are you?" He raced around the house but couldn't find him. "He's probably gone for a walk. Let's go find him."

If he wasn't here, Stella didn't know what she would do. "That's a great idea. I'll take my shoes off."

"Me, too."

They left them inside the sliding doors off the family

room. She followed him outside. Steps led down from the deck to the sand. The evening air felt like velvet. Her eyes took in the ocean not thirty feet away.

The pristine beach was just as she remembered it from years ago. "Come on, Mom. This is the way Papa took me for a walk."

She ran to catch up to him. "There aren't any people around."

"This is his private beach. He said that when he was growing up, their family lived like sardines in a can." She laughed at the metaphor. "He decided that if he ever made enough money, he'd build a place where he could walk around and be by himself."

Her eyes smarted. "Well he certainly accomplished that here."

"Yeah. I love it. Our house in Athens is old and full of people all the time, too."

Stella hadn't ever thought about it before, but he was right. Rich or poor, both her family and Theo's had been through a lot of togetherness.

As they rounded a small headland, her feet came to a stop. This was the little cove where Theo always brought her in the rowboat. This was where they'd made passionate love for the first time. Ari had been conceived here.

She lifted wet eyes to capture the scene. In the distance she saw the man she loved hunkered down on the sand in shorts and a T-shirt, watching the ocean. This part of the coast was protected, making the water as calm as a lake.

"Papa!"

He turned his head. By the way he slowly got to his feet she could tell he was shocked to see her with Ari.

Her heart pounded so hard, it seemed to give her wings as she started running toward him. Suddenly he was galvanized into action and raced toward her as if he could outrun the wind. They met halfway and clung in euphoric rapture while he swung her around.

"Darling," she cried breathlessly.

Theo didn't speak words she could hear. He did it with his mouth, covering hers hungrily, letting her know how he felt while they communicated in the way they used to when they found this special spot to be together.

"Thank God you came," he whispered at last. "I swear I—"

"Shh." She pressed her lips to his. "We're never going to talk about this again. We're never going to think about the past again. Don't look now, but I think we've embarrassed our son."

When Theo lifted his dark head, the last rays of the sun gilded his features. They were more striking to her now than ever before. His black eyes devoured her before shifting to their son, who stood a little ways off watching a sailboat in the distance.

"Ari? You'll have to forgive your mother and me. She just told me she'd marry me."

"You did?" He shrieked for joy.

She nodded.

"That's so awesome, Mom!" He leaped in the air, shouting like a maniac. His whole face was wet from happy tears. Her heart thrilled to see the smile that transformed him.

"'So awesome' is right," Theo murmured, kissing her again. "I kind of lost control for a minute."

Ari laughed and ran over to them. They all hugged for a long time.

"How soon is the wedding?"

"Three weeks," they both said at the same time. He smiled into her eyes. "That should give us enough time."

"Why do you have to wait so long?"

She slid her arm around their son. "The wedding banns."

"What are those?"

"An announcement that we're getting married," Theo explained. "It gives anyone time to object if they know a reason why we shouldn't be married."

"That's crazy! Who wouldn't want you two to get married?"

Stella's eyes sought Theo's. The moment was bitter-sweet until he said, "Nobody I know, and you're absolutely right. It *is* crazy, but it's tradition. Come on. Let's go back to the house and plan the wedding."

"Are you going to ask Hektor to marry you?"

"Who else?" Theo teased.

"Are you guys going to go on a honeymoon?"

That forlorn little tone had sneaked into his voice. Theo smiled at her before he said, "We're thinking either Disneyland or Disney World. We'll let you make the decision."

"Disneyland!" he cried out. "Dax said it's awesome!"

CHAPTER TEN

Eleven Months Later

"RACHEL? Would you do me a favor?" She and Stella were lying by the pool at the villa on Andros looking at baby magazines.

"What is it?"

"Don't look now but Theo's staring at me from the other end of the patio. My due date isn't for another three days, but you'd think I was on the verge of giving birth right now. Tell Stasio to take him somewhere for the day. I swear if he hovers around me one more minute, I'm going to scream."

"I know exactly how you feel. Stasio drove me crazy for the last couple of weeks before Anna was born."

"I'm getting there fast."

"He's in the house changing her diaper. As soon as he comes out, I'll ask him."

"Thank you."

"Uh-oh."

"What?"

"Theo's coming over here."

Stella lifted the magazine higher, pretending not to see him.

"You've been in the sun long enough, Stella. Let's get you inside for a little while. Too much heat isn't good for you."

"I haven't been out here that long."

"I disagree." In the next breath he picked her up off the lounge with those strong arms and carried her in the house to their bedroom.

Once he'd placed her carefully on top of the bed, he lay down next to her and smoothed the hair off her forehead. The anxious concern in his eyes baffled her.

"Darling, I'm as healthy as a horse. You don't need to worry about me. When I was carrying Ari, I never had any trouble. There's no reason to believe I'll have it this time."

"But I wasn't there to take care of you. Now that we can enjoy this spring break with the family, I want to wait on you."

"I know, and I love you for it, but watching me all the time is like waiting for water to boil."

His lips twitched. "Not quite. You're much more interesting." His hand slid over the mound, sending delicious chills through her body. "Is she kicking right now?"

"Not at the moment. I'll let you know the second she does. Come on. Close your eyes and take a little nap with me."

"That's kind of hard when I want to do more than that with you."

"I think you've done quite enough for one year, Kyrie Pantheras."

He chuckled deep in his throat and bit gently on her earlobe. "You're a fertile little thing."

"So I've found out. We're going to have to be careful after she's born."

His dark brows furrowed. "Is that your way of telling me the honeymoon's over?"

"No." She grabbed his hand and kissed his fingertips. "It's my way of telling you we could probably have a baby every year for the next ten years without a problem."

"I like the idea in theory."

"You would. You're not the one who feels like a walrus."

He grinned. "Yesterday it was a hippo. A very sexy one, I might add."

"Oh, Theo." She cupped his cheeks. "I love you too much."

Their mouths fused for a long time. "Now you know how I feel all the time."

"Pretty soon this baby will be born and you can stop worrying."

She heard his sharp intake of breath. "If anything happened to you—"

"It's not going to," she said.

"Have I told you Ari's latest idea for a name?"

"No. What is it?"

"We were looking at the Andromeda constellation the other night and he said, 'Papa? Can we name the baby Andrea?'"

"That's a beautiful name."

"I like it, too."

"Then let's do it. Ari will be thrilled."

"We'll tell him later. Right now I have other plans for us. Roll over on your side and I'll give you a back rub."

"That sounds heavenly." She'd had a low backache all week. It was the pressure of the baby since it had dropped.

The second Theo began touching her, her body quickened. Slowly his caresses sent sparks of desire through her, making her breathless. His mouth played havoc with hers. Stella wanted him with a need so powerful it turned into literal pain. She must have let out a little cry.

"What's wrong?"

"Nothing that a night of making love without our baby separating us won't cure."

"I probably shouldn't be touching you at all."

"If you didn't, I don't know how I'd go on living." She pressed her mouth to his and clung. All of a sudden she felt another pain that came all the way around to her stomach.

She grabbed Theo's hand and put it there. "Feel how hard that is?"

"Like a rock."

"I'm in labor, darling."

"You're kidding!" His voice shook.

"No. This is how it started before. We'd better call the doctor."

His face drained of color, Theo rolled off the bed and pulled out his cell phone. "His number's there on the bed stand."

The next few minutes were a blur while she timed her contractions. "They're coming every five minutes."

She didn't hear what Theo was saying, but after he got off the phone he told her they were leaving for the hospital. "The doctor says the baby could come fast because this isn't your first. Come on. We'll take Stasio's car."

"That's right," she quipped. "This beached whale couldn't get inside my sports car right now."

The joke was lost on Theo, who looked absolutely terrified. He helped her down the hall and the steps, calling to Stasio, who came running. By now the whole family had gathered around the car.

Rachel leaned inside the window. "I'll take care of the boys. Theo will take care of you. Don't worry about a thing."

It didn't take long to reach the hospital in Palaiopolis. She hadn't planned to have her baby there, but then you never knew what a baby was going to do. Andrea wanted to be born now.

Two and a half hours later she heard a gurgling sound and the attending doctor lifted up their little girl who was crying her lungs out. Knowing they were working and healthy meant everything.

"You've got a strong, beautiful daughter here, Kyrie Pantheras. Here—you cut the cord."

Theo, who'd put on a hospital gown and gloves, let out a cry of happiness. He'd lived through every second of the last few hours with her. Stella's tears ran down the sides of her cheeks. He hadn't been a part of any of this before. She was so thankful he had the opportunity now, she couldn't contain her joy.

A minute later the doctor laid the baby across her stomach so she could see her. "She's got a little widow's peak just like yours, darling!"

"She's got your hair and mouth."

"Oh, she's so sweet."

Theo buried his face in Stella's neck. "My two girls." She could tell he was overcome with emotion. She was, too, but so exhausted from the birth and filled with love for her new family, she could feel herself drifting off.

When next Stella came awake, she was in a private room. Theo stood at the side of the bed holding their daughter, who was all cleaned up and bundled. Her father had a five-o'clock shadow and his black hair was disheveled. Theo made a gorgeous sight!

Their gazes collided.

"You're awake!"

She smiled. "Yes. What do you think of our little girl?"

"Words don't cover it," his voice trembled.

"I know."

He lowered Andrea into her arms, then sat on a stool next to her. Together they examined their baby. "I've already checked everything. She's perfect."

Stella broke down laughing. "She is."

Theo covered Stella's face with kisses. "How are you feeling?"

"Good. Like I'm floating."

"You women are the stronger sex. I know that now." His eyes were pleading with her. "You've given me the world. What can I give you?"

"Just go on loving me. I need you desperately. I always will."

The baby started fussing. "She's hungry."

"She sure is," the nurse's voice boomed. "You'll have to leave for about a half hour while I help your wife start to nurse, Kyrie Pantheras."

He lowered his mouth to hers once more. "I'll be back."

"We'll be here waiting."

Theo drove back to the villa in record time. Ari and Leandros were waiting for him. "You have a new sister. We decided to name her Andrea."

He grinned. "Hooray. Can I go see her?"

"As soon as I've showered and shaved."

"Can I go, too, Uncle Theo?"

"Of course. Anyone who wants to."

"We'll all go." Stasio brought up the rear.

Ten minutes later they all piled in the car and left for the hospital. When they reached Stella's room, she was lying there propped up in the bed with the baby asleep on her shoulder. For a woman who'd given birth such a short time ago, Theo found his wife utterly breathtaking.

While everyone had a chance to hold the baby, he moved over to her side. "You must be exhausted, yet you've never looked more alive."

"That's because you were with me. We're the luckiest people in the world to be given a second chance at life. Oh, Theo…it was worth the six-year wait."

Theo had a hard time swallowing. "I can say that, now that you're alive and safe, but I wouldn't recommend it for everyone."

"No."

Unable to resist, he kissed her thoroughly. "I know there's a part of you that wishes Nikos could be here. One day let's hope he can find our kind of happiness and come around again."

Her eyes filled with liquid. "You can say that after everything he did to you?"

"I've forgotten it. It's true what they say. Love really does heal all wounds."

"Theo…"

"Hey, Mom? She kind of looks like Cassie except she doesn't have red hair."

"Do you know something, Ari, honey? Every day you look at her, you're going to see someone else in the family she looks like. It's part of being a baby."

"She's cute."

"Of course she is," said Theo. "I'm her father!"

Ari laughed. "Did you hear that, Mom?"

"I heard it."

Theo had come back to Greece not expecting to claim her or their son. Instead he had both and their adorable Andrea. That was her joy and her blessing.

* * * * *

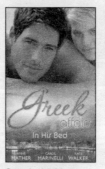

 *Have Your Say*

You've just finished your book.
So what did you think?

We'd love to hear your thoughts on our
'Have your say' online panel
www.millsandboon.co.uk/haveyoursay

- Easy to use
- Short questionnaire
- Chance to win Mills & Boon®
  goodies

 Visit us Online Tell us what you thought of this book now at
www.millsandboon.co.uk/haveyoursay

YOUR_SAY